# Summer House

**Center Point
Large Print**

Also by Nancy Thayer
available from Center Point Large Print:

*Moon Shell Beach*
*The Hot Flash Club Chills Out*
*Stepping*

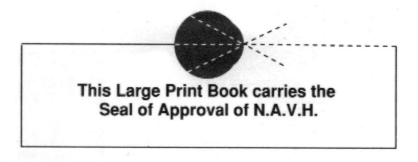

# Summer House

## NANCY THAYER

CENTER POINT PUBLISHING
THORNDIKE, MAINE

This Center Point Large Print edition
is published in the year 2009
by arrangement with Ballantine Books,
an imprint of Random House Publishing Group,
a division of Random House, Inc.

*Summer House* is a work of fiction. Names, characters,
places, and incidents are the products of the author's
imagination or are used fictitiously. Any resemblance
to actual events, locales, or persons, living or dead,
is entirely coincidental.
The text of this Large Print edition is unabridged.
In other aspects, this book may vary
from the original edition.
Printed in the United States of America.
Set in 16-point Times New Roman type.

ISBN: 978-1-60285-491-8

Library of Congress Cataloging-in-Publication Data

Thayer, Nancy, 1943-
 Summer house / Nancy Thayer.
    p. cm.
  ISBN 978-1-60285-491-8 (library binding : alk. paper)
  1. Women--Family relationships--Fiction. 2. Nantucket Island (Mass.)--Fiction.
  3. Large type books. I. Title.

PS3570.H3475S86 2009
813'.54--dc22

2009014834

*This book is for my beautiful grandchildren*

*Ellias Samuel Steep Forbes*

*and*

*Adeline May Wilde Forbes*

# Acknowledgments

*For this book about a family,* I want first of all to thank my own family, who surrounds me with the love and support and chocolate a writer needs. Thanks to my mother, Jane Patton, for giving me my father's WWII scrapbook and for sharing family stories with me. Thanks to my sister Martha Foshee for keeping me sane, or at least laughing when I'm not. Thanks to my uncle, Commander Lee Bert Findly, and his wife, Marjorie, for everything over the years, from walking me down the aisle to the current email jokes.

To Josh Thayer and David Gillum, and to Sam Wilde and Neil St. John Forbes, and to Ellias and Adeline, thank you over and over again, for the joy. I love the way you're changing the world, and I'm so proud of you all. Let's have a conversation!

Thank you, Charley Walters. You're my husband, my best friend, my reliable earth, and my blue-eyed heaven.

Thanks and hugs and kisses to Pam Pindell, Deborah Beale, Mimi Beman, Jill Hunter Burrill, Laura Simon, Jean Mallinson, and Charlotte Kastner. Your radiance continually illuminates my life.

Thanks to Jean Gordon for all your help here on Nantucket.

Thanks to Junessa Viloria for her continual swift

and spirited assistance, to Janet Baker for her eagle-eyed copyediting, and to Kim Hovey, Cindy Murray, Sarina Evan, and Diana Franco for their creative support. Much gratitude to Libby McGuire and Gina Centrello for the important work they do to make it all happen.

Thank you, *thank you,* Meg Ruley, for being such a great agent and for having the best laugh of anyone I know.

And to my editor, Linda Marrow, your intuitive and generous mind is as fabulous as your beauty. Thank you for all you have done for this book.

# Early Summer

# One

*Charlotte had already picked* the lettuces and set them, along with the bunches of asparagus tied with twine and the mason jars of fresh-faced pansies, out on the table in a shaded spot at the end of the drive. In July, she would have to pay someone to man the farm stand, but in June not so many customers were around, and those who did come by found a table holding a wicker basket with a small whiteboard propped next to the basket. In colored chalk, the prices for the day's offerings were listed, and a note: *Everything picked fresh today. Please leave the money in the basket. Thanks and blessings from Beach Grass Garden.* She hadn't been cheated yet. She knew the customers thought this way of doing business was quaint, harkening back to a simpler time, and they appreciated it. Perhaps it helped them believe the world was still a safe and honest place.

The day was overcast but hoeing was hot work and she had been up since four-thirty. Charlotte collapsed against the trunk of an apple tree, uncapped her water bottle, and took a long delicious drink. Nantucket had the best water on the planet: sweet, pure, and clear. It was shady in this overgrown spot, so she lifted off the floppy straw hat she wore, in addition to a heavy slathering of

11

sunblock, and sighed in appreciation as a light breeze stirred her hair.

She couldn't linger, she had too much to do. She took another long drink of water, listened to her stomach rumble, and considered returning to the house for an early lunch.

When she heard the voices, she almost jumped.

People were talking on Bill Cooper's side of the fence, just behind the green tangle of wild grapevines. Hunky Bill Cooper and his gorgeous girlfriend. From the tense rumble of Coop's voice and Miranda's shrill whine, they weren't happy.

"Come on, Mir, don't be that way." Bill's tone was placating but rimmed with an edge of exasperation.

"What way would that be?" A sob caught in Miranda's throat. "Truthful?"

The moment had definitely passed, Charlotte decided, when she could clear her throat, jump up, and call out a cheerful hello. Vague snuffling sounds informed her that Bill's dogs, Rex and Regina, were nearby, nosing through the undergrowth. She thought about the layout of Bill's land: along the other side of the fence grew his everlasting raspberry bushes. The berries wouldn't be ripe yet, so Bill and Miranda must be taking the dogs for a walk as they often did. She was glad the berry bushes grew next to the fence, their prickly canes forming a barrier between Bill's land and Nona's. A tangle of grasses massed around barberry bushes was wedged against the fence, and then there were the tree trunks. They would pass by any moment now. She would keep very quiet. Otherwise it would be too embarrassing, even though she had a right and a reason to be here.

"I never lied to you, Miranda. I told you I wasn't ready for a long-term commitment, especially not when you're in New York all winter."

"You could come visit me."

"I don't like cities," Bill argued mildly.

"Well, that's *pathetic*. And sleeping with that— that *slut*—is pathetic." Miranda was striding ahead of Bill. She cried out, "Rex, you stupid, stupid dog! You almost tripped me."

"Mir, simmer down." Bill sounded irritable, at the end of his patience.

Miranda didn't reply but hurried into the orchard of ancient apple trees. Bill followed, crashing through the brush. Charlotte could hear a few more words—*I'm not kidding! It's over, Bill!*—then she heard the hum of their voices but no words, and then they were gone.

"Gosh," Charlotte whispered to herself.

Charlotte had had a crush on Bill Cooper for years. Coop was a hunk, but so easygoing and funny that when you talked with him you could almost forget how handsome he was. She seldom saw him, even though he lived right next door. Of course, "right next door" was a general term. Nona's property consisted of ten acres with fifty feet of waterfront on Polpis Harbor, and the Coopers' land was about the same size. With all the plantings, you couldn't see one house from the other, even in winter when all the leaves had fallen.

Like the Wheelwrights, the Coopers mostly summered on the island, the Wheelwrights coming from Boston, the Coopers from New York. Eons ago, when they were all little kids, Coop had played a lot with Charlotte's brother Oliver, even though Oliver was younger, because Coop was an only child, and the two families got together several times over the summer for cocktails or barbecues. Then came the years when they rarely saw each other, everyone off in college and backpacking in summer instead of coming to the island.

Coop lived in California for a while, but three years ago his parents moved to Florida and Coop moved into the island house, telling everyone he wanted to live here permanently. He ran a computer software business from his nineteen-sixties wandering ranch house, mixed his plasma TV and Bose CD player in with his family's summery bamboo and teak furniture, and was content. Mostly he allowed his land to grow wild, except for a small crop of butter-and-sugar corn famous for its sweetness. At the end of the summer, he held a party outdoors, a clambake with fresh corn, cold beer, and icy champagne.

Charlotte had seen Coop and Miranda about town now and then, when she went in to catch a movie or pick up a prescription at the pharmacy. It was obvious why any man would fall in love with Miranda Fellows. She was a dark-eyed beauty hired to run Luxe et Volupté, an upscale clothing shop on Centre Street. She was British, and her accent thrilled the young, beautiful, rich, social-climbing set, men as well as women. She was such a snob, and Coop was such a genuine good guy, they seemed like an odd pair, but Charlotte hadn't allowed herself romantic thoughts about Coop.

She hadn't allowed herself romantic thoughts about any man for quite a long while.

Her own move to Nantucket had not been a light-hearted, impulsive act. She'd thought about it a lot. She'd searched her soul. She came to Nantucket to get away from men—at least from one particular man—and to somehow balance with good acts the wrong she'd done. Her organic garden was her own self-imposed penance and repentance, and she'd been diligent and hardworking and nunlike for three years. She didn't know when her penance would be over . . . but she knew she would find out when the time came. Until then, she forced herself to work hard, every day.

She stood up and stretched. On this June day, the sky was overcast, but Charlotte wore a long-sleeved T-shirt, a pair of striped bib overalls, and the floppy straw hat. She'd been burned too many times after carelessly exposing her pale skin to the sun. She'd learned her lesson.

Gardening seemed endlessly full of lessons, ones that had to be learned through personal experience instead of research and memorization. She liked that about working in a garden—the directness of it, the intimacy. It was so *personal.* No wonder people talked to their plants. Sometimes Charlotte sang to hers. And there was one stubborn wild rose, a rogue at the far end of the rows of winter onions, that had proudly kept a few green leaves all through the frigid winter. Charlotte actually *visited* it, touching its chilled leaves and whispering to it to cheer it on. When a failing plant began to thrive, she felt it as a personal victory; she believed it was her good work that somehow brought about good results.

Now she scrutinized the long rows of plants shining beneath the sun. At the far end, Jorge, her part-time employee, was plucking weeds and tossing them into a bucket. Jorge was a good, fast worker, and she was lucky to have him, because hand weeding was backbreaking work and absolutely necessary for an organic garden. There were many positive aspects about growing lettuces on the island—lettuce liked sandy soil and cool weather, and Nantucket had plenty of both, even in the summer. And since her lettuces were harvested while they were still young, they were seldom in the soil long enough to develop insect and disease problems. But weeds were her nemesis. By U.S. Department of Agriculture standards, chemical weed killers couldn't be used in an organic garden, and Charlotte didn't want to use them. The first year, she had tried to do everything herself, the seeding, planting, weeding, watering, and picking, in addition to taking the lettuces and other veggies to the various posh restaurants that would pay her prices for fresh locally grown produce, and at night she'd tried to keep up with the necessary paperwork for taxes and for her records. She just hadn't been able to do it all. Fortunately, Nona's landscaper, who had tended her formal garden regularly for years, recommended Jorge, and Jorge had saved the day.

Jorge was weeding now and would weed most of the day. Charlotte ran down her mental list of duties. She wanted to plant more lettuces and arugula and, if she had time, pot the double impatiens people bought the instant they were available. She walked back to her work shed, trying hard not to think about Coop.

She would think about her family. *That* would provide sufficient distraction!

Three years ago, she'd presented her plan at Family Meeting and no one, not her brothers and not her cousins, had objected to Charlotte's use of the roadside end of Nona's land for a trial market garden. Even when she had the ground rototilled so that the familiar bronze tones of wild brush and grasses were transformed into shining rows of dark sandy earth, even when dump trucks unloaded good soil and manure that smelled to high heaven, even when men came to build an unattractive wire fence around the garden to keep out deer, rabbits, and other wildlife, and especially not when Charlotte contributed sweet fresh strawberries or crisp lettuces to the family meals, did anyone in the family object.

But last year Charlotte had made a profit of four thousand dollars, and suddenly everyone—well, her aunt and uncle and her cousins—was having fits of jealousy, claiming that Nona was giving more to Charlotte than to the rest of them. Which was crazy of them, because to them four thousand dollars was just *nothing*.

It was not the four thousand dollars, really, Charlotte knew, that was the issue. It was the whole property, land and house and beach, worth several million, that everyone wanted—and, rightfully, had a claim to. Nona was almost ninety; she couldn't live forever, even though everyone wished she might and Nona herself seemed to think it possible. Nona had two living children— Charlotte's father, Worth, and his sister, Grace— two in-laws—Charlotte's mother, Helen, and Grace's husband, Kellogg—six grandchildren, and—from Mandy, Grace's daughter—two great-grandchildren. Nona had not, would not, disclose the details of her will, even though at each annual Family Meeting her children pressed her. When the time is right, she would respond, and it didn't matter if they claimed to be insulted, she wouldn't change her mind.

The three acres of land constituting Charlotte's garden didn't belong to Charlotte. There had never been any kind of arrangement like that, and in fact Charlotte had insisted on paying a token rent to her grandmother for the use of the land. But no one in the family had ever expected her to stick with gardening; they had all assumed that sooner or later Charlotte would think up some more appealing project and wander away, letting the acreage revert to its natural state.

Well, she was proving them wrong. Her grueling, dogged physical labor had paid off in unexpected ways. No one had expected her garden to be a success; she could understand that completely. She'd never been dedicated to anything before.

When she was younger, she'd had trouble settling down to any kind of career. In college, she'd never known what she wanted to major in. She spent her early twenties drifting from place to place and job to job. She'd tried writing for a newspaper in the Northampton area where she went to college, and then she tried selling ads for them, and then she went backpacking in Europe and forgot about the newspaper. In Italy she met an old friend from college who was starting a chic shop on Newbury Street, and in a moment of enthusiasm and too much Chianti, she'd agreed to return home to manage it. She'd done all right, but she'd grown bored with retail, so she waited tables for a while, thinking she might learn about the restaurant business, but that hadn't captured her soul either.

When her father suggested again that she try to learn the family business, she surrendered. She'd always known she would, sooner or later. She adored her father and wanted to please him, and she had worked in the bank for three long years. She'd started as a lowly teller, and then worked in residential lending and for a while in operations. She did her best—and she'd hated every minute of it.

Oh, in the very beginning, she'd had fun with the dress-up aspect of office work. She'd bought some clever little suits and killer high heels. Her parents gave her an expensive coffee-dark leather brief-case with gleaming brass buckles for her birthday, and she carried it to the bank daily, but in truth she was more impressed with how it looked as an accessory than what it ever had in it. Numbers numbed her mind. Graphs, rows, charts, and bank language made her eyes roll back in her head. "Liquidation" made her thirsty, and "asset class" made her think, childishly, of her bum. But Charlotte knew her father hoped at least one of his children had inherited his passion for banking, and she always wanted to make her father happy, so she tried. She really did try.

But she'd hated it. She'd been not just bored but

*miserable.* Perhaps that explained why she had an affair, but it did not make it right.

Nothing could ever make it right. But she could try, somehow, to make amends.

When she decided to attempt a market garden, she did so from the deepest part of her heart. She truly believed that one person could change the world—just a little bit—for the better, every day, and to do this through hard physical labor made a kind of sense to her. Plus, her idea was good. Everyone was trying to buy locally now, and on Nantucket there were plenty of posh restaurants and wealthy people who would pay top prices for organic produce. After her decision to leave the bank, Charlotte had determined not to appear like a feather brain in front of her family. She prepared a business plan and made copies for everyone, and she kept records, paid taxes, and worked her butt off. Also, she was living with Nona, which meant free room and board for Charlotte but relieved the family of no small amount of financial obligation, not to mention personal duty.

After Charlotte's grandfather Herb died five years ago, Nona had surprised her family by stating that she wanted to sell the Boston house and move permanently to Nantucket. Worth and Grace had objected strenuously. You are eighty-five, Nona, they reminded her. Nantucket is an island with a small cottage hospital. Your health might be fine now, but what if something happens?

And think of the winters, so long and dreary. You'll be so isolated. None of your relatives lives on the island, and most of your island friends have died of old age. And that house is so huge—think of the expense of heating it! And what if you fall down the stairs? In the middle of the night! We will worry about you every moment of every day!

Nona was never one to admit to any shortcomings, and the truth was that she was in excellent health for a woman her age. She insisted on moving to the island house, and to satisfy her anxious offspring she hired Glorious Wellington from Kingston, Jamaica, to live with her and act as housekeeper and, if necessary, nurse, for Glorious was an LPN. Glorious was in her thirties, a tall, broad-shouldered, voluptuous woman with a gentle voice and an easy laugh.

Nona's children weren't thrilled with this expenditure of money for live-in help, but it was Nona's money, after all. And after the first year, they had to admit that Nona seemed to do very well indeed, living in that drafty old wooden yacht of a house, even in the winter. She had friends over once a week to play bridge, and she attended lectures, plays, and concerts, driven to all events by Napoleon Posada in his ancient Cadillac taxi, where Nona sat in the front seat and caught up on all the local gossip, for Napoleon knew it all.

Still, as each year passed, Nona slowed down

just a little. Arthritis crippled her, so she needed a cane to walk and could no longer jump up and rush up stairs the way she had all her life. Her hearing and sight were diminished, and more and more she seemed to be forgetful, absentminded. When Glorious had to fly back to Jamaica when her own mother was ill, Nona assured everyone she was fine alone for a few days. But Helen had made a little spur-of-the-moment trip down from Boston and discovered that for three days Nona had pretty much forgotten to eat. When Helen pointed this out, Nona had argued that at her age she didn't need much to survive.

Luckily for Charlotte, this was just a month before Family Meeting, and when she submitted her market garden plan, everyone in the family saw at once how helpful it would be to have a member of the family living full-time in the house with Nona.

The arrangement had worked out nicely for everyone. Or it had, until her relatives learned that she'd actually made a profit on her harebrained scheme.

Would it be better, somehow, if her garden enterprise failed?

Carrying a long woven basket piled with weeds for the compost heap, Charlotte headed back through the rows of growing plants to the greenhouse. Her back and arms ached pleasantly. She liked this feeling, liked having worked hard. How different it was from the bank, where she had spent each day with a cramped back and a crashed brain. Now she felt healthy, clear-eyed, well-used.

And she felt guilty for even this much pleasure.

## *Two*

*Nona spent* much of her day tucked up in a lawn chair in the garden, dozing beneath the sun. If it was stormy, or overcast like today, she settled on a chaise at the window with the tea service on a table by her side and a good book in her lap. She seldom read. More often she napped or looked out at the garden and remembered all that had happened over her ninety years.

Today she could not seem to get comfortable. She wedged another pillow behind her back and smoothed the mohair throw over her legs, but she was still restless. Well, of course she was; everyone would be arriving at any moment, and the peace she had come to crave in her dotage would be shattered.

From where she sat now, she could see out into the garden terrace, with its walls of high privet hedge, and just a bit farther through the arched opening onto the white gravel drive. She would spot any arriving vehicle.

Although the main entrance to Wheelwright House with its pretentious Doric columns faced Polpis Harbor, the descendants of its builder, old

Horace Wheelwright, never understood why. It wasn't as if the mailman, neighbors, or friends regularly arrived at the house by water. When any of the family took a boat out, they set off from the dock at the boathouse on the far side of the property, and they got to the boathouse by leaving the mudroom at the side entrance of the house and following an ancient slate walk carpeted with low-lying mosses and determined periwinkle. The mudroom door was also the entrance for anyone in the family carrying armfuls of groceries or luggage from the garage or the half-circle white shell drive. Guests parked on the drive, walked beneath the arch in the high wall of privet hedge, and followed the path over the slate terrace to the French doors. These opened into the long living room, with its sofas and chairs and piano and fireplace and, at the far end, its expansive view of the harbor.

Back when she was a new bride and still known by her given name of Anne, she had learned how to keep the hedge healthy and trimmed from her mother-in-law, the ironically christened Charity Wheelwright. Anne would have preferred to allow her three children to play in the garden, but Charity Wheelwright was adamant. Children would spoil the elegance and symmetry, they'd poke holes in the thick green tapestry with their careless games. So Worth and Bobby and Grace were sent out the side door, through the mudroom, with their nanny, to play on the windy moors and in the high lofts of the barn—before it was converted to a garage. Perhaps Nona—Anne—longed to go with them, to jump, shrieking, down into the old piles of hay, to chase them through the slender trunks of the forest behind the barn, to feel the tickle of low wild grasses beneath her own bare feet. But in those days, a woman, a *good* woman, was responsive to the demands of her mother-in-law. In those days, a good woman put her husband first and her mother-in-law second. And children were tended by others until they were old enough to sit quietly at the dinner table and appreciate adult conversation.

Still, Nona believed she had been a good mother. An approachable, reasonable, generous-spirited mother-in-law. And an affectionate, adoring, devoted grandmother. It gave her a sense of satisfaction, even smugness, to know that all her family was arriving today to help her celebrate her birthday. That would be fine. She even looked forward to it, although at her age she hated being the center of attention. Still, Grace had arranged a party at the yacht club, and Nona always loved parties.

No, it was Family Meeting that was making her nervous. Family Meeting was just two weeks away, and she was uncomfortable—*anxious, really.* Nona shifted her knees beneath the mohair blanket as her thoughts stung at her like tiny insects.

The silly business about Charlotte's little garden!

Three years ago, when Charlotte asked to use the three acres of Nona's waterfront property that fronted Polpis Road for an organic market garden, Nona had readily agreed. After all, the land was just lying there, fallow, low scrubland with no endangered plant species and all the beauty of a forlorn prairie. You couldn't even see the land from the first floor of the house because the formal garden, walled in by its high privet hedge, blocked the view. Nona had thought that Charlotte's business plan was well considered and supported with research and statistics, and the others—Charlotte's parents, Worth and Helen, Worth's sister, Grace, and her husband, Kellogg—had thought so, too. When they discussed it at Family Meeting, no one had objected. Not Charlotte's siblings, not Grace and Kellogg's three daughters.

Of course, everyone thought privately that Charlotte wouldn't really follow through; Charlotte's enthusiasms were like firecrackers, explosive and brief. Everyone assumed she'd tire of the endless manual labor of gardening, and the land would soon be covered again with wild grasses.

No one had expected that Charlotte would love the work, that her garden would flourish, that she would, so soon, be making a profit from the place. Oh, Charlotte wasn't close to making a living off it, not yet, but Grace and Kellogg and their daughters were already mumbling about "balancing out inequalities." What did they want? Nona thought irritably. Should she give them each a check for a pitiful four thousand dollars or whatever little amount Charlotte netted last year? Would that keep them from becoming jealous, from believing that Charlotte was her favorite and receiving more than the others?

It was all nonsense. Nona would not be bullied, no matter with what enormous charm. For that matter, she'd gladly write a few checks to Grace and Kellogg's children. As for Charlotte's brothers, Teddy might not even show up and Oliver was sweet and easy about everything. Oliver was quite happy in his life out there on the West Coast, and both he and his partner had work they loved, so they didn't worry about money. Also, they were Dinks. Nona congratulated herself for knowing, at her age, the term Dinks, which meant Dual Income, No Kids. And she was pleased to remember that she had always treated Oliver and Owen with love, acceptance, and unconditional welcome.

Some days she succeeded better than others. Some days the present rushed toward her like a storm, wild with gale-force winds, rogue lightning strikes, and thundering rain, and she found herself taking refuge in the past. Not all her memories were easy. No one's were. Yet over the years time had spun her memories into a kind of nest, a comfortable silken cushion into which her mind fit as tidily as a ring into a jewel box. She felt snug there. She escaped the failures and frustrations of her aging body and was young again. Surely those memories of her youthful passions would help her be a good grandmother to her passionate descendants. She hoped that was the case.

## 1943

"*Please. Son.* Are you marrying this girl because you have to?"

"For God's sake, Mother!" Herb's voice was low but angry.

Anne had just that moment paused at the head of the stairs with her hand on the banister as she bent to smooth her stockings, checking that the seam was exactly in the middle, because, from all Herb had told her, his mother would notice that sort of thing. Would care. Her footsteps had been muffled by Persian carpets when she walked from the guest bedroom at the far end of the back wing—Mrs. Wheelwright had sequestered her as far from Herb's bedroom as possible—so she was standing in shadow at the top of the stairs when she heard their voices.

"We understand, son. We're grown-ups here." His father's words were lightened by a boys-all-together tone. "With the war, and you shipping out so soon, this—this *urgency*—is only natural."

"But marriage, surely, is not necessary." Charity

29

Wheelwright moderated her voice. Anne had to hold her breath and strain to hear.

"I don't know how the two of you can speak this way!" Herb was angry and hurt. "I explained in my letter to you. I love Anne, and I want to spend my life with her."

Anne's heart knocked in her chest so fiercely she could scarcely breathe. It was a pitiful and demeaning act, eavesdropping in the shadows like this, but she could not move away; she was impaled by her own fascination like a butterfly pinned to a board.

Now Norman Wheelwright was offering his son a drink: Scotch, the excellent single malt he seldom brought out, but nothing was too good for his son. The family's words seemed to blur as they moved toward the far end of the living room. Should she go down now? Anne wondered. She had to go down sometime. She couldn't hide up here for the rest of her life. What could she do to warn them of her approach? Clear her throat loudly when she reached the bottom of the stairs? Something bristled inside her at the thought. Why should *she* protect *them* from embarrassment? Her future in-laws did not seem to have taken any measures to secure privacy for this conversation, to shelter Anne from their disdain. They'd left the door open from the living room to the hall. They hadn't even waited until evening was over and Anne tucked away in bed to assail Herb with their fears. Anne had scarcely said more than hello. She doubted that Herb had even had a chance to unpack; his parents were rushing at him as if Anne had set him on fire and they had to smother the flames.

This was not completely unexpected. Herb had described his parents in all their haughty snobbery to Anne—he had made fun of them, really—at first. After Anne accepted his proposal, he discussed his family members and their elevated regard for their station in life more seriously. The Wheelwrights were bankers. They had lived in Massachusetts since the late 1700s, and they had always been careful to marry within a small select group whom Herb's mother, Charity, called Our Kind. Herb's mother was a Folger by birth. *Her* mother had been a Cabot. Herb's father's mother had been a Saltonstall.

"But I'm not some hick with straw in my teeth!" Anne had protested.

"Of course not. I never meant to imply that you were!" Herb had pulled Anne close, caressing her as if she were some kind of little beast with its fur on edge.

Anne wriggled against his embrace. "And if you want to talk about *money,* my family could buy and sell your—"

Herb brought his mouth to hers so she could feel his lips move; his words puffed against her as he said, "But we don't. Want to talk about money. *It's not done.*"

"That's ridiculous." Anne shoved him away. Sitting up on the edge of the sofa, she pushed her hair back from her face. They were in the small Back Bay apartment Anne rented with her best friend, Gail. Gail had gone out with her own beau this evening but would be back any moment. Anne didn't want to get caught with her dress all rumpled and twisted, even though as soon as Herb left, she and Gail would curl up on the sofa with a warm mug of Postum and tell each other every detail of their evenings, giggling and snickering at the ways of men.

Anne and Gail were both from the Midwest, Anne from Kansas City, Gail from Chicago. They'd met at Radcliffe, where they were majoring in English, and they'd become best friends at once. Anne had intended to go home and teach high school English, but her father, who owned large stockyards in Kansas City, persuaded her to stay in the East for the duration of the war, to lend her considerable energy and organizational know-how as a secretary in the office of the Stangarone Freight Company, the Boston-based shipping company responsible for loading the food products and supplies onto the Liberty Ships that crossed the Atlantic Ocean in convoys, escorted by U.S. destroyers, carrying necessary goods to the troops. The army, desperate for vessels, couldn't build cargo ships fast enough and had commandeered the use of just about anything that would float. The office in Stangarone's shipyard warehouse was always chaotic, frenzied with paperwork, phone calls, and telegrams as they liaised with governmental directives. Anne loved it. It made her feel she was doing her part for the war effort.

Gail was an energetic, plump little bumblebee of a woman, full of laughter and eager to see new sights, but she missed the wide open spaces of the Midwest and planned to return home when the war was over. She wanted to raise quarter horses and have lots of children, but she hadn't yet chosen a husband, and she wouldn't, not now. *I'm not going to marry some guy and then lose him to the war,* she declared, and Anne admired the way Gail believed she could control her own destiny.

Anne's destiny was set the moment she looked into Herb Wheelwright's eyes.

They met on a hot September evening at a party on Commonwealth Avenue given by the family of Hilyard Clayton, who had just finished officer training. Gail was dating a nearly cross-eyed reporter for the *Boston Globe,* Quinn Probst, who'd gone to school with Hilyard, and Gail told Anne to come along, because the party was really one of those wartime crushes where anyone in uniform was welcome to a drink and pretty girls were welcome to two. Gail worked at the *Globe* as well, as a secretary, with no aspirations to be anything else. She just loved being where so much action was unfolding.

The Clayton house was enormous, with high ceilings, walls covered with oil paintings of disapproving ancestors, and a great many valuable, breakable, porcelain cachepots and vases set about on heavy furniture.

"I feel like I'm stepping into a book by Edith Wharton," Anne said to Gail, as they stood in the front hall taking their bearings.

"More like Edgar Allan Poe," Gail quipped.

Quinn took Gail's hand and pulled her into the noisy crush of the party. Gail grabbed Anne's hand and yanked her along. A bar was set up at the far end of the dining room, and waiters moved through the rooms with trays of drinks. Above the babble of the party, a record played a new Benny Goodman song, "Why Don't You Do Right?"

Hilyard Clayton and many of his buddies were on leave for a month before shipping out to Arizona for special training. Because of this, his parents and the other older folk had thoughtfully gathered in the father's den, leaving the larger living and dining rooms for the younger crowd, most of the men in uniform, most of the women adorned with deep red lipstick, all of them smoking Camels and Chesterfields. Smoke spiraled above their heads, drifting up to the crown molding, and to the elaborate plaster rosette around the chandelier sparkling over the dining room table.

Everyone was drunk or getting there; they were young, excited, sexy, and perhaps just a little bit scared. They all felt very much on the brink. Perhaps, that night, they missed the reassuring presence of the older ones. Perhaps it felt to the young people that the mature generation, their parents, were settled comfortably in the well-fortified inner sanctum, while they crowded at the front of a moving vessel, without guide or sage or leader. They did not articulate this. The party was noisy, raucous, explosive, but something was absent—or something unwanted was present. Anne couldn't help but think, as she looked at the lanky men in their uniforms, leaning against the massive walnut sideboard laden with silver trays, chafing dishes, buckets, and bowls, that those inanimate objects, already heirlooms, might outlast the living heirs.

Somehow Gail and Quinn had gotten over to the other side of the room. Anne could hear Gail's bubbling, irrepressible laughter, and she was ticked off at herself for being melancholy in the middle of a party. She was wearing a white dress with red polka dots and round red earrings and high red heels, and she knew she was pretty enough, and several men stopped to chat her up, but she was out of sorts. She decided to go sit on the front steps and cool off.

She squeezed her way to the front hall, delicately balancing a pink gin. In the wide double doorway between the hall and the living room, a group of men was gathered in a rough noisy circle. In the middle, a short soldier with blazing red hair held a very pale blond waiter by his shirt collar. The soldier was shaking the waiter and yelling at him. It took Anne a moment to understand what he was saying. "Kraut! Damned Kraut! Get out of this house!" The crowd of men around him bellowed agreement.

The blond waiter held his hands up, protesting but not fighting, obviously trying not to exchange blows.

The waiter's passivity seemed to irritate the soldier even more. "Well! What do you have to say for yourself, you miserable rat-eating Kraut?"

An officer, tall and wide-shouldered in his dress uniform, strode down the hall, shoved through the crowd, and grabbed the redhead. "Watkins! *He's* Dutch and you're *drunk!*" Wrapping an arm around the soldier's neck, he manhandled him away from the waiter, dragging him through the crowd, down the hall, and out the open front door. The crowd, as much disappointed as relieved, muttered and laughed and went back to the bar for more drinks.

Anne went out to the front steps. The red-haired soldier was vomiting into the bushes. When he was through, the officer handed him a handkerchief.

"Thanks, Herb," the soldier said.

"You should go home," the officer told him. "Get some sleep."

"Yeah, I should, but I'm not going to. When will I have another opportunity for free booze?" Watkins stumbled past Anne, up the stairs, and back into the hot crush of the party.

Anne leaned against the front door, looking at the officer named Herb. "How did you know that waiter was Dutch?"

The officer grinned. "I didn't."

She laughed in surprise and admiration.

He laughed, too, then added, "But you know, we've got a lot of people in this country whose parents came from Germany. Hell, one of my best friends is part German. Fortunately for him, he's not as blond as that waiter." He climbed up the steps until he was on the same level as Anne. He held out his hand. "Herb Wheelwright." He was almost as blond as the waiter, with eyes as blue as the sea.

She smiled. "Anne Anderson."

"Do I detect a southern accent?" He leaned against the opposite side of the doorway, reached in his pocket, brought out a cigarette case, and offered it to her.

"No, thanks, I never could get the hang of smoking. You're half right about the accent. I'm from Kansas City."

"And how did you manage to be in Boston on this fine evening?" Herb lifted out a cigarette and lit it.

"Well, I went to Radcliffe. Graduated a couple of years ago. My father thought I should stay here in Boston and work for Stangarone's."

"Liberty Ships." A slight breeze carried the smoke into the sky.

"Right. And Gail, my best friend, is working for the *Boston Globe*, so I moved in with her. We're having a grand time."

"You like the East Coast?"

"I do. Well, I can't say I've actually seen the *East Coast*. I mean, I've mostly just been in Boston, and of course I've taken the train down to New York a lot to see the sights." Anne considered. "How about you? Where are you from? No, let me guess. Say something so I can hear your accent."

He said: "I think you're beautiful."

She knew he was only flirting, but the way he looked at her when he said those words made her blush. "Well"—she took a sip of her gin—"I think you're from Boston."

"You're right."

A group of soldiers with their arms around a gaggle of what Anne's mother would have called "fancy women" staggered up the sidewalk toward Hilyard's house. As they climbed the stairs, one of the soldiers pinched a woman's fanny and she shrieked with laughter. Some of the men saluted Herb Wheelwright as they wedged themselves, two or three at a time, through the open doorway and into the party, which had spilled out into the front hall. Explosions of laughter rolled through the air, followed by Cab Calloway singing, "Hi-De-Ho!"

Herb asked, "Could I take you out for a cup of coffee before we both go deaf?"

Anne laughed and agreed. She set her gin glass just inside the door, on a long rectory table laden with other empty glasses. She considered telling Gail she was leaving the party, but one look at the mass of singing, drinking, laughing, shouting people made her change her mind.

The night air was fresh against her skin. The silence of the streets, broken by the occasional honking of a taxi horn or the slamming of a door, seemed like peace. They walked through the Public Gardens and Boston Common, admiring the lush green trees and flower beds, and up and down the rather European-looking residential streets leading away from the Common, past the private clubs and the stately town house residences with their elaborate architectural features in marble and stone. Past Trinity Church and the public library. Past the Arlington Street Church and up Beacon Hill to the State House.

"So much history here," Anne murmured, looking up at the golden dome.

"But we're here *now*," Herb told her. "And I wouldn't be anywhere else."

He took her hand.

They walked and talked, and sometime after

midnight they stopped at an all-night diner for coffee and apple pie. Anne took Herb back to her room that night—that morning, the sun was coming up. They didn't make love. They just lay down, fully clothed, on her narrow bed, and snuggled together and fell asleep. They were tired, but they didn't want to go their separate ways. They felt at home with each other. And when they did wake up, they made love, and it was Anne's first time, and it felt just right.

But she had certainly not set her cap for Herb Wheelwright. She'd had no idea that he was so wealthy or that his family owned a bank in Boston, and when she did find out she didn't care. Why should she? *Her* family owned half the stockyards in Kansas City. She knew, if she married him, she'd have to move to Boston after the war, but while that didn't bother her, it didn't excite her either. She didn't care whether they had ten children or none, whether he went into politics like his parents were hoping or not, whether they lived on Beacon Hill or in a tent in the middle of the Public Garden. She just wanted to be with him, and he wanted to be with her.

After two weeks, Herb asked her to marry him. She threw her arms around him and kissed the word yes all over his face. They wanted to marry right away.

Anne telephoned her parents, who gave her

their preoccupied blessing and said they'd try to come east for the wedding, but they couldn't promise. Anne wasn't surprised. Her father had turned executive control of the stockyards over to his wife so that he could direct his attention to the management of a factory producing and packaging meat "products" that were compressed in twelve-ounce gold-tone tin cans and shipped to the overseas troops. Augustus—Gus—Anderson was everywhere at once in the factory, working day and night, scrutinizing the quality of production like an eagle—this food was going to the boys fighting overseas. Even on the telephone, Anne could hear the exhaustion in her parents' voices.

"Darling girl," her mother said, "we're so happy to hear good news during this horrible time. I'm glad you've found this man, and I hope you'll both be very happy."

"And we will all meet up as soon as possible, God willing," her father added.

Herb also phoned his parents, who were ensconced in their summer home on the island of Nantucket, and today he and Anne had taken the stately old steamer from Woods Hole to Nantucket so that Anne could meet his family. They'll be aloof, Herb warned Anne. Judgmental. But it was important for the future that Herb and Anne do this, now. It was the right thing to do.

• • •

So here she stood, at the top of the stairs, eavesdropping.

Not for the first time, Anne missed her own
father. If he were with her now, he'd take her arm
in his and tap beneath her chin until she lifted her
head proudly. He'd sweep into the living room
with Anne beside him, and he'd beam his
welcoming, expansive, generous, Midwestern
smile, and even Herb's mother would gawk,
because Anne's handsome father, Gus, radiated the
natural-born charm of an optimist. Herb's father
would like him, too. Gus would shake Herb's
father's hand with his own large, muscular work-
toughened paw, and Herb would know at once
that Gus was an ally.

Anne had once exuded a similar relaxed and easy
charm, but she quickly discovered that here in the
East, because she was young and untried, she
appeared to people as simply naïve and even a little
silly, more like a girl than the woman she was. So
here at the Wheelwrights' summer home, she had
to monitor her own wide smile. She had to tamp
down her natural enthusiasm. She had to summon
up some kind of dignity. She had to act, for
heaven's sake, with *decorum,* and if Gail knew,
she'd fall out of her chair laughing.

But this was important. Herb's family was
important to him. Anne's family was important to
her too, but they'd recognized her as an adult long

ago. They'd turned her loose. She knew that after the war she would be living in Boston with Herb and coming here to this very house in the summers, where Wheelwrights had come every year since the 1800s.

"You going to turn and run, honey?"

Anne squeaked with shock as a soft voice sounded just at her shoulder. Herb's sister Holly stood there with a big grin and one eloquently arched eyebrow. She wore a red wool suit with a Christmas wreath of diamonds, rubies, and emeralds on the lapel.

"I was straightening my seams," Anne insisted, striving for dignity even though, the one time she'd met Holly, she'd liked her immediately.

Holly's glance whisked up and down Anne's figure. "They're straight as rulers, Anne. But let me warn you, my mother is a rat terrier disguised as a human. If she can get you by the throat, she'll shake you till you're dead, so don't let her take hold. And don't look so shocked. I've had to live with the woman all my life, remember." Holly linked her arm through Anne's. "You're the first woman my brother has dared to bring home, did you know that? I can tell he loves you, so I would be hugely disappointed if you let the old battle-ax beat you down."

"I love Herb, too," Anne whispered as they descended the stairs.

"Chin up, then," Holly ordered.

The living room swept across the entire side of the house, with a fireplace at one end and, at the other end, windows full of sky and sea in daytime but draped with heavy velvet now. Enthroned in a wing chair by the fire sat Herb's mother, in a white wool dress and pearls. She looked like she was chewing nails.

Anne smiled tremulously. "Hello."

"*Would you like* a cup of tea, Mrs. Wheelwright?"

"What?" It was with effort that Nona abandoned her memories. Where was she?

She was still in the living room of the Nantucket house, but in the present, or what other people thought of as the present. After the war, Holly had married and moved to Montana, where she and her husband raised cattle, horses, and several unruly children. Holly had happily given up all claims to the Nantucket property long ago. She and her family never enjoyed coming east. Nona and Herb had visited them several times over the years, impressed by the spacious, bustling, western life Holly had chosen for herself.

Now Holly was dead. She'd died—my goodness—fifteen years ago. Holly's husband had died not long after, and their children remained in the area where they'd grown up. Nona seldom saw them, but they were dutiful in sending cards on her birthday. Nona kept a birthday book and always remembered to send them birthday cards, too.

And Nona's beloved husband, Herb, was dead. He had passed away five years ago.

But Nona wouldn't allow herself to brood. She was reasonably fit, active, and lucid, and she was not alone. She had Charlotte's engaging company, and Glorious to brighten her life and take care of her.

Any moment now her family—*her* family—her children and their children and all their noise and turbulence and demands and excitements—would scatter into this house like a flock of gabbling geese, and she would have no more time for little voyages into the past.

Nona had to think of her family, had to think of their comfort and appetites and emotions. She had to *focus*.

"Yes." Her voice, not so often used these days, was dry and croaking. To her Jamaican housekeeper, she said, "Yes, please, Glorious."

At that moment the telephone rang and, as Glorious hurried off to answer, Nona heard the first automobile pull into the drive.

## Three

*H*elen decided she wouldn't make coffee. She was trying to figure out, without resorting to a visit to her doctor, what was causing her headaches. They troubled her almost daily now, sometimes operating with a fierce viselike action, squeezing her temples, but usually they were mild, weighing down her skull with a kind of bovine heaviness. Today she would go without caffeine and see if that helped.

Slipping a silk wrapper over her nightgown, she padded barefoot down the hall, down the stairs, and through the quiet house into the kitchen. She poured herself a glass of orange juice and sipped it standing at the kitchen sink, gazing out at their long backyard rolling down to the Charles River.

Today she and Worth were flying down to the island for the weekend, to celebrate Nona's birthday. Nona was going to be *ninety!*

It would be a grand celebration. All spring Worth had plotted with his sister Grace. They rented the yacht club for a party, made out a guest list, sent out handsome invitations. Helen had phoned her sister-in-law twice to assure her she would like to help. *We'll let you know when we need you,* Grace had replied. Helen felt more relieved than rejected. Grace and her husband, Kellogg, were methodical and organized. And bossy Grace loved to nitpick and criticize.

Helen's headache began its bass note hum. She set her glass in the sink and went into the den. Pulling out her office chair, she settled at her desk and opened her engagement calendar. This small act centered her, smoothed down the ruffled fur of the flustered little beast of her mind.

She'd known when she married Worth that she

was taking on the entire Wheelwright family, but she had been too ferociously in love to worry about it. As an only child, she'd welcomed belonging to a large family, especially a family like the Wheelwrights, so well known and respected. Worth's parents, Anne and Herb, had a kind of glamour, and they were very much in love with each other. That seemed like a good omen for Helen's own marriage.

And who could complain about spending two months every summer in the wonderful old Wheelwright house? Grace and Kellogg played doubles tennis with Helen and Worth, and the four of them joined Anne and Herb for dinner dances at the yacht club. They played badminton and cro-quet on the neatly mowed lawn, and when the wind was calm they sailed on a rippling silver path in the moonlight.

It was when their three children—Charlotte, Oliver, and Teddy—were born that Helen truly fell in love with the summer house. There, the long summer days were glorious. Grace's three daugh-ters—Mandy, Mellie, and Mee—were close in age to Helen's brood, and the children all tumbled around like puppies in the spacious sunlit rooms in the big old house on the harbor. If it rained, they'd do jigsaw puzzles or play wild games of hide-and-seek and board games. When the sun was out, the hours of the day were like honey.

Years ago, when Worth and Bobby and Grace

were young, their father had had sand delivered to make a small beach where the harbor waters lapped at the grassy shore. Over time, as the wind whipped low dunes along the lawn's end, beach grass and wild roses found homes there, creating a natural wild seaside garden, which in the summer, when the roses bloomed, filled the air with a sweet perfume. Anne and Herb's children played on the beach and then, as the years passed, Anne became Nona, and Herb became Grandpa and their grandchildren played there.

Grace married Kellogg and had three children. Worth married Helen and had three children. Like their parents, the children built elaborate fantastical sand castles or spread their towels on the hot sand and lay soaking in the sun and warming up after a dip in the shimmering blue shallows of the harbor. Later, they learned to sail from the Wheelwrights' wooden dock and played beach volleyball in the shallows, coming in for dinner drenched and salty, their smiles flashing white against their tanned skin.

Over the years, Grace's husband, Kellogg, and Worth stayed in Boston at the bank all week, so Helen and Grace were thrown together without their husbands. This was usually okay, although Grace could be a bit intimidating and officious. Grace had such high standards. Helen didn't really mind if the children had mac and cheese two nights in a row, but Grace wrote out menus for the week and stuck to them, rain or shine. With her own children, Grace was a bit of a dictator, but while she often made "suggestions" to Helen about how she should raise her children, she was never pushy. She just sort of exuded a smug perfume of superiority.

Helen had always *liked* Worth's family. But she could never *be* like them. She remembered the time, ten years before, when she told them at Family Meeting she would like to run an art gallery on the island. They'd reacted as if she'd suggested boiling puppies. Wheelwrights were bankers! Their bank had been founded in 1878 by Worth's great-grandfather. Once simply named The Fourth Bank of Boston, over the years it had changed names and added owners and directors. Worth was co-CEO, sharing duties with his old friend Lew Lowry and Grace's husband, Kellogg. Grace had chosen to remain in the background, running their home but always keeping informed. The bank was the hub of the Wheelwrights' lives. No Wheelwright did anything as frivolous as run an art gallery.

"Well, I think you're all stuffy and unimaginative," Worth had told the others at that Family Meeting. "Helen's got a great eye for art and she's a wonder at networking. I'll stake her the start-up money personally, and I'll bet you I get it all back and more."

Helen had been pleased that her husband had championed her, but after that meeting she lost her momentum. Even then she was aware that her children were breaking away from the Wheelwright traditions, and she didn't want to seem to be widening the breach. And perhaps she didn't want to risk failure; perhaps that was a small part of her decision.

Now a small bolt of pain forked through Helen's head. Could it be nervous tension? Because she was headed for another season on the island?

She focused on her engagement calendar. When her three children grew up and left home, Helen had joined several volunteer organizations, helping with church fairs, volunteering in libraries both in Boston and on the island, and tutoring students in English as a Second Language. All this work brought her great pleasure, a sense of accomplishment, and—she could never admit this to anyone—a kind of self-awareness she hadn't even realized she was missing.

In July the Nantucket library would hold a book sale. She was cochair. She was also in charge of the auction of the needlepoint quilt for the church. But she wasn't worried about these responsibilities. She had them well in hand. Her volunteer work was not the cause of her headaches.

Helen closed her calendar and allowed herself to admit the truth.

For the first time ever, she was dreading the two months at the summer house. Dreading being around Worth's sister and her perfect family.

Helen's own children seemed so feckless in comparison.

All three of Grace's children had made good marriages with people from Nona's circle. Mandy and Claus had presented Nona with two healthy great-grandchildren. Mandy and Mellie's husbands both held prominent positions at the bank.

But Helen and Worth's children showed no interest in banking. They were, at the best, eccentric and at the worst—well, the worst didn't bear considering.

Charlotte, the eldest child, had tried working at the bank. Charlotte adored her father and wanted to please him. She had put in three years before suddenly handing in her notice. At the next Family Meeting, she'd surprised them all with her naïve little scheme for an organic garden. Helen sympathized with Charlotte, who was trying to save the world, as Worth secretly joked, one head of lettuce at a time. And she thought Charlotte appreciated the fact that the family were all being supportive of her oddball endeavor. Well, they were all *comfortable* with Charlotte in an oddball endeavor. Charlotte's enthusiasms were always genuine and passionate but seldom long-lasting. The family could indulge Charlotte one more time. She'd settle down eventually—she was their best hope for being what the family would consider normal. Perhaps she would return to the bank.

Oliver, Helen's second-born and secretly her

most beloved child, would never work at the bank. Staggeringly handsome, Oliver had always been the most like his mother, interested in art and music, bored with sports and banking, mild-mannered and dreamy. Helen and Worth had not been surprised when, at sixteen, Oliver announced that he was gay. Back then, Worth was still trying to groom Oliver to take over the bank, but Oliver combined his father's facility for numbers with his mother's love of art and became an architect. Now, at twenty-eight, he was living and working in San Francisco with his partner, Owen. Oliver and Owen were planning a commitment ceremony this year.

Their third child, Teddy, was the real problem. He was becoming—could she actually say it?—a drug addict and alcoholic. Harsh words. Painful, frightening words. She wasn't sure they were accurate. Teddy had always been moody, volatile, and, she had to admit it, spoiled. Possessed of the same charismatic good looks all her children had—the shining maple sugar hair, the sapphire eyes rimmed with thick dark lashes—Teddy was the baby of the family. If Helen had spoiled him, so had everyone else. Helen had often wondered just how much difference it made that Herb, Teddy's grandfather and the stern commanding patriarch of the Wheelwrights, had died during Teddy's teenage years. She'd always believed that Herb might have talked some sense into

Teddy. She and Worth had not managed to do that, no matter how hard they'd tried.

Since they couldn't change Teddy, somehow they had, without conscious agreement, changed themselves. Changed their standards. Teddy hadn't been subjected to the tongue lashings and groundings they'd imposed on the two older children. But Teddy was so sweet!

As a child he was simply a mischievous elf, playing pranks. Somehow all that had blurred, until, when he was eleven, he'd sneaked out one night and driven Worth's Mercedes around the neighborhood and into a wall. That time, they'd been so glad he wasn't injured that they hadn't gotten angry. And really it was hard to be angry with Teddy. He had an infectious laugh and a lightning-quick wit. He had the same easy charm Worth and Oliver had, too. He was kindhearted and gentle, never mean. At boarding school he got into trouble for all kinds of silliness, but he was always simply playful, roguish, not destructive, at least not on purpose.

Worth thought it was his fault, the way Teddy had turned out. Worth had a sense of humor— Helen thought he'd gotten Grace's share, as well— and especially with his family he indulged his flippant side. He loved pounding on the piano, and all through the years Worth had often entertained his family by spontaneously transforming their daily activities, successes and woes, into a musical comedy. He'd roll up his shirtsleeves, seat himself with a flourish at the baby grand, and bang out the theme from *Sound of Music* as if it had been written by Wagner. "Teddy wants a dog, but Mom's allergic, Oliver has a cold, but Charlotte's fine!" he'd bellow, or something just as silly.

When the children were learning to sail, Worth had concocted elaborate pirate fantasies that lasted for days. He'd arrive at the island with a multitude of plastic "gem"-encrusted swords, ravage the trunks in Nona's attics for dress-up clothes, and charm Nona into turning her old hats and scarves into tricornes and black eye patches. Grace had always scoffed at her brother's foolishness, but her daughters followed Worth into his games with stars in their eyes.

Worth had taught his children to ski, to play tennis, and to sail. During blizzards, he'd spend hours playing board games with them, and if it rained for several days during the summer, he'd invent an indoor scavenger hunt that involved the entire family, Grace and Kellogg and their daughters and Nona, too. He worked hard, and he played just as hard.

How had that love of fun been transmuted into an addiction to drugs and alcohol for their third child?

A year ago, Teddy had dropped out of another college—the third he'd been admitted to after failing out of the first and being banned from the second for being drunk and high and mooning a professor on campus. He'd raided his college fund to travel around the continent, phoning from time to time to assure them he was okay. He'd phoned three weeks ago, and he'd promised to arrive on Nantucket, in time for Nona's birthday.

Perhaps when they were all together, all her children, safe on the island, enfolded in family routines as polished by the years as soft-buffed silver, perhaps then Helen's headaches would cease. She would be so grateful for that, even if it lasted only a few days.

*Nona's birthday.* Helen would focus on that. She needed to get ready for the trip. She rose. Worth might be awake now, might enjoy sitting down to a proper breakfast for once. She'd ask him.

Worth didn't often eat breakfast, even though Helen reminded him that doctors said it was the most important meal of the day. Her husband sprang from bed wide awake and energetic, ready to take on the world. Even coffee didn't interest him. But then, Worth was a good sleeper, not a continually exhausted insomniac like Helen. Worth fell asleep when his head touched the pillow around eleven at night, and he snored, twitched, and slumbered luxuriously in what was obviously a refreshing, rejuvenating state until, around seven thirty, he awoke in full consciousness, threw back the covers, and strode into the bathroom for a brisk shower. He dressed entirely, crisp shirt, cuff links, suit, tie, and wingtips, without even a sip of juice. If Helen tried to press breakfast on him, he told her he'd grab something when he got to the office, and he'd snatch up his briefcase, peck her on the forehead, and march out the door.

It still seemed wrong to her, separate bedrooms, even though it had been her own relentless insomnia brought on by hot flashes that, a few years ago, drove Worth out of their marriage bed and down the hall to one of the guest rooms. It suited them both, really, since they went to sleep and woke at different times, but she missed the warmth and weight of Worth's body in the bed, missed the accidental touch of his knee against the back of her leg, which often inspired them toward lovemaking.

Although, now that she thought about it, in the first few months after his move, they had made love more than usual. And it had been better. Worth had taken the trouble of seducing her, and she had returned the favor. It had been like having a lover.

When had that changed? They still made love occasionally, not as often as Helen would like but, as Worth reminded her, he was sixty. He showed affection in other ways—he brought her flowers, and books, he complimented her on her hair, he noticed when she looked good—but it seemed to Helen that marriage was not just about dutiful displays of fondness but profound physical encounters. Perhaps not as often now, but still, even at their age.

Worth must be awake by now. She could make eggs Benedict. Or even pancakes. Her spirits rose as she headed up the stairs and down the hall to Worth's bedroom.

As she drew close to Worth's door, she heard him talking on his cell phone. *Good,* she thought, because he was awake, and then, *Oh, dear,* because she hated it when his work, his important over-riding work, invaded their home on weekends.

"Come on, Sweet Cakes, don't be that way. You know I'm thinking about you every minute. You know the only thing I want to do is take you back to bed."

*What?* Helen stopped dead in the hall, as if she'd run into an invisible wall. What was Worth saying? Who was he talking to? *Sweet Cakes?*

"You know I do. And you know I will. I promise. But I've got to get through this family business first. I've explained it to you. Come on, talk nice to me."

*Talk nice to me?* Worth's voice held a low, playful, sexual urgency Helen hadn't heard for years. The very sound of it made her blush. She stood there, paralyzed in the hall, eavesdropping on her husband and flushing with a painful heat.

"I don't think she's awake yet. I don't smell coffee. But she'll be up any minute so I really should get off the phone. Oh, Sweet Cakes, you know I'll phone you." His voice grew louder, as if he were moving closer to the door, to the hall, where Helen stood paralyzed.

Then the primitive fight-or-flight survival instinct shut down her thoughts and shocked her into action. Heart pounding, she raced down the stairs and into the den, where she paced around the room, wringing her hands together.

My God. Worth was having an affair.

She had known something was wrong. She'd sensed it, the presence of a parasitic vine twining around her life, draining her marriage of its nutrients.

Growing green and supple, while she grew gray and brittle.

But perhaps she was wrong! Perhaps—but no. She had heard her husband say it. All he wanted was to take Sweet Cakes to bed.

All right, then, perhaps it wasn't *serious*. But what if it was? Worth was a handsome man with enormous charm and charisma. He was a powerful man with many friends. She was sure he hadn't had affairs before now. For one thing, he was always so busy, either at the bank or with his family. Of course she was not naïve; she knew a man could always find time to have an affair, but Worth was a Wheelwright, and Wheelwrights were all about family.

Worth's father would not have tolerated any kind of insult to the family. But Herb had died five years ago. He was not here to judge. Nona judged, and harshly, but she didn't have the kinds of access Herb had had to the world of men. She did not have the enormous range of contacts.

Was this why Worth was having an affair? Because his father had died and his mother was aging? Nona's hearing and strength were failing. Worth was always her favorite, and Nona's slowly flagging energy had to be very hard for him to see.

And his children were refusing to go through the golden doors Worth had opened for them, into the business of the family bank. Perhaps he considered himself a failure because of this, and Worth did not like to fail.

*Oh, come on, Helen,* she told herself. It doesn't take a convoluted Freudian reason for a man to have an affair. It only takes Sweet Cakes and chemistry. What should she do?

What *could* she do?

Should she confront him? No. Not now. Not today. It was Nona's birthday. Her children were already bringing enough disorder into the clockwork perfection of the Wheelwright family. She would not allow herself to distract anyone from this weekend celebration of their revered and beloved Nona.

But she was almost shivering with a frantic energy that outdid any caffeine hit she'd ever had. Was she hysterical? Probably. She had reason to be!

She had to think about something else, or she'd

simply explode. Hurrying to her desk, she forced herself to focus. *Book sale,* her calendar said. Book sale. She needed to sort books for the island library sale.

One wall of the den had shelves built in from floor to ceiling, and the shelves were full. In some places, books had been placed in front of or on top of the original rows. Pacing back and forth, she scanned the titles, and then she began to empty the shelves. *The Scarlet Letter*! They hadn't read that in years. And all those Hemingways were her college texts. And Edgar Allan Poe was so weird and depressing. These editions, handsomely bound, would bring a pretty penny.

Her stack grew. She would box these up and take them down to the island when they moved down for the summer.

And the children's books! She could pack those too, all of them! Who knew when she would ever have grandchildren? She *longed* for grandchildren, but would she ever have any? Oliver and Owen wouldn't have children. Teddy was practically a child himself. And she couldn't press the responsibility on Charlotte. Charlotte already had enough on her plate, with her father's constant reminders that he'd love her to return to work at the bank.

"What are you doing?"

Helen jumped, startled, heart pounding, as if she'd been caught in some dire guilty act. "Books," she managed to say. "I'm sorting books."

"Why now? And why are you crying?" Worth came toward her, an expression of genuine concern on his face. "Helen? What's wrong?"

Helen turned away and hid her face in her hands.

"Grandchildren," she sputtered desperately. "I'll never have grandchildren to read all these wonderful books to."

Worth put his arms around her and pulled her close to his body. "Of course we'll have grandchildren. Everyone has their families late these days. Charlotte's only thirty."

Helen sniffed and wiped her cheeks with her hands. "I know. I'm just being silly."

"Not silly. Not at all. I'd like grandchildren, too."

She pulled away from him. His warmth and understanding made her feel like an emotional nutcase; he was having sex with Sweet Cakes and yet he could be so loving to his wife. She couldn't process it.

"I need to shower and pack," she said, without looking at him. "We don't want to be late."

Without waiting for a reply, she left the den and hurried up the stairs to her bedroom. She crossed her room, entered the bathroom, shut the door and locked it, stripped off her gown, and stepped into her shower. Pain slammed at her head. She wrenched the water taps open to the fullest, grateful for the onslaught of noise and water. She bent over, put her hands on her knees, and gasped for breath.

The hot water beat against her bare back. She unfolded to her full height and sagged against the tiled wall, letting the steady flow of water comfort her.

But the thought would not recede: Worth was having an affair.

Had Nona ever run down the hall and thrown herself into a shower to collect her thoughts? Helen doubted it. Nona was always composed. Nona was perfect.

Helen turned off the water, stepped out, dried off, and ran a comb through her heavy, curly salt-and-pepper hair. She'd always been secretly proud of her hair, thick and wavy and luxurious. She never wore makeup, except for lipstick on formal occasions. Her skin was pretty good, considering all the time she'd spent in the sun. Her mother had been an early devotee of sunblock and straw hats. Her blue eyes were her best feature, she thought; she needed glasses only for reading. And although she'd gained weight over the years, the various sports she pursued in her own mild way and the hours spent on the exercise bike or treadmill when she thought about it had paid off. Perhaps she was not slim, but she was not fat, either. Until now, she'd considered herself just pretty much *healthy.* And at sixty, healthy was fabulous.

But obviously not fabulous enough for Worth. Helen returned to her bedroom and pulled a loose floral sundress over her head. She slipped into a cashmere cardigan in the same dreamy pinks and sat down on the side of the bed to buckle her sandals. As she stood before her mirror, fastening her necklace, a tinkling dangle of silver with beads and nuggets of reds and yellows and blues, her hands trembled. *Sweet Cakes.* The name conjured up a soft blond beauty, someone with delicious flesh and adorable dimples. Someone irresistible.

Someone who could change all their lives.

How different would this summer be? Would Worth still fly down every weekend, to swim, sail, and play tennis, to enjoy lobster dinners and clambakes? Or would he remain in Boston, claiming the exigencies of work, when in truth he wanted to be with his—his what? His *mistress?* That sounded rather Victorian and frivolous. His *girlfriend?* She couldn't imagine Worth with a girl.

Well, then, a *lover.* She hugged herself and rocked slowly as she sat on the side of her unmade bed.

"Helen?" Worth called from the bottom of the stairs. "What's taking you so long? We've got to leave for the airport."

Helen steadied herself. "I'll be right down," she called.

# Arrival

# Four

*From her chaise,* Nona heard the white shells on the driveway crackle and then doors slammed, voices called out, and a baby cried.

She looked out to see them file beneath the curved arbor, through the hedge, her daughter Grace and Grace's family—Kellogg, the nicest and most boring man on the planet, and their three daughters: Mandy, thirty-five; Mellie, thirty-three; and Mee, twenty-eight. When they were infants, their names had been cutely abbreviated from Amanda, Amelia, and Amy, and of course they were referred to as the Ms. The fact that not one of the girls, when she became an adult, insisted on reverting to her full name suggested to Nona that all three granddaughters chose to exist in the infantile state their parents preferred.

But Nona had to admit that nicknames were rampant in the Wheelwright family. Long ago, Oliver had referred to Kellogg, his daughters' husbands, and Worth as the Bank Boys, and the name stuck. That was, at least, a useful moniker. Secretly, Nona thought of Kellogg and his daughters' husbands as the Nonfiction Husbands: no romance, no mystery, no suspense. She wished she could share this witticism with someone without hurting anyone. Perhaps someday she would tell Oliver. He could keep a secret, and he'd appreciate the humor.

But she would never want to hurt her grand-daughters. They were nice girls, the Ms, never the least trouble, and pretty, but they lacked the spirit, what Nona thought of as *spunk,* that inspired Worth's children. Ms had made good marriages, all three—although Mee had just gotten a divorce.

Something rather strange had been happening to Nona over the past few years, and it worried her. She'd even considered discussing this with a psychiatric doctor, and Nona had always scorned therapists and psychology. The older she grew, the more she seemed to love *people in general.* When she voyaged across the water on the ferry, she watched the other passengers and felt an unexplainable rush of affection for them all—the gawky teenage boys wearing their jeans so low they trod on the cuffs; the young women with their glossy hair, multicolored nails, and cell phones; even the (probably illegal) Hispanic immigrants clutching their shopping bags full of the inexpensive merchandise one could always buy on the Cape and never on Nantucket. Or if she watched television—for example, one winter evening she'd watched the Super Bowl with Charlotte and some of Charlotte's friends. A good-looking blond-haired man named Tom Petty sang during halftime, and the cameras panned around to show some faces of the individuals swaying to the music, smiling, singing, waving light sticks, all of them young and in jeans, and Nona was swept with something she could only call bliss at the sight of so many beautiful and happy young people. It was odd, but she felt related to them all, as if they were all her grandchildren. This is how God feels, she thought, looking down at an infinity of faces.

And yet now that her real grandchildren were arriving, what she felt was a kind of dread. She seemed to have lost her enthusiasm for *people in particular.* Or, rather, for particular people. She loved having Charlotte around, and when Oliver visited she was in heaven. But plodding Kellogg and his three bland daughters often bored and sometimes just plain irritated her. That in turn made her feel guilty. She and Herb had tried their best not to show favoritism to any of their children or grandchildren, and she thought they'd succeeded.

What had caused this change? It had to be this business with Charlotte's garden. It was peculiar and almost amusing, how Beach Grass Garden's paltry net income of four thousand dollars had sent the family into a maelstrom of jealousy and greed. Of course no one, and Nona included herself, had expected Charlotte to make a go of her garden. It had seemed just one more of the idealistic, save-the-world, bubble-headed schemes that all the grandchildren had proposed at one time or another. Even Mee had taken time off from college to travel the country telling fortunes at state fairs. She'd set off in an ancient rattling VW camper with her boyfriend Sky, a handsome, emaciated fellow who seemed to survive on whatever nutrients he inhaled from marijuana plants. They had gotten as far as Indiana before the VW broke down. She'd called her parents, who sent her a plane ticket. Mee flew home and went back to college that January. Sky had stayed in Indiana and, as far as Nona knew, Mee never heard from him again.

But remembering this about Mee made Nona feel a surge of affection for her, and the timing was propitious, for here they were, three of the four Wheelwright granddaughters. Mandy carried her baby, Zoe, and her husband, Claus, had four-year-old Christian riding on his shoulders. Sweet little children, really. Mellie lumbered along behind, hugely pregnant, with her husband, Douglas, following, his forehead wrinkled in concentration as he barked into his cell phone. Mee came last, by herself.

They swept toward Nona in a wave of greetings, kissing, hugging, and, in Zoe's case, drooling. Behind them strode Kellogg, bags in each hand and one hooked over each shoulder. "Hello, Nona!" he called heartily from behind his flock. "Girls, where do you want the luggage?"

Grace struggled in through the French doors, also laden with bags. She blew Nona a kiss. "Mother! You look lovely! Does it matter where we sleep?"

"Not at all. Charlotte's in the attic, you know."

"I'll take another attic bedroom, then," Mee declared. "We spinsters can have our own floor."

"Can't be a spinster if you've been married," Mandy corrected. "It's too bad Charlotte's taken up the attic. The playroom's up there. It would be much easier if *we* could have the attic bedrooms."

"Don't be silly, Mandy," Mee retorted. "The attic bedrooms only have single beds."

"Well, *I* don't want an attic bedroom," Mellie pouted, rubbing her round belly. "It's going to be hard enough for me to climb stairs as it is."

"I'll take an attic bedroom," Mellie's husband, Douglas, said. "Maybe I'll be able to get some sleep without being bounced about by a great white wh—" He was skewered by his wife's glance. "Sorry, Mellie."

"Why don't you and Claus take the front bedroom," Grace suggested to her oldest daughter. "The children can go in the old sewing room, and Daddy and I will stay in the room across the hall so we can help with the children."

"Is the crib still set up in the old sewing room?" Claus asked. "Christian, you're getting heavy, Papa's going to put you down."

"These *bags* are what's getting heavy!" Kellogg announced. "I'm taking them up to the second floor. You can sort them out up there."

Bulging and joining and separating like some kind of amoeba shown on a Nature Channel special, the dynamic mass of Grace's family made their way from the living room into the large hall and up the front stairs. Interesting, Nona thought, that Charlotte hadn't come in from the garden, rushing into the room to hug her cousins and aunt and uncle. Well, Charlotte was serious about her work, and although she had to have seen the vehicles arrive, driving over the sandy path from the main road, she might have only waved and then returned to her weeding or watering or whatever she was doing. The years when they would have hurried to greet one another, all of them squealing like piglets, had passed.

Mandy fluttered into the room. "Do you think you could hold the baby for just a minute? I'll be right back with her diaper bag and her bouncy chair. There's so much paraphernalia required for a baby." She plunked the baby down in Nona's arms and hurried out to the garden and through the hedge to her SUV.

Nona gazed down at her great-granddaughter. Zoe's skin had the smooth iridescence of the inside of a shell. She remembered this luminous skin from her own babies. Zoe was awake and looking around, puckering her mouth as if she were about to pronounce judgment on what she saw. When her eyes fastened on Nona's, she smiled a toothless baby smile.

"You darling," Nona whispered, stroking the baby's soft face with her gnarled, wrinkled old witch's finger. She remembered this, too, from when her grandchildren were babies, how infants could somehow see past the disfigurements of age to the love within.

Claus entered the room. Tall, thin, Scandinavian, he gave off the nervous energy of a purebred borzoi. "I was going to ask you to look after Christian, but I see Mandy got to you first. I need to bring in the co-sleeper for Zoe." He looked hopelessly burdened.

Kellogg appeared. "I'll bring in the co-sleeper. Which room did you take? Come on, Christian, let Grandpop give you a ride." He swept the four-year-old up onto his shoulders. "Nona, we're going through the mudroom, okay? It's closer to the cars."

Mellie waddled in and collapsed in a nearby wing chair. "I have the worst heartburn! I never dreamed pregnancy could be such a torment!"

"We have baking soda in the kitchen," Nona told her. "Mix some with a glass of water. It works wonders."

"Baking soda! Nona, you just have *no idea* the ferocity of this heartburn! Baking soda wouldn't touch it. I've tried every over-the-counter medication there is; I *live* on Rolaids and Tums." Her husband passed through the hallway, lugging duffel bags. Spotting him, Mellie said loudly, "I just wish Dougie had to experience some of what I'm going through. I just wish he could experience it for *one day.*"

"Mmm," Nona agreed vaguely. "Mother Nature always was unfair."

Grace came in, wiping her hands on an embroidered kitchen hand towel that Nona's mother-in-law had once used. "Glorious and I are making several gallons of iced tea. We're all so thirsty. I assume no one wants a real drink, not until evening, right?"

Claus, wrestling two bulging duffel bags into the hall, stopped at the bottom step. "No alcohol for me. I want to play tennis this afternoon."

Behind him, Kellogg was struggling with the co-sleeper. "Yes, and I want to get the boat into the water."

The two men toiled up the stairs with their heavy burdens.

"Okay, iced tea it is," Grace told them, and went off.

*I could use an alcoholic beverage,* Nona thought but did not say. So many people needing so many things.

It was different with Charlotte. She was just one person, and she cared about Nona's pleasure. Nona had found Charlotte good company over the past three years, while Charlotte lived in the attic and worked in her garden. Charlotte always made time to stop and chat with Nona, and she made the long winter months deliciously cozy, building a roaring fire, making cocoa from scratch, playing backgammon or cards with Nona. Also she had discovered a trove of brilliant British films on DVDs at the local library, and Friday nights had become their "date night," when they sat together in the den, watching movies and eating a delicious and completely disreputable meal of pizza and ice cream. All that played havoc with Nona's bowels the next day, but it was too delightful an occasion to give up.

Other than that, Charlotte did not really impinge on Nona's sensibilities. If she played music, she did so either on her headphones while she worked in the garden or up in the attic, from where the sound did not travel. Charlotte also had her computer up there, and a television of her own, so she did not interrupt Nona's routine.

Glorious had a large room on the far side of the kitchen, fitted out with a big new TV and a small sofa as well as a comfortable bed and private bath. Glorious had many friends in town and loved to socialize—needed to, Nona imagined, after a day spent dealing with an old bat like herself. Glorious didn't complain about helping Nona. She was relaxed and seemed actually happy about everything. Still, Nona felt guilty about keeping Glorious later than six o'clock. It made a long day for Glorious, and of course Nona paid her well, but still she hated to be a bother. Nona never liked being a bother.

So even before Charlotte had come to live in the house, Nona had hit upon a routine that satisfied her. She simply retired at six o'clock. She brushed her long white hair, braided it, and tied the braid with a plaid grosgrain ribbon. She cleaned her teeth, set her bridge into a glass of denture cleaner, and washed and creamed her face. She slipped into one of her flannel nightgowns and settled into bed, resting in the clever chair pillow Glorious had given her one Christmas. Its back was soft and plump and Nona could rest her tired arms on the arms of the pillow. That done, Glorious would settle the bed tray over Nona's lap, and on the tray was Glorious's latest splendid culinary effort for Nona's dinner. Also, a glass of red wine. Also, the remote control. Glorious would kiss Nona on the forehead and hurry downstairs. Soon a friend would come by for her in a rackety old car and Glorious would go giggling out the front door into the evening. Nona would eat, watch the news, and shout her opinions at the overly groomed news-casters, and sometimes she watched her favorite television shows: *As Time Goes By. Keeping Up Appearances. Masterpiece Theater.* Often, she read. And more and more often, she dozed. She seldom slept for more than four hours straight any-more. She was amazed at what sorts of things one could see on the television at three in the morning.

When Charlotte moved in, she made it clear she didn't want to alter Nona's routine. Of course Nona could hear Charlotte rattling around the big old house, preparing herself a meal—the aromas drifting temptingly up the stairs—or talking on her cell phone, or leaving the house and returning later after a movie or a meal with a friend. Nona enjoyed those signs of life. Somehow they had tacitly agreed that Charlotte would greet her grandmother in the morning but not at night. It had to do, Nona thought, with the fact that she didn't like her family to see her without all her teeth.

It was not just vanity. It was also about dignity and, more than that, about power.

Every summer of her life since she was twenty-three, Nona had spent in this house surrounded by family. The summers had been splendid when she was young. When she had energy. She'd run the house, raised her children, and found time to go sailing or play a game of tennis. She'd orchestrated birthday parties, Fourth of July celebrations, clambakes for seventy.

But not until five years ago, when Herb died, had she been responsible for Family Meeting.

No one could ever call Nona self-effacing. But there truly was a generational difference in the way wives responded to their husbands. When Nona was a bride, women were more submissive. That was simply the way the world was. Nona wasn't responsible for that and she would not accept any kind of guilt. In turn, she did not try to judge or condemn her daughter-in-law Helen for Helen's attitude toward Worth. In fact, she admired Helen and thought Helen handled Worth pretty well.

Worth was a lot to handle. He was the most handsome of Herb and Nona's children, and the one who shouldered the inheritance of the bank. Of the three children, he was the achiever, bright, charming, ambitious, and political.

Worth and his younger brother, Bobby, had always fought—there were only two years between them. Perhaps Bobby would have been more rebellious or perhaps he would have straightened out. No one would ever know. Bobby had been killed in Vietnam in 1970.

One thing Nona was certain of, although she never had spoken of this with anyone, was that Worth's sense of family responsibility increased the moment he heard of his brother's death. It was understandable. Herb himself had changed when his second son died. He became driven. He spent less time at home and more time at the bank. It was as if the bank suddenly took Bobby's place, and he needed to see it prosper and grow as if it were a living creature.

True, the bank was one of the oldest institutions in the Commonwealth of Massachusetts, founded in 1878 by Herb's great-grandfather, and in a way it did seem part of the family. Once simply named The Fourth Bank of Boston, over the years it had changed names and added officers and shareholders. Now Worth, Kellogg, and Lew Lowry were in charge. Lew's son Whit, who was Charlotte's age, worked at the bank, and Nona knew that Worth wanted Charlotte to date him.

Nona still owned shares in the bank, but she had little power there and didn't care to have more. She did have control of the Wheelwright personal monies and trusts, and she ran Family Meeting in Herb's place. It had been subtly suggested to her that Family Meeting was too much of a burden for a woman of her age, but she had no intention of letting go of the reins just yet.

The truth was, she was worried about Worth. She felt a need to keep her eye on him. Something wasn't quite right. It was not just the fancy of an old lady, either. She was clear-sighted enough to see how Worth put pressure on his children. Well, on two of his children. He demanded the most of Charlotte, because Charlotte was the child who most adored her father. Charlotte had tried working at the bank and had disappointed Worth when, after three years, she told him it was not for her. Worth wanted his second son, Teddy, to quit his rogue ways and stop drinking so much. Well, everyone wanted Teddy to stop drinking so much. But Worth's methods and manners of relating to his two younger children had changed. Worth could be so persuasive when he tried. He was handsome, charming, energetic, humorous—but this past year he had become a bit of a tyrant, which only turned his children more definitely against him. Even Charlotte, who worshipped her father, had begun to argue with him. The sound of their raised voices was not pleasant, nor was it in any way effective.

It was not just Teddy that was worrying Worth. Nona wondered if perhaps Helen was having an affair. So often sex was at the root of an upheaval. Worth and Helen had just turned sixty, a dangerous age. Helen was hardly a siren, but in her own untidy way she was attractive. Perhaps she was sleeping with another man; that could explain Worth's disposition. Nona cared for her daughter-in-law, but she did think Helen was a dark horse. Helen had never allowed herself to become a true part of the Wheelwright family. She had been and continued to be a good mother, though, and Nona thought her children were still her top priority. Perhaps it was only the burden of Teddy and his difficulties that was weighing Worth down.

Oh, daughter Grace and her contingent were surely noisy and chaotic, but it was the thought of Worth's arrival that made her feel so tired. Was this because she loved her son just a little bit more?

## Five

*H*elen *felt scattered* as she settled into the limo.

Worth, next to her, touched her hand. "Fasten your seat belt."

She did, hoping he wouldn't notice how her hands were shaking.

He didn't.

Lounging back in the buttery-soft cushioned leather of the limo, Worth talked on his cell phone with colleagues and assistants about bank business or tapped on his laptop computer.

In self-defense, Helen opened her own laptop and tapped away too, making lists and memos for her various committees. Amazing, she thought, how her stifled emotions supplied a geyser of energy. Interesting, how all the modern technological gadgets designed to bring us closer together really provided a polite means for people to ignore one another.

At the airport, they went through the rituals of checking in and getting their boarding passes pleasantly, automatically, as they had done a thousand times before. Their strides matched evenly as they walked swiftly through the crowded halls, past newsstands, fast-food boutiques, and coffee shops, from security checkpoint to gate. Worth tapped memos into his BlackBerry as they sat on the hard plastic chairs at the Cape Airlines gate waiting for their flight to be called. Helen read a book, or pretended to.

In fact, her mind whirled with questions. With whom was Worth having an affair? Someone from the bank, a sleek young secretary or administrative assistant? Perhaps a widow or a divorcée? No. Worth would never call a woman of Helen's age "Sweet Cakes." It had to be a younger woman, a much younger woman, with her breasts still riding high above her rib cage and her skin free of stretch marks. How long had this been going on? What kind of wife was Helen, to have been so oblivious—to have gone about her life in such a carefree manner, unaware that her husband was having sex with another woman?

Their flight was called and they boarded the nine-seater prop jet that carried them to Nantucket. It skimmed south, above the coast, humming and rackety and too noisy for conversation. The day was brilliant with sunshine, the water below infinitely blue.

Worth's sister, Grace, was at the airport to meet them in her father's beloved 1949 Chrysler woody convertible.

"Worth! Helen! On time! Good for you!" Grace hugged them, then grabbed one of their suitcases and led the way out to the car.

It was a relief to be with Grace, who jabbered away enthusiastically about all the plans she'd made for Nona's birthday the entire time it took to drive out to the house. Not that Helen could hear her. Grace liked to drive with the top down, and it was a beautiful day for a ride in a convertible, but Worth with his long legs got the passenger seat in front behind the windshield, and Helen was wedged into the back with the luggage, where the wind beat at her face and tugged at her hair. She felt oddly calmed, caught like a leaf spinning on the stream of the family's life. She could only let herself be carried along. Other thoughts had to wait.

Grace slowed on Polpis Road for the turn onto Nona's land, and there was Charlotte's little market-garden stand. Charlotte was there, too, and now Helen's thoughts receded in a wave of love and delight at the sight of her wonderful daughter.

Charlotte was dressed like a farmer in striped overalls and boots and a straw hat, and Helen remembered all the costumes Charlotte had worn in her life. Her favorite pastime as a child was to play dress-up, raiding the trunks in Nona's attics. Charlotte was Helen's Gemini child, with at least two personalities. She was smart, hardworking, and kindhearted, but she had never been very practical. She was idealistic, a dreamer, and in spite of her attempts to seem businesslike with this garden, Helen was afraid Charlotte still had her head in the clouds.

"Hello!" Helen waved at her daughter, who waved back.

Charlotte was talking with Bill Cooper from the house next door. He was a handsome man, and Helen looked forward to seeing his parents tomorrow at Nona's party. They were on the guest list, Grace had informed Helen, and she was glad. They weren't close with the Coopers, but they'd known them forever, played tennis with them occasionally, had cocktails on the Coopers' deck or in Nona's garden or on the Coopers' yacht. Felicity and Mark Cooper had had only one child, Bill. Helen thought Mark had wanted his son to follow him into his business in real estate. Instead, Coop had wandered around, trying different jobs, a bit of this, a bit of that, a bachelor's degree in English literature, which would help him get no job at all, and, later, a master's degree in computer science, which did, after a few years, pay off. Coop was self-supporting now with his software business, at least that was what Felicity had told Helen last summer. Of course, "self-supporting" was a relative term when someone lived at home without paying rent or mortgage as Coop was doing on the island.

Still, Helen didn't think Coop had ever caused his parents any serious concern. One summer night, when he was sixteen, he'd gotten drunk with friends and thrown up on the beach in front of Nona's house, but Mark Cooper had given him holy hell, and Nona, playing the role the Coopers had asked her to play, gave the boy an old-fashioned tongue-lashing which had put the fear of God into him. Helen smiled, remembering how the grown-ups had conspired to terrorize Coop out of his reckless overindulgence in alcohol.

And then Helen frowned as she remembered that she and Worth had played out many scenes of censure, anger, and threat with Teddy, and with Teddy their condemnations did not seem to work.

The ride was bumpy as Grace sped the convertible along the dirt lane leading up to the house. To the west lay Charlotte's garden, rows and rows of plants, which might have looked attractive except for the ugly wire enclosure. Charlotte said the fence was necessary to keep the deer out, and Nona didn't mind; she couldn't see the area from her living room or from the formal garden, where she liked to spend her summer days. They passed the old barn, which had been converted into a garage and toolshed, with the long new addition of Charlotte's potting shed added on, the wooden shingles still pale gold, not yet weathered to silver. The driveway circled around a large concrete vase spilling over with ranunculus and pansies. Slate stepping-stones led right, to the boathouse and boat ramp, and left, across the lawn to the mudroom and kitchen. But Nona would be in the living room, so Helen and Worth went under the opening in the high privet hedge and through the formal garden and in through the French doors, where Nona was seated in her chaise by the window.

"Hello, darlings." Nona held up her arms. She wore one of her trademark tailor-made outfits, silk slacks and a matching silk top with a mandarin collar, toggle closures, and embroidered cuffs. Today, it was coral with white trim. Helen thought Nona probably had thirty of these outfits in a range of colors. They had a simple elegance to them which Nona completed by adding her pearl choker and pearl earrings, just the luminous white of Nona's hair. The older woman's face was creased with age, but when she smiled she was young and beautiful.

"Mother. You look wonderful." Worth bent to kiss his mother's cheek.

"Thank you. What's that in your hand?" Sharp-eyed Nona didn't waste a moment. "You greet me with your cell phone in your hand?"

Worth grinned sheepishly. "I've got just one more piece of business to conclude."

Nona gestured imperiously. "Take it outside. Or into the library. No business in the living room or in my garden." She held her arms up to Helen. "Honestly. How do you put up with him?"

"Actually, I have no idea." Helen kept her voice bantering as she bent down to kiss her mother-in-law.

Nona patted the side of the chaise. "Sit here a moment, dear. Let's catch up. Grace and her tribe have already invaded—"

"I heard that, Mother!" Grace yelled from the hallway.

Nona laughed. "The great-grands are darling, and Mandy and Claus ride herd on them very capably. Mellie, however, as the first woman on earth ever to endure pregnancy, is languishing, and Mee—well, poor Mee is taking this divorce really hard."

*Divorce,* Helen thought, and wasn't sure whether

the idea frightened or tempted her. Perhaps a bit of both. Absentmindedly, she said, "Your party will cheer her up."

Sharp Nona caught something. "You look tired, Helen."

Helen put her hand to her windblown hair. "Not tired, really, just disheveled."

"Grace drives that convertible like a maniac. I told her I will never ride in the backseat again."

Helen laughed. "I don't blame you. How's Charlotte been treating you?"

Nona lay back against her pillows with an affectionate smile. "I see very little of her these days. It's her busiest time in the garden. She's up at four-thirty every day. I know, because I'm awake then, too, but I'm too lazy to get out of bed. I just lie there, watching the sky lighten and listening to the birds singing. I can hear her coming down the stairs, tiptoeing like a little children's-book cherub so she won't wake me. I hear the door to the mudroom open and close; I always mean to have someone oil those hinges, and I forget it as soon as I remember it. I love lying there, imagining her out in her garden, smelling the fresh morning air, gathering up all her tools, hearing the world wake up."

What a gift it was, what sheer delight, to hear her mother-in-law speak with such fondness about her daughter! A rush of love and gratitude swept through Helen, and she said, impulsively, "That reminds me, Nona! I made a present for you. I'll get it now."

Nona held out a hand to forestall her. "But my birthday's not until tomorrow."

"I know, but if I give it to you now, you can use it first thing in the morning."

Nona quirked an eyebrow. "Now you've got my curiosity aroused."

"I'll be right back." Helen hurried out into the hall. Her bulging duffel was there on the floor, and from the dining room came Worth's voice as he paced around, still on his cell phone. Helen unzipped the duffel, lifted out the package, and carried it in to Nona. Smug as a child, she presented it to her. "Happy birthday."

Nona said, "Thank you, dear." She untied the ribbon and carefully unfastened the tape; Nona always saved wrapping paper. She lifted out a mound of lavender mohair, as soft as a cloud. "A shawl?"

Helen shook her head. "A bed jacket." Eagerly, she reached out and unfolded the garment, holding it up for Nona's inspection. "I know how you enjoy reading in bed. Sometimes I've seen you with a blanket tossed over your shoulders for warmth, and I thought this might be lighter and warmer."

"It's lovely, Helen. Did you actually make it yourself?"

"I did. I chose the yarn and I knitted it." She swallowed her innate shyness. "I love you, Nona, and I wanted to give you a birthday present especially and only from me."

Nona took the bed jacket and held it against her. "It's as light as feathers."

"But it will be warm," Helen said.

"Yes. It will be perfect. And the color is dreamy. You are so thoughtful, Helen; I'm touched. I'll put it near me so I can slip into it tomorrow morning. It will be my first present, starting off my ninetieth birthday just right." Nona reached out a wrinkled hand and patted Helen's.

Worth came in, Helen's duffel over his shoulder. "I'm going up, Helen. Do you want to come choose a room?"

"Look what Helen gave me, Worth." Nona held up the bed jacket.

"Nice." Worth shifted impatiently from one foot to the other.

"I'd better go up," Helen said.

*Nona's summer house* had plenty of bedrooms and bathrooms, but anyone who had stayed there once or twice knew from experience that some of the baths had showers and not bathtubs and some had old claw-footed bathtubs but no showers, and these were lovely for long soaks but impossible for washing one's hair. Some of the bedrooms had high four-poster twin beds, and some had old lumpy double beds, and some had queen beds, and no one claimed any room as theirs because personal sleeping arrangements changed almost every year. For example, Mee had been married for three years to Phillip and they'd insisted they couldn't have a room with twin beds; they wanted to sleep together. But now here Mee was, divorced, so she would take, she had announced like a good brave martyr, any little room with a futon or something, someplace for one person alone.

Because Helen and Worth were late arrivals on Friday, they ended up with a choice of one of the cramped attic bedrooms or a second-floor room with a lumpy double bed. It was a pretty room. All the rooms were nicely wallpapered and softened with thick silky rugs, and the bed linens were old but clean and crisply ironed.

"This will have to do," Worth said, and dumping his bag on the bed he began to unpack, setting his striped pajamas in the bottom drawer of the dresser, allowing Helen, as was his habit, the top two drawers.

All at once panic rinsed down Helen's back. She could not share this pretty little room, that narrow double bed, with Worth, lying, philandering, cheating, deceitful Worth. It would be sickening to feel his large hairy male body shoved up against hers, knowing he had been lying on top of, inside of, another woman, and it would be heartbreaking if he should curl up against her—and how could he not in such a small bed—without becoming aroused and initiating sex.

"You know," she said, and her voice seemed higher than usual, "I am too familiar with the lumps in that bed to want to attempt a night's sleep there, and you don't want to deal with my insomnia. I think I'll try the sleeping porch."

Worth kept unpacking. Socks in the drawer with the pajamas, and ironed boxer shorts, and a couple of short-sleeved polo shirts in the deep blues that brought out the blue of his eyes. "No one sleeps on the sleeping porch," he said.

"Then why is it called a sleeping porch?" She sounded lighthearted, flippant, as she left the room and walked down the hall.

The sleeping porch, at the end of the house, had three walls of screened-in windows, a wooden floor with an old rag rug in an oval puddle of blues and browns, and a disreputable daybed shoved up against the inner wall, covered with a white chenille bedspread that probably dated from the 1930s. The spread was stained with dubious spots that looked like blood, but Helen knew it was from pizza or chocolate ice cream, because not so very long ago, when they were teenage boys, Oliver and Teddy had turned this room into their private and unassailable lair. Mismatched furniture that Nona couldn't quite give up but didn't know what else to do with had migrated from other rooms to the sleeping porch: a white wicker rocking chair with unraveling wicker and chipped paint, a handsome ladies' desk with a wobbly leg, a standing brass lamp with sockets for three bulbs, only one socket of which worked, and a very ugly card table that someone—Grace, no doubt—had covered with Con-Tact shelf paper in a white-and-pink rose print. The paper was coming unstuck at several places along the edges of the tabletop.

Helen dropped her bag on the floor and collapsed on the daybed. This gave her a view of the ceiling, which was a yellowed white with a water stain in one corner. It would be cool out here at night, perhaps even cold. Nantucket Junes were notoriously unpredictable. But there were plenty of wool blankets in the linen cupboard. Besides, Helen liked a cool bedroom. The room had no closets, but someone had once hung a couple of black wrought-iron plant holders near the windows. The plants were gone, but the little metal arms would serve very well to hold a few hangers. And she didn't need a chest of drawers. Well, she would when she returned for the summer. If she intended to sleep here for the entire summer. . . .

From the hall came Grace's voice. "Mandy? I'm taking Christian down to the beach with me, all right?"

"Thanks, Mom!" Mandy called. "I've got to nurse the baby."

Oh, fortunate Grace, to have that darling bright-eyed little grandson! Helen could hear the child's high sweet voice as they went down the stairs. "Will the seals be on the beach this time,

Grandma? Maybe the bottle with our message will be there in the sand! Can I take my shoes off now?"

Helen had been surprised at the satisfaction she'd felt when Grace's daughter gave birth to Christian, the Wheelwrights' first grandchild. She remembered visiting Mandy in the hospital, and being given the infant to hold, and gazing down at that perfect baby boy with his pearly skin and pursed mouth. He is the future, she had thought with a surprising surge of optimism. Look at the generosity of the universe, giving us this perfection, this potential, this reason for joy and hope.

Would she ever have grandchildren?

Lying on the sloping daybed, Helen thought that if she had a grandchild she wouldn't mind so much about Worth and his affair. She had shared an extravagance of love with Worth during their lives together. When she first met Worth, her heart had warmed, as if a well-fed cat had jumped up on a windowsill, turned around, and settled down, purring, in a square of sunlight. Worth had been a lovely lover. His present affair could not erase the memories of all those past embraces.

And it did not make those memories false, did it? Worth was a splendid father, and he would be a doting, involved, attentive grandfather. If only Charlotte would fall in love! If only she would get married—never mind marriage, if only she would fall in love and have a child! Then, perhaps, Worth would lose interest in this other woman and, sharing the new adventure of grandparenting with Helen, return his attention to his family. To his wife.

But perhaps not.

And would she want him back on those terms, or was everything broken between them?

## *Six*

*Charlotte saw* the cars arriving: a Yukon with Mandy, her husband and children, and a desolate-looking Mee crammed in the backseat; a Volvo with Mellie and her husband, Douglas; and then Aunt Grace and Uncle Kellogg in a cab.

Charlotte waved from her row of strawberries, feeling torn. She loved the drama of arrivals, everyone hugging and talking at once, and she didn't want anyone to feel that she didn't care that they were here, but she really did need to take advantage of every daylight minute on warm days. Also, she wanted to impress upon her relatives that she was out here *working*.

She continued picking strawberries, delicately tugging the sweet crimson fruit off the plants and dropping them in a wicker basket lined with a blue-and-white-checked napkin. She'd found a trunk of these old hand linens in the storage room in the attic, and Nona gave them to her readily. Charlotte used them to line baskets when she took the lettuces and vegetables to the restaurants that bought her produce, and everyone seemed to appreciate the attractive presentation. Even the lettuces seemed to frill a little more briskly, lying there against the crisp cotton cloth.

A squawk from a car horn made her look up. Aunt Grace waved from Granddad's beloved Chrysler convertible, which had slumbered in the garage patiently all winter, then tore off down the road toward town and the airport. Charlotte waved back, grinning. Aunt Grace loved to drive that car.

She reached the last plant, chose the ripest berries, and then she was done. She stood up, put her hands on her back, and leaned far back, looking up at the sky, feeling the welcome stretch in her spine. It was after seven. Everyone would be more or less settled now, having cocktails, waiting for the others to arrive before sitting down to dinner.

Carrying her basket, Charlotte walked between her long rows of plants and along the edge of the garden until she came to the far end gate. She went out, double-checked that the gate was fastened with its loop of wire, and continued walking down the dirt path to the main road and her little farm stand.

Bill Cooper was there, wearing jeans, a T-shirt, and a Red Sox cap, holding a bunch of radishes in his hand. "Hey, Charlotte."

"Hi, Coop. What's up?" Remembering the conversation she'd overheard earlier in the day, she felt herself flushing.

"Do you have any more of that arugula?"

Charlotte scanned the table. Only a bag of mesclun remained of all the lettuces she'd picked and set out this morning. Her wicker basket was full of bills and coins. "Sorry. No more until tomorrow."

"Damn. That arugula's tasty." He picked up the mesclun. "Well, I'll take this. It will keep for a couple days, won't it? I mean, I'll eat half tonight, half tomorrow."

Charlotte felt her flush deepen. Was he trying to inform her indirectly that he was eating alone now? "Sure," she replied. Then she remembered. "Oh. Wait. Aren't you coming to Nona's birthday party?"

"Absolutely. How could I forget? Ninety. What a milestone. She's an incredible woman, your grandmother."

"She is. The amazing thing is how good her hearing is. And her memory. She has to walk with a cane, and she can't go far, but mentally she's exceptional."

"She always was exceptional." Coop leaned a blue-jeaned thigh against the long picnic table. "Mom and Dad tell some great stories about her."

Charlotte thought she was probably staring at Coop like a teen seeing her favorite rock star. She was absolutely *beaming* at him. "Are they coming?" Charlotte picked up the bills and patted them into a neat pile as she spoke, then tucked it and the coins into the little money bag she wore on her hip. When she got back to the shed, she'd count the money and record it on her computer.

"They wouldn't miss it for the world. They're flying in tomorrow morning. Staying with me." As Charlotte lifted the red-and-white-checked table-cloth and shook it out, he asked, "Can I help you with anything?"

"No, thanks. I just don't like to leave this out overnight." She folded it neatly in half and then again and draped it over her arm.

"Is Oliver coming?"

"Of course! He flies in tomorrow."

"Great. I haven't seen him for years. Will Owen be with him?"

"Yes. They're staying at an inn in town. Nona thinks it's so they can have mad homosexual sex, but I know it's because they can't handle the chaos and clamor the Ms cause."

"Well, little children make noise. . . ."

"Mandy's children are adorable. They're not the noisy ones. *You* know, Coop, you remember what it's like in the summer, the Ms tripping around together squawking like some kind of bird with three heads."

Coop laughed. "Still, I'll be glad to see them again." He reached over and plucked one strawberry from the basket sitting on the table. "Yum. Do you have more?"

"I'm picking more tomorrow morning. You'll have to get to the table early. The strawberries go fast."

"You're developing quite a name for yourself, aren't you?"

"I hope so. I know I'm a novice, but in some ways that might be good. At any rate, I sell everything I can grow."

"You need a better sign."

They both stared at the piece of plywood nailed to the tree. Two winters ago she had spent days on it, using patterns to trace *Beach Grass Garden* in Lucida Calligraphy font, which was clear but slightly curly, just a little bit Victorian, just a hint old-fashioned, like her little farm. She'd painted berries, potatoes, tomatoes, and onions around the edges of the board and slashed long green beach-grassy knolls in each corner, and when she had finished she was quite pleased with the result. But two summers of sun and rain had faded it slightly, and it did look amateurish, and now she wasn't so sure she liked it anymore.

"Mmm," she said. "But what?"

"A quarter board. Gold letters."

Charlotte squinted. "I'm not so sure. Gold letters might be too upscale for me. Plus, I think people like the idea of a real local home-run garden."

A car came down the road from town, the woody

convertible. Aunt Grace slowed when she turned off onto the drive and Charlotte's mother stuck her head out the window. "Darling! Hello! We're here!"

"And everyone's starving!" Aunt Grace yelled.

Charlotte's father waved from the passenger seat, rolling his eyes at his sister's bossiness.

Charlotte grinned. "I'll be right there."

Aunt Grace gunned the motor, and the convertible disappeared down the lane in a little cloud of dust.

Charlotte looked up at Coop. He was truly handsome. But she had to stop gawking at him this way. "So, okay, so I'll see you tomorrow night."

"Great." He held up his mesclun. "Off I go, to my lonely bachelor's salad."

Now that *was* a hint. Charlotte couldn't ignore it. "Where's Miranda?"

"I have no idea," Coop told her. "We've broken off."

"Wow, Coop. That's huge."

He shrugged. "Not so huge. It was never very serious in the first place."

From a nearby juniper, a catbird began to chatter. She'd never thought of Coop as a cad or a playboy, but really, wasn't this a little careless, breaking up with a woman in the morning and smiling about it that evening? Charlotte was confused.

"I'd better get to the house now that the parents have arrived." She picked up the basket of strawberries. "See you tomorrow night."

"Looking forward to it. Am I right, you're having a band?"

"We are. Jeremiah and the Blue Fins. They can play it all, Ginger Rogers to Tina Turner."

"Great. Save a few dances for me, okay?"

His grin made her breathless. "Sure. And hey, that mesclun, just keep it in the crisper and it will last for days."

He waved and headed back along the grassy verge to the dirt lane on his land. Soon he was out of sight, hidden by a forest of pines, scrub oak, juniper, and tupelo trees.

The sun was still high as Charlotte went along the lane to the shed. It was almost June 21, the longest day of the year. Summer always came late to the island, but in the past few days a kind of steady warmth seemed to emanate from the earth, as if winter's frost had dissipated and the ground had become soft and receptive to the sun's rays. Birds flitted high in the sky. From here, this lane leading to the house, her market garden, neatly protected by the wire fence, seemed tidy and flourishing, and the slant of sunlight made the green leaves luminous. She was physically tired. She'd been up almost fifteen hours. But her work gave her such satisfaction. She was surprised at how she had come to love her garden. Love was not a frivolous word, either. After three years of tending it, fertilizing it with organic matter, manure, and horrid-smelling fish entrails, and all her careful study and research and plant selection and planting, and the endless weeding and watering— after all that, each clod of earth seemed personal to her. Sometimes in the very early morning, when she came out in her work boots and floppy sun hat, she'd feel the garden perk up when she entered the gate. Silly, of course, and yet the plants did perk up when she watered. They lifted their heads as if the slender stalks, replenished, were stronger, and more eager to meet the heat of the sun.

Kicking the dirt off her boots, Charlotte stepped into her work shed. She'd paid someone else to pour the concrete floor and install the electricity, but she'd done much of the construction herself: bought the boards, hammered the nails, combed the Take It or Leave It shack at the dump for tables at just the right height. It didn't matter that they were old or scarred or cheap to begin with, she needed them to hold her trays of seedlings beneath the overhanging fluorescent lights. Nona had a small greenhouse off the library, and she'd allowed Charlotte to cram it with as many plants as would fit, but Charlotte was going to have to build a bigger greenhouse up here by the shed. If she continued to make money, perhaps she could have it built this winter.

For now, she was happy with this little place. Water had been piped up from the main well for an outdoor shower on the side of the big building that had served, long ago, as a barn and was now used as a garage and storage shed. Charlotte had built her toolshed on the outer wall of the barn, and it had been a simple matter to have a deep sink installed and a faucet for hoses. During the winter she had pottered around happily in the shed, cleaning it, making it a bit more cozy for herself and for the baby plants she would set into their little seed trays in early spring.

Now she stripped off her work gloves, washed her hands at the sink, and rubbed creamy lotion into her skin. She'd hung a little mirror in the shed, to reflect light and make the room seem bigger, but she found it useful for checking herself for stray bits of dirt on her nose, and she did so now. In spite of her sunblock and floppy hat, her face had tanned and her cheeks and the tip of her nose were rosy. She lifted up the basket of strawberries, shut the shed door and latched it, and walked down the driveway toward the house.

She went through the mudroom, sat on a bench to unlace her boots, kicked them under the bench, and went into the kitchen. Glorious was busy at the stove.

"Hey, Glorious, I've brought some fresh strawberries for dessert!"

"Want me to cut and sugar them?"

"Mmm . . . let's just rinse them. We can put out some powdered sugar if anyone wants to dip them. They're pretty sweet." She handed one to Glorious, who tasted it.

102

"Yummy. Okay, I made some oatmeal cookies; we can serve those with the berries."

"Great. Where is everyone?"

"In the living room having drinks." Glorious lifted a pot and checked the rice. Steam swirled up into the air.

"Sounds good to me. I could use a medicinal bit of wine to help my aching back."

Charlotte went out into the long hall and down to the living room. Here everyone was gathered, all talking at once, it seemed. Nona, her cane resting against her leg, held court from her wing chair next to the fireplace. She still wore one of the outfits Charlotte had jokingly dubbed her Public Pajamas, and she'd added a pair of ruby and sapphire Victorian earrings which, as everyone had been told a million times, had once belonged to her own grandmother. Pregnant Mellie sprawled on a sofa, her husband, Dougie, dutifully at her side, ready to fetch water, a shawl, antacid. Claus perched on another wing chair, so long, thin, gawky, and pale that he really did resemble the proverbial stork who brings babies. Aunt Grace and Uncle Kellogg and Mandy were on the floor, playing Chutes and Ladders with little Christian, and Mee was sulking at the far end of the room, sitting at the foot of Nona's chaise, looking out at the garden, her back to the party. Charlotte's father was at the piano, his tie loose, his shirt-sleeves rolled up around his strong arms, his fingers drifting from "Old Black Magic" to "Hey, Jude."

And Charlotte's mother sat on a sofa facing pregnant Mellie, the skirt of her dress spilling around her like flowered tissue. She held Mandy's baby daughter Zoe in her arms. *Of course* Helen was holding a baby. Helen might as well tattoo GIVE ME A GRANDCHILD on her forehead, she was so unsubtle.

"Hi, everyone! Hi, Mom." Charlotte bent over the back of the sofa and kissed her mother's forehead. She gazed down over her mother's shoulder at Zoe, who gazed back at Charlotte and then brought up a tiny fist and waved it like a miniature sign of solidarity. "What a nice fat pink little bundle, Mandy!"

"I know," Mandy agreed proudly from the floor. "Christian, it's your turn now."

Charlotte knelt next to her nephew and pecked his cheek. "How's it going, Christian?"

Christian wiped her kiss away. "I'm *thinking,* Auntie Charlotte."

Charlotte walked over to the piano and sat on the bench next to her father. She'd never really learned to play the piano, but she and her father had over the years worked up several duets, starting of course with *Chopsticks* and segueing into a slightly bizarre version of *The William Tell Overture* and finally, *Oklahoma!* They pounded away at the piano keys, laughing, and when they were done, everyone applauded.

Still sitting cross-legged on the floor, Aunt Grace reported in her "The rest of you are wastrels but I soldier on" voice, "I know Glorious might appreciate some help with dinner. And is the table set?"

"I've got to nurse Zoe," Mandy said.

"I can't move." Mellie groaned, rubbing her belly.

Charlotte was bone tired from working, but she left the piano and plopped down on the chaise next to Mee. Charlotte was closer in age to Mellie, but closer in spirit to Mee, who was the most spirited and imaginative of her cousins. Mee, two years younger, had once kind of idolized Charlotte, who had babied her in return, but since Mee's divorce, Mee had grown cranky and short-tempered.

Mee was rolling and unrolling the cuff of her shirt, her face downcast, her shoulders slumped.

"Hey, good-lookin'," Charlotte joked, nudging her cousin with her arm. "Want to set the table with me?"

Mee twitched her shoulder irritably. "Oh, right, because that would be so much fun."

Charlotte sat quietly for a moment, then tried again. "Your shirt is gorgeous, Mee."

Mee sniffed, disdainful of Charlotte's attempts at flattery. "Yes, and that's why I don't have a husband."

Charlotte laughed. "You're just a tad irrational, don't you think?" Mee shot Charlotte a surly stare.

"Okay, fine." Charlotte stood up. This was just

the sort of task she'd determined to perform, whenever she could. Another penny in her over-drawn cosmic account. "I'll set the table," she announced, and went into the dining room.

# Seven

*S*aturday morning, Helen was in the kitchen helping Glorious make casseroles for lunch when Grace came marching in. Mandy sat at the long kitchen table, nursing Zoe, while Christian lay beneath the kitchen table, unbuckling his mother's sandals. Mellie was collapsed at the table, puffing and munching on bacon and toast and chatting with Mee, who was wearing entirely too much blue eye shadow, one apparent result of having been dumped by her husband. Helen reminded herself that no matter what, she would not begin wearing blue eye shadow.

"Nona wants to see you," Grace told Helen offi-ciously. She had a clipboard in her hand and a pencil behind her ear.

"Do I have time to finish my coffee?" Helen asked. She'd decided she had quite enough to deal with, pretending she didn't know about Worth's affair, never mind the general stresses of this day. She needed coffee, so she was going to drink coffee, as much as she wanted. She was on her fourth cup.

Grace just breathed through her nose like a bull.

"What does Nona need?" Helen asked reasonably.

"She wants you to help her choose which dress to wear tonight." Grace's lips thinned. "Although why she needs *your* opinion, I don't know."

Mellie looked up from her breakfast. "Duh, Mom. Look at yourself and then look at Auntie Helen."

Grace wore sensible khaki shorts, a green polo shirt, and leather moccasins. Helen wore a filmy, flowery sundress, the sort of thing she loved wearing here in the summer, and even though she had basically the same sensible chin-length cut as Grace, Helen's hair curled in the island humidity, giving her a softer, more feminine appearance. Also Helen loved jewelry, and wore it, and not just the staid pearls Grace brought out for dress. Today Helen had on a glass flower on a silver chain, hung with bits of beads, and her favorite bracelet, a cuff of thick twisted silver. She wore it when she needed courage, knowing that this sort of superstitious thinking was another quality that set her apart from the real Wheelwrights.

Grace didn't react to her daughter's remark. Grace didn't care about vanity, she cared about virtue and considered herself the more responsible mother. The better mother. Helen and Grace had always done their best to get along, and over the years they'd developed a kind of vigilant cooperation, like two mama tigers carrying a bone too heavy for one. Helen admired Grace, even if she didn't especially like her; she thought Grace secretly liked her a little bit but didn't admire her.

Helen set her cup down and rinsed her hands in the sink. "I'll go up."

"I don't think Mrs. Nona's had her tea yet," Glorious told Helen. "I've got the hot water boiling, but somehow with all this"—she spread her hands to indicate the counters cluttered with chopped vegetables and grated cheese—"and then Grace was going up."

"It's probably too hot for tea," Grace said.

"She's an old lady," Glorious reminded her. "Her bones are cold."

Helen set the tray with a pretty porcelain teapot and cup and saucer, no mugs for Nona. She took a cloth napkin from the drawer in the butler's pantry. Glorious added a china bowl filled with Cheez-Its—"About all Mrs. Nona will eat in the morning."

"Wait, Helen!" Grace pointed her pencil at Helen. "What time did you say Oliver and Teddy are arriving?"

"I don't know, Grace." Helen lifted the tray and headed for the back stairs. "But you know Oliver and Owen aren't staying here at the house. And they know what time the party starts. And Teddy—"

"Yes. Well," Grace said peevishly, "it would help if we knew what time they're arriving. What if we're in the middle of something and they need to be picked up?"

"Mom." Mandy held the baby to her shoulder and burped her. "They're big boys. They can grab a cab."

Another martyred sigh from Grace. "Yes, but I was hoping to get a group photo before the party begins—"

"I'm sure they'll be here in plenty of time for that," Helen assured her sister-in-law.

"Auntie Helen, just *go*." Mee waved a lazy hand toward the stairs. "Or Mom will have you here picking over details until that tea turns cold."

"You're an ungrateful daughter," Helen teased Mee, but she turned to climb the stairs.

Interesting, she thought to herself, how quickly a person can slide into schizophrenia. All morning she'd bantered with her nieces, chatted with Glorious, and moved around the house just as if everything were normal.

The truth was she hadn't slept last night. Her entire body ached with fatigue. Her mind had gone haywire, like a CD set on continual loop, replaying yesterday morning in her own home, when she'd overheard Worth talking to Sweet Cakes.

Pain cramped her right in her midriff. She stood still on the stairs a moment, bent almost double, catching her breath. *Don't think about that now,* she ordered herself. Not today. This was Nona's big day. Be a grown-up, for heaven's sake! She straightened and climbed the stairs.

Nona's room was at the far end of the hall, stretching across the east wing of the house, with windows facing the harbor. Helen knocked and entered. Nona was still in her enormous bed, linen-cased pillows tucked behind her against the carved mahogany headboard. She looked very old and Victorian in her white cotton nightgown with her funny little white braid hanging over her shoulder. The lavender mohair bed jacket lay around her shoulders.

"Good morning, Nona!" Helen smiled brightly. "Grace said you wanted to see me. And I've brought you some tea."

"Good girl, thank you." Nona patted the bed beside her. "Put the tray here, will you? No, don't perch on that chair, I can't see you properly, sit here beside me on the bed."

Helen obeyed, pouring Nona's tea, adding cream and sugar, handing it to her, then arranging herself at the end of the bed where she could lean against the footboard. It was more comfortable this way. The room was filled with sweet cool air. Nona always liked the windows open at least a bit unless there was a blizzard.

"You look very pretty in that bed jacket," Helen said.

"It feels lovely, warm and light. Thank you, Helen."

"Happy birthday, Nona," Helen said.

"The dreaded day begins!" Nona took a sip of tea.

"Grace said you wanted my opinion on which dress to wear tonight?"

Nona leaned back against her pillows. "Yes, I told Grace that, but what I want to talk with you about is Worth."

"Worth?" Helen's heart kicked.

"What's going on with him? He looks terrible, Helen. He looks aged and worried. Ever since he's been here he's been distracted and abrupt."

Helen looked down at her hands. She venerated her mother-in-law and had great respect for Nona's intelligence. She was shocked, and yet not entirely, that Nona was so perceptive. But whatever was going on between Worth and another woman was, first of all, a matter between Helen and Worth. It was a temptation to spill out a confession to Nona, because Nona would take charge of the matter in no uncertain terms. Nona would make Worth end the affair. But was that how Helen wanted the matter resolved? Worth chastened like a schoolboy and forced back into his marriage by his powerful mother? No. Helen was not yet sure how she was going to deal with this, but she would not come crying to Nona to make things right.

"I think it's Teddy." Helen met Nona's eyes. Nona would see the anxiety there, she would believe. "Nona, we are very worried about him."

"I understand it's a matter of alcohol?"

"Yes, and also drugs, perhaps."

"What kind of drugs? Marijuana?"

"That would be the least of it."

"Is Teddy coming today?"

"He said he is. He left a message on our answering machine. He should arrive at any moment."

"And Oliver?"

"He arrives this afternoon."

Nona sipped her tea. "I've enjoyed Charlotte's company."

"Oh, good. I'm glad. And her garden is flourishing."

"Yes. A mixed blessing, it seems. We are all glad to see her persevering with something, but I know Worth would like to have one child follow him into the bank."

"Yes. Charlotte did try."

"It's not such a concern for me, Helen, I want you to know that. It is sufficient for me that Mandy's husband is at the bank. They have two children and may have more. Perhaps the Wheelwright bloodline will carry on the bank even if not the Wheelwright name."

Helen felt her heart lighten slightly. "I'm very glad to hear that, Nona. I wouldn't like my children to be a disappointment to you."

Nona reached over and squeezed Helen's hand. "Don't talk nonsense. You know I adore Oliver, always have, always will. In fact, I told him I'd like him to hold his marriage ceremony here at the summer house."

Helen's hands flew to her heart. "Nona! How lovely of you!" Nona was like this, she could be formal and cool and then surprise everyone with a splendid gesture of love.

Nona continued, "And Teddy is a problem, I understand, but he's young—"

"Twenty-two is not so young," Helen murmured.

"It is these days, I believe. I read things, you know, Helen. I watch the news. Adolescence seems to be lasting longer. Young people of twenty and even thirty are moving back to live with their parents. Children are taking longer to find their place in the workforce. It's not like it was when *I* was a girl, or even when *you* were young." Nona sipped her tea again. "If thirty is the new fifteen and, as I read in the ladies' magazines, sixty is the new forty, that should make me about—oh, fifty-two, don't you think?"

Helen laughed. Nona could be charming when she wanted; Worth had inherited that character-istic. And she was being very kind. "Well, Worth and I are worried about Teddy. For different rea-sons. I want Teddy to do anything at all, as long as he gets off this frightening alcoholic path he's been on. And Worth—"

"Worth wants Teddy to go into the bank."

"Eventually, yes."

"And Teddy is your rebel. Your rogue."

Helen shrugged. "I suppose all three children are."

"You look a little frazzled, too," Nona observed.

Helen raised her hand to her face. "I didn't sleep well."

"Perhaps the bed on the sleeping porch is too bumpy."

Of course, Helen thought. In this house, Nona knows everything. "I like fresh air. Cool air. I'm still having hot flashes." That would head the older woman off at the pass. Nona was not comfortable discussing female physicality.

"I keep worrying about Worth." Nona's voice sharpened. "Charlotte is certainly being given her way in the matter of career. And she's thirty now. She's had plenty of time for summer romances and playing the field."

Helen felt skewered by her mother-in-law's clear blue gaze. "You think Charlotte should marry Whit Lowry."

"Well, he *is* a catch. From all I hear, Whit is proving to be quite capable at the bank. He's a handsome young man, and a good sailor and athlete. No blots on his copybook as far as I know."

Honestly, Helen thought, this family! She made an attempt to keep her tone reasonable, but she did feel angry. She was not going to sacrifice her daughter to the Wheelwrights' legacy. *If you only knew what your precious Worth has been doing!* Helen wanted to cry. She heard the emotional quaver in her voice when she replied, "This is all true, Nona, but you can't engineer love. We aren't living in feudal times."

But Nona only sipped her tea. "Perhaps you're right," she said at last. "Perhaps you can't *engineer* love. Yet Whit and Charlotte will be thrown together over the summer. Whit and his family are coming tonight for my birthday party, aren't they?"

"Yes, of course they are. But Nona, Charlotte has known Whit since she was a child. She worked with him at the bank and nothing sparked between them."

"That was three years ago," Nona reminded Helen. "Let's just sit back and see what happens. And you, Helen, try to get Worth out on the dance floor, will you? Be sure he drinks a lot of champagne. I'd like to see him enjoy himself. I'd like to see him smiling."

"Of course." Helen rose. "Shall I take the tray down?"

"If you would."

Helen lifted the tray and crossed over the thick blue and gray Aubusson rug to the door.

When her hand was on the doorknob, Nona said, "Oh, and Helen?"

"Yes?"

"I will be wearing the navy blue dress tonight. It displays my grandmother's diamonds best. Should anyone ask."

"The navy blue dress it is," Helen agreed, admiring the way Nona closed their little tête-à-tête with a moment of light conspiracy.

*Instead of returning* to the kitchen, Helen went down the hall to the sleeping porch. She wanted to take just a few minutes to regain her equilibrium. She had made her bed after showering and dressing and before breakfast—one did, in Nona's house—but even so, the room appeared, not messy, but occupied. Her dresses hung from the wrought-iron plant hangers, her evening sandals sat tidily against the wall, her paperback novel and her purse and some toiletries were on the card table, and her stained-glass silk wrapper lay where she'd tossed it, at the foot of the daybed.

Sinking into the wicker rocker, Helen planted her feet on the floor and counseled herself to breathe, just breathe. She forced herself to relax her hands in her lap. *Worth. Sweet Cakes—*

"Mom!" Charlotte's voice was sharp. "What in the world are you doing out here?"

There in the doorway stood her beautiful daughter. Overalls again today, and an old white shirt, her butterscotch hair pulled back and held with a bit of gardening twine.

"Hi, Charlotte. I thought you'd be out in your garden."

"I was. I came in to grab a bite of breakfast."

She glanced over her shoulder, then skewered Helen with a look. "*Why* are you sleeping out here?"

Helen shrugged, amused. "Why shouldn't I sleep out here? I never have before, not in all the years I've stayed in this house. I'd think you'd understand, Charlotte, the appeal of being almost outdoors, and yet—"

"But what about Dad?" Charlotte plunked herself down on the edge of the daybed.

"What about him?"

"Why aren't you sleeping with him?"

Helen snorted with exasperation. "Charlotte, Dad and I have had separate bedrooms for ages. He can't sleep with me prowling around the room, or reading in bed, or flipping from side to side in one my insomniac fits. You know that."

"Yes, but that's at home. Here—" Charlotte scraped a bit of dirt from her wrist.

"Here, what?" She knew what her daughter meant but she was also feeling very cranky with Charlotte, who always assumed Worth could do no wrong and that Nona was nothing less than an angel from heaven.

Charlotte squirmed. "Well, there aren't as many bedrooms here. What about everyone else?"

"Everyone has a bedroom, Charlotte. Except for Teddy, and he can take an attic room. And you know Oliver and Owen are staying at a B and B in town."

Charlotte slumped. "But what will Nona think? If you're not sharing a room with Dad?"

"Charlotte, Nona is well acquainted with the aggravations of old age. She knows I have trouble sleeping. As for the others, I'm sure Grace and Kellogg have nights when they sleep separately, too. It doesn't mean anything." Rising from her chair, she crossed the small room to sit next to her daughter. She put an arm around her. "Sweetie. What's bothering you?"

Charlotte leaned against her. "Oh, I don't know, Mom. I just want everyone to be happy."

"Everyone is happy, Charlotte." She squeezed her child's shoulder. "Tell me," she said briskly. "What are you doing in your garden today? And can I help?"

Charlotte perked up. "Are you serious? About helping? Gosh, if you could do some weeding—"

"I'd love to."

"But it's hard work, Mom. It really stresses the back."

"Why don't I do what I can, and I'll stop when I get tired?"

"Great!" Charlotte jumped up. "Okay, I've got to get back outside, and you need to put on work clothes and sunblock and a sun hat."

"Aye-aye." Helen stood and saluted. How easy it was, just for now, to make her daughter happy. Smiling, she remembered what she and Cecilia, her best friend, had agreed when their children became teenagers: they couldn't think about what would happen in the future. They had to be grateful for the present moment. They had to take things one day at a time. Even if, sometimes, it was one hard, confusing, maddening day at a time.

# Nona's Party

# Eight

*N**ona spent Saturday** in her room, saving her energy for the evening's festivities. It was a little appalling, how easily she dozed through the hours in her chaise near the window. It wasn't so much that she slept as that she daydreamed, and not even that, it was more a kind of drifting, as if her chaise of its own accord transformed into a hot-air balloon or Aladdin's magic carpet, lifting her effortlessly up and away from her present life, out the window, above the clouds, and smoothly through her past.

She could look down on herself as a girl, galloping her enormous old quarter horse across the fields, riding western, not that prissy eastern way, as wild as an Indian, her hair flying straight out behind her and her springer spaniel loping alongside, pink tongue hanging out, smiling, because Pup loved to run. She could spy herself as a young woman, giddy and silly and crazy with love for the dashing officer she'd met, Herbert Wheelwright. She could watch herself keeping her back straight as she endured her mother-in-law's barbed "compliments," and wasn't amused by those memories; the old wash of anger flooded through her, as heated and potent as it had been all those years ago. She saw her babies again, and her heart sang with joy, and she heard the knock on the door of their Boston house in 1970, when Captain Bruce Moore came to inform them that their son Bobby had been killed on the battlefield in Vietnam. Such grief. Such darkness. She attended Grace and Kellogg's wedding—what a fuss that was!—and Worth and Helen's, and she saw the pink baby faces of her grandchildren, and the hot-air balloon carried her just a little farther, and she was at Mandy's wedding, and Mellie's, and Mee's, and she saw the sweet precious faces of her great-grandchildren, Christian first, with his great thatch of brown hair, and then bald little Zoe.

What a lot of life she had lived! No wonder she was tired!

All day long she was aware of the unusual commotion in her house. It always took awhile, at the beginning of summer, to get used to the noises of a full house; it was like going to sleep in a library and waking up one day to discover that overnight it had become a train station. Baby Zoe wailed like a siren. As Christian waited in the upstairs hall for his mother to change his baby sister's diaper, he kicked a ball up and down the hall, yelling "Goal!" when it thumped into the wall. Nona didn't mind. Long ago she'd packed away all the valuable antique vases and heirloom bibelots, and she didn't miss them. Downstairs, the doors slammed and squeaked and voices rose and fell, Grace's chipped soprano answered by Glorious's slow deep hums. Water ran through the pipes as various members took their showers, and the uncarpeted back stairs resounded with footsteps running up and down.

At four, a knock came on Nona's door. "Yes?"

Helen peered in. "Are you awake, Nona?"

"I am now." Nona waved Helen into her room.

Helen was wearing a brilliantly colored silk wrapper and a pair of rubber flip-flops, and her hair was freshly shampooed, hanging in those ridiculous Shirley Temple ringlets that no grown woman should sport, but of course Helen couldn't help it if she had naturally curly hair. Although Nona secretly wondered if that rebellious hair didn't have a genetic link—like white cats and deafness—with an insubordinate personality.

Helen said, "We thought you might like to have a little bite to eat."

Nona frowned, perplexed. "I ate lunch today, didn't I?"

"Yes, you did, but that was at noon. We thought you ought to have something substantial before the party."

The hardest part about becoming truly aged was having to take suggestions, which were really velvet-gloved commands, from younger people. Nona tried not to bristle. They were, after all, only thinking of her own good. "Won't there be food at the party?"

"Of course. A buffet dinner. But you know how it is, impossible to eat with people all around you talking to you. We thought perhaps a nice hot pot of tea and a cheese sandwich?"

Nona snorted. "How about a nice big Scotch and some Cheez-Its."

"Nona! Cheez-Its?"

"I'm old. They settle my stomach. And I have always drunk a Scotch every day of my life, you know that, Helen." She peered closely at her daughter-in-law. "Your nose is red."

"I know. I helped weed in Charlotte's garden today." Helen put her hands on her back. "I'm not as young as I used to be."

"Who is? But you've got just a bit of a burn, a glow, actually; it becomes you."

Helen blushed. "I'll go get your drink and your Cheez-Its."

Nona wedged herself up off her chaise, leaned on her cane, and wobbled off into her private bathroom. She urinated, washed her hands, and studied her reflection in the mirror. She looked as old as Moses, and about as attractive. From this room, she could hear Grace in the next bedroom.

"I *knew* they'd do this! Helen's children have always been unreliable! They're going to ruin everything!"

Kellogg's voice was soothing. "Grace. They'll be here, or they won't; it doesn't matter. You have arranged a magnificent party, and Nona will be thrilled."

Nona sighed. Why did Grace not have Worth's

ease? Was it her fault? Of course it was her fault. She would have to be fulsome in her compliments to Grace. Grace was such a worker.

She hobbled back to her bedroom and lowered herself into the old wing chair by the fireplace. She knew from experience it was easy to pull up the old lacquered octagonal Chinese table, for eating. She was glad Helen had suggested a little treat. She *was* peckish.

Through her open window, she heard the crackle of gravel. Doors slammed. Voices called out. More commotion. Laughter and more laughter. Then the pounding of feet up the back stairs, and her door opened.

Into her room burst two gorgeous young men, their confident air of health, strength, and sheer love of life billowing around them like an invisible perfume. Oliver and Owen.

"Nona! Forgive us for being late! Our plane had an emergency landing in Kansas City! It was such a drama!" Oliver strode over to Nona, talking, gesturing, smiling, while Owen stood shyly in the background. Tall, slender, elegant, Oliver had honey-brown hair, shining azure eyes, milk-white teeth, and the overall aura of a knight straight from King Arthur's round table. He was wearing a three-piece tight black suit, and his hair had been cut and gelled into one of those bizarre thatches pointing straight up, and he hadn't shaved for a day or two, so his square jaw was dotted with whiskers.

"You look very metrosexual," Nona said, as her grandson bent to kiss her. She was pleased with herself for knowing the modern term.

"Well, Nona, get you!" Oliver pulled a chair over next to hers and held her hands. He cocked his head. "And you look as beautiful as always."

"Flatterer." She gestured to Oliver's partner. "Owen, come kiss me."

Owen approached, moving as gracefully as a dancer. He was smaller than Oliver, and somehow neater, and if he didn't watch out, people would say he was *dapper,* which Nona knew Owen would find insulting. Owen wore a black suit, too, but with a black turtleneck instead of the white shirt and blue tie Oliver sported. His hair was ebony, his eyes chocolate, his eyelashes long and thick, like brushes.

"Hello, Nona. Lovely to see you again. Happy birthday." Owen bent to kiss her cheek.

"Room service," Helen called from the door. "Oliver, move that little Chinese table closer to Nona—that's perfect. Thanks." She set a Waterford tumbler and a basket of Cheez-Its on the table.

"Thank you, Helen." Nona eyed the Scotch. "My drink looks suspiciously pale."

"Grace fixed it," Helen retorted. Plopping down on the chaise by the window, she smiled at her son and his partner. "You two look wonderful."

"Wait till you see us in our tuxes," Oliver told

her. "What time is the family going to the yacht club?"

Grace stuck her head in the door. She wore a long silk dress, printed with geometric shapes, and pearls. She resembled, slightly, Barbara Bush—or was it Mamie Eisenhower?

"Cocktails start at seven, but we want to be there around six-thirty. I'm going to take some family photos before we set out, so drink up, Nona, so you can dress." Grace looked at her watch and frowned. "Oliver, I don't know if you two will have time to go back to the inn, change clothes, and return in time for the photos."

"Well, we'll have them taken at the club, then."

"But I want to take them *here*. At the house."

"But who will know?" Oliver argued softly. "With so many people in the photo, the background won't show up."

Grace's lips tightened. "*We'll* know." A blush of frustration blotted her neck and face.

Oliver said, placatingly, "Okay, then, we'll just stay here and have our photos taken, then change into our tuxes on the way to the yacht club."

Grace crossed her arms under her bosom, battle-ax pose. "Yes, and ruin the photo. Everyone else will be in formal dress."

"We *are* in suits," Oliver pointed out. "We'll stand behind everyone else," he added. "You'll just see our heads."

"I know!" Brightly, a little desperately, Helen

made a suggestion, "I'm sure we have some nice black bow ties in some closet out here, and some white shirts. You can look formal from the shoulders up; that's all that will show."

"Oh, that's just like you, Helen!" Grace snapped, losing her cool. "I'm trying to create a historical record of Nona's dynasty, and you're turning it into a comic routine."

Nona watched and listened, munching away at her cheese crackers and sipping her Scotch, thinking Grace could use a hearty slam shot of alcohol herself right now. The matter was finally decided when Glorious arrived to help Nona dress for the evening. Oliver and Owen assured Grace they could race to their inn, change clothes, and be back in time for the photo if they left now. And they ran out the door. Through the open window, their hearty male laughter floated, and then came the sound of their rental car peeling away down the drive.

"It's *not* funny!" Grace declared, hands on hips.

Oh, the poor responsible child, Nona thought. "I know it's not funny," she said soothingly. "And Grace, I do appreciate all your thoughtfulness and preparations. I know how much work has gone into this, and I'm very grateful. Now I'd better get dressed so I can attend this magnificent occasion."

Grace, appeased, kissed Nona on the cheek and marched off down the hall to help Mandy dress the babies. Helen waved at Nona from the hallway and went off to change. Glorious, already garbed for the evening in red satin, shut the bedroom door. "All right, Mrs. Nona, let's get you beauteous."

Nona had been in her seventies when she first realized that simply taking a bath and arranging her hair took energy and stamina. She had expected, as the years passed, that she would have less ability for such things as charity committees and sailing, but it never occurred to her that some days she might feel just too tired and weak to brush her own hair. In her eighties, she had considered cutting it, but when she finally seated herself in the hairdresser's chair, an emotion like fear swept through her, as if her hair were life itself and she did not want it cut short. She had always considered the expense of having one's hair done a waste, especially for simple daily life, but that day, instead of a cut and style, she had a simple wash and blow-dry, and after that she had what the salon called a "standing" appointment.

Nona soon came to enjoy the luxury of lying back in a chair with her neck braced on the cool porcelain as Brad's capable hands caressed her scalp. And she looked forward to the hour of gossip at the salon and seeing other people, people whom she didn't know: young girls getting ready for proms or bridal parties, growly-voiced men having their heads shaved as they raved about the deer on the island. It opened the world up to her a bit, and she came away looking much better than she did when she washed her own hair. It was something about a product they used that made her fine white hair look silky.

Brad had begged to be able to do her hair in some fancy style for this birthday party, but the thought secretly terrified Nona. She didn't want to show up in front of everyone who knew her with her hair all puffed out or curled, and she hated hair spray. For thirty years at least she had worn her hair the same way, pulled back from her face and fastened in a chignon at the back of her head. She'd worn it this way for so long she was surprised she still needed to use hairpins, surprised the hair didn't just go into its little snail roll and stay there of its own accord.

But of course it didn't. She needed Glorious's help to make it neat. But first she had to bathe, which she did with Glorious sitting outside the closed bathroom door, ready to rush in to Nona's aid if she slipped or simply didn't possess the power to step out of the tub. And getting out of the tub did take muscle and determination. After her bath, Nona sat for a few moments on a little stool, catching her breath. Glorious had seen her naked, of course. There had been the occasional sickness, when Nona was really too weak to get in and out of the tub herself. Glorious was patient, kind, even affectionate, but Nona still preferred her privacy as she pulled on and fastened her various undergarments. Afterward, she considered herself in the mirror. She appeared rather Germanic, girded for battle. Her braid still hung over her shoulder. All she needed was a shield, and she could be a Valkyrie. There her heavy breasts were, pooling into their cups like a pair of vanilla puddings. What pleasure they had given her all her life! She patted them gratefully. "Good girls," she said.

Then she opened the door and hobbled back into her bedroom. She sat on the bed and held up her arms like a little girl while Glorious slipped her floor-length navy-blue dress over her head.

"I can't remember when I wore this last," Nona told Glorious. "It's been at least a year. I wonder if I've shrunk some more. I hope the gown hasn't gotten too long, I don't want to step on the hem."

"Stand up and let's see."

Glorious held out her wonderful strong arms. Nona put her own hands on them and used Glorious for support as she heaved herself up off the bed.

"Oh, dear. Far too long. I've become a midget!"

Glorious laughed wonderfully. "You don't have your shoes on yet!"

Nona held on to the bedpost while Glorious went to the closet and returned with Nona's black court shoes. Glorious slipped one knee-high stocking and then the other over Nona's legs, while Nona observed that her legs were not bad at all, for her age. But her feet were a disgrace. Her nails were cracking and yellow, and she had bunions, and everything was crooked. After wearing nothing but comfortable sneakers, the leather shoes felt like little prisons to her feet.

"Oh, dear, Glorious. I don't know if I can wear these. Do you suppose anyone would notice if I wore sneakers?"

"Oh, Mrs. Nona, I almost forgot! I have a present for you." Glorious reached into the pocket of her skirt and pulled out a package of foot inserts filled with turquoise bubbles. She maneuvered them into Nona's shoes. "Now try."

Nona stood. "Glorious, it's miraculous!" It was like standing on cushions. "How can something so thin feel so soft?"

"It is a wonderful world we live in," Glorious told her. "Now, look. Your dress is the perfect length."

"It is."

On her pillowed feet, Nona walked to her vanity and settled onto the stool. Her face was mirrored back to her in three different panes. She was ninety years old in each one. Glorious unbraided Nona's white hair and brushed it—Nona closed her eyes and was a girl again—and coiled it into a crescent at the back of her head. When Glorious had finished, Nona patted her face with white powder and covered her thin lips with a bright red lipstick. She opened the vanity drawer and brought out a handsome black box, opened it, and lifted out her grandmother's diamond brooch and matching earrings.

"A young girl should wear these," Nona said, as she screwed on the earrings.

Glorious bent to pin on the brooch. "No, no, this is serious jewelry. Young girls are too frivolous. These are like medals of honor."

"Interesting perspective," Nona said. She shook her head impatiently. "All right, I'm not going to get any younger staring at myself. Help me up, Glorious, I think it's time I got myself downstairs."

The hall was silent as Glorious and Nona processed toward the stairway. Nona knew she was late and everyone else was waiting for her, but that was as it should be. It was her birthday. Her family should be in attendance.

"You look beautiful in that red dress," Nona told Glorious.

Glorious smiled shyly. "Thank you. I like wearing it."

"You know, I think we're going to enjoy this evening," Nona confided, leaning on Glorious's arm.

"I think we are," Glorious agreed.

Suddenly, before Nona had reached the bottom of the stairs, an explosion of noise swept through the house, as if every one of her family were talking at the same time as loudly as they could.

Nona clutched Glorious's arm more tightly. "I wonder what's happened."

"Perhaps some flowers have arrived for you?" Glorious suggested.

They walked as swiftly as Nona could into the living room. Everyone was there, and it was not flowers that had arrived but Nona's youngest grandchild, Teddy.

"Teddy!" Nona gasped.

Teddy wore shabby jeans, filthy sneakers, a wrinkled cotton shirt in yellow covered with dancing martini glasses, and a camel's hair blazer Nona remembered he'd had back in boarding school. His long caramel-colored hair hung over his shirt collar, and his shirt hem hung over his sagging low-slung jeans. But his eyes were clear and his smile was contagious as always. "Nona, you look like a queen!" he said.

Then Teddy took a slender young girl by the wrist and tugged her forward. "Nona, this is Suzette. Suzette, Nona."

Nona managed to keep what she hoped was a welcoming expression on her face as she extended her hand. "Hello, Suzette."

Suzette ducked her head shyly. She was petite and short and extremely thin. Her hair was as multicolored as a tabby cat and stuck out strangely, as if bits of paintbrushes had been glued on. Her eyes were a lovely blue, and her face was heart-shaped, but her nose was pierced with a little gold ring, a number of earrings sparkled from the rims of her ears, and she wore a tattoo of wings on her upper arm.

Her outfit was strange. Riding low on her hips, a skirt swirling with shades of green fell to her feet. A white cotton off-the-shoulder gypsy blouse ended at her midriff. Between the two garments, Suzette's round belly protruded nakedly. Nona could see the girl's belly button, also pierced and sporting a gold ring. And she couldn't miss the fact, so proudly displayed, that Suzette was exceedingly pregnant.

# Nine

*Charlotte was trying* not to meet Oliver's eye, because every time she did, they began to snicker, and they didn't want their younger brother to feel they were conspiring against him. Although they often had, in their childhood. Charlotte and Oliver, older than Teddy by eight and six years, had been not really distant to Teddy as much as close to each other. Charlotte had always been a good girl, hating disorder and mess, and Oliver, though flamboyant and theatrical, had always wanted to please. Their younger brother's continual rebellious antics were funny, or shocking, and often even irritating, in a salt-in-the-sugar-bowl kind of way.

But this, even in Charlotte's amused opinion, was going a little too far. It was probably to be expected that Teddy would show up for this occasion ill-dressed and late enough to make everyone else late, too. Adding a pregnant girl was over the top. The poor little thing was making the parents and even the Ms nervous. Mellie, who had draped her own belly like a piano in winter storage, had taken one look at Suzette's basketball and collapsed into a chair. Charlotte's father was red in the face; Charlotte was afraid he might have a heart attack. Auntie Grace and Uncle Kellogg both looked smug, exchanging glances and quirked eyebrows that telegraphed clearly their pleasure that once again it was Worth's child who was causing trouble.

But Nona was cool, as she clasped Suzette's hand. "Lovely to meet you, Suzette. And Teddy, come let me hug you."

Teddy loped forward to embrace Nona, and for a moment Nona's face softened with pleasure as she patted her youngest grandchild's back, and everyone else in the room could see Nona remembering how she had once held this man when he was a baby boy, how she had loved him then and loved him now.

Aunt Grace trumpeted, "We'll be late!" Shoving her way past her cluster of daughters, she reached Nona. "Nona. We need to take the photographs *now.*"

Nona released her grandson and turned to her daughter. "Yes, dear, of course."

Grace went into directorial mode. "Nona, you sit here." She gestured to a dining room chair she'd had Kellogg carry in. "Worth, you and Helen stand on Nona's left, with your children in front of you, and Kellogg, you and I will stand on Nona's right, with our family here and here." She handed Glorious her digital camera. "You remember how to take the pictures?"

"I do." Glorious leaned against the wall, focusing the camera as everyone took his place.

Grace ranged up and down the little assembly, checking and rechecking to be sure they were perfectly grouped. She bent to arrange Nona's full skirts.

Charlotte stood just behind Nona, with her mother just behind her, and Oliver on her left.

"Owen, come stand next to Oliver," Worth told his son's partner.

Grace bridled. "Worth. Is that appropriate? Sorry, Owen, I don't mean to offend but it's not as if you and Oliver are actually—um, married."

"They'll be married this summer," Nona reminded Grace smoothly. "I'd like Owen in the picture."

"Down, Daddee," Christian whined, squirming impatiently in Claus's arms. Next to him stood Mandy, holding baby Zoe, and on Mandy's other side was pregnant Mellie with Douglas close to her, supporting her with his arm, and Mee had squeezed in close to Douglas, pouting at being alone.

"For pity's sake, try to look happy, Mee!" Grace

commanded her youngest daughter. "Everyone, let's have your best smile!"

"Teddy," Worth said, "you stand next to Owen."

Teddy stepped into the arrangement. "Suzette, you'll be here, kind of in front of me," he said.

"Oh, *really!*" Grace turned red. "Teddy, this is a family photograph. A family record. This is your grandmother's ninetieth birthday." She approached Suzette, put a controlling hand on the girl's arm, and tried to pull her out of the family group. "Suzette, it is lovely to meet you, but I'm sure you understand: only family members just for now."

"Auntie Grace," Teddy said, with his sweet smile, "Suzette and I are married."

"Married!" Everyone in the room cried out the word simultaneously.

Charlotte couldn't help it. She looked at Oliver, and Oliver widened his eyes, and they both burst out laughing.

"Married?" Worth was not amused. "Teddy, are you serious?"

Helen left her place in the group and went to her son. "Teddy. Why didn't you tell us? Why didn't you invite us to the wedding? We didn't even know you were—seeing someone." She put a hand, not controlling but gentle and soothing, on Suzette's arm. "My dear." She studied the pregnant woman's face. "You are having Teddy's child."

Staring at the floor, Suzette said, "Well, maybe."

Another informational bomb. *"Maybe?"* everyone said.

Charlotte struggled to contain herself. She collapsed in helpless hysteria against Oliver, who whispered into her ear, "Steady on." The babble of voices filled the room.

Grace said, "I need a drink."

Nona said, loudly, "I think we should get this picture taken or we'll be late for my party. Grace, stop pacing around and come stand next to Kellogg, here on my left. Glorious, are you focused?"

Glorious took several shots and showed them to Grace, who found something wrong with each one but finally threw up her hands and cried that they had to leave for the yacht club *now*. She insisted that Nona ride with her and Kellogg in the old Chrysler, and Nona objected, saying she wouldn't ride with the top down, so Grace put the top up and Kellogg helped Nona fold her body into the front seat, then held the door for Glorious to squeeze into the backseat with him. Helen and Worth crowded with all the Ms into the Yukon and the Volvo. Charlotte told her brothers she was driving the Jeep and she thought she could fit everyone in—Oliver, Owen, Teddy and Suzette—if Suzette sat on Teddy's lap, but to her immense surprise Teddy said thank you, no, he had rented a car and he'd prefer to drive Suzette in that, it would be safer, and they would have the use of seat belts.

Charlotte looked at the vehicle parked on the white gravel and saw that it was a Taurus sedan.

With much slamming of doors and rumbling of engines, the family set off, white gravel crackling and spewing up from the tires. Charlotte's Jeep was at the end of the convoy. All around them the summer evening fell in gentle swaths of muted light and warmth, and for just a moment the peace of the island drifted by.

Then Oliver leaned forward from the backseat and said, "Teddy has really outdone himself now. A wife! And a baby!"

"And a *Taurus!*" Charlotte cried. "I thought I was going to faint."

"I can't wait to get Teddy alone," Oliver said. "I can't imagine why, of all the females our handsome Teddy could have chosen, he picked Suzette. I would never say this to Teddy, but Suzette is—"

"Weird," Owen suggested.

"Yes, but more than that. I don't want to be catty—"

"Oh, please, Oliver, you're with me." Charlotte urged him on.

"Well, folks, she's so sallow." Oliver sat back in his seat. "I'm sorry. I'm being a bitch."

"She looks as if she hasn't had the best medical care in her life," Charlotte pointed out, and the mood in the car plummeted.

"You're thinking drugs, aren't you?" Oliver's voice was serious now, too.

"Oh, Oliver," Charlotte said. "Drugs and a baby? I've read such terrible things about what babies have to endure when their mothers are on drugs."

No one spoke. Charlotte drove rapidly and carefully through the small town of Nantucket and out along Madaket Road toward the yacht club.

Into the glum silence, Owen suggested, "Is it possible that Teddy is—well, *tricking* you all? That he's hired this young woman to help him play a kind of practical joke?"

"Oh, Owen, you're a genius!" Charlotte leaned across to the passenger seat and kissed his cheek. "That is exactly the sort of thing Teddy would do."

"I'm not so sure," Oliver said, from where he'd subsided into a corner of the backseat. "I mean, he's always ready to torment Mom and Dad, but Nona? He adores Nona. He wouldn't want to ruin her birthday."

"Nona didn't look particularly tormented," Charlotte remarked. She turned into the yacht club parking lot. "Look at all the cars! It's going to be a fabulous mob for Nona's party!"

Owen said, "Charlotte, let me get in the driver's seat and find a parking space. You and Oliver go on in."

Charlotte put the Jeep in park. "Good idea, Owen, thanks."

*They squeezed* their way through the foyer with its tables set with gigantic spilling vases of flowers into the huge main room, as large as a basketball court, with wooden floors and a high ceiling hung with burgees and banners. At one end of the room, a band was playing soft jazz; the dancing wouldn't start until after the buffet. All around the edge of the floor, tables and chairs were set up, each table set with flowers and a candle centerpiece on blazing white linen tablecloths. At the far end Nona was holding court, greeting her friends who flocked up to wish her happy birthday. Beside her chair was a long table, also covered in white linen, decorated with more flowers and holding a guest book for people to sign, and the table was quickly becoming laden with beautifully wrapped presents.

"Drinks first, I think," Oliver told Charlotte.

"Absolutely."

Passing through a wide double door, Charlotte and Oliver entered another reception room, with a bar set up at one end and a buffet table just being organized at the other. Stewards in white jackets hurried to and from the kitchen, bearing great wooden bowls of salad and heavy stainless steel trays.

Against one wall was a giant peg-board covered with photos of Nona at different ages.

"Auntie Grace really did an amazing job organizing this," Charlotte told Oliver. It was so noisy in the room she had to shout to make herself heard.

"You're right. I'm going to make it a point to be

grateful to her, the poor old obsessive-compulsive bat." Oliver turned to shout their drink orders at the bartender, then handed Charlotte a flute of champagne. "I never did tell you how beautiful you look tonight."

"Oliver, thanks! You look pretty smashing yourself, but then you always do."

"I want to hear all about your garden," Oliver began, but at that moment an old friend threw herself upon him.

"Oliver! Darling! I was hoping you would be here! I don't see Owen! Have you broken up? Have you gone straight, by any chance? Oh, please say yes."

With a grin, Charlotte allowed Oliver to be idolized and made her way through the crowd in Nona's direction. She didn't get far. Everyone stopped her, kissed her cheek, told her she looked lovely. These were her friends, after all, or her parents' friends, or her grandmother's friends, or her aunt or uncle or cousins' friends. She'd sailed with these people or played tennis or badminton with them ever since she could walk, she'd gone to parties with them, and to boarding school and college, and had dated some of them. She'd even been in love with one or two.

"Hello, Charlotte. Great party."

Glancing up, she saw Whit Lowry standing there, in his tux and red tartan cummerbund and bow tie, his black hair falling over his forehead, looking like an ad for a very expensive Scotch. She'd always thought Whit looked like a male version of Snow White, with blue eyes and pale skin and natural roses in his cheeks.

"Whit, hello, how are you?" Charlotte always felt awkward around Whit. He was her father's best friend's son, and she knew he was as irked as she was by their fathers' barely concealed desire that they would fall in love and marry. He *had* been very kind to her when she'd tried working at the bank. He'd saved her ass several times, actually. He was very good at what he did, he understood stocks and bonds and foreign currencies and asset classes and diversification, and sometimes she had just wanted to kick him because he was such a reliable, unrebellious son. She hadn't seen him for almost a year—it was here, last summer, when she saw him last.

"Did you see Oliver?" Charlotte had to yell to be heard. Guiltily, she was glad she was wearing this wonderful dress, a long streak of gold silk that made her hair, worn loose to her shoulders tonight, appear gold, too. She was glad the dress had a plunging neckline.

"I'm just on my way over," Whit yelled back. "Did Owen come?"

"He did. He's somewhere in this crush. And Teddy is here. Have you seen him yet? He's brought a girl with him."

"Wow, I haven't seen Teddy in years. How is he?"

"As mischievous as always." Before she could say more, one of Nona's dowager cronies swooped down on her, embracing her in a cloud of talcum powder and bugle beads. "Hello, Mrs. Burton," Charlotte said, and was released from the hug in time to see Whit wave a quick goodbye and head off in Oliver's direction.

A waiter came along, smartly bearing a tray of drinks at shoulder level. Charlotte snagged a second champagne flute and held them both up high, so people would think she was taking a drink to someone as she squeezed through the crowd. Finally, she arrived at the end of the room where most of the family stood. So many people crowded around Nona, Charlotte could see only the top of her grandmother's white head, and her parents and other relatives were equally engaged by friends. Charlotte took a moment to study her mother. Helen had always been a little eccentric about her clothing. Aunt Grace and the Ms and the group Helen ran with on the island tended to wear L. L. Bean for day and something like Lilly Pulitzer with a string of pearls for dress. No one ever tried to be fashionable, nor was Helen actually fashionable, she was just colorful. More—Charlotte had heard Grace use this word often—*Bohemian*. Certainly she was tonight. She wore a crimson floor-length silk skirt with a high tight waist and a long-sleeved white shirt with a scoop neckline. Her ornate necklace of brass studded with huge ruby, emerald, and sapphire stones looked antique, as if it had been made from old Romanoff medals, crosses, and rosettes. Her gray hair had become, with the evening's mist, something between a cloud and a tangle. She looked good. To Charlotte's eye, her mother looked suspiciously attractive.

Charlotte's father was talking to Whit's father, Lew Lowry. Both men were tall and, for their age, relatively slim in their tuxes. They stood slightly apart from the crowd, the very set of their shoulders giving off an air of superiority and self-satisfaction. Their handsome heads were bent close to each other. They were scheming about something. Those two always were, always had been since they were boyhood chums.

Charlotte was searching for Teddy and spied him backed up against the wall by a cluster of admirers. Suzette stood next to him, staring down at her bare extended belly as Teddy bantered with a little herd of young women with silk headbands and yacht-club teeth. Teddy had a possessive arm looped around Suzette's shoulders, and from time to time he would sort of jostle her affectionately. Suzette would force a smile in response, but she never glanced up from her belly. She looked out of place and miserable.

"Suzette!" Charlotte put the champagne on a nearby table and swept up, as brisk and commanding as Nona often was. "Sweetie, what on earth is Teddy thinking, making you stand up this way! Come sit down with me. We have so much to talk about!"

She took Suzette's limp hand and drew the girl out of the circle of Teddy's admirers. "Here," she said, pulling out a chair.

"Thanks." Suzette slumped down.

Charlotte pulled her own chair close. "You must find this bewildering, thrown into the pack all at once like this," she said encouragingly to the young woman. "Teddy is a little thoughtless sometimes."

"It's okay," Suzette mumbled. "I know what Teddy's like."

"Well!" Charlotte leaned closer. "Tell me about yourself, Suzette. Where did you and Teddy meet?"

Suzette continued to stare at her belly. "At AA."

"Oh! Well, that's good. Um, where?"

The girl shifted, looking peeved. "In a church basement."

Charlotte laughed. "No. I mean, what town?"

"Tucson. Tucson, Arizona."

"So! You're from Tucson."

"No."

Charlotte stared at the girl. Was she being purposefully rude or was she socially inept? Perhaps she was just painfully shy. Charlotte softened her voice. "I hope Teddy told you all about his crazy family."

Suzette shrugged.

Charlotte grabbed up her champagne and knocked it back. "Do you have anything to drink, Suzette? Would you like me to get you some sparkling water or some juice?"

"I have juice." She nodded at the other side of the table.

"Well, let me get it for you!" Charlotte made her way around the table, got the glass of juice, set it before Suzette, and sat down again. "So you know all about Nona, our grandmother; she is wonderful. We all adore her. I don't know if you got to meet Oliver and Owen, it was so rushed back at the house with the photographs and everything. Oliver's over there talking to that really tall woman, and Owen is trying to get to Oliver with some drinks. Aren't they just about the handsomest men on the planet?"

Defiantly, Suzette declared, "Teddy's handsome."

"Yes, he is. I have two handsome brothers." After a long inspirational sip of champagne, Charlotte asked, "Do you have any brothers, Suzette?"

Suzette didn't answer for a few moments. "A stepbrother," she conceded. "But I haven't seen him for a while."

Charlotte looked desperately around the room. Everyone else seemed to be having a fabulous time, exchanging gossip and laughing uproariously.

"Well, I'm the oldest of three children. I'm Teddy's big sister. I guess he told you that. And I've been trying to build up a little market garden business here on the island. Perhaps you noticed my little farm when Teddy brought you to the house?" She waited for some kind of response, got none, and plunged ahead. "I grow lettuces and other produce and flowers. I sell the produce at posh restaurants, plus I have my little roadside stand."

Suzette continued to stare at her belly.

All righty, Charlotte thought. "So, when is your baby due?"

"September."

"Oh, lovely. And do you know whether you're having a boy or a girl?"

"No." But for the first time Suzette lifted her head. She smiled shyly. "I hope it's a girl." She ducked her head.

"Oh, I do, too!" Charlotte agreed. "Girls' clothes are much more fun!" Before she could continue her friendly chatter, the piercing ring of a tapped mike sounded, and she heard her father's voice.

"Hello, everyone! We are so glad to have you all here to celebrate Anne Anderson Wheelwright's ninetieth birthday! After dinner, there will be dancing and a few extremely brief speeches, but for now the buffet line is open, so please begin!"

The noise level changed as people flocked out of the large room into the smaller reception room to line up at the buffet tables.

"Would you like me to get you a plate?" Charlotte asked.

"I can do it." Suzette pushed herself up off her chair.

Teddy appeared from the squeeze of bodies. Wrapping an arm around Suzette's shoulders, he leaned forward to kiss Charlotte's cheek. "Hey, Char. You're looking well."

Now that she had an opportunity to see him close up, Charlotte studied her brother before answering, "You look good, too, Teddy. Really good." She studied his jeans, his wrinkled dirty cheap martini-glass-dancing shirt, his worn camel's-hair blazer. There was a hole in one of the sleeves, and part of the breast pocket had come loose. "But couldn't you have come just a little bit earlier? We didn't get a chance to meet Suzette properly, and this must be a pretty overwhelming way for her to meet your family."

"Don't be such a big sister," Teddy scolded. "*Any* way of meeting this family would be over-whelming."

Charlotte relented. "That's true. Well, I'm glad you're here, Teddy. I can't wait to have a long long talk with you, you and Suzette, about everything. What are your plans?"

"My plans?" Teddy's grin glinted with the old mischief. "Suzette and I plan to stay at Nona's for the summer. So you and I will have lots of time for long long talks."

# Ten

*It was not* the first time Helen had felt emotionally apart from the other Wheelwrights. But this was separateness of an entirely different magnitude. Everyone else was talking, laughing, gobbling up the delicious food, and tossing back the drinks, and Nona, now seated at a table enjoying her own dinner, seemed glowing and happy and right in the moment. Helen sat next to Owen, with Oliver on Owen's right, and Suzette next to Oliver, who was trying to make conversation with the young woman. She wasn't responding much, mostly staring down at her belly, although Helen was glad to see that she ate rapidly and finished everything on her plate. Teddy was on Suzette's other side, with Nona on his right. The glass in his hand, a tall tumbler filled with ice, seemed to be only water. Helen had been watching and she didn't think he'd had an alcoholic beverage yet. Teddy leaned toward Nona, chatting and laughing, and Nona glittered under his attentions. On Nona's other side sat Charlotte, talking with her father, both of them as fascinated with each other as if they hadn't been together for months.

What a handsome family. What a fortunate family. All this champagne, this wealth of friends, this summer evening, this celebration. Helen allowed Oliver to engage her in a lighthearted conversation about current movies; she hoped she was managing to keep her anxiety concealed.

She had believed that once her children were adults, out of college, moving forward in their own lives, she would be less burdened with worries, or that the worries would be less compelling. She had been wrong. When her eye fell on Suzette, Helen's thoughts went wild. Was Suzette's baby Teddy's child? Were they really married? Had Suzette been on drugs or alcohol earlier in her pregnancy? Helen had heard heartbreaking stories of fetal alcohol syndrome. What were Teddy's plans? How could he support a child? He'd received a small inheritance when his grandfather died, but he'd run through that already, and had nothing substantive to show for it. And Teddy had always been unstable.

She was so concerned about Teddy and this new twist in his life that her grief over Worth's affair receded into the background, but it did not disappear. From experience, she knew how to compartmentalize her thoughts and emotions, and she thought she was doing it pretty well. But she felt as if she had been dropped from a great height. She was shattered, every cell of her being in shards and sharp pieces, and she was holding herself together with a thin layer of skin and teeth-gritting determination.

She and Worth hadn't spoken intimately since they set foot on the island. No chance, really, not with the rest of the family slamming in and out of the house. When they arrived tonight at the yacht club, they were, as always, separated by their good familiar friends, with gossip about marriages and babies in Helen's case and tips about the stock market in Worth's. Helen spoke mostly with other women, Worth with other men, but occasionally Helen would glance across the room to see one of Worth's female friends sidle up to kiss him on the cheek and, laughing, straighten his tie or take his arm. She was pretty sure none of his yacht club friends could be Sweet Cakes. But she was glad it would be Worth and Grace doing the master of ceremonies bit tonight. Helen thought that if she tried to speak aloud she might choke on the clot of misery in her throat.

People were through eating. The waiters had cleared the plates away. From a nearby table, Grace waved at Worth, who nodded and rose. They went to the bandstand together and took turns speaking into the mike. Grace was her usual clipped bossy self—she was a good leader and a great captain of a racing boat—but it was Worth who made the crowd laugh and applaud and cheer. Helen couldn't concentrate on his words. She was staring at Worth, thinking of his body, that elegant, healthy male body, naked with another woman.

She would have understood if Worth had had some kind of *flirtation*. Worth was sixty also, and while time had not ruined his body quite as much as it had Helen's, he was a bit heavier, his skin was looser, and when he stood up, his knees creaked and he limped for a while, muttering "no more tennis," although he still played. Helen often grieved—weeping, in real pain—for the loss of her youth, for the erosion of her beauty. She missed receiving the spontaneous attentions of unfamiliar men the way she once had—a wink and a grin from a man in line at the post office, a flattering flourish of the arm when a strange man held the door open for her, a double take from a man at a restaurant. And she missed the electricity of attraction that had once connected her to Worth.

But they had been married for so long: thirty-five years. They had truly grown old together. Helen had thought that the sexual passion of their marriage had been gradually replaced by deep affection, shared memories, and a sense of comradeship equal to that of old soldiers who once fought side by side in the trenches. People said that a sense of humor was important in a marriage; how many women said, "I married him because he made me laugh." Worth still made her laugh. They still shared so much, especially their family: their children, Nona, and Grace and her clan. They shared friends.

Perhaps that was not enough for Worth. Over the past few years, banking as an industry, and the world money market, had changed enormously. He couldn't do it all himself. He couldn't even oversee it all himself. So his sense of self-worth might have suffered, and his power had definitely faded. Helen could understand that he might want a fresh young woman to remind him that he was still, in all ways, virile. She did not want her husband to be unhappy, after all.

But she could not bear his infidelity.

She wondered whether Worth was *in love* with Sweet Cakes. She wondered whether he would ask for a divorce.

She realized she was wringing her hands under the table like a madwoman. But her hands were freezing cold.

People were making toasts now. Applause. Laughter. Appreciative sighs. The invisible bubble surrounding Helen set everything apart; she felt like an anthropologist surveying the rituals of a strange tribe.

The band launched into an old-fashioned Strauss waltz, that familiar lilting melody of a birthday song, and Worth stepped down from the platform, bowed to Nona, and gently helped her up from her chair. He led her to the dance floor, put one hand on her waist, and with the other took her hand in his. Slowly, with great dignity, he waltzed with his mother, who gazed up at her handsome son with adoration. With her stiff carriage, in her splendid floor-length deep blue gown, Nona looked like royalty. Helen felt bits of ice sparkle against her face. When she touched her cheeks with her fingertips, she felt tears. But that was all right, other people were weeping, too. It was a moving and wonderful sight.

After a few minutes, Kellogg stepped out onto the floor and with great ceremony tapped Worth's shoulder. With a flourish, Worth ceded to his brother-in-law. Kellogg danced with Nona, and then Oliver cut in, and now Helen's tears flooded down her face, to see her eldest son dance with his grandmother. Mandy's Claus cut in, and then Mellie's Douglas, and finally, handsomely, Teddy. By this time, Nona wasn't so much dancing with her partners as being supported by them. Soon Worth came to her side and whispered something to Teddy, and together they helped Nona off the dance floor, to return to her seat. The music swelled. Douglas led Mellie out to dance, and Kellogg offered his hand to Grace, and Claus bowed to Mandy.

"Mother?" Teddy stood before her, holding out his hand.

She went with him to the dance floor. She had to reach up to put her arm on his shoulder. "I didn't know you could waltz."

His grin was wicked. "There are a lot of things you don't know about me."

Well, *that* was true, she thought. She took her time replying. His skin was healthy and slightly sunburned. His blue eyes were clear. "Do you realize it's been almost a year since I've seen you?"

"Well, you know, Mom, not all families are as ingrown as the Wheelwrights. I know dozens of people who don't see their families for years at a time and still manage to be perfectly sane and productive citizens."

Lightly, Helen asked, "What are Suzette's parents like?" Seeing Teddy's face grow cloudy, she hastened to add, "I mean, where do they live? What do they do? How did you and Suzette meet?"

"Why don't you type up a questionnaire and I'll have her fill it in."

"Stop it, Teddy. I'm only asking normal questions any mother would ask."

Just then, the song ended. The music stopped. People applauded, and Helen forced herself to smile gaily at the couples surrounding them.

"May I?" Oliver was there, smoothly relieving Teddy of the burden of his mother.

With a toss of his shaggy head, Teddy left the dance floor.

"Oliver to the rescue," Helen joked.

"You spoil him, Mom; you always have, you always will," Oliver told her.

"Oh, Oliver!" Helen bit back her words. She didn't want to take the frustration Teddy made her feel out on her other son.

The music was faster now, a sixties rock-and-roll medley, fun for dancing, impossible for conversation. It raised the noise level in the room, so that people laughed more loudly and, it seemed, more often. Helen danced for a long time with Oliver, who was without a doubt the best dancer in the room. He moved as if he had no bones, he flowed. He was the handsomest of her three children and the most at peace with himself, Helen thought. But then Owen appeared next to them, with Charlotte as his partner, and subtly Oliver and Owen shifted directions, so that for a little while the two men danced opposite each other, while Helen danced with her daughter. Perhaps Oliver's aura of peacefulness was partly an act, Helen thought, and deep inside him a great discontent burned, because here at the yacht club he and his partner were not really able to dance with each other, not to a fast dance and especially not to a slow one.

The music changed. Helen started to leave the dance floor, but Lew Lowry took her arm. "Dance?" he asked. And she liked to dance, so she did. She danced all evening, with all her husband's friends and all the husbands of her women friends. When she danced with her brother-in-law Kellogg, she felt like a piece of luggage being manhandled around the room. And both Mandy's husband, Claus, and Mellie's Douglas *plodded*. She'd always felt that Grace and her family had none of the charm Charlotte, Oliver, and Teddy had, but of course she, as their mother, would think that. Truly, Worth was effortlessly more attractive than his sister. Well, Worth was his mother's favorite. He moved through life as if a red carpet were unrolling before him while the crowd stood back, eyeing him with admiration. It was the way he had been raised, really. Was Worth unfaithful to her because she didn't smother him with idolatry like some giddy girl?

She was breathless when she returned to her place at the table. Tomorrow her back would kill her. All that weeding in Charlotte's garden, and now all this dancing. Sipping champagne, she surveyed the room. Nearby, Charlotte was paired off with Bill Cooper. Helen looked for Miranda Fellows but didn't see her. Bill had an appreciative grin on his face as Charlotte undulated, her arms high above her head, her gold gown swaying provocatively against her perfect slender body. Oh, my. Charlotte had had a crush on Bill when she was a girl, and it looked as if she had a crush again. Across the room, Whit Lowry leaned against a wall, trapped by a young woman who was practically crawling on top of him in her efforts to keep his attention, but Whit kept looking over at Charlotte. God, Whit Lowry was handsome! And from the way he looked at Charlotte—goodness, he was interested in her!

Helen couldn't prevent her mind from flipping into the future: Charlotte married—to Whit or to Coop—and having children! At last, Helen would be a grandmother.

Although it was possible she'd be a grandmother in a matter of months. During dessert, she had tried talking with Suzette but found the girl unresponsive and monosyllabic. Suzette did not wear a wedding ring, but that wasn't proof that she wasn't married to Teddy. And marriage or not, Teddy seemed to believe there was a strong possibility that the child Suzette was carrying was his. Perhaps Teddy was ready to be a father to the child no matter whose genes it had, but Teddy was an impetuous, unreliable fellow, like a bead of mercury, gleaming like silver but rolling in all directions, never still and not always there when you needed him.

"The girl's a gold digger."

Helen startled, almost knocking over her water glass. She had turned her chair around so she could watch the dance floor, and Grace had swooped down next to her, dragging a chair parallel to Helen's. Helen leaned close to her sister-in-law. "Grace, she might hear you."

"Are you kidding? Over this din? I can scarcely hear myself. Besides, what if she does hear me. The little skank needs to know that we're not buying her act."

"Don't call her a skank, Grace! Why are you being so uncharitable? I'm concerned, too, but Teddy said they're married, and as Teddy's wife she deserves our respect. And our assistance. The poor thing looks like she hasn't had a decent meal in ages."

"She's a drug addict, Helen, of course she hasn't eaten."

"You don't know she's a drug addict! Give her a break, Grace. Teddy loves her."

"And Teddy is such fine judge of character, being such a fine character himself."

Helen turned to face Grace full on. "Are you drunk, Grace? Because that's the only excuse for your speaking this way."

"Maybe I am drunk. But I'll be damned if I allow some little piece of trash your druggie son's dragged in to lay claim to any part of the Wheelwright legacy."

Helen sat perfectly still. She had never been close to Grace, but they had gotten along all right. They'd shared so much over the many years, cooking for their large intertwined families, organizing beach picnics, sailboat races, tennis matches. She'd never imagined Grace felt anything like this. She'd never seen Grace quite so vitriolic. In fact, she'd never seen Grace so passionate about anything.

From the corner of her eye, she saw the black gleam of a tuxedo, and then her husband was standing in front of them. He leaned down to his sister. "Grace, may I have this dance?"

Grace rose without another word. Helen just sat there, staring out at the dance floor, watching all the smiling, happy, well-fed people dancing by. Did anyone else have a family like hers? Were any other women forcing gaiety when inside they burned with grief? Did any other women feel separate from their own families? Helen's parents had gobs of money, and Helen had had a sterling education. She played a decent game of tennis and could sail a boat well enough. She'd chaired committees and supervised events, and back in Boston she'd given all the cocktail parties Worth had wanted.

But in her heart, she was not a Wheelwright. So then—who was she?

The wildest thing she'd ever done was to suggest—merely suggest—that she open an art gallery on the island. When the idea was vetoed by the rest of the Wheelwrights, she let the matter drop. Helen had never wanted a career. All her life had been about her family—*her* family, Worth and their three children. She just hadn't cared about being a Wheelwright. She didn't care now. She wanted her three children to be happy and healthy. If she wished for anything else, it would be to have more presence in her children's lives. She liked her children so much, even roguish Teddy. No matter what Grace said, Helen's children were wonderful, amazing people, good people, and perhaps Teddy was facing more challenges than most, but he was still a good person, and she would stand by him and his choice of a wife, and to hell with the Wheelwrights!

Grace returned to their table, obviously avoiding Helen and seating herself next to Nona. Helen saw Worth slow-dancing with Harriet Hingham, an old friend of Worth's and a maniac sailor who crewed for him anytime he asked.

Suddenly, there was a commotion. Nona gave a little cry and slumped sideways. Grace shrieked. People jumped up from nearby tables and rushed over. Nona's body was limp. Worth pushed through the crowd and knelt at his mother's side, taking her weight in his arms. Roger Parsons, their island doctor and a friend, pressed his way through the crowd.

"Come on, folks, give her air." He leaned down to feel for Nona's pulse at the side of her neck. He looked up. "Call nine-one-one."

## Eleven

*Cuddled in dreams* like a china doll among soft cotton puffs, Nona became aware of a man bending near. She could sense the rumble of his deep voice, the force of his male presence, a large masculine hand on her crooked old chicken claw, and then his voice.

She tried to open her eyes, but her lids were too heavy. Still, she could glimpse through her lashes, just a bit. . . .

It was Bobby! Her heart quickened. Her darling beloved son—but no, it was Worth. Or was it Herb? It wasn't Kellogg or one of her grand-daughter's husbands—this male was hers, belonged to her; she knew it in the way she knew a familiar scent.

"Nona?"

It was Oliver.

It was Oliver, and with that knowledge rushed a plethora of information: she was in her summer house, in her dear comfortable bed, and the cotton puffs were pillows, and it was day. She could somehow feel the light through the windows, and the windows were open; bless Glorious for keeping the windows open.

"Nona?" Oliver sat carefully on the side of her bed.

He smelled delicious. She had never approved of men using cologne, but Oliver did smell delicious, like a mixture of gin and pears.

She managed to open her eyes. "Oliver." Her voice was a whisper.

"She's awake!"

It was Grace shouting from the doorway, of course it was Grace, she had always wanted to be the first with any good news, as if she would somehow be given credit for it, a gold star somewhere on her cosmic lifetime behavior chart. Grace liked to be the first with bad news, too, for that matter.

The air of the room roiled as Grace rushed to the bed, elbowed Oliver out of the way, and bent over Nona.

"Nona! How are you?"

"I'm fine. Don't fuss."

"You fainted last night at your party."

"Of course I did. I was overwhelmed and exhausted."

"You gave us all such a fright!"

"I'm sorry, Grace. I didn't mean to."

"The doctor said you'd only fainted. We brought you home in an ambulance, and you've just slept eight hours straight!"

"Could I have some water, Grace? My throat is dry."

"I'll get it." Grace flitted away.

Nona was still holding her grandson's hand, and now she squeezed it. "Are you leaving?"

"Yes, Nona. We have to get back. Owen has a conference tomorrow morning that he has to attend. But we'll be back in two weeks, for Family Meeting."

"And for your wedding."

"Yes. And for our wedding." When Oliver smiled, he looked like an angel.

"Where's Owen?"

"I asked him to wait downstairs. I didn't think you'd want too many people crowding around you right now."

"That's thoughtful, Oliver, and you're right. I'm tired, and not feeling especially social at the moment. But kiss Owen goodbye for me, will you?"

"Of course." Oliver bent down and kissed her cheek. "Goodbye, Nona."

He was her first grandson. She could remember

holding him when he was only a few hours old. She had trembled at the exquisite completeness of him, his little bald head, his squinting eyes, his birdlike rib cage. She could remember thinking how *smart* he was, and now she smiled at her memory. How could she have thought that a newborn was smart? And yet Oliver was, wise and intelligent and clever. She had known it when she first set eyes on him, and she knew it now.

"Goodbye, Oliver." It was an effort to speak.

To her surprise, he grinned a wicked grin and shook his head. "Don't even think it. You're absolutely not going to die on me, Nona. We want you there for the ceremony. But you're not going to die for years and years anyway, you know that."

"What are you saying!" Grace swept up, water glass in hand. "Oliver! Don't talk about death in front of Nona!"

"Right," Oliver responded archly. "Because she'd never think of it on her own."

The bed jiggled as Oliver stood up. "Goodbye, Aunt Grace." He waved at Nona and left the room.

"He's not as cute as he thinks he is." Grace settled on the bed. "Can I help you sit up, Nona? So you can have a sip of water?"

"Thank you, Grace, I can do it alone." But Nona was dismayed at how weak her arms were. It was only sheer pride and cussedness that fueled her as she struggled, managing to hoist herself just a few inches higher on her pillows. When Grace held out the water glass, Nona was horrified to discover that she didn't have enough energy to say *Wait a moment.* She rested, just breathing. After a few moments, she was able to reach out for the glass, but her hand was shaking.

The water was cool, a slide of crystal elixir down her throat. She took another sip. And another. Oliver was an unusually handsome man, she thought. She had handsome children. But no one was as handsome as Herb.

"I'm going to sleep some more," Nona whispered. Seeing the concern on her daughter's face, she said, "Don't worry, dear. It's just sleep."

## 1943

*The steamer* Nobska rounded Brant Point on its voyage across Nantucket Sound to Woods Hole. Anne slipped her high heels off and tucked her feet up under her for warmth and comfort. Herb hadn't warned her about the cobblestone streets and brick sidewalks of Nantucket, and the walking tour he'd taken her on of the quaint village center this morning had been hard on her feet. They ached. Her heart ached even more.

"So," Herb said. He settled across from her on a bench, looking handsome and relaxed in his civvies. "What do you think?"

Anne gazed out the window at the long sandy beaches and gray shingled houses, the moderate waves breaking gently against the easy shore. "I think Nantucket's beautiful."

"And? You're looking mighty pensive." He reached into his breast pocket for his cigarette case, held it out to her, and, when she shook her head, took out a cigarette for himself.

Anne forced herself to be brave. To face him straight on. "Herb, I can't marry you. At least not yet."

He recoiled in surprise. "Why, Anne, what's gotten into you?" His face changed. "My parents are *that* bad?"

"I didn't say they were bad. I didn't say anything about them, Herb. I'm not calling anyone names. But you can't deny that they didn't take to me."

"Look." Herb leaned forward, elbows on his knees, earnest in his speech. "I know my father's a cold fish and my mother's—well, she's *formal.* That's just the way they are."

"Herb, your parents didn't like me. Not even a little bit."

"My sister liked you!"

"Yes, and I like Holly. But your parents—"

"Damn it, Anne, we're not going to live with my parents!"

"Well, perhaps not, but you're going to work in the bank, aren't you? And won't you want to spend every summer on Nantucket, in that big old house, sailing and all?" She had to look away. Every fiber of her being yearned to kiss him, touch him, be with him—that was all that mattered. But she couldn't *let* it be all that mattered. "Besides, Herb, maybe they're right. Maybe we're rushing things. Well, we *are* rushing things. We've only known each other three weeks."

Herb said, "Anne, I knew I wanted to marry you the moment I saw you."

She couldn't hold back the tears. She buried her face in her hands.

"You said you felt that way, too," Herb quietly reminded her.

She nodded. "I know. I did. But we shouldn't be *hasty*."

"Anne, I have never taken a woman home to my parents before. I have never asked a woman to marry me before. I have gone out with several women, and been a little bit serious about one or two, but when I saw you, it was like—like getting hit right in the gut." He paused. "That doesn't sound very romantic, does it?"

Anne couldn't help but smile. "It sounds very romantic. I know exactly what you mean." She unclasped her purse, took out her embroidered handkerchief, and wiped her eyes. She was determined to be dignified about this. "But that doesn't mean we have to get married right away, does it?"

"I leave for special training in Arizona tomorrow," he reminded her.

"And we can spend the night together," she said. "And I'll be true to you, Herb, and I'll write you

171

letters, and when you get home from the war we can get married."

Herb's mouth set and he drummed his fingers on his knees, thinking. Then he said, "What if we didn't have a war on? What if I weren't getting sent away? You know what? I'd still want to marry you right away, and not to sleep with you or to keep you from sleeping with other men, and not to start a family or be sure a baby's legitimate if we accidentally did start a family. I'd want to marry you because I want you to be my wife. Right now. Right away. I want to be officially connected to you. You are my person. I finally *found* you. Why do I have to wait any longer?"

Anne looked out the window, trying to compose her thoughts. The ferry steamed away from the calmer waters of the shoreline and hit rough water, the early October winds transforming the waves into troughs. The ferry reared and dropped, reared and dropped. Salt spray dashed against the windows and the horizon tilted alarmingly. Anne's stomach turned.

She put her hands on her midriff. "I'm going to be ill."

"Lie down," Herb advised her. "Try to sleep."

She slid down on the long bench, pulling her light cloth coat over her. Herb rose, folded his overcoat into a pillow, and gently placed it beneath her head. It did help to lie down. She shut her gaze against the way everything slanted.

She could feel Herb looking at her, and she remembered the first day they spent together just three weeks ago.

That morning, their first morning together, when Anne and Herb finally made it to Anne's little kitchen for breakfast, they saw the sun blazing in the high blue perfection of the sky. It was late September. Anne had the windows open, and a fresh breeze occasionally stirred the curtains. As she moved around, fixing scrambled eggs and bacon and toast and coffee for Herb, she was well aware of the domesticity of the moment, she felt as if she were trying to form a mold or pattern for their future life so that this simple event would be stamped into time like a phonograph record, to be played over and over again. She wore her summer wrap, a lightweight silk peach kimono. Herb had tried to put on her white chenille bathrobe, but his shoulders were too large. How they had laughed! He pulled on trousers and an undershirt. She wanted to sit on his lap while he ate. She wanted to be the food that he ate.

Herb set his coffee cup back on the saucer and leaned back. "That was great. Thanks, Anne." He looked out the window. "What shall we do with this fine day?"

"Well, we could stroll through the Public Gardens. The trees are just starting to turn, and I love the trees in the autumn."

"You'd rather do that than go to a museum?"

"Oh, always!" She shot a quick glance his way to see how he took this. "I guess I'm just a Midwestern outdoor girl at heart. Anyway, Herb, I've been in Boston for four years. I've pretty much seen the museums."

"Have you ever been out to Concord?"

"You know, I never have. I don't have a car. Well, I do at home, of course. But when I was at Radcliffe I never needed a car, really. I just took a bus or a cab if necessary. I was so busy all the time with my courses, and every social event was with the boys at Harvard. Sometimes we went down to New York on the train, but otherwise I never even thought of leaving Boston and Cambridge. Do you think I should see Concord?"

"I do. Absolutely." He stood up, suddenly awake and energetic. "Let's get dressed. We're going for a ride in the country."

Anne wore a blue dress with a white belt, tied a red sweater over her shoulders in case they were out late, and knotted a silk scarf around her long brown curls. They walked up to Herb's family home on Beacon Hill. While Herb changed into a fresh uniform, Anne waited in the living room, which was much like Hilyard Clayton's parents' stuffy old mausoleum. All she could think about was how glad she was that Herb's parents were down at their summer home on Nantucket Island, because she wouldn't have wanted to meet them this way, the morning she and Herb had become lovers. She was vaguely aware of the quality of the oil paintings on the walls, the porcelain on the tables, the high dignified ceilings, but it was really a small place compared to her parents' home in Kansas City, so she wasn't overwhelmed or even impressed. She was just thinking about Herb. She was just aching to be back in bed with him, to do all those things she'd learned to do this morning, while the sun rose.

Herb raced down the stairs, two at a time. "Okay! We're off!" Behind the house, on a narrow cobblestone lane, sat his own automobile, a 1938 Terraplane convertible. It was aqua, with a shining curved chrome grille and white sidewall tires. The seats were natural leather, the dashboard a shining curve of wood—teak, Anne thought.

"What a beaut," Anne said, and Herb grinned proudly.

The top was up, so for a few minutes they occupied themselves in folding it back, and then they settled onto the leather seats, and Herb turned the key and pulled out the choke and gunned the gas, and they were off.

Herb steered knowledgeably through the cramped and winding Boston streets. He glanced over at her. "Did you know that the streets of Boston were originally old cow paths? That's why they're so confusing."

Anne said, "I must confess I don't pay attention

to streets. I think I navigate by buildings, landmarks. Like, my apartment is two blocks away from the little diner where Gail and I like to have breakfast." She waved an arm through the air. "This is all new to me."

When they reached Route 2, they picked up speed and their words were lost in the wind. The sun beat down on their shoulders and the wind blew at them, ruffling Anne's scarf against her face. She lay back against the warm leather and allowed herself to soak in the soft magic of this day. Even without turning to look, she sensed Herb's every move, downshifting the gears, smoothly passing a slow dump truck.

Concord lay about fifteen miles northwest of Boston, away from the growing city, nestled among forests and neat farms. A perfect little village, with handsome colonial mansions and tidy stores and banks in discreet brick buildings, it slumbered beneath the sun like a town dreaming of the past.

And it was a town in love with its past, a venerable past. Herb parked the car near the long grassy rectangle named Monument Square and ushered her around the village, pointing out historic spots. Emerson had lived in Concord, and Thoreau and Nathaniel Hawthorne as well. They strolled along Lexington Street, and stood in silent thought in front of Orchard House, where Louisa May Alcott had written *Little*

*Women.* Walking a bit farther, they came to another house, where the Alcotts had lived; then, Hawthorne; and, much later, Harriet Lothrop, writing her book *The Five Little Peppers and How They Grew.*

"So much history in one place," Anne mused.

"And you haven't seen my favorite spot yet." Taking her arm, he turned her back toward the center of town and his car.

"Walden Pond?" she guessed.

He only shook his head and smiled.

They got back in the car and drove out of town along a narrow wooded road, not much more than a lane; the houses fell away, and they were in the countryside. Trees lined the road, shading them from the sun, making the light seem to flicker as they rolled along. Twice a bright orange maple leaf drifted down into the convertible. One landed on Anne's lap, the other on Herb's head, and they laughed.

Herb steered the car into a small car park, and said, "We're here." They got out, crossed the road, and walked along a path between more august old trees. The lane was sprinkled with fallen leaves, like flags or trail marks.

Anne saw a modest wooden bridge. Before it stood a small obelisk, indicating that the stone wall was a memorial stone for the British soldiers killed and wounded here during the Revolutionary War.

"For the *British* soldiers," Anne whispered, and she couldn't help but think of them, those boys in their red coats, so far away from home, having survived crossing the Atlantic in order to march this far and then, on foreign soil, to die.

They crossed the bridge, their feet thumping solidly against the wood. On the other side rose a statue by Daniel Chester French of the Minuteman. Beneath the plinth, carved into a plaque, were words from Emerson's memorial hymn:

> *By the rude bridge that arched the flood,*
> *Their flag to April's breeze unfurled,*
> *Here once the embattled farmers stood,*
> *And fired the shot heard round the world.*

"I've memorized that poem," Herb told her. "We had to, in school."

"I'd like to hear the rest," Anne told him.

Herb cleared his throat.

> "*On this green bank, by this soft stream,*
> *We set today a votive stone;*
> *That memory may their deed redeem,*
> *When, like our sires, our sons are gone.*
> *Spirit, that made those heroes dare*
> *To die, and leave their children free,*
> *Bid Time and Nature gently spare*
> *The shaft we raise to them and thee.*"

"Oh, Herb." Anne hugged herself, tightly.

"I know," Herb's voice was hoarse. "I'm always moved, every time I come out here. I think of those farmers, that raggedy band of men fighting against the British troops, but I think of the British troops as well, who were probably all yearning to return to their own homes and families and farms and green fields and lush meadows." He cleared his throat. "And of course those words—*that made those heroes dare to die, and leave their children free*—well, that's what we're going to be doing over in Europe, isn't it?"

Anne looked straight ahead, at the gentle arch of the bridge. "Are you afraid, Herb?"

He chuckled, putting an arm around her shoulders and hugging her against him. "Of course I'm afraid, only a fool wouldn't be. But I'm not superstitious, if that's what you mean, I'm not—well, *dreading* the battles. And I do believe what we're doing is right, I believe in the cause, and I've always thought a man had to have a cause to believe in, a cause he would die for, if he was going to be a real man."

Her throat was swollen with unshed tears. She managed to say, "You *are* sort of an old-fashioned guy, aren't you, Herb?"

"No, I don't think I am. Or if I am, so are most of the men in the country. But don't you see now, Anne, why it's important to me to marry you? I don't know, maybe it's old-fashioned of me, but I'd like to have a wedding ring on my finger and a wife to write letters to, and not just any old wife. I'd like to know *you* were my wife. Here, in my country while I'm off fighting."

He was such a romantic man. Anne had never met such a romantic man. "You know I love you, Herb."

He tilted her face up so he could look in her eyes. "Then marry me," he said.

She had said, "I will. Yes. I will . . ."

"Anne?" Herb leaned over and gently touched Anne's shoulder. "We're almost there."

She sat up, smoothing her skirt down over her legs. She ran her fingers through her hair. "I'm not a very good sailor, I'm afraid."

"It was a rougher crossing than usual."

She stood, pulling her sweater up against her shoulders, and looked out the window at the long harbor with sandbars and long stretches of beach and gray shingled cottages among the low dunes. Fishing boats motored past, and a handsome orange and black Coast Guard vessel was pulling away from the dock. She saw cars on shore, and people standing in the sunshine waving at the approaching ferry. She liked seeing the bustle of normal life. It made her braver. Herb's parents were only two people, after all, in all the wide world, and as Herb said, in all this wide world they had found each other.

Herb stood behind her. He didn't touch her, but she could feel his breath on her hair. "How do you feel?"

"Better." She looked up at him. "Much better. I was being silly before, and I'm sorry. I want to marry you, Herb. As soon as possible."

# Twelve

*The very early mornings* had come to be Charlotte's favorite time of day. She'd wake to her alarm, pull on her work clothes, and tiptoe through the sleeping house, down the stairs, and out to the mudroom, where she sat on an old wooden bench and laced up her boots. Then, careful not to slam the door, she stepped out into the fresh morning. As she hurried to her shed for her tools and then strode up the drive toward her garden, dawn slowly revealed itself like a secret shared with her alone. She had become so acquainted with the few magic moments when the sun, with stately royalty, rose, that she could sense it on her shoulders before her eyes saw the light. She felt a primitive response in her belly and across the back of her neck; it was if someone invisible leaned toward her, whispering. She felt a breath.

She knew, scientifically, this was only the routine turning of the planet, but personally she believed it was much more than that. Sometimes she felt as if it were a kind of message, or that a message was displayed in the rising of the sun in a language she could not yet decipher but might be able to, someday. And if it was absolution, would she know?

She carried her supplies out to the table by the roadside. With an old rag, she wiped the dew from the surface of the table, shook out the checked tablecloth, and spread it over the table, smoothing the cloth down with her hand, standing back to ascertain that it hung evenly all around. She put the woven basket on the table and added five dollars' worth of nickels, dimes, and quarters, in case her customers needed to make change. Double-checking the list she kept in her notebook, she wrote the items for sale and their prices on the whiteboard and propped the board and the wooden sign against a cookbook stand that had been collecting dust in Nona's pantry. Then she went to her garden to collect the day's wares.

During the past three years, she had trolled the Take It or Leave It shed at the local dump for vases, mason jars—anything that could hold a bouquet of flowers. In the winter, during days when it was too cold to go out, she put all the containers through the dishwasher, stacked them, clean and dry, in cardboard boxes, and lugged them to the shed. Now she walked across the sandy stretch of untended low moorland to her garden. She unlatched the gate, entered, and walked down her rows, eyeing her various plants, until she came to the flowers. Kneeling, she snipped away, carefully placing the blooms in her basket. She carried them to her shed, set out the containers, filled them with water from the tap, and occupied herself for a while, making pretty spring bouquets, mixing ranunculus and pansies, iris, peonies, and poppies, inserting long slender stems of beach grass and beach peas or wild chokecherries for height and whimsy. These arrangements went for seventy dollars, but they were fresh, unique, and worth it—she always sold as many as she put out.

Next, she cut several bunches of asparagus and lettuce. She filled her basket with arugula and loose lettuce leaves, rinsed them, and tucked the leaves into plastic bags. Later, at seven-thirty, when Jorge arrived, he would cut and rinse more lettuces. She picked tiny bright-green pea pods, radishes, herbs, and onions, tied the clusters up with green twine, and laid them on the table. She had only just finished stocking her little stand when the first customer arrived, a woman named Muffy Nerwell, who was Charlotte's mother's age and drove a Hummer, on this island where the speed limit was never higher than 45 miles per hour. Muffy came every morning, early, wanting to have first choice. She told Charlotte she arranged her evening meal according to what Charlotte had fresh that day. She was frustrated because Charlotte didn't have carrots, potatoes, and corn like the local Stop & Shop did, and when Charlotte was present to wait on her, she expected Charlotte to give her a five percent discount.

Charlotte was glad to finish with the transaction. She returned once again to her shed, where she went into a kind of Zen mode as she sowed more spinach and lettuce seeds into little plastic trays. For the first time in months, her concentration was divided, and this irritated her. A lot was going on in the house, and she wanted to know about it first-hand.

Most important, she knew Nona would be all right. The doctor had said so, and Nona had wakened briefly last night, murmured that she was fine, and then fallen back into sleep, which Charlotte was sure was exactly what the nonagenarian needed after such an unusual day of socializing.

Oliver and Owen were leaving this morning. She hadn't had a chance to spend much time with them, but they would be back in two weeks and she'd catch up then. They were fine anyway; she could tell.

Charlotte's father was flying back to Boston sometime today. Her mother had planned to return with him, to continue packing and organizing for the move to Nantucket for the summer, but then she had told Worth she'd fly home later; she needed to talk with Teddy and Suzette. Charlotte was glad her father would be absent for this conversation. Worth was hard on Teddy, he always had been. Well, Teddy had always been a rascal. As far as Charlotte knew, her father had not approached Teddy or Suzette since their arrival last night. Certainly, her father, who could be the most charming of men, had not been welcoming.

But really, Charlotte thought, there had hardly been time. After Nona went off in the ambulance, everything was in chaos and the party was pretty much over. It had been almost midnight when Nona was returned to her own house and her own bed. Any sense of celebration had dissipated, replaced by simple relief that Nona was alive, and everyone drifted off, exhausted, to bed. Charlotte had heard Teddy and Suzette in the attic room next to hers. She hadn't been able to make out the words, but she caught the mood, Teddy's low rumbling, Suzette's soprano counterpoint. Suzette had talked a lot. Good to know the strange young woman *could* talk a lot, Charlotte had decided, as she fell asleep.

Now her hands moved swiftly, in a sure rhythm, as she poked holes in the dark prepared soil, inserted the minuscule seeds, and smoothed the holes closed. Her mind was not so orderly. It was more like an oscillating sprinkler, flipping from image to image, from concern to concern. Why did her father look so worried? Were Teddy and Suzette really married? Was Teddy the father of Suzette's baby? Her father cared about that sort of thing, and even though it didn't matter much to

Charlotte, she could understand her father's point of view.

And there was Coop.

Would Coop ask her out? When?

For a moment she leaned against her worktable, remembering last night. Coop had danced with her almost all evening. He was a great dancer in a reckless, funny, high-spirited way, moving effortlessly from jitterbugging, with one hand on hers and the other in the air, to a jerky version of hip-hop, then into the twist, and suddenly, hands on hips, torso stiff, jigging out an Irish river dance that had Charlotte nearly in hysterics and the crowd around them applauding and cheering him on. With Coop, Charlotte tangoed, fox-trotted, and jived. They had laughed a lot, and then the music slowed and Coop had pulled Charlotte against him in a slow dance that was pure seduction, his long thighs moving against hers, his warm breath on her hair.

Did she deserve this? Could she allow herself to be happy, to fall in love? She needed a sign from the universe.

If he had asked, she would have gone home with him. To bed with him.

But he hadn't asked, perhaps only because Nona had fainted, changing the course of everyone's evening. And that was probably a good thing, Charlotte told herself now in the clear light of a new morning.

She heard footsteps and a knock on the shed door, and then Jorge was there. "Good morning, Charlotte." He lived on the island with a community of Hispanic friends who dropped him off at her farm on their way to work. He was hardworking, well-mannered, and diligent, and since Charlotte spoke little Spanish and he spoke little English, they didn't waste a lot of time chatting. She got him started replanting from starter trays into the freshly hoed garden rows, then went into the house for a bite of breakfast and a much-needed cup of coffee.

Sitting on the bench in the mudroom, unlacing her boots, Charlotte couldn't help but hear the conversation in the kitchen.

"It's just not fair," Mandy was saying. "I can't do it."

Mandy's husband said, "I don't understand the problem. You've done it ever since Christian was born."

"Yes, well, when Christian was born, Mellie wasn't a gigantic whining pregnant sow, so she helped me with him, and Mee wasn't a theatrically depressed divorcée, so she helped me, and Charlotte wasn't playing happy idiot farmer in her stupid little garden, so *she* helped me! And Teddy wasn't around with that—that *person* sucking up all the air."

"Suzette has hardly spoken a word."

"Oh, Claus, don't be so perverse. You know what I mean!"

"Mandy. I have to go back to the bank. I have responsibilities. I'll be here next weekend."

"And I'll be here taking care of a four-year-old and a new baby!"

"Glorious will help you. Your mother will help you. Aunt Helen will help you." Claus made a huffing noise. "Or, for goodness' sake, hire a nanny!"

Their voices faded as they left the kitchen for the front hall. In her stocking feet, Charlotte padded into the kitchen, poured herself a cup of delicious hot coffee, and opened the refrigerator door.

Her father came into the kitchen, coffee cup in hand. He was already dressed in a suit, crisp striped shirt, silk rep tie. "Good morning, princess." He kissed the top of her head, and went to the coffeepot.

"How's Nona?" Charlotte took out a couple of brown eggs, cracked them into a bowl, and set a skillet on the stove.

"Alive and kicking. Well, sleeping, actually, but she woke for a few moments and she's lucid. She's fine. Just tired."

Charlotte dropped a pat of butter into the skillet. "Want me to scramble you a couple of eggs, Dad? I'm having some."

"Thanks, no. Got to watch my cholesterol. Anyway, I've already eaten. But I'll join you while you eat." He settled in a chair. "You've already been outside?"

"Since four-thirty." She couldn't help the pride in her voice. "I have to use every daylight hour I've got. We're approaching prime season."

"Ah, youth." Worth shook his head ruefully. "Only someone young could dance until midnight and get up at four-thirty."

Charlotte spilled the eggs into the skillet. She found grated Parmesan in the cheese bin and sprinkled it into the eggs. She popped some bread into the toaster. "Last night was really fun, wasn't it?"

"You certainly seemed to enjoy yourself." Worth toyed with his spoon, polishing it with a napkin. "Coop is quite the dancer."

Charlotte grinned. "Wasn't he funny? He was great." She flipped the eggs onto a plate, buttered her toast, sliced it, and carried it to the table. She sprinkled her eggs with salt and pepper and smoothed her own homemade strawberry jam on her toast.

"I thought he was engaged to Miranda Fellows."

"Uh-uh," Charlotte said, around a mouthful. She swallowed. "They were never engaged. Anyway, I guess they broke up. He didn't bring her last night."

"I like Coop." Worth leaned back in his chair and crossed his arms behind his head. A relaxed pose, but Charlotte knew his mind was working. "I like his parents."

"But." Charlotte felt the drums of rebellion hammer in her chest.

"Oh, I don't know, Charlotte. Coop just has always seemed kind of unreliable to me. A little reckless."

Charlotte concentrated on her eggs, shoving them into her mouth as if she were starving, which she kind of was, but now she couldn't enjoy the creamy, cheesy taste. After a moment, she said, "Come on, Dad. I only *danced* with him."

Worth nodded. He stirred his coffee with his highly polished spoon, then set the spoon on the table, neatly aligning it with the cup and saucer. "Two things matter in life, Charlotte: work and family. You must admit I've been completely supportive in your attempt to make an idyllic green life as a country gardener."

"I do admit that. And I'm grateful."

"So that leaves the matter of family."

"Dad." Charlotte had lost her appetite entirely. "Dad, I'm not even dating anyone."

"True. But perhaps you should be. Whit Lowry—"

*"Dad."* Charlotte shoved her chair back and stood up. She scraped the remains of her breakfast into the compost barrel under the sink and she tossed back the rest of her orange juice as if it were alcohol. She sensed it was the wrong thing to say but she said it anyway. "Look, Teddy's home with a wife and a baby. You've got your grandchild, your heir, on the way!"

Her father's expression was rueful. "Oh,

Charlotte, I doubt very much if that is Teddy's baby. She said herself that the child might not be his."

Charlotte wanted to cry, *You want entirely too much from your children!* but she bit her tongue. Teddy had to work out his problems with his father, and she had to work out hers. She stood quietly, her anger simmering.

Worth rose. He carried his coffee cup and saucer to the sink, rinsed them out, and put them in the dishwasher. When he turned to face Charlotte, his face was sad. "I have to go back to Boston today. We've got some problems at the bank. In the meantime . . . Look. If Teddy asks you for money, give it to him and I'll reimburse you, okay?"

"Well, of course, Dad." She hesitated, then blurted, "Teddy told me they plan to stay here for the summer."

Her father's face sagged. "Honey, Teddy and his friend can't stay here. You know that."

She hated being in the middle like this, but still she challenged him. "What does Mom think?"

Worth rubbed his forehead. "We haven't had a chance to discuss it. She's still sleeping."

"Dad—"

"Charlotte, just bear with me, okay? I'm trying to practice tough love. Your mother and I have consulted counselors, attended meetings, read books—we need to make Teddy stand on his own. We need to force Teddy to get real about the world. It's not easy, but it's got to be done."

"Suzette is pregnant!"

"I know. But we need to remember all the pranks Teddy has pulled on this family. Remember when he disappeared on his boat and we thought he'd drowned, and he was over on Tuckernuck for an entire night? He thought that was *fun*."

"He was fourteen."

"He's still fourteen, mentally. My point is, Charlotte, this girl could be someone he picked up at a bus station, someone he's paying to play a role."

Charlotte nodded. Teddy did love to play tricks.

Her father continued. "Look. Teddy probably doesn't really want to stay here, but he may not have the money to leave. He might ask you for money. He won't ask me. He might ask your mother, but I don't think she'd give him much. He'd better not ask Nona. He'll ask you. I'd like you to give it to him. Would you do that?"

She'd given Teddy money before, countless times. "Sure, Dad. If Teddy asks me for money, I'll give it to him."

Worth sighed. "Thanks, Charlotte." He crossed the room and hugged his daughter. "I knew I could count on you." He pecked a kiss on the top of her head. "See you next weekend."

Charlotte scrubbed the skillet clean and put everything else in the dishwasher. She could hear voices upstairs, and the thud of footsteps, and for a moment she considered going up, but this was a good clear day and she had a lot of work to do, so she filled a water bottle, twisted the cap shut, and went back out to the mudroom to put on her boots.

*She spent the morning* transplanting the seedlings of flowers into various terra-cotta and resin pots, some she'd discovered at the Take It or Leave It shed, some at the back of Nona's garage. Cosmos, impatiens, geraniums, salvia, alyssum, nasturtiums. Coleus and portulaca. Using Nona's wheelbarrow, she moved them out into the sun and watered them generously. Soon they'd be ready for the roadside stand. A taxi came for Oliver and Owen, and in a while Aunt Grace went past, taking Charlotte's father to the airport. Charlotte waved and kept on working.

She checked on Jorge's progress and carried the two baskets of loose lettuces he'd cut back to the shed, where she rinsed them, spun them dry, tucked them into plastic bags, and carried them out to the stand. She was on her knees in the dirt, transplanting lettuces, when a shadow fell over her. She looked up.

"Hey," Coop said. He wore swim trunks, deck shoes, and a faded polo shirt.

"Hey!" With a little groan, she stood up.

"How's Nona?"

"She's fine. She was just completely exhausted by the festivities." Cocking her head playfully, Charlotte said, "I think it was your version of the river dance that pushed her over the edge."

"You should let me teach you sometime. We could be a team. We could perform at anniversaries and weddings."

"Right," Charlotte said. "They'd pay us to stay away."

Coop laughed. "Anyway, Charlotte, I had fun last night."

Flushing, Charlotte reached down for her plastic bottle and tilted back her head, filling her mouth with the cool water.

Coop didn't seem to notice her awkwardness. "So I was wondering, it's such a great day, want to come sail with me over to Coatue? We could take a picnic lunch."

"Oh, Coop, I wish I could! But I've got to keep working."

"Oh, come on, you can take one little day off. You've got Jorge over there, he can take care of things."

Charlotte shook her head. "This is my crunch time, Coop. I've got to get as many things out into the garden as possible. I've got trays of transplants waiting."

Coop reached out and touched the side of her neck, where a strand of her hair had come loose from its band and clung, damp with sweat, to her skin. "But you're so hot."

The double entendre, Coop's touch, made Charlotte's breath catch. "Coop, really. . . ."

"Come on, Char," Coop urged. "Play hooky. The wind is just right for an easy sail. And think how good a swim would feel."

"I know, Coop, but really, I've got to resist temptation and keep working. Every day is important."

Coop opened his mouth to argue, then relented. "All right, then, I guess I'll just have to go alone." He stepped back, unknowingly crushing a lettuce plant. "Some other time?"

"After dark," Charlotte told him, growing warm again at the suggestion in her words.

"Sure." Coop tossed the word off carelessly as he turned and strode down the row toward the gate.

## *Thirteen*

*H*elen was dizzy from lack of sleep. It wasn't the fault of the sleeping porch. The cool night air acted like a soporific, but her mind bubbled with anxieties and anger. She wasn't worried about Nona; Dr. Parsons had assured them she just needed rest. Helen thought she could use some rest, too—from her thoughts—but instead she had tossed and turned, as she imagined Worth with Sweet Cakes, replayed the insults Grace had flung at her at the party, and then, worst of all, envisioned the possible problems that odd little unhealthy-looking Suzette might be causing her baby.

At some point, though, sleep had overtaken her.

She woke sprawled on the daybed, drooling into her pillow, the full light of sun falling onto her left arm. It was a bright day; it would be a hot day. She showered and slipped into a fresh sundress and sandals and went swiftly down the stairs. She needed coffee.

It was almost ten o'clock. The kitchen, she was glad to see, was empty. The coffeepot was still full. She poured a cup and drank gratefully. As she gazed out the window toward the drive, a taxi crept up the white gravel, parked near the other cars, and honked.

Oliver and Owen came thumping down the stairs and into the kitchen.

"Mom! Great! We didn't want to leave without saying goodbye."

"I just woke up," Helen confessed.

"Lazy thing." Oliver grabbed up an apple from the bowl. "While you snored, we dressed and packed and checked out of the inn and came out here to see everyone before we took off." He held another apple up to Owen and tossed it to him when he nodded.

"And did you? See everyone?" Helen asked.

"I saw Nona. She's as feisty as ever. And I spoke with Dad, briefly. He's getting ready to go back to the city, too. I haven't seen Charlotte. Tell her goodbye for me, will you? Oh, and I saw Aunt Grace, who seems especially Wicked Witch of the West today." Oliver hugged his mother, and Owen came around the kitchen table and hugged her, too. "We left our luggage out on the drive. Hey, is that our cab?"

Owen said, "I'll go out and tell him we're ready."

Oliver did a quick scan to be sure no one else was around. "Look, Mom. About Teddy. E-mail me, okay? Or call me. Let me know if there's anything I can do."

"Did you talk to him at all?"

"I tried. I got a lot of sarcasm and evasion. Sorry, I'm not trying to be harsh. I know it must have been tough on him, walking into all this."

"Well." Helen shook her head. "Perhaps it was tough on him. Or perhaps he enjoyed it."

"Anyway. Let me know."

"I will. And Oliver, let me know about your wedding. What can I do to help you get ready?"

Oliver's smile was like the sun coming from behind clouds. Sometimes Helen couldn't believe this amazingly handsome young man was her son.

"We're not inviting many people, really, so it won't be a fuss, but we would like a bit of a party. The minister is a friend of ours, he's flying in from California—" Seeing his mother's face change, he quickly added, "No one is planning to stay here. Owen and I have rented a house out near Surfside for the month of July, and all our friends are going to stay there. We're hoping the weather will cooperate and we can have a beach wedding with a casual reception here at the house—just champagne and nuts, Mom, nothing elaborate."

"But you must have a wedding cake!" Helen said.

"Okay. Well, could you do that? Could you order a cake?"

"I could make one. What kind? Chocolate? Maybe a yellow cake with strawberries?"

"Anything at all. We're easy." Oliver hesitated. "We're planning to have a real party back at the rental house in the evening. With a DJ and lots of dancing and serious booze. So you all can come or not."

Helen quirked an eyebrow. "Are you going to be indulging in outrageously gay activities that would traumatize your old parents?" she teased.

Oliver grinned. "Not until after midnight." And he went out the door.

Helen watched through the window as Oliver and Owen settled into the taxi and were driven away. Her heart was lightened now. She took a banana from the fruit bowl and was peeling it when Grace came into the room, dressed for the day in khaki shorts and a polo shirt.

Seeing Helen, Grace stopped short. Her face fell. Grace looked miserable and hungover and old and sad. "Is there any coffee left?"

Helen took a cup from the cupboard, poured coffee into it, and handed it to Grace. She didn't speak.

Grace hunted around for the milk pitcher, found it, added a dollop of milk, and stirred in several teaspoons of sugar. "I feel hideous. I didn't sleep at all last night."

Helen turned her back to Grace and stared out the window.

"Look, Helen." When Helen didn't respond, Grace said angrily, "I apologize for what I said last night."

Helen shrugged. "It's fine, Grace."

Worth came into the kitchen, smelling of shaving cream and soap. He wore his suit trousers and a crisp striped shirt. "Has Kellogg come down?"

"Not yet," Helen told him.

"Grace, do you want to drive me to the airport?"

"I'm driving Kellogg, Douglas, and Claus. They've got an eleven o'clock flight. Can you wait?"

Worth looked impatiently at his watch. "All right. I can make some phone calls." He turned to go, then looked at Helen. "Are you flying back with me?"

"No. I . . . I've got some work to do here for the book sale." It was easy to talk to her husband with someone else in the room. Even Grace's critical presence steadied her.

"So you'll be home later today?"

Helen almost said, *What's it to you?* But now was not the time. "I think so. I'll let you know."

Worth nodded and left the room.

Grace said, "Well, *I've* got more than enough to do today. Glorious is with Nona. After I take the Bank Boys to the airport, I've got to hit the grocery store. And the house." She sighed.

Helen frowned. She and Grace had managed to divide the housework and cooking for thirty years. She couldn't imagine why Grace was making such heavy going of it now. "I'll do the house." She put her coffee cup in the sink. "I'll start in the living room." She left the kitchen.

The long front living room was littered with champagne flutes and teacups and bowls half filled with peanuts and crackers. Helen carried them into the kitchen, washed the flutes, emptied the snacks into plastic bags, set the teacups in the dishwasher. She dug the dust cloths out of the laundry room and went around the living room, dusting end tables, straightening chairs, plumping up sofa cushions. She shook out the draperies and opened the French doors and took the vacuum from under the stairs and dragged it over the various ancient thick Persian rugs. It was all very satisfying, putting things into place, so when she found the kitchen empty for a change, she quickly swept and mopped the flagstone floor.

At some point, Grace came down, trailed by Worth, Kellogg, Douglas, and Claus, all businesslike in their suits and ties and briefcases. Helen said goodbye to them all and stood beneath the arbor, waving at them as they left in one of the

SUVs. She returned to the kitchen to boil some eggs for egg salad and was chopping celery when Glorious came down.

"Mrs. Nona's sleeping," Glorious said. She carried a basket piled with diapers and tiny little bits of clothing. "Oh, good, you've started lunch. And Grace said she'd go by the grocery store."

"Where are the little ones?" Helen called to Glorious as the other woman went into the laundry room.

"They went out early, down to the beach— Mandy, Mellie, and the two children. Their father carried down the beach umbrellas. He took some beach chairs down, too."

"Have you heard any rustlings from Teddy?" Helen called.

"Not a sound."

Glorious came into the kitchen with a basket of clean laundry in her arms. She stood at the end of the table, folding baby blankets and little boy's T-shirts. "Do we know how many will be here for dinner tonight?"

Helen set the eggs under cold running water and began to chop an onion. "Well, you and Nona, although she doesn't eat much, and Grace, Mandy, Mellie, and the two children. And Charlotte, of course. And maybe Teddy or Suzette, but I don't know their plans."

"You staying?"

"I'm not sure if I'll be here tonight or not. I had

planned to fly back after I spent some time with Teddy and Suzette, but I thought they'd be up by now."

Glorious stacked the folded laundry in the basket. "I think I'll just thaw a pan of lasagna. That will work for a few more or less."

"Good idea. I'll make those oatmeal raisin cookies Mandy approves of for Christian."

"I'll do that."

"Oh, Glorious, I can—"

Glorious shook her glossy head. "No, no. You go on and take a rest. I heard you down here with the vacuum. I've just been sitting there listening to Nona snore. I need to move. And I love eating the raw dough," she added, smirking.

Helen hated to admit it, even to herself, *especially* to herself, but it had been a great relief when Glorious came to work for Nona. Glorious was cheerful, easygoing, and self-starting. Most of all, she was young. Years ago, Helen had been able to help Grace run the house and still find time and energy to enjoy herself, go for a little sail, lie in the sun with a beach read, play a game or two of tennis. But for the past few years, Helen found she needed a nap simply to refuel for the rest of the day. Grace did, too. They had always had a cleaning company come through the house once a week, and there had been a space of years when all their children were college age and off traveling through Europe or visiting friends. Then, entire weeks would pass by with only five or six people in the house needing meals prepared and laundry done and sunblock bought and messages taken. Those had been restful times, although not as much fun. When the summer house filled up again, with weddings and wedding parties and baby showers and babies, Helen and Grace had discovered they were older. They didn't have as much stamina.

Today, Helen felt especially ancient. She stirred mayonnaise and a sprinkling of curry powder into the egg salad, covered it with plastic wrap, and set it in the refrigerator.

"I think I *will* take a nap. I didn't sleep well last night. But listen, Glorious, will you tell Teddy to wake me when he gets up?"

"Surely will."

Up on the sleeping porch, the air was warm and still. Helen lay down on the daybed and was asleep the moment her head hit the pillow.

*When she woke*, it was after one. The sun fell in long rectangles across the wooden floor, and the air seemed to hum with light. She yawned. From the other end of the house, she heard a baby's thin cry. Little Zoe must be awake from her nap as well. She heard a child's high sweet voice raised in song and the plinking tones of a xylophone: Christian entertaining himself. The xylophone had been one of the Ms' first toys, and Helen's three children had played with it, too. Helen remembered sitting on a bedroom floor with Grace as their toddlers played together. Way back then, they'd worried that the little ones were too aggressive and would never learn to share. Grace had worried that Mee would never learn to talk. Helen had worried that Teddy would spend his life in casts—he was such a daredevil and so accident prone. And here they all were now, their children safely grown. Grace had grandchildren. And Helen might have a grandchild on the way.

She sat up, ran her hands through her tangled hair, and stretched, then went to the window facing out over Nona's hedged garden. Far in the distance on the rolling land was Charlotte's garden. Helen couldn't see her, but she knew her daughter was out there working.

She wasn't sure what she thought about Charlotte's funny little plan to live her life as a farmer here on Nantucket Island. Grace had been right. Helen's children *were* different. Charlotte digging in the dirt, Oliver gay and intelligent but completely without interest in the Wheelwright bank, and Teddy . . . well, *Teddy.* Wasn't he awake yet?

She went down the hall to the bathroom, splashed water on her face, and made an attempt to comb her hair. She wouldn't try to get back to Boston today. Why should she? Let Sweet Cakes fix dinner for Worth. Although Worth probably treated his paramour to dinners at expensive restaurants. Oh, God, what should she do?

*Helen found Teddy* and Suzette in the kitchen, sitting at one end of the table, dunking cookies into cups of milk. Glorious was standing over the sink, scrubbing the cookie sheet. Both Teddy and Suzette wore the clothes they'd worn the day before. Actually, they looked like they'd slept in them. A twist of maternal irritation tightened beneath Helen's rib cage.

Still, she tried to be upbeat. "Good morning, lazybones!" She pecked a kiss on top of Teddy's head and put a hand, gently, just for a moment, on Suzette's shoulder.

Suzette didn't respond, and Teddy just mumbled something around a mouthful of soggy food. Please, could they be more childish!

"I hope you ate some real food before you started filling up on cookies," Helen said. She went to the sink and filled a glass of water.

Another mumble from Teddy.

Glorious was drying off the cookie sheet. "Honey, those cookies are oatmeal and raisins. Let's pretend it's breakfast."

But Helen couldn't let it go. "A growing baby needs protein."

"Milk's protein," Teddy said.

"At last! He speaks!" Helen sat down across from her son.

"I'll be taking a little rest now," Glorious said, and left the room.

It was very quiet in the kitchen. The faucet dripped into the sink: *plink, plink.*

"Your father's gone back to Boston," Helen said. "So have your Uncle Kellogg and Claus and Douglas. And I think Mee might have gone back while I was resting."

"So it looks like I'm the man of the house." Teddy wiped cookie milk off his upper lip.

"Well, yes, you and Christian."

Teddy laughed. "Well played, Mom."

Helen crossed her arms on the table and leaned forward. "Teddy, let's talk a bit, okay?"

Teddy pretended innocent confusion. "I thought we were. Talking."

"What are your plans?"

*"Plans? Who says we need plans?"* His tone was arch and teasing.

*"I* do!" Record time, one part of Helen's mind noted, between Teddy's first word and her first blastoff. "Teddy, your wife is going to have a baby. Has she had prenatal checkups? Ultrasound? Is she taking vitamins? Where will she have the baby, in a hospital or by the side of the road? Does she have a personal physician? And what about you? How are you going to support a child? Babies take a lot of care and a lot of paraphernalia!" Teddy opened his mouth to speak but Helen held out her hand, forestalling him. "And

please don't give me your holier-than-thou speech about the evils of materialism. Your baby can't ride in a car in this state unless it's in a car seat. It's Massachusetts law. Your baby will need diapers and clothing and a bouncy seat and medical care. Babies need to have drops put in their eyes when they're born, did you know that? And you and Suzette could both use at least one change of clothing, judging by what you wore yesterday and what you're wearing today. And—"

Teddy held his hands up in surrender. "All right, Mom, I get it. Listen, I thought Suzette and I would stay here for the summer."

Helen was speechless.

"What's the big deal? I've always stayed here in the summer. Nona has plenty of room."

Helen nodded. She took a sip of water, just to give herself a few seconds to recover. "That's fine," she told him. "That's good, really. It's just that we hadn't seen you for a year, or heard much from you, so this is a surprise. So . . . Suzette, when is your baby due?"

"September," Suzette mumbled.

"So you'll have the baby here. On the island."

"Is that a problem for you?" Teddy's voice took on a defensive tone.

"Not at all," Helen hastened to assure him. She turned toward Suzette. "We've got a great hospital here. A good obstetrician and several good mid-wives, if that's the way you want to go. And I'm sure the attic is crammed with baby stuff. We might even have a few maternity dresses somewhere. Oh, this is exciting! I'll have to make a list." Caught up in a more optimistic mood, Helen turned back to Teddy. "And you. *You* need to get a job."

Teddy moaned. "Oh, brother, here it comes."

"Teddy. You're twenty-two. You're about to become a father. Unless you have some money stashed away which I know nothing about, you're going to have to buckle down and grow up and get a job like everyone else."

Teddy squirmed. "I won't work in the bank."

Helen snorted, exasperated. "Did I mention the bank?" She looked at Suzette. "I don't know how much your husband has told you about his remorselessly evil family, but most of the men related to Teddy work in a Boston bank that Teddy's great-great-grandfather started in the eighteen hundreds. Worth and I had hoped Teddy might work there. Frankly, Worth would love it if *one* of his children carried on his work, and if you went to Boston you could stay in our house and save money. In case you want to buy—oh, say a car. Or a house, with a yard, for your baby."

"It's not going to work, Mom," Teddy said, his face dark.

"What's not going to work?"

"You're not going to convince Suzette that I should work in the bank."

"Fine. You still need to get a job."

"Or what? Or we can't stay here this summer?" Teddy stood up so abruptly his chair rocked. "Do you need me to contribute funds because otherwise there won't be enough money to feed us all? Look at this place! There's probably enough food stashed in the pantry to keep us all from starvation for months!"

"Teddy, it's not about that. It's about your self-esteem—"

"Which is fine!" Teddy paced the length of the kitchen, looking terribly young in his stupid yellow martini-glass shirt. Everyone had always said that Teddy combined his parents' physical attributes. His dark-blond hair curled tightly like Helen's, and when he ran his hand through it in exasperation, it recoiled right back into place.

Softly, Helen said, "It's about growing up. Teddy, you have to grow up."

"I am grown up," Teddy protested. "You just don't get it, Mom. You think you're so wildly different from Dad and Aunt Grace—"

Stunned by Teddy's insight, and hot with guilt because she secretly *did* think that, Helen said, "I never said—"

"Oh, you've always been the champion of the underdog, the rebel; how can you think I haven't noticed? But you see, you think of me as an underdog, a rebel, because you're just as brainwashed as the rest of them. You really believe, in your heart, there is only one way to be!"

"Teddy! I don't!" They had argued before, a hundred times, a thousand times, with as much heat and anger, but all this was new and it cut deep.

"And you know why? You want to believe there's only one way to be, because you are so stuck in your life. You never ever got to spread your wings and fly."

Helen stared at her youngest child, her beautiful son. "My children were my wings, Teddy," she said. "My children were my flight."

*"Were."* Teddy tossed his head.

*"Are,"* she corrected herself. She looked over at Suzette, who had stopped dunking cookies to stare at Teddy and Helen, her mouth hanging open. Her bare belly protruded, the little belly button sticking out like the tied-off end of a balloon. "When you have your baby, Teddy, you'll see what I mean."

Suzette awkwardly shuffled her body around in her chair, so she could face Teddy, and gave him a look. Helen couldn't see Suzette's face, so she didn't know what Suzette meant to convey, but after a few minutes Teddy shrugged and, with one of his easy smiles, relented. "Fine. I'll get a job."

# Family Meeting

# Fourteen

*Two weeks* after her birthday, Nona lay on her chaise in the garden. It was unusually hot for this early in July, but Nona welcomed the heat and relished these few moments of solitude. Tomorrow was Family Meeting. The house would be full again, the air trembling with the strong emotions and real or imagined wounds and desires and disagreements of her family.

The birdbath, with its recirculating water fountain, made a pleasingly musical trickling sound and, if she kept very still, all sorts of birds, not only the bold mourning doves, lighted there to give themselves vigorous baths, splashing water up under their wings, glancing around to be sure they were safe, and then dunking their heads right down into the water. At the far end of the garden, shaded by the wall of hedge, a pair of robins pecked in the alyssum bed. Nearby, a catbird called. Nona called back, "Hello, pretty fellow." Catbirds were friendly, and she'd always thought they were quite dapper, with their neat black and gray plumage.

"Hello?" The sound was scarcely more than a whisper.

Nona looked up. Suzette loomed next to her, as swollen as a ship under sail. Gradually, over the past ten days, Suzette had become a bit less shy. She'd pretty much kept to her room right after

Nona's birthday party, but Nona didn't blame her for that. She'd kept to her room, too. So much folderol was exhausting. And poor Suzette had been just thrown to the lions by Teddy's showing up with her like that, without any warning or explanation.

"Hello, dear." Nona nodded toward a wicker rocking chair. "Sit down. It's nice here in the sun. How do you feel?"

"Icky." Suzette lowered her bulk into the chair. She wore a pretty swirly skirt and a T-shirt, and her rounded belly protruded in all its naked glory into the sun. "I can't get a good night's sleep. The baby kicks."

Nona laughed softly. "I remember those days. I was sure Grace was going to be either a ballerina or a quarterback. And the head wedges up against your lungs so you can't get a deep breath."

Suzette extracted a fingernail file from her pocket and began to shape her nails. Nona found the little grating sound—well, *grating*. "How's Teddy?"

Suzette's chin jutted out as she asserted stoutly, "He's gone to AA every day."

"And has he found a job?"

Suzette scratched away even faster. "He's looking."

"From the little I've seen of him, I gather he's been playing a bit of tennis. And sailing."

Loyally, Suzette insisted, "He's *networking*. Teddy thinks he might meet an old buddy who could steer him toward a decent job."

"Has he checked the classified ads in the news-papers?"

Suzette poked at her belly button with the nail file. "I guess. But the jobs are all for dishwashers and stuff."

"I see." Nona wanted to be careful here. Suzette was about as skittish as the birds in the birdbath. At the slightest hint of criticism, she vanished, whisking her pregnant self back upstairs to hide away in the attic bedroom she shared with Teddy or to find refuge in the den, paralyzed in front of the television set. "The problem is that any job available now on the island is bound to be pretty much a summer job. Is that what Teddy's looking for?" Nona didn't want to pry, but she as well as the rest of the family were curious about just how long Teddy planned to stay here and what his long-term plans were.

"Teddy's smarter than most people think," Suzette said. "Just because he didn't finish col-lege—"

"Oh, I understand that." Shifting on her chaise, Nona turned to face Suzette. "And believe me, I have no intention of pressuring him to work in the bank."

"I know." Suzette smiled shyly at Nona. "You're nice to him."

This was as friendly as the girl had been since she arrived. Nona settled back. "I wonder, what sort of work would Teddy like to do?"

"He says—"

"Good morning, Nona!" Mellie waddled out into the garden, hands supporting her back, which was curved like the moon with her pregnancy.

"Good morning, Mellie. How do you feel?"

"Like a kangaroo. *Oh.*" Mellie's tone changed when she saw Suzette in the rocker.

"Won't you join us?" Nona invited. "The sun is lovely."

"No. No, I'll—" With a listless wave of her hand, Mellie waddled back into the house.

"I should go." Suzette put her hands on the arms of the rocker, trying to lever herself up.

"Nonsense. Sit still. You just got settled." All this domestic drama made Nona just tired. "Mellie's irritable because of her pregnancy, that's all."

But Suzette had achieved standing position. "That's okay. I'm tired anyway. I think I'll take a nap."

"All right then, dear."

Nona sighed. Any sane person would assume that Mellie, being pregnant, would befriend the pregnant Suzette so they could commiserate. But Mellie acted as if Suzette carried a fatally contagious virus. Partly, this was Grace's fault. Grace was unashamedly disparaging about Teddy and his wife. It didn't help that Helen was still in Boston. She was to arrive today for the summer, but without her balancing opinions, Grace's bitter suspicions filtered through the house like that expensive perfume Grace used, the one that smelled like cat pee.

Dear Lord, Nona thought, if her own family—her fortunate, wealthy, healthy family—couldn't get along, how would world peace ever be achieved? For that matter, to bring the issue down to practical terms, how would they manage to get through Family Meeting without confrontations? Nona was dreading Family Meeting. She had never enjoyed them. All the statistical analyses of funds bored her. When Helen and Grace presented the charitable distributions and their suggestions for the coming year, Nona often received a rush of pleasure at imagining someone somewhere receiving comfort, and over the past few years there had been little reason for altercations. But now Teddy was here, so very much here, and not shaping up into any kind of practical, reliable man. And Charlotte, out there grubbing in the dirt, had made four thousand dollars from her little garden, which was driving her millionaire relatives wild.

"Oh, good." As if summoned by Nona's thoughts, her daughter appeared in the doorway. "I want to talk to you," Grace said.

In khaki shorts and a hunter-green polo shirt and sneakers, Grace had the appearance of a camp counselor or Girl Scout. All she needed was a whistle around her neck. Actually, Nona thought, Grace would love to go through life with a whistle around her neck.

"Please." Nona gestured to the rocking chair. "I'm always so popular the day before Family Meeting," she observed lightly.

Grace arranged herself in the chair, resting a sheaf of papers and a clipboard on her knees. "Joke all you want, Mother, but we do have some important matters to discuss."

"Would you like to wait a little while? Helen's flying in this afternoon, and—"

Officiously, Grace cut in. "No, Mother, I need to talk with you in private first. My concerns involve Helen's children, actually, and I think we need to get our ducks in a row before Helen gets involved."

"And these ducks would be?" Nona could feel her blood pressure begin to simmer as it always did when Grace cornered her.

"Don't be coy, Mother, you know exactly what I'm talking about. First of all, I'll just be blunt: Owen. I know Oliver and Owen are going to have their ridiculous little *marriage* ceremony, but I feel very clear on the matter: Owen should not be allowed to attend Family Meeting."

"Oh, Grace."

"And second, Teddy should not be allowed to bring Suzette into Family Meeting unless they provide written documentation that they are actually married."

"Oh, Grace."

"Mother." Grace's face turned florid, her lips

thinned, and her head jerked high, like a beast hearing a battle cry. "I don't think you realize how much you favor Worth's children and ignore mine."

"What?" Nona shook her head sadly. "That's ridiculous."

But Grace was up and away. "I don't think you appreciate the devotion of my side of the family. Kellogg works in Daddy's bank. Mandy's Claus works in the bank. Mellie's Dougie works in the bank. Our side of the family is carrying on the Wheelwright tradition."

"Worth works in the bank," Nona reminded Grace quietly.

"Oh, yes, Worth!" Grace spat his name bitterly. "We all know Worth is your favorite child. He's the charmer; he's the Mary talking while I'm the Martha doing housework. But consider his children, Nona, seriously! Oliver has no interest in the bank, and he is not furthering the Wheelwright name in any way; he's not going to provide you with an heir, do you think? Oh, perhaps he and Owen someday will adopt some homosexual AIDS child from Africa, *just* what we need to carry on the Wheelwright name. And Charlotte? She's playing farmer in the dell or pretending to; Charlotte's the smart one in the family, and just because she's pretty, you think she's incapable of duplicity, but you just wait! She'll play out there in her little garden, and when you die, she'll claim that all that land is hers and she'll sell it and make a fortune."

Nona straightened in her chair. This was uglier than she'd expected. "I really don't think Charlotte—"

"No, you think Charlotte hung the moon, don't you? And what about Teddy? He's a fool and a freeloader. He'll never be anything but a useless alcoholic. And that *Suzette*!"

*"Grace, lower your voice."*

Grace recoiled as if Nona had slapped her. More quietly, she continued. "All you have to do is look at that girl to see she's not much more than a whore."

Nona's heart wrenched. "Honey. Why are you so venomous?"

"Because I feel these things deeply. Because I have to be the one to say these terrible things, which is only what we're all thinking, but no one else is brave enough to speak out. Mother"—Grace drew herself erect—"when that baby's born, I insist on a DNA test to prove it's a Wheelwright."

Nona raised her hand to her forehead, which felt congested. Her hand, her left hand, still ringed with a simple platinum band—she'd given the four-carat diamond engagement ring to Worth when he told her he wanted to marry Helen, and that was another decision Grace could not forgive her for—her hand was trembling. *Frail old crone,* she told herself. Yet crones were supposed to be wise, and she did not feel wise at all. She felt very tired. She rubbed her forehead lightly and strained to hear birdsong. She only heard her daughter breathing like a bull in the ring.

"Aren't you going to give me the honor of an answer?" Grace demanded.

"Grace, please remember I am ninety years old. I am tired; I am very tired. I don't quite understand what more you want. To me, it seems you have so much. But I do comprehend your concerns, and I'll consider them."

"Mother—"

"That's all I can say for now. I need to rest."

Nona leaned her head back against the chaise. Now, as more and more often these days, life seemed to dissolve into a kind of gel around her, a warm, soothing, buoyant, cradling substance, rather like an ocean combined with a hot bubble bath. She was safe, nestling into this cushion; she was supported. She sank into it gratefully.

## *1943–1944*

*Anne didn't wear* a wedding dress when she married Herb in September of '43. There wasn't time for that sort of fuss. She bought a pale rose lightweight-wool suit with a little jacket and a hat with a half veil that tilted quite adorably. Anne's best friend, Gail, was her bridesmaid, and Hilyard Clayton was Herb's best man. Both men wore their dress uniforms and were proud to do so.

Herb's parents attended, looking stern and disapproving, and his sister, Holly, came, brightening the occasion, and Anne's parents flew to Boston for the event, for which Anne was fervently grateful. At the celebration dinner at the Ritz, her parents charmed Herb's parents so much that the Wheelwrights seemed to soften their opinion of Anne. Still, the entire event was overshadowed by world events. It was difficult, in spite of the occasion, to talk about anything except the war. They spent their wedding night at the Ritz, and Herb joined his battalion the next day and moved out to Arizona for special training.

Herb's parents made it clear that it would be inappropriate for her to continue to remain in the apartment with the single, convivial Gail. They invited—commanded—Anne to come live with them. Herb said he would like that, too; he would know Anne was safe. Anne intended to continue as a secretary at Stangarone's. She believed her work was, in its own small way, important. Because she would be gone all day and could meet Gail and other friends for dinner on weeknights and for fun on weekends, Anne reluctantly agreed to move in with her in-laws, even though the thought both terrified and bored her.

Living with her in-laws wasn't quite as ghastly as she'd feared. In fact, it was rather nice to come home from the noisy, overwrought, disorganized, frantic shipping office to the calm of a delicious meal and a nice glass of wine. The war curtailed

much of Charity Wheelwright's social appoint-
ments. Instead, women were getting together to
knit stockings and pack goody boxes filled with
tins of homemade cookies. Once in a while, Anne's
mother-in-law insisted Anne join them at a cocktail party or a concert or an afternoon tea. "We
want to show you off, my dear," Charity said
smoothly. "Our new daughter-in-law." *Right,* Anne
thought. *You want to show off my nice neat waist-
line, proof that your son didn't* have *to marry me.*

On weekends, Herb's sister, Holly, drove up
from Rhode Island, where she taught sailing and
math at a private school. Holly was engaged to
another teacher, now an officer in the U.S. Army
Air Corps, stationed in England. If Anne didn't
know about the fiancé, she would have believed
Holly was a lesbian, because Holly was such a jock,
very no-nonsense and abrupt. Plus, she wore really
dowdy clothing. Often Holly was joined by some
of her girlfriends, who nattered away loudly about
their tennis, their squash, their dinghies, their
Indian sailboats, their trips fly-fishing in Montana
and golfing in Florida, and how amazing it was
that Anne had landed the handsome Herb when
she didn't sail or play tennis. There was no malice
in their remarks, though, no sense of threat. The
group of athletic women regarded Anne with the
fond amusement of human beings watching
another species. When they went out at night to a
movie or a party, they always invited Anne along

and, best of all, whenever Charity Wheelwright began to criticize Anne for one thing or another, loyal Holly jumped to her defense.

In May, Charity and Norman Wheelwright went down to Nantucket to open their summer house. They left on a weekday, so Anne couldn't go with them, and they took Mrs. O'Hara, their house-keeper, and for a few blissful nights Anne had the large old mansion on Beacon Hill all to herself. At first it seemed eerie, being alone in the empty mausoleum, but Anne revved up her courage with a glass of wine and decided to snoop. Perhaps she might learn something about her in-laws that would help her be more comfortable around them. She had seen Holly's bedroom, and the bedroom Herb slept in as a boy, and Anne was using the guest bedroom, which happily had a private bathroom. But she'd never seen Herb's parents' room, so she bravely set off up the stairs and down the long wide hallway to the room at the front of the house. She paused outside the closed bedroom door, asking herself what she was looking for, what she wanted to find. Well, she answered herself, she hoped she'd find signs of the small secret passions that make life rich. A stack of romance novels or mysteries. A bedside drawer stuffed with expensive chocolates. Even satin sheets, or a drawer of silk underwear. Perhaps—these were wealthy people, after all—perhaps a charming little Impressionist original oil over the fireplace.

"Ta-da!" she yelled, giving herself courage, and threw open the door.

The room could have been anyone's. It was a handsome, comfortable room, with lots of heavy Empire furniture and brocade draperies and a thick Persian rug, but the signs of an individual personality were not in evidence. On the bedside table: a clock, a crystal water tumbler, a small china box holding nail clippers and an emery board. On the walls: framed photographs of Holly and Herb as children, framed photographs of distinguished, straight-backed, prune-mouthed citizens who had to be Charity and Norman's parents. On Charity Wheelwright's vanity table, a silver-backed brush and hand mirror, a small jar of cold cream, and a small wooden jewelry box holding Charity's best pearls. Everything was set at right angles and aligned as if by a ruler. Anne pulled open the closet door. Charity's dresses hung at attention, straight and proper, as if Charity never once had pulled something out, put it on, groaned at herself in the mirror, and tossed it back in the closet. She opened a drawer in one of the bureaus and saw not a rainbow of silk nighties, or a shocking quantity of satin underpants, but a large quantity of rubbery girdles. She decided not to open the other drawers. She could keep her fantasies that Charity Wheelwright had secret luxuries. She closed the drawer, looked around the room to be sure she hadn't disturbed anything, and left.

She went downstairs, through the house, and into the kitchen, where she ate a cold dinner of cheese, crackers, and sliced ham and had another glass of wine. Where did Holly and Herb get their sense of humor? she mused as she ate. Perhaps Herb's parents came alive on Nantucket Island. Perhaps they relaxed there, and Anne could get to know their real selves.

*July 22, 1944*

*Darling Anne,*

*Arrived safe and sound after a very boresome and uneventful trip. My location is a military secret as far as you are concerned so please do not attempt to locate me. If my mail ceases in the not-too-distant future you will know that I am on an extended fishing trip. I've never tried ocean fishing but expect to enjoy it.*

*I hope you and my parents are knocking around all right together. They will warm up, I promise you. I miss you constantly and dream of the days when we can start our married life together in a safe and free world.*

*With all my love,*

*Herb*

Anne carried Herb's latest letter in the pocket of her trousers. She liked being able to reach in whenever she wanted to and feel the crisp folded paper. It was as if she were touching a bit of Herb, as if he were safe and alive in her keeping. Gwendolyn Forsythe, her immediate superior at Stangarone's, had insisted that Anne take two weeks off that July. "You need a break, kid," Gwen told Anne. "Don't worry, the war won't end without you."

So Anne rode down to Woods Hole with her in-laws and took the ferry to Nantucket Island, where a friend of the Wheelwrights met them, loaded his car with their luggage, and drove them out to their summer home on Polpis Harbor.

It was a luxury to be here; Anne realized that at once. Back in Boston, the July air was punishingly muggy, and in spite of fans set on top of filing cabinets, the humidity made papers stick together, made hair frizz or hang lank, made tempers short. On the island, the air was also humid, but the temperature was almost ten degrees cooler, and a light sea breeze stirred freshness into the atmosphere.

Anne was given the guest bedroom at the opposite end of the house from Herb's parents. She set her suitcase on the needlepoint luggage rack, opened it, and started to put away her clothing. Then she shuffled through her things, dug out her black bathing suit, and stripped off her clothing. She pulled on her bathing suit, grabbed a towel from the bathroom, and ran down the stairs.

The housekeeper, Mrs. O'Hara, came into the hall, wiping her hands on her apron.

"Hello, Mrs. O'Hara! I'm going for a swim!" Anne announced.

"Yes, I can see that. Use the mudroom door when you return, so you don't track sand in any farther than necessary."

"Right." *You old Puritan,* Anne thought as she hurried into the living room, down to the French doors leading to the harbor side. She went through them, her bare feet touched on soft green grass, and she sighed with pleasure. The lawn was man-made and needed a lot of tending, for wild shrubs of bayberry and barberry and *Rosa rugosa* crowded in luxuriant untamed abundance down to the shore. A narrow boardwalk extended between these bushes—the boards were hot to the soles of Anne's feet—and then she was at the water's edge, her feet sinking into the warm sand, the sun blazing down on her, light shimmering everywhere. Across the harbor, several sailboats were anchored, and in the distance a motorboat grumbled along. She waded into the water and plunged off away from shore until the water was deep enough for swimming.

She stroked through the water, swimming until she was breathless; then she flipped over and floated, gazing up at the blue sky. Oh, how she'd missed this—the sense of open space and the solitude. And the sensual pleasure. She missed Herb.

She didn't think she'd been wrong to marry him—she loved him like crazy—but she thought perhaps she'd been wrong to marry him just before he went off to war. It was as if she were a wild horse who had found a mate with whom to gallop full speed, mane flying, over an endless pasture, only to find herself suddenly inside a fenced corral, ruled by strangers cracking whips to make her obey.

Oh, come on, Anne told herself. You have it so tough, living in luxury while Herb is overseas with bullets flying over his head. Stop whining. Grow up.

But how she missed him! Their few times together had wakened her senses in ways she'd never expected. Plus she had so much to tell him. And she wanted to hear everything he had to tell her. Missing him was a kind of pain, almost a grief. She remembered his long legs, his wide shoulders, his deep laugh, the sweet breath of his kiss. She needed that. She needed that again, and *now.* And he was so far away. She didn't know where he was. She didn't know when he would be coming home. She didn't even know whether he would be coming home, and her heart ached with worry.

This, she told herself, is why you shouldn't be alone in wide open spaces, because then you start worrying and remembering and you get maudlin and imaginative. Be a big girl, for heaven's sake!

She swam back to shore, dried off, and walked back to the house.

. . .

"Would you like to see my garden?" Charity
Wheelwright asked.

Anne smiled, pleased. "Yes, of course." She had
showered and dressed in a neat blue checked seer-
sucker shirtwaist, slipped her feet into sandals, and
pulled her hair into a chignon, to keep her neck
cool. When she entered the living room, she found
Charity Wheelwright seated by open French
doors, working on a needlepoint sampler. The
invitation surprised Anne and pleased her. Could
there be an invitation more charming, more full of
hope, than one to "my garden"? Now, perhaps,
she'd discover her mother-in-law's soft side. And
Anne, who had never paid attention to flowers
before, would learn all about gardening from her
mother-in-law. She would carry on Charity's gardening traditions! They would have a common
pursuit to discuss!

Charity walked out onto the raked gravel. Anne
followed. They stood for a moment, blinking in
the early evening sun. When Herb had introduced
Anne to his parents, it had been winter, and they
had not come out this way. As Anne looked about
her, she saw high walls of crisply clipped privet
hedge cut at natty, sharp right angles.

"The high hedges for privacy, you see," Charity
said.

Yes, Anne thought, you really need privacy out
here on an island a thousand miles from anywhere,

on an isolated chunk of land populated by deer, birds, and rabbits.

"Also," Charity continued, "the hedges provide a sense of civilization and order in the midst of all this"—she waved her hand vaguely—"wilderness."

Anne knew she had to say something appropriately complimentary. "Yes, I see," was the best she could do.

Charity walked along the gravel path, and Anne dutifully followed. The hedged garden was essentially one long rectangle. Inside was another, shorter rectangle of privet, and inside that was yet another, even shorter privet box. At the center of all the boxes was a stone plinth and a small sundial.

Charity Wheelwright stood before it, smiling. "What do you think?"

Anne said, "It's charming. Really charming." Actually, she thought, it's absurd, these rigid lines closing space in and in and in. She could see how it would be considered horticulturally interesting, and certainly it was unusual, but it made her feel claustrophobic. But if this was what made Charity Wheelwright happy, Anne would learn to love it, or at least admire it. She would do whatever would help bring peace between them. More than anything, Anne wanted peace.

# Fifteen

O*n the morning* of Family Meeting, Charlotte woke to a steady downpour. The air held a chill, so she yanked an old sweatshirt on over her work clothes and headed downstairs. The house was quiet, everyone else, even the children, still asleep. She was careful to ease the mudroom door shut without a sound as she stepped into the rain.

It must have rained all night. The ground was sodden, and that made her feel a bit better about missing an afternoon in the garden because of Family Meeting. She entered the shed, grateful for its warmth and light, peeled off her yellow rain slicker, picked up the clipboard she had hanging on a hook, and reviewed her scribbled daily notes and reminders. One thing for certain, she couldn't set up her farm stand when the rain was so heavy. It would wash the bags of lettuce right off the table, tear the flower petals, and turn the money box into a miniature bathtub. She needed to think of a way to protect that table, so she set the thought in the back of her mind and concentrated on seeding more lettuce and filling ornamental pots with vibrant mixtures of flowers.

As she worked, she allowed her thoughts to wander out of the shed, across Nona's land onto Coop's, and into the house where Coop no doubt lay sleeping. Three days after Nona's birthday party, Coop had again dropped by the garden to invite Charlotte out for a sail and again she had had to refuse. Coop had understood. He'd even joked about booking her for the first of November. Two days ago he'd phoned to ask her out to dinner tonight, and once again she'd had to decline. Today, she told him, was Family Meeting, and it was the family's custom to go out to dinner afterward. This is the third time I've refused, she thought, a bit desperately, so she quickly added, "How about tomorrow night?" She would ask her mother, or even Teddy, to deliver the fresh produce to the three restaurants she supplied. Coop had agreed. He'd suggested sailing across to Coatue. He'd bring a picnic dinner. Wear a bathing suit, he'd said, and now Charlotte experienced a little frisson of excitement at the thought of the two of them together, on a solitary beach, in the warm evening air. . . .

Jorge stomped into the shed, stripped off his rain poncho, and said, "It's raining cats and mice out there."

Charlotte grinned. "Cats and dogs." She gave him his instructions for the morning and allowed herself a break. She needed coffee. As she ran to the house, she couldn't avoid splashing through puddles, so water sprayed up against her legs and by the time she got to the house her boots were thick with mud. That's why Nona has a mudroom, she told herself, and sat down on the bench to undo the laces.

She heard voices from the kitchen. This old house

had peculiar acoustics. In some rooms you couldn't hear someone speaking from five feet away. In other rooms, conversations from next door came through as clearly as if on speakerphone.

"Helen, I agree with you about Owen." It was Charlotte's father speaking, his voice low and intense. "He and Oliver have been together for five years. They behave like adults. They're self-supporting. They're holding a commitment ceremony, another sign of their stability. I have no problem with Owen attending Family Meeting. As Oliver's life partner, Owen *belongs* at Family Meeting. But Suzette is a completely different matter."

Charlotte sat paralyzed on the bench, holding her breath. She didn't want her parents to know she could hear them.

Calmly, Helen asked, "Would you like some more coffee?"

Charlotte relaxed.

"No, thank you. Listen, Helen, you and I have both asked, at separate times, for Teddy to provide us some proof that Suzette is actually his wife. And Teddy has not complied."

Helen's voice sharpened. "Oh, Worth, your language. *Teddy has not complied.* This is not a business matter."

"Well, Family Meeting absolutely *is* a business matter. I don't want some stranger knowing the details of our financial holdings."

"She's not a stranger."

"No? Who is she? Where is she from? Who are her parents? Does she have any kind of education? How did she and Teddy meet? And if her baby is not Teddy's, then he or she is not entitled to any of the Wheelwright money."

"Come on! Teddy loves her. And since he's been with her he's been drug and alcohol free. Isn't that enough?"

"Enough? I don't think so. It's certainly wonderful, Helen. I love Teddy. I want to see him live a good healthy life. But we've been through so much with him before. I'd like to see a few months go by before I consider Teddy cleaned up. And I'd like to see some proof that they're married. That the child is Teddy's."

"You know how Teddy is! He's dug his heels in. The more we ask, the less he'll tell. I think we have to take his word for it that they're married and that the baby is his."

Worth's voice mellowed with a kind of amused humor. "You just want to have a grandchild, Helen. You want one so much you're willing to take an outsider. Tell me I'm wrong."

"Oh, Worth, you're so—*stubborn*."

After a moment's silence, Worth said gently, "Am I? Really? I didn't think we should allow Teddy and Suzette to stay here this summer. I thought we should force Teddy to support himself. But you felt very strongly about the matter and so I agreed."

Very quietly, Helen admitted, "I know. I know you did."

"I love Teddy just as much as you do, Helen."

"I know you do," she said. After a moment, with a sigh, she said, "All right. But who's going to tell Teddy Suzette isn't invited?"

"We'll tell her together," Worth said, just as Helen sneezed. "Are you catching a cold? It's not very smart, spending the night on a sleeping porch during a rainstorm."

"As a matter of fact, Worth, I enjoy sleeping there very much." Helen's voice trailed off as she went out of the kitchen.

Charlotte waited a few more minutes to be sure her father had left, too. In the kitchen she drank her coffee automatically, as if she were fueling a machine, and she didn't even bother to scramble eggs or butter a muffin, she just munched cold cereal, her thoughts too troubled for pleasure.

*Family Meeting was held,* as always, in the dining room of the Nantucket house. It began just after lunch and continued for most of the afternoon. Because it was hot in July, no one dressed formally. On the other hand, no one came to the table in shorts or grubby clothes after a morning of sailing. They showered and put on fresh clothing, and the women wore skirts or dresses.

At noon, Charlotte drove in to deliver fresh produce to the restaurants she supplied. When she returned, she gave Jorge a long list of instructions and stomped through the rain to the mudroom. Grateful to find the kitchen empty, she quickly made herself a peanut butter and jelly sandwich and raced upstairs to the attic, where she showered and dressed. She wore a blue button-down shirt with a khaki skirt; she had thought hard about what to wear to Family Meeting and decided this was best. It was as close as she could get to looking like a man. It made her look sexless, efficient, sober, and levelheaded—at least she hoped it did. While she ate her sandwich, she opened her folder and reviewed her notes. And then the clock struck one, she heard the voices of the family on the stairs as they headed toward the dining room, and, with her heart in her throat, she joined them.

Nona sat at the head of the long wide dining table, in the chair Grandfather Herb had used until his death. Nona wore one of her Public Pajama outfits, this time in a staid gray, and she wore her pearls and a touch of lipstick. The rest of the family sorted itself out around the table, pulling out chairs, taking care to sit next to someone from the other side. Once all of Grace's family had sat on one side, facing all of Worth's family, and it had seemed too antagonistic. It had been uncomfortable. It was, after all, a *family* meeting. All in all, there were fourteen people today, the most ever: Nona; Worth, Helen, Charlotte, Oliver, Owen, and Teddy; Grace and Kellogg, Mandy and Claus, Mellie and Douglas, and Mee.

Nona opened the session by thanking them all for her birthday celebration. "But please," she invited, with a smile, "I beg you, help yourselves to the plunder. I've stacked it on the table in the front hall. I must have received seven boxes of lavender toilet water, even more boxes of perfumed soaps, and quite a bit of very nice Crane stationery. I intend to live a long life, but even so, I won't be able to use up all my loot."

She turned the meeting over to Worth and Grace. Grace reminded them of various far-flung relatives and friends who had passed away over the last year. She handed out printed schedules of the charities the family supported and asked for comments or suggestions. Then Worth and Kellogg together presented a formal review of the family's financial holdings. The presentation was detailed, complete with color-coded charts and graphs and footnotes and investment-objective assessments.

Charlotte doodled on her yellow pad, half listening, half studying the faces of the others. Oliver and Owen sat at attention, handsome and solemn, seeming truly interested. Teddy, seated between Mee and Charlotte, was restless. He'd taken the trouble to change out of one of his ridiculous Hawaiian shirts into a white button-down with the sleeves rolled up, and he looked good. Perhaps thin, but good. His butterscotch hair could use a decent cut, but still he looked respectable.

Worth spoke for a long time about how the

Internet and ever-improved new technology were changing banking in ways no one could ever have foreseen. Customers were no longer coming into their familiar neighborhood bank where they knew the faces of the tellers and the reputations of the bank directors. More and more transactions occurred online. One way this impacted their bank was in personnel. Wisdom, experience, and a track record were less important than technological capability. The bank now hired, of necessity, young people, often very young people, because they needed employees who were technologically savvy. Also, because of technology, a global market had opened up and could not be ignored if the return on the bank's assets was going to be maximized. Many older employees were finding it difficult to adjust to the rapid changes in their profession. The bank directors had instituted a number of educational options, from in-house computer training seminars to a six-month leave of absence for intensive technological education. But many of their oldest employees found the computer programs too confusing, and they chafed against working with and being taught by younger, hipper staff members who seemed to have no respect for their elders. The problem was not one to be solved easily. After one hundred and thirty years of business, the Wheelwright Bank was assaulted by challenges it never could have foreseen.

Bank business had always taken the majority of

the time allotted for Family Meeting—so much so, in fact, that ten years ago Grandfather Herb had insisted on a limit. After all, he reminded them, it was a family meeting, not a meeting of the bank's board of directors. Today Nona gently enforced the time limit by interrupting Kellogg, who would have droned on forever, saying that she needed a little breather; they would reconvene in fifteen minutes. The Bank Boys shoved back their chairs and charged off into separate corners to check messages on their cell phones and text directives, and Oliver and Owen did the same. Teddy raced off to check on Suzette, and Helen and Grace and their daughters carried in the pitchers of lemonade and ice-filled tumblers and plates of cookies that Glorious had made for the occasion.

When they were all seated around the table again, munching cookies and sipping lemonade, the atmosphere was less formal.

"The next item on the agenda," Grace announced, "is the matter of Beach Grass Garden."

Charlotte's heart thumped. The atmosphere in the room was still inharmonious, as if they'd geared up for a battle which had dissolved, leaving them ready to fight about anything. Still, she had done the best she could to prepare. She handed around neatly printed copies of her annual report. For a few moments the room was silent except for the rustling of papers as everyone skimmed her figures.

Finally Kellogg spoke. "You show a profit of four thousand dollars for last year. Well done, Charlotte. Most small businesses don't show a profit for at least three years. You're ahead of the curve."

"And yet," Mandy said, "you only made that profit because you are using Nona's land."

"I'm paying Nona rent for the use of the land," Charlotte replied.

Mee barked out a laugh. "Yes, a pittance of what the land is really worth."

"I see much of the profit deriving from 'container gardens,'" Claus said, tapping his forefinger on a line item on her financial statement. "What does that mean?"

Charlotte had been hoping someone would ask this very question. "In the off season there's not a lot I can do to make an income. The garden is basically done after the middle of November. But I discovered there is a huge demand for container gardens, as gifts and decorations." Reaching into her folder, she brought out a few photos she'd printed off and passed them around the table. "These are container gardens."

The first garden was a fishbowl filled with sand, a variety of seashells, and a miniature evergreen tree made from a twig of pine, all of it sparkling with soap-flake snow. The second was an old wicker tray piled with gourds, autumn leaves still vivid with color, bits of barberry and ivy, and plumes of beach grass. The third was a china water pitcher filled with dried hydrangea.

"These are cool," Oliver said.

"Did you make them yourself?" Grace asked.

"I did." Charlotte started to elaborate, but Mandy cut her off.

Mandy said, with a bite in her voice, "Under the expense column, I find no item for *containers.*"

Charlotte smiled. "That's because there *was* no expense. I get all the containers at the dump."

"Oh, *gross!*" Mee said.

"Not gross at all," Charlotte told her. "You have no idea of the quantity and quality of items that are dropped off at the Take It or Leave It shed. This island fills up with fifty thousand people in the summer, and the flower shops deliver centerpieces, arrangements, bouquets, and thank-you gifts to many of them. The containers—inexpensive glass vases and bowls—end up at the shed and I retrieve them. Then I give each one a thorough cleaning in the dishwasher, with hot water and a strong disinfectant soap."

"Ah!" Claus pounced. "So you are using Nona's electricity and water for your own private gain."

"As you can see," Charlotte coolly replied, "I pay for a portion of Nona's electricity in addition to the rent I pay her for her land." She looked around the table. "By using these containers, I'm holding to the guiding principle of Beach Grass

Garden. A return to the natural, a return to local production and recycling."

"That's all very nice," Grace said, her voice tight. "Yet I am uncomfortable with your use of Nona's land. You are setting a precedent here. You are making a profit from Nona's land."

"I'm paying Nona rent for the land."

"True," Nona agreed, leaning forward. "And I've put the money into a savings account, so that when I'm gone you can divide it equally among yourselves."

"Still." Grace chewed her lip, discontent. "It's the land," she said finally. "It's the use of the land. What if Charlotte continues to run Beach Grass Garden for *years?*"

"Aunt Grace," Charlotte replied, "that land has lain unused for years."

Oliver spoke up. "Here's a thought. Charlotte is using three acres of Nona's land. Why don't Aunt Grace and her family choose three acres to use as *they* see fit?"

"That seems like a fair suggestion," Nona said.

Grace and her daughters and all the husbands exchanged glances.

"That's a good solution," Worth told his oldest son.

"The three acres would be for *rent,*" Oliver stressed. "This would not affect the matter of ownership."

Grace and Kellogg nodded stifly.

"But we don't want to do anything with the land!" Mellie protested.

Grace clearly wasn't happy, but she admitted, "But we could if we wanted to." She looked at her brother. "This might work, at least for a year, and then we can review matters at the next Family Meeting."

"Blessed be the peacemakers," Nona murmured under her breath.

*After Family Meeting,* it was customary for the family to go to the yacht club for a long, indulgent meal. This was Nona's innovation. She'd realized long ago, and she was still right, that family issues could not be discussed in public, and a friendly, familiar atmosphere where no one person had to carry dishes, cook, or clean up would go a long way toward lessening any tensions caused by Family Meeting.

By evening, the rain clouds had been blown away, leaving the sky a clean rinsed blue and the air sparkling with evening sun. Charlotte wore a sleeveless low-backed white sheath dress with a clever short jacket and very high heels. It was fun to change out of her work clothes, and fun to see her cousins and her mother and aunt and grandmother all dolled up again. Even Suzette wore a floaty yellow dress that covered her usually bare belly. It wasn't the best color for the sallow young woman, and she could use a decent hairstyling as well, but she was certainly what Aunt Grace called *presentable.* As the family entered the yacht club, Charlotte felt proud of her family as she often did, so many of them they took up two long tables, all of them good-looking separately and, together, a striking pack.

Tonight Mee chose to attach herself to Charlotte, complimenting her on her dress and earrings, making jokes and touching Charlotte's arm. Perhaps Mee, newly divorced, wanted the company of another single woman. Mee was the least attractive of the three sisters, but since the settlement of her divorce from Phillip, she'd become by far the wealthiest. She was announcing her return to single life as brazenly as she knew how, with too much makeup and low-cut tacky clothes. Charlotte gave herself a mental demerit for her cattiness and reminded herself she had a lot of karmic work to do.

"Mee," Charlotte said, "where did you get that necklace? I've never seen it before."

"Do you like it?" Mee's face lit up at Charlotte's compliment. "It's awfully gaudy, I know, but aren't people wearing big stones now?"

"Absolutely," Charlotte assured her. "You look smashing."

The group was led to their tables and seated. Charlotte saw Suzette being gently tended by Helen, who helped Suzette into a chair, slipped off the silk shawl draped over her own shoulders, and wrapped it around Suzette. Helen's gestures were so nurturing—so *maternal*—Charlotte felt a twinge. Why, she was jealous of Suzette—or at least of the attentions Helen was paying her. And Suzette was going to give Helen a grandchild, a gift beyond measure. Charlotte was ashamed of her emotions, but she could not erase them. She wanted a child, too, but she wanted to be married to a man she loved first.

Oliver was seated on Charlotte's right. He noticed her glance and drew close to her, whispering, "So what do you think of Suzette?"

Charlotte shrugged. "I don't know. She's hardly said a word to me, and I've really tried."

"She seems to like Mom."

"It's easy to like Mom." Charlotte flicked her linen napkin into her lap and picked up the menu.

"Aunt Grace is really on a tear this summer." Oliver spoke softly, picking up his own menu and pretending to discuss entrees with Charlotte.

"I know. I've noticed that, too. Mom's not her normal self, either. What's going on, I wonder?"

"Perhaps now that Family Meeting's over, everyone will relax." Oliver turned his attention to the waiter.

*They were finishing dessert* when Mee clutched Charlotte's arm. "Look who's here!" she squealed. "And he's coming this way!"

Charlotte followed her cousin's gaze and saw

Whit Lowry walking across the room toward their table. His navy blue blazer made his dark hair and dark blue eyes flash. He made Charlotte think of a blue jay.

"Very dishy," Oliver whispered into Charlotte's ear.

"Talk to me!" Mee hissed at Charlotte, jerking her arm. "Say something funny!" Without waiting for Charlotte to speak, she tossed her blond hair and laughed trillingly.

"I didn't know you had a crush on Whit," Charlotte said softly, as Whit stopped at the head of the table to speak with Nona and Worth.

"Oh, Charlotte, duh. Everyone has a crush on Whit."

"I didn't know that."

"Well, I'm not saying I want to *marry* the man, although I sure wouldn't turn him down. I'd just like the opportunity to—spend a night with him."

"Well, you randy little thing," Charlotte teased, and then Whit approached her.

He put a hand on the back of Mee's chair, and a hand on the back of Charlotte's. Bending close, he said, "Hey, Charlotte. Mee. Remember Devin O'Conner? He's been in Tibet for the past year. He's visiting us, and he's got some fascinating tales. We're having some people back to the house tonight, and I thought you might like to come over."

"We'd *love* to," Mee gushed. "Wouldn't we, Charlotte?"

• • •

*The Lowry house* was an enormous old shingled Victorian off Cliff Road. The front door was open, and laughter and chatter floated out on the night air. Charlotte and Mee went up the steps, across the porch, and into the hall and followed the sounds to the back of the house, where the party was gathered in a family room that opened onto the patio. Seated on sofas or leaning against walls or lounging on the rug, backs against a couch, were twenty or more friends they'd known forever. Mee left Charlotte to make a beeline for Whit. Charlotte went to the drinks table, poured herself a glass of seltzer, and joined the group around Devin O'Conner. Devin had been a short, muscular, energetic little boy, and now he was a short, muscular, energetic man whose flaming red hair had turned auburn since Charlotte had last seen him. His hair might have calmed down, but Devin himself was as enthusiastic as always, happy to be the center of attention, describing his trip with great flourish and drama. Charlotte allowed herself to be entertained for a while; then she grew bored and slipped away, out the door, into the fresh night air.

At the far end of the garden, a cluster of people were smoking, and the sweet smell of pot drifted through the night air, mingling with the stronger, darker smell of tobacco. In the brick wall delineating one edge of the property, a bronze cupid spilled water into a shallow pool. Charlotte sat on the low stone side of the pool basin, dipping her fingers in the cool water. It was after eleven. She should go home and get a decent night's sleep. But Mee's laughter bubbled from the party, and she didn't want to spoil Mee's fun.

"May I join you?"

She looked up. Whit stood there. He'd taken off his blazer, and his white shirt gleamed in the moonlight.

"Hi, Whit. Of course. Great party."

He settled on the edge of the pool, carefully setting his glass next to him. "Devin is still the entertainer, isn't he?" Whit leaned his elbows on his knees. "Charlotte, I'd like to talk to you about something."

"Oh?" Charlotte was surprised at how her heart kicked. She'd always thought Whit was good-looking, but when she'd worked at the bank, she'd hated him, or at least resented him, Mr. Goody Please-the-Father Bank Boy. It was also true, she admitted to herself, that she'd felt he was judging her—and he *was* judging her, judging her ability to do the sort of work her mind could not seem to find engaging.

But out here, on this warm summer evening, with the fountain trickling its musical notes and laughter drifting on the air, she really *felt* that he was, as Oliver had said, absolutely *dishy*.

Whit leaned closer to Charlotte and spoke in a low voice. "Oliver told me Teddy's looking for a job."

Charlotte gave a little snort. "The entire family's looking for a job for Teddy. Except maybe Teddy."

"Well, I think I've found the perfect thing for him. You know Gray Lady Antiques? On Centre Street?"

"Sure, although I've never gone in. The last thing we need out at Nona's is another antique."

"George Jameson and his wife, Audrey, own it. It's got good stock, pricey but worth it. Well, Mom told me that George is having some surgery, prostate trouble, not uncommon for men his age, but he and Audrey will have to be going off-island a lot this summer. They need someone to run the shop."

"And you think Teddy could do it?"

"Why not? He's intelligent, friendly, well-spoken. The Jamesons know your parents and Nona; I'm sure they know Teddy, too." Whit shifted on the pool's edge. "I know Teddy might not want to work in retail, but he doesn't have a college education or, as far as I can tell, any particular skills, so I'm not sure what sort of work he's prepared for. The antique shop is classy, so Teddy might think it suits him more than—"

"—than selling T-shirts," Charlotte finished for him, with a grin. "Whit, I think it's a brilliant idea. You are so great to think of it!" Impulsively, she leaned over and pecked a kiss on Whit's cheek.

Her action surprised them both. She felt her breath catch as Whit turned to look at her more fully. In the moonlight, his blue eyes seemed black and serious and compelling. She felt drawn to him—she felt *paired* with him—she felt spellbound, as if her spontaneous deed had been a kind of magic wand, and now they were enclosed together in a shimmering world of sensation; everything else in the world was distanced, muted, and all that mattered was this small magic sphere.

"Charlotte," Whit said.

"Hi, guys!" Mee pranced up, her high heels clicking on the patio stone. "What are you two doing all alone out here?" With much flipping of her full skirt, Mee plopped down next to Whit, close to him. "Great party, Whit!"

"Actually, Mee, I was just saying goodbye." Charlotte stood up. "I'm sorry, but I get up at four-thirty. I have to, to use all the daylight."

Whit rose. He put his hand on her wrist, lightly. "I'm glad you came."

"Well, I don't want to go home yet." Mee pouted. "I'm a free woman, I want to enjoy myself!" She waved her arms above her head. "I'd stay if I could get a ride home." She smiled encouragingly at Whit.

"Perhaps Devin could drive you when he leaves," Whit suggested.

*"Devin."* Irritated, Mee jumped to her feet. "He's a—a leprechaun."

"Well, if you want a ride with me, you have to leave now," Charlotte told her cousin.

"Oh, you are such a party pooper." Mee sighed, made a face, then threw herself against Whit and kissed his mouth quickly. "Thanks for the invitation, Whit. It was fun!" Grabbing Charlotte's arm, she pulled her toward the side of the house and the drive where Charlotte's Jeep was parked. "See you!"

As Charlotte looked back, Devin's younger sister Fiona came out of the house, heading toward Whit, her long curly red hair floating around her head, her body slim as a reed in a silk dress. She put a possessive hand on Whit's arm.

"I thought you wanted to go home," Mee snapped.

Charlotte realized she'd stopped walking, was standing there staring. "Right," she said. "Right." She forced herself to turn away, to walk with her cousin to the Jeep, to drive through the warm fragrant night to her lonely attic bed.

# Oliver's Wedding

# Sixteen

*O liver and Owen's* rehearsal dinner party, held at the yacht club, was a great success, but Helen was afraid, as she slid between the cool sheets of her sleeping-porch bed, that she had eaten too much. And perhaps had one too many glasses of celebratory champagne. She wanted to get a good night's sleep, because tomorrow would be a memorable day. Tomorrow her older son would be married.

Lying on her side, she shoved and folded the pillow beneath her head, trying to ease her body so it would relax her mind. *Marriage.* What did it mean to Oliver, that he wanted to hold this ceremony with the man he loved? If nothing else, Helen was glad she had kept her silence about Worth's affair over the past three weeks. That Oliver wanted to be married surely was a sign that he believed marriage was a worthwhile state, an enviable commitment, a circumstance graced with honor and hope. She did not want to stamp his days of joy with the imprint of his parents' disillusion.

She flipped onto her back, rearranged her limbs, and still she was uncomfortable. Rising, she padded across the floor to the little table holding her vanity items. She found the bottle of aspirin and her glass of water and took two pills. She stood for a moment, appreciating the fresh velvet night air, but she was too tired to stand for long. Was this going to be one of *those* nights, when her mind fretted and her muscles cramped and her brain pleaded for the relief of sleep but her body would not oblige, would not pull her under into sweet oblivion? Tomorrow was the wedding! She would be hollow-eyed, with dark bags on either side of her nose; she would be dizzy and short-tempered. She threw herself back onto the bed and tried to compose herself. Concentrate on happy moments, she instructed herself. Count your blessings.

*When she met* Worth, Helen had just graduated from college with a degree in art history. She'd taken a job working at a posh art gallery on Newbury Street while she tried to decide what she really wanted to do. An inheritance from her grandparents meant that she wouldn't have to work at something she hated but could find the time to search out work she loved, whatever that would be. She enjoyed working in the gallery, especially when there was a new show to be hung and an opening to be organized and publicized and orchestrated.

One day in early summer, she was seated at the Chippendale writing desk, trying to look busy but really doodling on a notepad, when a tall man about her age walked in. He had thick gold hair, real gold, not light brown or strawberry blond, and eyes as blue as heaven. He wore a suit and tie, and his shirt was crisp, and he moved with a confident, comfortable stride, a man happy with himself and with life.

Helen rose and walked toward him. "May I help you?"

He smiled at her. She smiled at him. For a long moment they just looked at each other. He seemed to cast a magic circle, and she was included.

"Have we met before?" Worth asked.

Thank goodness she had chosen the sleek black dress and high heels today. "I don't think so." She couldn't stop smiling at him.

"Well." He seemed as stunned by her presence as she was by his. "Well," he repeated, shaking himself, "I'm looking for a wedding present. For my sister, Grace."

"Lovely! What sort of art does she like?"

He chuckled. "I'm not sure she likes any kind of art, actually. She's more of an outdoor type. Loves sports. Big jock."

"Ah. Does she sail?"

"She does."

"We've got some lovely water scenes by a contemporary Impressionist." She turned and walked into the back room, stopping in front of several large oil paintings.

In one painting, two people were silhouetted by the setting sun as they steered their sailboat toward a sandy shore.

"This might be nice," Helen said. "Two people, together." She turned to see how he was reacting to the painting.

He was looking at her.

He said, "Two people, together."

She blushed.

"Look," he said suddenly. "Who are you? I'm sure we've met before."

"I really don't think so," she told him. "I'm sure I'd remember meeting you."

"Yes. Yes—me, too. Well, how about a drink? Or let me take you out to dinner. Or lunch? Or tea?" He walked toward her.

The space between them shimmered. She was absolutely *dazzled*.

"Breakfast?" he asked desperately, and they both laughed.

She agreed to have dinner with him that night. From that point on, they were a couple.

When she took him to Hartford to meet her parents, she worried that he might find them a little dull, because, in fact, they were. Her father was an executive at an insurance company and her mother was a homemaker and committeewoman, and both of them required a great deal of routine and tranquillity. This was the early seventies, which Helen's parents found more frightening than stimulating, and Worth, with his navy blazer and good manners, bowled them over. Helen was amazed at how easily he managed to create a conversation with her father, asking him about his opinions, his childhood, the insurance business, drawing him out. Helen learned things about her father that she'd never known before.

When Worth took her to meet his family, Helen felt like Dorothy in *The Wizard of Oz*—the black-and-white world became Technicolor. Worth's family was so *active* and such a *tribe*. On Nantucket, they sailed together, played tennis together, swam together. Went on picnics together. Had parties together. In Boston, everyone except Worth's mother, Anne, worked at the bank: Worth's father, Herb; Worth himself; his sister, Grace; and her fiancé, Kellogg. Anne had a rule that no bank business could be discussed at home, and Helen could often see and feel the difference in Worth once he walked through the front door; he became lighter, brighter, happier. During the winter months, the family went north to ski, and at home in Boston on weekends, they would sit around the dining room table, playing poker or board games, or they'd gather in the kitchen to try out a new, complicated recipe. All the men cooked. That alone would have perplexed Helen's father, who didn't.

Often, someone in the family would mention Bobby, Worth's younger brother, who had been killed in Vietnam in 1970. Worth would say, "Remember during that blizzard when we played poker and Bobby got a royal flush? I've never ever seen another real live royal flush." Or Worth's mother would say, "Kellogg, there's a handsome plaid jacket of Bobby's that would look great on you. Grace, take him up and show him." She knew the family was trying to keep him with them somehow, by including him in normal conversation.

Once Helen said to Worth, "Kellogg doesn't say much, does he?"

"I know." Worth grinned. "Kellogg's a bit of a stick-in-the-mud. But he's reliable and honest and kind, and he's willing to live with my sister, so that's good enough for me."

Helen quickly learned not to criticize Worth's relatives. The Wheelwright family had always been close, and the loss of the second son had made them treasure one another even more.

*All these years later,* as Helen lay sleepless in bed before the wedding of her own older son, she assured herself that family was still first in Worth's heart. He wouldn't want a divorce. She was pretty sure of that.

But then, she had never expected him to be unfaithful.

She hadn't yet confronted Worth with her knowledge of his affair. She knew that when she did, the ground under their marriage would crumble. A divide had already opened between them, but a bridge still joined their parallel lives, a necessary union, supporting their family. First, to celebrate Nona's birthday with the attention it deserved, and now, three weeks later, to honor Oliver and Owen's wedding.

Oliver's wedding was the last big event for the family. Then the summer would truly have arrived. Nona's house would remain full of her children and grandchildren and great-grandchildren until fall. Worth and the other Bank Boys would come and go, dividing their lives between Boston and Nantucket, but Helen would stay on the island as she always had, helping Glorious and Grace buy groceries, cook, and clean, and also swimming, sailing, playing tennis, and attending concerts and plays. It was always a luxurious, idle few weeks. This year, Helen wanted to get to know Suzette better; the young woman seemed to trust her more each day. She thought Suzette felt comfortable with Charlotte and Nona, too; she certainly hoped so. Suzette would have her baby in September.

And Teddy? Teddy was working! He was managing Gray Lady Antiques. Helen didn't care what Suzette's background was, she was a miracle worker where Teddy was concerned. Teddy was not drinking or doing drugs, he wasn't playing stupid practical jokes or getting speeding tickets or sneaking out to the garden to smoke pot. He was working and attending AA meetings every day, and he was obviously in love with Suzette and happy about the coming baby. This was a fragile peace for Teddy, an unusual and delicate state. Helen didn't want to upset it by a breath of dissension, and certainly not by the torching explosion of her anger at Worth.

Helen twisted onto her left side and punched her pillow. This bed *was* lumpy. The summer air was gradually increasing in humidity, and in her irritated state she thought she could feel her hair frizzing. She forced herself to take deep, calming breaths.

Suddenly she heard a noise, and then she felt someone on the bed. She raised her head and saw her husband sitting there in his striped cotton pajamas.

"Worth?"

"I have melancholy," Worth said, and, lifting the sheet, he climbed into bed with her, lying on his side so that she spooned against his back.

*I have melancholy*—that was a family catchphrase. When Oliver was a very small child, he'd said that to them the day after Christmas, and since then they used the remark whenever nothing was really wrong but something seemed missing, some essential but invisible thing.

How very strange, almost shocking, it was to have Worth's warm solid bulk sinking into this narrow bed with her. His shoulders rose up, his bum nudged against her belly, and as she adjusted herself to his girth, scooting closer to the wall, he eased a hand over to pull part of her pillow over to cushion his own head. Her arm had no place to go except over his torso, and when she laid her arm over him, he took her hand with his and held it. He gave off warmth, and his body made the bed sag down in his direction, so that she was rolled against him.

He said softly, "I've been remembering Oliver as a little boy. Remember when he spent one afternoon tying all those balloons to the picnic basket, thinking he'd be able to drift up into the sky?"

Helen smiled at the memory. "I'd forgotten about that."

Worth shifted slightly, nestling more closely. "Remember that summer he spent building houses from playing cards? What patience he had. Those houses were enormous, and he didn't cheat and use glue, he just carefully balanced card after card."

"He was an architect even back then," Helen said.

"Remember the plays the kids used to perform?" Worth chuckled. *The Vampires of Vaudeville.*"

"*Sherlock Holmes and the Missing Martian,*" Helen said. "They covered Teddy with green eye shadow and stuck on hideous warts made out of green Play-Doh." She shuddered.

Worth nodded, his head moving against the pillow. "We have wonderful children, don't we, Helen?"

She was touched. "We do."

"They're certainly individuals. Not who I thought they'd turn out to be. It's taken me awhile to get used to that." Worth's voice was sad. "I remember how much I wanted to be just like my dad. Go to work at the bank, share his knowledge about money and the state of the world. I admired my father above all other men."

Helen stroked her husband's hand. "Your children admire you, too."

"Not in the same way. I'm not trying to be maudlin, I'm just stating a fact. I keep thinking about my childhood, comparing it to that of our children, and I just don't see much of a difference, yet they don't hold any of the values I had at their age. Security, continuity, family, and community—these mean nothing to them."

As Worth talked, his voice low and confiding, Helen felt the puff of his breath and the hum of words in his chest and was carried back to all the other nights they'd lain together like this, talking over some problem or another. There had been so many problems, mostly with Teddy and his escapades. Ever since the boy was fourteen, he'd been caught drinking too much, or been brought home drunk, or was found stealing something from Oliver or Charlotte, and then it was as if Helen and Worth had been caught up in a whirlpool; they'd struggle to save their son, keep their own heads above water, and make it back safe to shore. Their bed had become a kind of life raft for them, a safe retreat; they would crawl in together and lie side by side, calming down, the warmth and bulk of each other's body providing reassurance in the troubled night.

"I feel I have a responsibility to my father," Worth said, moving so that his bare foot rested on Helen's leg. "And to my grandfather. And to Nona. To keep the bank strong. To preserve the Wheelwrights' place in the world. I know Grace's husband and sons-in-law can do that, *are* doing that, but I'm the oldest, I'm the male, and while that's not supposed to matter in this day and age, it does. My father counted on me to carry on his traditions, in the bank and at home. I feel I'm failing him."

"You're not failing him," Helen said, but the murmur of his words was making her drowsy. Sleep, like a dark seductive sea, was pulling her under, deliciously, and she wanted to surrender to it. A thought flashed up from the depths, through her mind. She should say, *And did your father have a mistress called Sweet Cakes?* But she couldn't summon up the energy to speak. The mistress would still be there tomorrow and the next day, and the pain—the anxiety of how their lives would change—would not disappear. But right now she felt so cozy, lying here pressed against her husband's back. It was a familiar and soothing situation; she had not been so physically pleased for a long time. The simple touching of his body to hers.

Not in sex but in marriage, friendship, companionship, and trust. Dear old friend, she thought, and with her hand still in her husband's, she fell asleep.

*Oliver and Owen* were married in the late afternoon. The officiating minister, who had flown in from California, was completely bald, with pointed ears and a grave, still manner; he resembled Mr. Spock. The ceremony was held on the beach, and the weather blessed them with blue sky, a blazing sun, and a gentle sea breeze. Owen's parents had flown in for the occasion. They stood at Owen's side, and Worth and Helen stood by Oliver, while the vows were spoken. Earlier in the day, Charlotte had decorated a twisting piece of driftwood with flowers, a kind of little altar, and Grace flitted from place to place, shooting photos of the ceremony.

Afterward, they filed back up through the wild rosebushes and over the lawn, through the house, and out into the hedged garden, where a long table had been set up with a dramatically high tiered cake in the place of honor. Champagne was poured and handed out by Kellogg and Grace, because Oliver and Owen wanted to keep things informal, and Oliver's aunt and uncle were pleased to be able to repay some of the many duties Worth and Helen had performed at the various marriages of their three daughters. There were about fifty people in all. Most of the guests were friends of the wedding couple, handsome professional men who would, later in the evening, leave for the house Oliver and Owen had rented for the real party. The families were invited to the later party, too, but Oliver had been thoughtful not to entertain the group, which would drink and dance into the small hours of the morning, at Nona's house, disturbing the peace of his grandmother and his cousin's little children.

Helen moved among the crowd, loving the flow and drape of her long turquoise skirt against her legs, sipping champagne, talking with the guests. Phyllis Lowry, the wife of bank director Lew Lowry and one of Helen's oldest friends, was sitting on a bench, and Helen joined her.

"Do you know," she confided in a low voice, "I think I'm getting just a tiny bit tight."

Phyllis laughed. She was a tall woman whose black hair had gone a shining snow white. "It's the relief," she told Helen. "The ceremony is over, all the details are dealt with, and now you can relax." Leaning closer, she whispered, "Don't look now, but—Whit and Charlotte."

Helen allowed her gaze to drift over the crowd and, sure enough, there her daughter was, talking with Whit, smiling at Whit. These two had known each other since childhood. When she was thirteen, Charlotte had developed a painfully intense crush on Whit, but they had never really dated as far as Helen knew.

Helen looked away. "I will not get my hopes up," she told Phyllis. "Not with *my* children."

"Whit's probably telling her about his friend Laura Riding. She's started a new magazine, *Eat Local.*"

"Oh, I've seen it. Matte paper and lots of great photography?"

"Right. It's a national publication, with local articles inserted for each state. Whit told Laura she should write up Beach Grass Garden."

"How great! Charlotte will be thrilled." Helen linked her arm with Phyllis's. "Whit is so wonderful. He recommended Teddy for the antiques shop. Teddy's actually been working, every day."

"Well, good thing. He's going to be a father." Phyllis squeezed Helen. "You're going to become a grandmother."

"And about time, too!"

Helen was laughing as she continued to sweep her eyes around the garden. So many handsome young men. Why, she wondered, were gay men all so handsome? She saw Nona seated in her chair by the house, in the shade, regal in scarlet silk pajamas. Suzette sat next to her, looking sweet in a blue maternity dress Mellie had given her. Her multicolored hair had grown slightly, so that instead of sticking out in clumps it curled lightly, feathering close to her head. Every so often Nona would lean near Suzette and say something, and Suzette would smile and nod. Progress was being made there, Helen thought, and took another sip of champagne and allowed herself to be, for the moment, happy. Almost triumphant.

Then her gaze fell on her second son, Teddy, and her heart caught in her throat. Because the ceremony was held on the beach, the dress was casual. Teddy wore crisp white flannels and one of his more colorful Hawaiian print shirts. His blond hair was long enough now that he pulled it back in a funny little ponytail at the nape of his neck. He was talking with one of Oliver's California friends, and he held a flute of champagne in his hand.

Helen hurriedly corrected herself. Perhaps it wasn't champagne. Perhaps it was water—but no, it wasn't water, the color was wrong, it was the pale sunshine yellow of champagne. Could it be grapefruit juice? As she stared, Teddy tilted the glass and drank. He downed the glass in one swallow, then said something to the other man and left to walk to the drinks table, where he set his glass down and picked up another, a glass Helen had just seen the bartender pour from a champagne bottle.

Perhaps champagne didn't really count as alcohol, Helen thought quickly. Who really ever got drunk on champagne? Perhaps Teddy felt obligated to drink at Oliver's wedding—but no, that didn't work, because Teddy had drunk water at Nona's birthday party.

"Excuse me, Phyllis." Helen set her own glass on

the brick path and rose. She headed toward her younger son, but people stopped her to congratulate her and praise gorgeous Oliver, and when she got to where Teddy had been, he was gone. She turned, scanning the crowd.

Teddy was with his brother and one of Oliver's California friends—right now Helen couldn't remember the man's name. As Helen watched, Teddy aimed a hearty slap at Oliver's shoulder. Oliver was a few inches taller than his younger brother, and while both men were slender, Oliver's posture was erect, his limbs muscular. Beside him, Teddy looked too thin.

"Congratulations, big brother!" Addressing the California friend—*Brad,* Helen thought; *his name is Brad*—who stood next to Oliver, Teddy announced jovially, "You know, every time I see Oliver, it's to congratulate him for something. Graduating from high school, graduating from college, getting his architect's degree, winning that award in San Francisco—Oliver's a golden boy, aren't you, Oliver? You're a real golden boy."

Oliver dipped his head and said something softly to Teddy.

In response, Teddy tilted his glass and drained it. "But it's a party!" he declared. "A celebration. Another celebration! For *you,* Oliver, handsome handsome Oliver, talented Oliver, and of course you *would* find a mate from a terribly terribly socially accepted family. You're just a golden boy,

Oliver!" Keeping his hand on his brother's shoulder, Teddy roughly shook his brother in rhythm to his words, "A golden boy, a golden boy, that's what you are, a golden boy!" He lurched aggressively toward Brad. "Right? Am I right? Don't you think Oliver's a golden boy?"

A deep, exhausting sadness possessed Helen, and the iron brand of a headache scorched her forehead. She had been in this place before, many times before, with Teddy drunk after a beach party in high school or college, or drunk at home in Boston when he showed up for one of his unannounced visits. So she knew better than to try to lead him away from the party. Teddy would never hurt her—Teddy was not a mean drunk—but even as thin as he was, he was stronger than Helen, and if he swayed or stumbled against her, he could knock her over. He *had* knocked her over before, accidentally. She saw her husband headed toward Oliver and Teddy, a strained smile on his face.

"Oh, no!" Teddy broke into a crowing laugh. "Here comes Dad! It's crackers and milk in my room again! Crackers and milk for me, because I'm the bad boy. Champagne and cheers for you, Ollie, old chap, you're the golden boy."

By now Teddy's voice was loud enough to summon everyone's attention, and Helen was aware of the crowd pausing in their conversations and turning to stare. Helen looked to see how Nona was taking all this. In state on the bench, Nona resembled some kind of gigantic beetle with her fat torso and stick limbs, and she was just about as nimble as an overturned beetle, unable to rise without someone's assistance or at least the use of the cane lying next to her. Nona's gaze was on Teddy. Suzette, like another, differently colored beetle, was awkwardly pushing herself up from her wicker chair. Her face was grim as she lumbered toward Teddy.

"Teddy." Somehow Worth managed to get between his two sons. He clamped a hand on his younger son's shoulder, but instead of drawing Teddy away as Helen thought he would, he said, "Grace? Where's your camera? I want a picture taken of me with my sons. With both my sons."

*Oh, thank you, Worth,* Helen thought, grateful that he was trying to ease them all out of an unpleasant situation.

Grace practically ran through the gathering, holding her digital camera up, giddily giving directions, "Stand closer together, Teddy, Oliver. That's right. Now Worth. Smile, everyone. Come on, a nice big smile."

But Teddy wasn't smiling. His drunken jubilation had morphed into depression. Helen had seen this transition before, too. She hoped they could maneuver him into the house and away from the party before he started one of his self-pitying rants.

"Great!" Grace cried. "I have several wonderful shots."

"Thanks," Worth said to his sister. He had not taken his hand off Teddy's shoulder, and now he moved him away from Oliver and toward the house. Suzette approached Teddy and said something Helen couldn't hear.

"Oh, come on," Teddy roared back. "I've gotten started, at least let me finish, let me have one good intoxicating event. If I'm going to be sick with guilt tomorrow, I might as well do it right."

Kellogg appeared at Teddy's other side. He exchanged a glance with Worth, and the two older men gripped Teddy's arms and half carried him through the garden and into the house. Suzette followed. Helen followed the others. She heard Oliver say to the crowd, "This seems like a good time to move the party over to Surfside. You all know the address, right?"

Teddy heard, too. "I want to go to the party!" He wrestled away from his father and uncle. "Hey, no fair, I want to go to the party." He sounded like a child.

Worth and Kellogg escorted Teddy to one of the sofas in front of the fireplace. "Come on, Teddy, sit down here a minute. You can go to the party, but there's no hurry. It's going to be awhile before the others have unblocked the drive with their cars." Worth kept his voice moderate, friendly.

Glorious, who had seen Teddy's fits of drunkenness before, appeared from the kitchen holding a cup of coffee.

"Thanks, Glorious," Worth said. "Teddy, sit down. Drink this."

"Oh, there you go, such a Puritan. Why are you making such a big deal of this? I don't need any coffee, I'm celebrating the golden boy; you should be celebrating him, too. Well, you *are* celebrating him—or you were, weren't you?—until I messed things up for you." Teddy suddenly sat down, hard, on the sofa. "Did I ruin Oliver's party? That is so pathetic. My God, I'm a hopeless fool."

From outside came the noises of the departing crowd. Car doors slammed. Voices called out. Someone laughed. At the far end of the room, Grace was helping Nona in from the garden.

Suzette awkwardly lowered herself next to Teddy. She took his hand. "Teddy, it's all right. It's fine. Everything's fine. You haven't ruined anything. Now drink your coffee."

Teddy clutched Suzette's hand hard. He looked up at his father. "Isn't she wonderful? Suzette is wonderful. I wouldn't be here without Suzette. I wouldn't be anywhere without Suzette. And you wouldn't let her come to your stupid lockjaw Family Meeting!"

"Let's discuss this matter tomorrow, son," Worth said.

"Oh, right, let's not talk about your cold-shouldering now, not while Golden Boy is on stage."

"You know what?" Worth said, his voice angry. "That's right. It *is* Oliver's wedding day."

Teddy glared up at his father. "Yeah? Well, when are you going to celebrate my marriage to Suzette? When are you going to throw *us* a party?"

"When you show me a marriage certificate," Worth shot back.

Helen's headache was nearly blinding her, but she noticed from the corner of her eye that Glorious had gone to Nona and put a supporting arm around the old woman. She left the group gathered around Teddy and went to her mother-in-law. "Nona. Are you all right?"

"I'm fine, dear. Just very tired. This has been such an exciting day. Time for bed for me." Nona's voice was scarcely louder than a whisper.

Behind her, Teddy continued to rage, his words becoming looser and less well formed, and soon, Helen knew, he would launch into an unattractive, petulant blubbering that no amount of gentle reassurance could stem. He was this far into his inebriation. The only way out from this point was to keep him away from more alcohol while preventing him from doing something potentially harmful to himself. Helen's heart ached for her son. And her head ached, as if she were very weary, as if she'd been awake for several weeks without sleep.

Charlotte swept in from the garden, her pale saffron silk skirt swirling around her ankles. The evening's humidity had made her long hair rise slightly around her head like a halo. She leaned over her brother and tugged on his hand. "Come on, Teddy, let's go for a walk."

Teddy pulled away. "No, no, you want to go to Oliver's party."

"No, I don't. I want to walk with you. On the beach. It's such a beautiful night. Let's kick off our shoes and get sand between our toes."

"Suzette—"

"Suzette needs to rest. You and I need to walk." She yanked on him and, reluctantly, Teddy rose.

Suzette pushed herself up to a standing position and watched Charlotte draw Teddy away from the sofa. Without another word, she crossed the large room, walked out into the hall, and up the wide stairs.

"I ruined Oliver's party," Teddy groaned. "I'm an asshole."

"You're an asshole," Charlotte agreed, "but you didn't ruin Oliver's party. Tell me about the antiques shop, Teddy. How do you like working there? Have you made any fabulous sales? If I know you, you've persuaded quite a few people into some pretty pricey deals."

Helen watched, relieved, as Charlotte steered Teddy out the French doors toward the grassy lawn and the low brush and the beach. Charlotte knew the drill. They all did. Now it was just a matter of keeping Teddy moving until he wore out his drunk. He would be boring, repetitive, and maudlin, but he wouldn't drink any more alcohol. Helen didn't think he'd had the chance to get shit-faced enough to vomit like he had in college. It was good of Charlotte to deal with her brother.

She walked back to where Worth and Kellogg stood. "Charlotte saves the day."

Worth's face was as dark as thunder. "Charlotte shouldn't have to save the day. I've warned Teddy I won't put up with this behavior. I want him out of the house tomorrow."

## Seventeen

*N*ona *hated* hearing her son fighting with his wife about her grandson. She didn't want to be in the room. She wanted to be in *bed,* she needed to rest—but at this moment she didn't have the stamina or the breath to climb the stairs. She gestured to Grace to help her to a chair.

"Just for a moment," she told her daughter. "I just need to catch my breath."

"Of course, Nona," Grace said, with a saccharine smile.

*Oh, don't be so smug!* Nona wanted say. It was so unbecoming, the way Grace relished her brother's discomfort. "Could I have a glass of water?"

"Yes, Nona, I'll get it," Grace cooed.

"I'll help!" Kellogg noticed his wife leaving the room and hurried after her, eager to escape the living room battlefield where Worth and Helen were speaking in low, tense voices.

"Worth, please," Helen pleaded. "Teddy wasn't so very awful this time. He was only a little bit drunk."

"Helen, look. We've been through this all before, more times than I want to remember. You know as well as I do that with Teddy there's no such thing as a little bit drunk. The point is, he's *drunk.* And we agreed that we were not going to enable him."

"But the situation is different now," Helen argued. "Teddy's married. His wife is going to have a baby, our grandchild! Teddy is employed, and he's showed up every day, and he's doing a good job, and it's work he enjoys. Really, Worth, he's changed. We should give him another chance."

"How can you say he's changed?" Worth shook his head angrily. "Because he's married? You think he's *really* married? This is Teddy we're talking about here."

Grace returned with a crystal tumbler filled with ice and water. "Here, Mother," she whispered dramatically.

"Thank you, dear." Nona took a long, soothing drink. "Now I need to go to my room. Would you ask Kellogg to help me up the stairs?"

Grace looked alarmed. "Nona! Are you okay?"

"Darling, I'm just exhausted, that's all. I want to get these clothes off and crawl into bed."

In a flash, reliable Kellogg appeared at his wife's side; reaching down, he put his hands on Nona's waist to help her out of the chair. This was always awkward, and sometimes Nona thought it was funny and crumpled into a fit of giggles, but she was too tired for laughter just now. Doctors had instructed Glorious and all the adults who helped Nona that they should not try to help her stand by pulling on her arms. That might actually pull them right out of their sockets. The helper was supposed to put his arms beneath Nona's, but in Nona's case, the gelatinous mass of her ancient enormous bosom made it difficult to reach her back. So Kellogg secured his hands near Nona's waist, and she put her hands on his shoulders, and he heaved her to a standing position.

It took her a few moments to catch her breath.

"Give him another chance," Helen said again from the other side of the room.

"How many chances have we already given him, Helen?" Worth demanded. "And every time—*every time*—he's let us down."

"Worth, for God's sake, it's not a matter of letting us down. It's not about us. It's about Teddy. This is a weakness of Teddy's. It will not go away. It will be with him—with us—for the rest of our lives. But Teddy is doing his best to rise to the challenge, and we are his family. We need to stand by him."

"Helen, it's not as simple as that, and you know it. Teddy isn't just an alcoholic, he's manipulative, he's a troublemaker, and he's a spoiled brat. Why can't you see what's right before your face? Teddy getting drunk on Oliver's wedding day? Why today, of all days?"

Nona didn't want to listen anymore. "Kellogg, I'm ready," Nona told her son-in-law.

Kellogg wrapped a supporting arm around Nona's back, beneath her arms, and very slowly they made their way out of the living room, into the hall, and up the stairs. The sounds of the argument followed them, and Grace followed them, too, looking pious. *Oh, I'm such a critical mother,* Nona thought. *Here Grace is helping me, and she's so proud to be helping me; why can't I admire her for that?*

While Kellogg arranged Nona in a sitting position on her bed, Glorious appeared. "I've got the dishwasher packed and running," she told everyone. "But there's still a lot to be brought in from the patio."

"We'll get it, Glorious," Grace announced in her capable voice. "You help Nona. Are you okay now, Nona?"

"I'm fine, thank you. And thank you so much, Kellogg, for your strong arms."

Kellogg blushed with pleasure. "Glad to do it."

"Come on, Kellogg," Grace said. "Let's clear up the patio."

The excitement and effort and beauty of the day had told on Nona, and she let herself relax the way she could with Glorious, the way she never could with her own children, because she needed to keep at least some small sense of distance and dignity with them. With Glorious, who was so voluptuously large, whose hands were so soft and gentle, whose personality did not *come at her* the way her children's did, Nona could relinquish all endeavors to be competent, lucid, and in charge. She let herself slump. She was like a child as Glorious knelt to lift one foot and then the other, Glorious slipping off Nona's court shoes. As Glorious gave each foot a brief, friendly little massage, Nona took a deep breath of pleasure. She leaned against the bedpost then, while Glorious unbuttoned her silk shirt and unsnapped the technological wonder that held Nona's breasts in check. Like a little girl, Nona raised her arms for Glorious to slide her nightgown over her head. Then Glorious unfastened Nona's silk trousers and pulled them off Nona's ancient, unresisting body.

Glorious pulled back the covers, plumped the pillows, and helped Nona into bed. Nona was so very tired that Glorious had to pick up Nona's legs, one after the other, to lift them onto the mattress. Then she arranged the covers, smoothing and tucking them into the tidy, wrinkle-free expanse Nona liked.

Nona subsided against her pillows. "Oh, Glorious. Just what I need. Thank you."

"Would you like something to eat, Mrs. Nona?"

"No, thank you. I just need to sleep."

"I'll check on you in a while, then."

Nona felt the slight stir of air in the room as Glorious moved from the bedside to the door. She couldn't keep awake any longer. She slept.

## 1945

*May 1, 1945*

*Darling,*

*Tonight I write you under candlelight and I am not green with envy, just short of paper, so I borrowed these sheets from my German host for the night. The family were just preparing supper when we moved in. I have to say the pan-fried potatoes left on the kitchen stove looked very tempting. The family left the food for us and moved out in their customary German rush when American troops told them their home would be used to billet troops. So I have a roof over my head. I don't know how long we'll remain here. But now that the war is almost over I can give you a sketchy account of our activities since leaving the States.*

*We left New York on July 26 aboard the U.S.S. William G. Mitchell and debarked at Liverpool August 6. We went by train to South Wales. After living in the field for several days, we departed for Carmarthen to live in a tank* camp near Pembroke. From September to November, we traveled via rough seas and complicated routes, listening to and ducking buzz bombs, until we finally hit combat in the northern flank of the Bulge with the 30th Infantry Division. Then we worked a long time with the 82nd Airborne Division, shoving the Jerries back within their famous Siegfried Line. I'll never forget our bitter weather and the fighting during the latter part of December, January, and February. During this period I earned the Bronze Star.

Now we are up north and nearing the Baltic Sea and a linkup with the Russians and with the 8th and 82nd again. We are working with the 9th U.S. and 2nd British armies.

This information is not for all your friends or newspapers as yet; however, our folks can know.

My date for the cessation is May 7, and I pray the damn thing will be over before this letter reaches you. Fighting is sporadic and disorganized now; it is merely a matter of contacting the Krauts for them to surrender, and then we occupy the territory.

I suppose America was all agog over the big, false, and unofficial news recently. I can't see why people couldn't wait for an official statement from General Eisenhower or President Truman. Now Americans will have to locate a new supply of liquor to celebrate officially. From *reports received here, about all the celebration liquors were consumed.*

*Honey, I shall close now. This is not a romantic letter, but it does tell you why I haven't written you for so long. I love you.*

*Herb*

Anne didn't receive the letter until early June. She wept with relief when she read it, even though by then the war in Europe was over. Herb was alive, that was what mattered; that was all that mattered. Soon they could begin their real lives.

The Stangarone Freight Company was busier than ever, as the Army of Occupation settled in Europe to deal with thousands of prisoners of war and even more thousands of displaced persons, families who had lost their homes, their communities, their real lives, and now were dependent on the relief offered by Americans. Food and supplies for the troops had to be shipped over the Atlantic, and now, in addition, the necessities for survival for everyone else.

When July rolled around, Gwendolyn Forsythe once again insisted that Anne take a two-week vacation, and once again Anne joined her in-laws in their old white whale of a summer house on Nantucket, but this time she felt restless and rebellious. She was tired of being around her hypercritical, unaffectionate, dull, and dreary in-laws and their rigid routine. She found some relief playing tennis or sailing at the yacht club, but even those activities did not bring real pleasure. She was only treading water, killing time, waiting for Herb to come home.

One morning as she sat on the patio sipping her third cup of coffee and listening to her mother-in-law run down the list of menus for the week, groceries that had to be bought, cocktail parties, luncheons, and bridge groups to be attended, Anne looked at the long rectangle of space closed in by tall privet hedges and thought she'd lose her mind.

"Mrs. Wheelwright?" Anne asked, because that was what her mother-in-law insisted she call her.

"Mmm." Charity Wheelwright did not look up from her pad of paper.

"I'd like to do some gardening. Would you mind if I—"

"We have a gardener to attend to the hedges. You wouldn't be able to do it properly anyway, Anne; there's a real art to snipping them so they are straight and true."

"Oh, of course; I didn't mean that. I mean, I'd like to—fill a few pots with flowers and set them around, here and there."

Charity Wheelwright gave Anne a look she couldn't decipher. "Go ahead," she said.

That was sufficient encouragement for Anne. She asked to borrow the car, found her purse, and soon she was driving across the island to Bartlett's Farm. It was late in the season for planting, they told her, but they had a number of plants left, growing root bound in their terra-cotta pots. Anne went wild at the sight of so much color: vivid yellows, dreamy blues, explosive reds, cheerful whites. She got out her checkbook and loaded up the trunk of the car with daisies, geraniums, cornflowers, petunias, calendulas, black-eyed Susans, and, best of all, sunflowers, the pride of the Midwest. She bought wooden tubs and the largest terra-cotta pots she could find, and she bought bags and bags of potting soil.

Driving home, she found herself not just singing but absolutely bellowing out all the optimistic, hearty ballads she'd grown up singing during Girl Scout meetings or from a wagon piled with hay, drawn by horses, on the way to an autumn bonfire. "You Are My Sunshine," and "Daisy, Daisy, Give Me Your Answer, Do," and—for no reason except that it was so much fun to sing—"The Battle Hymn of the Republic." With a flourish, she brought the car to a halt on the gravel drive and set her purchases near the mudroom, because she knew Charity Wheelwright would not want the mess of potting inside her hedged garden.

She got a late start. It was almost dark, and she had to content herself with the time-consuming matter of giving all the plants plenty of water. Her mother-in-law did not possess a watering can, so

Anne found an old metal bucket, filled it at the outdoor spigot, and carried it to the flowers. By the time she'd soaked them all thoroughly, darkness had fallen, and suddenly she realized she'd missed the evening meal with her in-laws. In the kitchen, she washed her hands and prepared herself a plate of cold ham and potato salad, which she enjoyed with a glass of wine. Then, pleasantly exhausted, she brushed her hair and went into the living room to join Mr. and Mrs. Wheelwright by the large standing radio. They all listened to *Fibber McGee and Molly*, Jack Benny, and, finally, the last broadcast of the day's news.

The day's physical exertion had tired her, and for once she fell asleep easily, dreaming of sunny petals, emerald leaves. The next day she woke full of exuberance and plans. She pulled on her loose trousers, buttoned up a camp shirt, tied a scarf around her hair, and hurried downstairs and out the door, not bothering with breakfast or even coffee. All the plants waited for her, grouped together by the mudroom door, some of them already in bloom, others, like the sunflowers, still growing, their green stems and leaves vibrant in the sunlight.

She spent a good deal of time considering how she wanted to group them. All in one color massed together? But perhaps a mixture of colors would be more gay. She had never gardened before; she'd never had the interest. Her mother was her father's right-hand man at the stockyards and limited her gardening to paying a gardener who mowed their expansive lawn. Sometimes Anne's father sent his wife flowers, and then the heady fragrance of roses drifted through the house, and when they had dinner parties, guests often brought bouquets, and when they had buffet dinners or more formal parties, Anne's mother ordered elaborate arrangements for the table, but Anne had thought no more of those plants than of the vases holding them.

Now in full sunlight, she realized how very satisfying it was, working with flowers. The crumbling soil was warm and soft against the palms of her hands, and each plant appeared so singular, flowers and stems and delicate white angles of roots. She filled the terra-cotta tubs with soil, then carefully tucked in the plants, pressing the soil flat, ascertaining that the plants were standing happily on their own, not tipping sideways. She watered the flowers. Then she bent to heave the first tub up so she could carry it into the hedged garden. She was shocked at how heavy the tub was. She could lift it, but only by using all her strength, and carrying it was awkward.

She persevered. She stepped through the high arched opening cut into the privet hedge and stood for a moment on the slate path, surveying the interior of the hedged garden. Honestly, she thought, could her mother-in-law have been more boring? It was like standing inside a room with no roof and three high green walls, the fourth wall being the back of the house with its large windows. Near the house, on the slate patio area, a few deck chairs were set out, but that was the only sign of human habitation. Charity Wheelwright had decreed three long rectangles of privet, one inside the other, the outer wall eight feet high, the ones inside only four feet high, and, in the very center, a marble sundial. Slate of various colors, roses, grays, browns, had been painstakingly laid to be flat and even for walking around the hedges and into the center to observe the sundial. Somehow Anne's mother-in-law had contrived to make nature boring.

*Well,* Anne thought, *she would liven things up!* All morning she lugged the tubs and pots into the hedged garden, setting them here, and here, and here, wherever she saw a spot that cried out for brightening. As she worked, she hummed to herself, feeling very industrious and diligent. The war was over. Soon Herb would be coming home. She would get pregnant! She would walk around theses slates, holding her toddler's hand, and she would say, "See the pretty flower," and, "No, don't touch."

When she returned to Boston, she found Stangarone's Freight Company just as chaotically busy as ever. Gwendolyn Forsythe barely said hello before handing her a pile of bills of lading to be double-checked, noted, and filed. After work, she would join the other girls in the office for drinks and dinner and sometimes a movie: Abbott and Costello made them laugh, and *The Lost Weekend*, starring Ray Milland as an alcoholic on a four-day drinking binge, made them cry, and Bing Crosby made them happy, and John Wayne made them feel safe. The days flew by, and yet Anne was restless—and, she realized one morning, she was also oddly anxious. She couldn't figure out exactly what it was she was so worried about. The war was over. But she was full of dread.

At the end of August, Anne took a long weekend and traveled to Nantucket. It was Charity Wheelwright's birthday, and Anne knew she was expected to help celebrate the occasion. She bought an expensive set of Chanel perfume and talcum powder and wrapped it prettily and stashed it in her overnight bag. The ocean was as calm as a sheet of glass as the ferry trundled from Woods Hole to Nantucket, and the sun blazed high in the heavens. This is not such a terrible fate, she assured herself, to be forced to spend a long weekend on a beautiful island. Charity Wheelwright is not Satan, she reminded herself. However snotty and critical she was, she had raised Herb, and Herb was a wonderful man.

Norman Wheelwright met Anne at the ferry. He did not hug her; he wasn't that kind of man.

He did smile and extend his hand. "Welcome back, Anne." He picked up her overnight bag and carried it to the car.

As he drove home, he asked Anne for details about her work at Stangarone's. "It's kind of interesting," he said, "that Herb is in Germany, receiving supplies, and you're in Boston, helping send them."

It was one of the kindest things either of Herb's parents had ever said to Anne. It made her feel linked with Herb and accepted by his family.

"Yes, that's true. But I wish we were in the same spot. I miss Herb. I wish he'd come home."

"Well, we should be grateful he wasn't redeployed to the Pacific. And he's doing important work, Anne. Necessary work. They've got to maintain order in Germany. The fighting's over, but the world will never be the same as it was before."

Anne nodded, feeling not chastised but certainly sobered. She was being selfish, yearning for Herb this way, wanting him back *now*. But her life and certainly her marriage seemed to be on hold; she was treading water and all she had to show for it were the days of her life drifting past.

Norman Wheelwright turned off onto the long white gravel drive, and Anne's heart lifted. How odd, she thought, because nothing about her mother-in-law brought a song to her heart. It's my flowers! she realized. She couldn't wait to see all those beautiful, cheerful, fresh flower faces. Especially she longed to see the sunflowers, those flagpoles bearing bright banners of yellow. The moment the car stopped, she jumped out, raced across the gravel, and through the entrance in the hedge.

There was the patio, next to the house, shaded by the hedge walls. There were her pots and tubs—

Her hand flew to her bosom. The containers were just as she'd left them, but the plants in them were thin, unformed, and scraggly. She hurried from pot to pot, bending over, touching the thin, unhealthy leaves, searching for signs of petals and finding none. She stuck her fingers into each container. The soil was moist. But the flowers looked sickly, deprived, failing. Tears sprang to her eyes. What had she done wrong?

"You should have used plants meant for shade," a voice said.

Anne jumped. Turning, she saw Charity Wheelwright standing there, crisp in a pale blue dress and pearls, her hair tidily smoothed back into a chignon. She was smiling, just a little, and her expression was triumphant.

"Plants meant for shade?" Anne echoed.

"I thought you knew. You were so keen to garden. I thought you knew that many plants will not thrive in the constant shade of a hedged garden."

"No," Anne admitted sadly, "I didn't know that." She felt like a fool. Worse, she felt guilty—all those lovely plants, destined to struggle for the sun and not find it, and fall ill, fail, and flounder.

"Pity," Charity Wheelwright said. "All that work for nothing."

# Summer

# Eighteen

*Charlotte lounged* at the stern of Coop's catboat, her face lifted to the sky as she watched the light dwindle and the stars, one by one, twinkle on, as if someone up there were walking through the heavens, lighting them like candles. In the soft evening air, the harbor waters spread around them in a gleaming quilt of indigo, while fishing boats and sailboats sped toward the distant shore, stitching ivory lines through the water with their wakes.

It had been two weeks since Oliver's wedding, and for all that time the family had existed in peace. Their father had relented, giving Teddy another chance. Teddy had stayed sane and sober, driving off to work every morning, showered, shaved, and whistling, returning immediately after work for a swim or sail or to accompany Suzette as she waddled off for what Nona called "a constitutional" after dinner. When their father and the Bank Boys came down for a long weekend, Teddy remained respectful and polite, although on Sundays, his day off, he disappeared, driving Suzette around to show her the island and keeping out of his father's radar. Their mother also seemed to be avoiding Worth, but perhaps it only seemed that way. Helen was so busy with committee work.

"You look relaxed," Coop said. He was lazily

steering them back to his dock. He wore only swim trunks and an ancient pair of deck shoes that flopped open where the toes had worn through. The summer sun had bleached silver streaks in his blond hair, and Charlotte smiled, thinking how much a woman would have to pay a hair salon to get just that perfect effect. He was very tan, and his green eyes flashed like bright gems in his face.

"I am relaxed," Charlotte agreed. She wore her old one-piece black Speedo and flip-flops, and she'd pulled her hair back into a ponytail to get it off her face and out of the wind. This was the third time she'd sailed with Coop, and she knew by now that like most men he preferred to be in complete control of his boat. Sometimes people liked it if she moved to do something—change sides to balance the boat if it was heeling too much, or adjust the centerboard—of her own accord. But she had quickly seen that if Coop wanted her to help, he'd tell her. Her father was like that. She jokingly called him Captain Bligh.

As they glided toward Coop's house, Nona's house also came into view, with its ridiculous Ionic columns and unused front door. Lights were on in the living room and in some rooms on the second floor, and the light was on in Suzette and Teddy's room in the attic. From here, floating gently on the safe and increasingly shallow harbor waters, Nona's house looked blessed. Radiant.

Coop followed Charlotte's gaze. "How many of your relatives are there right now?"

Charlotte laughed. "The truth? I don't even know. The Bank Boys come and go all the time, and so does Mee."

"Man, I wish that woman would grow up and use her real name. I can't stand calling her *Mee.* Makes me think of a cartoon mouse. Or a little kid. It's not cute anymore, it's just embarrassing."

Charlotte chuckled. "Well, Coop, if you ask her out, I'm sure she'll change her name to anything you like."

Coop turned his glance to Charlotte and let his gaze linger on her. "It's not Mee I want to be with."

Charlotte felt herself flush, and she was grateful for the evening darkness that covered her. She supposed this could be considered their third date. Certainly it was the third time she'd spent an evening sailing with him, and now, as before, she was languorous with pleasure—although the icy gin and tonics Coop had brought in a cooler for their sail around the inner and outer harbor no doubt deepened her easy mood.

She stretched her arms wide. "Look at this night. Isn't this the most perfect night in the world? A soft breeze. Warm air. Calm water."

Coop dropped the mainsail and pulled up the centerboard. Jumping up, he walked carefully along the deck to the bow. He reached out, grabbed the buoy, and fastened the rope around it. His feet made solid thuds as he strode back to her side at the stern. "We can stay out here. But it's more comfortable inside."

Charlotte knew exactly what he meant by that, and she wanted to go inside with him. She wanted to press up against him, she wanted his mouth on hers.

Her heart knocked rapidly in her chest. "Coop, tell me about Miranda."

His body tensed. He looked toward the outer harbor, and took a deep breath. He hadn't yet spoken to Charlotte about Miranda. The first two times they'd gone sailing they had both behaved in an easy old-buddies friendship, but tonight something different was in the air.

"There's nothing to say about Miranda," Coop told her. "We dated, and now we're not together anymore. And we won't be together again."

"Why not?"

Coop shrugged. "We were never serious. She's a beautiful, fascinating woman, but we just don't have that much in common. I want to live full-time on Nantucket, and she doesn't. So I broke up with her."

Charlotte frowned as his words conflicted with her memory of the conversation she'd overheard. *I thought Miranda broke it off,* she almost said. *I heard you two arguing one day, and Miranda was in a fury because you'd slept with someone else during the winter.* Oh, don't be such a nitpicking priss, Charlotte ordered herself. After all, she had overheard only part of what was obviously an ongoing and complicated disagreement.

"Come on." Coop held out his hand. "Let's go ashore."

Charlotte took his hand. He steadied her as she dropped over the side of the boat into the cool thigh-high water. He grabbed the cooler, jumped over the side, and together they waded to dry land. They walked up the sandy beach, through the low wild bushes, across his lawn, and onto his patio. He set the cooler on a low table and turned to Charlotte.

"Will you come in tonight?"

He was standing very close to her, his arms at his side. He wasn't touching her, but the attraction between them was intense. The last two times he'd taken her sailing, she had gone right home after the sail, but tonight she wanted to enter his house.

"Coop." Her voice was shaking. "I'm not—I haven't been with a man for a long time. *Months.* Okay, three years. I'm kind of old-fashioned, I guess. I'm not asking for a commitment or any-thing, I just want you to know. . . ."

Coop lifted his hand and gently touched her cheek. "We'll go as slow as you want, Charlotte."

"But I mean—" How did people talk about this? It was so awkward! Moving away from him, she leaned on the back of a lawn chair, feeling a bit more in charge with the chair between her and

Coop's extraordinary magnetism. "I heard you were—seeing—someone else, too. This winter." *A slut, actually,* she wanted to say. *Miranda called her a slut, and that kind of scares me.* But she didn't want to let him know she'd overheard their argument.

Coop grinned. "Well, Charlotte, I did *see* another woman this winter. Saw several, in fact. But I'm not seeing her anymore. I'm not seeing anyone else. And I'm capable of being monogamous, if that's what you're asking. For the right woman, I could be monogamous. And if you're worried about STDs, I've got a report in the house. I usually get tested every six months. Want to see it?"

"Oh, dear." Charlotte tried to laugh, but her voice was shaking. "Here we are on this beautiful soft night with the moon and stars, and I'm asking about STDs. I'm sorry, Coop. This is so unromantic."

"Come inside, Charlotte," Coop said. "I think I can get you in a romantic mood pretty fast."

*Charlotte sat up* with a gasp, her heart pounding as if she were in danger. Looking around, she realized she was in a strange room, and then she heard Coop's rumbling snore and fell back against her pillows, smiling at herself. She glanced at the clock on the bedside table: 4:29. Good for you, she told her brain. She was glad she was so used to waking at this time that she did it without an alarm clock, but she wasn't very pleased about waking in a fright. It had been three years since she'd slept anywhere except her bed in her parents' home in Boston or her sweet private attic room at Nona's, but that was no reason to get neurotic.

She'd certainly fallen asleep easily enough.

She and Coop had made love—he was slow and gentle with her as he'd promised. Afterward, he'd served her pancakes and bacon, they'd gone back to bed and made love again, and sometime around midnight they'd fallen asleep. Coop was still sleeping, lying on his stomach, spread-eagled over the mattress, his pillow pulled over his head. Maybe she snored, too, Charlotte thought with a grin, and that wasn't a habit but a way to shut out sounds.

Morning light was beginning to illuminate the room. She had to get up, get dressed, and get out to her garden. She could tell it was going to be another hot day, and she didn't want to have to labor in the afternoon blaze. She scanned the floor, searching for her Speedo. Rex and Regina, his fat old labs, lay on their sides, snuffling and grunting, deeply asleep. Discarded clothing lay in heaps and mounds all around the room, and she remembered from last night how gritty the floor was with sand, and the sheets, as well. He had a cleaning woman in once a week, Coop told her, and she dealt with the laundry, putting clean sheets on the bed, and so on. Sandy sheets didn't bother him. Not much bothered him, Charlotte decided. The kitchen counters were piled with dishes and pots and pans waiting to be washed, and his living room was littered with CDs, DVDs, and video games, newspapers, and magazines.

Stepping quietly, Charlotte slipped from the bed, grabbed up her Speedo, and with a look over her shoulder, left the room. Coop continued to snore. She pulled on her bathing suit in the kitchen and looked around for a paper and pen. She settled for the side of a brown grocery bag and a fat marker.

She wrote: *I had a wonderful time.* She thought of adding: *I'll be in my garden,* but he knew that. He'd find her if he wanted to. She put the note on the table, weighted it down with the salt and pepper shakers, opened the sliding glass door to the patio, and stepped out into the morning.

She took a moment just to be in the day. Her body felt well used and content, like a racehorse that had been corralled for too long and finally allowed to run free. She wasn't tired, even though she'd gotten so little sleep.

A small forest of evergreens and brush divided Coop's land from Nona's, giving them both privacy. Charlotte walked down to the beach, across to Nona's beach, and up to her house. The mudroom door was unlocked. Doors were never locked on the island, there was no need. As quietly as she could, she hurried up to the attic, showered and shampooed her hair, and dressed. She went back down to the kitchen, poured herself a glass of orange juice, and drank it down, savoring the sweet brightness. Then she went out to her garden to make bouquets.

All around her, the world glowed with the freshness of morning. With each passing day, she understood that her self-imposed exile had turned into a kind of blessing. She loved her garden; she loved the work of it. As for romance—*love*—whatever she had going on with Coop was only lighthearted, nothing serious. She believed she could allow herself this much pleasure.

*By eight o'clock,* she was starving. The farm stand was always busy in July, so she left Jorge in charge and ran back to the house to grab a bite of nourishment. Jorge was a hard worker, but his English was difficult to understand and he often replied to any statement by smiling, nodding his head, and saying, lispily, "Yes." She decided to fill a thermos with orange juice and grab some of the oatmeal cookies Glorious had made.

She didn't bother to stop to unlace her boots. She was in a hurry, and the ground was dry today, she wouldn't track in mud. The only person in the kitchen was Suzette, just sitting at the table, her feet propped up on a chair.

"Good morning!" Charlotte pealed brightly.

"Morning." Suzette risked a quick glance at her.

"I saw Teddy drive off to work," Charlotte

observed, as she leaned into the refrigerator. "And I guess Mom and Aunt Grace and Mandy are taking the little ones to the yacht club for swimming and sailing. Are you going with them?"

Suzette shrugged. "I guess."

Impulsively, Charlotte said, "Suzette, are you bored?"

Suzette didn't speak. She just looked apprehensive and trapped.

"For heaven's sake, that was not a pass/fail question! I'm not criticizing you. I'm just honestly curious. You don't seem to read, and I'll bet you aren't swimming, and I can tell you haven't been learning to play tennis." She plopped down in a chair across from Suzette. "Tell me. Have you ever had a job?"

Suzette lifted her chin defiantly. "Of course. I waitressed for a while. And I worked at Donny's Coffee in Tucson. It's like Starbucks, only better."

Charlotte squinted at Suzette as an idea hit her. "So you can make change. You can deal with money." She grinned. "Suzette, want to try working for me? You could run my farm stand."

Suzette's face brightened. "Will you pay me?"

"Absolutely. Ten dollars an hour. And I'll take a chair out there so you're off your feet." Charlotte jumped up. "Come on."

*The day went* much more smoothly with someone at the farm stand. Charlotte made her deliveries to the three restaurants she supplied and still had time to weed and plant more lettuce. At six, Jorge's buddies clattered up in their ancient Chevy, Jorge went off, and Charlotte walked up to the farm stand to close it for the day.

"How did we do?" she asked Suzette.

"Damn, I can't believe how much people spend on a head of lettuce. And the flowers! Are these people crazy?"

Charlotte laughed. She'd never seen Suzette so animated. "Not crazy, Suzette, just very very rich and insisting on the best. You know, if I tried to sell that pot of asters and daisies for seven dollars, no one would buy it. But with some wildflowers and beach grass cleverly added, it's a real Nantucket arrangement, and at seventy dollars they snap it up."

"That's just wrong."

"No, Suzette, that's just the way it is. Besides, the vegetables are worth it. My farm is organic, and that means people aren't eating pesticides and fungicides along with my produce." As she talked, she picked up the cash from the basket, thumbed through it, and stuck it in her money belt. She saw Suzette watching her. "I'll bet you'd like to be paid right now."

Suzette just looked expectant.

"Seven hours, right?" Charlotte peeled off seventy dollars and handed over the money.

"Thank you." Suzette stared down at the money with an expression close to awe.

"Would you like to work again tomorrow?" Charlotte asked.

"Could I?" Suzette looked at Charlotte with such hope that suddenly the sullenness that had informed her features vanished, and she was pretty and cheerful and young.

"Suzette, you can work as much as you want," Charlotte told her. "This is my busy season, and things will be crazy until November. I can use you in bits and pieces like today, but I'd prefer to use you regularly, and put you on the payroll, and pay you as part-time agricultural help like I pay Jorge. That means you might have to pay taxes on what you earn, but since you're starting so late in the year, and since Teddy hasn't been working a lot, your annual income will be so low you two probably won't owe the IRS anything." She smiled. "Unless Teddy was raking in the dough out there in Tucson."

"I'd like to work regularly," Suzette said eagerly. She was almost animated. She gestured to the farm stand. "This wasn't really working, anyway. I mean, a lot of the time I was just sitting there; are you sure you want to pay me for it? I mean, I'm getting free room and board from your grandmother."

"Beach Grass Garden is independent of that. And if you're afraid you're not working hard enough, don't worry. I'll find more for you to do. For example, I close the farm stand around six—

people come by early in the day for fresh produce for dinner that night. If it's rained all day or I'm backed up, I spend some of the evening hours out in the shed, potting and arranging flower vases for the next morning."

Suzette smiled. "Oh, I'd love to do that!"

"Then we'll do it." Charlotte almost linked her arm through the young woman's but had second thoughts—she didn't want to startle her, and she didn't want to be too friendly, either. It was possible that Suzette would turn out to be slow, or sloppy, or unreliable. If she didn't turn out to be right for Beach Grass Garden, Charlotte still wanted to be able to establish a relationship with her as a family member—the mother of an expected niece or nephew.

Suzette smoothed the money with her hands. She said, "I'll be able to buy some things for my baby."

"Oh, Suzette!" Charlotte's heart twinged. "I'm sure Mom's dying to take you shopping for baby things."

"I guess. But still. It will be nice to buy something for my baby from *me.*"

"I get you completely," Charlotte said. "Let's go have dinner, then maybe we can work in the shed for a while."

*Coop had phoned* Charlotte that morning, when he woke up. His voice was warm and lazy; he admitted he was still in bed. He had made plans to go over to the separate and smaller island called Tuckernuck for a couple of days with an old friend, an old *male* friend, he hastened to add. He suggested they have a real date night Saturday; he wanted to take her out to dinner and perhaps to one of the local theater productions.

*Over the next* few days, Charlotte worked in the garden, and Suzette proved to be a quick and willing assistant. The thought crossed her mind that Suzette might be trying to prove herself in some way, to Charlotte and to the entire family, and she was very pleased by the idea of providing a way to impress the family.

Still, she should be careful. She didn't want to work pregnant Suzette too hard. Early one afternoon she showed Suzette how to use the Dutch hoe to slice off the weeds at ground level, carefully, without disturbing the plants.

"Are you sure you want to work outside in this heat?" she asked.

"This heat? This heat is nothing," Suzette told her, bragging slightly. "I grew up in Arizona. It reaches one hundred degrees and more in the summer. This is just a spring day for me."

The third evening, after they'd finished dinner, Charlotte and Suzette went out to the shed to prepare the flower vases for sale the next morning. They worked side by side, companionably, in silence, except for Charlotte's occasional suggestion or Suzette's question. Suzette learned quickly and had a knack for arranging flowers in unusual combinations. She focused intensely on her work, and Charlotte noticed with amusement how the young woman sucked her upper lip down with her lower teeth as she concentrated.

The door to the shed opened, and Teddy strolled in. "Hey, ladies." He'd changed out of the light linen Brooks Brothers blazer he wore to work at the antiques shop and wore only his swim trunks with a T-shirt. "So," he said to Charlotte, "I see you've turned my wife into a little factory girl."

Charlotte snorted. "Factory? Hardly." She gestured with her hands. The shed was full of flowers, picked fresh that evening and sitting in buckets of water while they waited to be arranged. The air was sweet and warm and moist.

"Stop it, Teddy," Suzette said, tossing him a glance. "I told you how much I like this work. Don't be a pest."

Teddy put his palms on the worktable and levered himself up to sit on it, swinging his legs like a kid at a playground. "Yeah, Char. Suzette told me how much you get for your little posies. Highway robbery!"

Charlotte didn't deign to look at him. "Right, and you know this because you buy so many flower arrangements here."

"I don't need to buy flowers," Teddy argued. "You fill Nona's house with yours."

311

"And this is a problem for you?"

Teddy backed down. "Of course not. They're great. But I'm saving my money so I can find a place for the two of us to live—well, the three of us, pretty soon."

"Do you want to stay on the island?" Charlotte asked, as she placed three hydrangea blooms in dreamy hues of periwinkle and sky blue into a milk white pitcher.

"No, thanks," Teddy said. "I prefer the warmth of the Southwest to the chill of the Northeast."

"I like it here," Suzette announced.

Both Teddy and Charlotte stared at the young woman in surprise.

"I thought you'd hate it," Teddy said.

Suzette snorted. "Is that why you brought me here?"

"I brought you here to meet my family. The entire snot-nosed perfect lot."

"I don't think Charlotte's so perfect!" Suzette shot back. She looked over at Charlotte, her face red. "Sorry. I meant that as a compliment."

"I take it as a compliment," Charlotte told her.

Suzette continued to arrange wild sweet everlasting from Nona's uncultivated moors in a vase with daisies and phlox. "I keep telling you, Teddy, you go through the world with expectations that are much too high. That's why you're always disappointed. Plus you always think the way anyone *is* is directly aimed at you."

Charlotte forced herself to stop staring. Suzette was speaking, entire sentences! And she was right. She had Teddy down cold.

Teddy sounded childish as he told Charlotte, "Whereas Suzette has *no* expectations."

"That's right!" Suzette agreed. "I am no one from nowhere. And I'm grateful for every day that I'm not drunk or living with a drunk."

During the long moment of silence that followed, Charlotte looked from Teddy to Suzette and back again, stunned by the intensity of their mutual gaze and by the current of love flowing between them. They were clearly meant for each other, and they were clearly bound to each other, perhaps by secrets and secret needs and humiliations and mistakes, but also by affection and a kind of acceptance Charlotte thought she'd experienced only with Nona. Her parents were too—not judgmental but *hopeful.* They were so proud of their children, their handsome, brilliant, capable, superior children, and with that pride came the belief that these children could win the tennis match, and the sailboat race, and get into the best boarding schools and colleges, and marry the best people, and live exemplary lives.

Teddy said to his wife, "You're trembling."

"Well, I'm mad," Suzette told him.

Charlotte spoke up. "You're probably tired, too. I know I am. Why don't you go put your feet up, Suzette. I'll finish in here."

"Okay. Thanks." Suzette washed her hands, and as she dried them she said to Charlotte, "Don't worry because Teddy and I fought. We fight all the time." Then Teddy put his arm around his wife's shoulders and ushered her out the door, into the summer night.

## Nineteen

*O*n a Thursday afternoon in the middle of August, Helen sat on a folding chair at a long table in the church basement, trying not to yawn in the stifling air. The committee for the annual church fair, which would be held the last week in August, was gathered for its final meeting. Most of the business had been concluded, but Bridget Houghton, the chairperson, continued to twitter on, bustling and self-important, like a fat robin rear-ranging all the twigs in an already perfectly fine nest. Helen looked across the table at her friend Phyllis Lowry. Phyllis rolled her eyes and Helen grinned. She had long ago surrendered to the eccentric power that was created by a dozen good-willed individuals and transformed by the presence of a table and a set of minutes into a creature called the Committee, with all its rambling, disjointed parts, like a centipede wearing different shoes on each foot.

The Wheelwright family gave a substantial amount to charity each year, but Helen believed the slogan Think Globally, Act Locally. She could not change the world. She could, however, change a few moments, a few conditions, in a few individual lives. In Boston, two evenings a week, she tutored English as a Second Language students at the local library, and she was on the library committee that held fund-raisers to pay for, among other things, the use of electricity and space for tutoring. Here on the island, she'd been co-chair of the July book sale, and it had done well this year. She was also in charge of the church fair's quilt committee. Every year, sixteen women each needlepointed a square designed by a local artist and then stitched them together to form a wall hanging of real and original beauty. Helen organized the women who made the quilt, and the women who sat on Main Street in Nantucket to sell raffle tickets to win the quilt, and the ticket drawing on the day of the church fair. Perhaps the money helped repair the toilets in the basement, or bought new hymnals, or supplied Christmas trees and turkeys to impoverished citizens. Whatever it was for, it was *something*. If it could provide a moment of grace in someone's life, she was glad to do it.

And of course it helped keep her mind off Worth and Sweet Cakes.

Finally, the meeting was adjourned. The room emptied gradually, and Helen joined Phyllis to walk out into the sunshine. The late afternoon was hot and humid and bright and still. Helen realized she was looking forward to returning to Nona's house and kicking off her shoes, perhaps taking a little swim before dinner.

For over a month now, the Wheelwright household had clicked along like a reliable clock. The Bank Boys had come and gone, spending weekends on the island, sailing and playing tennis and dining with friends. Nona's health had improved, probably because she spent most days in her garden, a book in her lap, pretending to read but really taking frequent and delicious catnaps. Teddy had stayed sober and begun to share details of his workday with the family at dinner. He was discovering that he liked antiques and had just the kind of personality needed to charm a reluctant buyer into making a purchase. He'd already been given a raise and the promise of a bonus at the end of the year, if he would stay on.

Suzette had brightened up, too. Charlotte was teaching her about garden vegetables and flowers, and every night now when they sat down at the dining room table, Charlotte pointed out a new arrangement of flowers done by Suzette. She did seem to have an artistic flair. With her straw tabby-cat hair growing out into its genuine silky light brown, and her skin glowing from work in the sun, Suzanne looked quite pretty. And she was happy. It was wonderful, how happiness could change a face.

Lost in her thoughts, Helen didn't catch what Phyllis was saying. "Sorry, what?"

"I asked whether Charlotte's still dating Bill Cooper," Phyllis said.

"Oh, groan." Helen shook her head ruefully as they continued along the sidewalk beneath the shade of the tall maples. "She is. I think they're serious. She spends a lot of her free time with him, and she's brought him in for dinner several times. He's attractive, I'll grant you that. Is Whit still seeing Fiona?"

"He is. Oh, dear, too bad." Phyllis laughed. "Remember when the kids were adolescents? We used to say that if they became adults and weren't in jail or dead, we would be happy." She stopped next to her ancient station wagon. "Here's me. I need to rush. I've got to get to the grocery store."

Helen and Phyllis kissed goodbye. Helen walked on down the quiet one-way street to her father-in-law's antique Chrysler convertible. Teddy was driving Nona's old Jeep to and from work, which left Helen with the convertible. She didn't mind. The handsome old heirloom had deep soft seats and a luxurious, stately ride. She drove home, savoring the trip, idly thinking about what there was for dinner that night. She hoped Grace and her gang realized that the vegetables Charlotte provided for their evening meals were not only delicious and nutritious, they also saved a lot of driving around to the other island farm stands for fresh produce. But hoping that Grace and her family would ever say anything positive about Charlotte's garden was a waste of time. It still made them uneasy. It made them think that Nona was favoring Charlotte. Families, Helen thought with a sniff of disdain. They must have been designed by a committee.

As she drove along the winding road, she felt almost young again. It was fun to drive her father-in-law's classic convertible, with the sun beating down on her shoulders. She'd tied a scarf around her hair and a light breeze whipped it around her face, making her feel a little like Audrey Hepburn in one of those blithe black-and-white movies. Well, she wasn't young and beautiful, and her life was not a romantic comedy, but still she was fortunate. Her children were happy and safe.

She hadn't decided what to do about Worth. She didn't see him often. He was away at work during the week, and when he arrived with the other Bank Boys on Friday afternoon, or sometimes Thursday evening, he wanted only to get out in his catboat and sail or play a round of golf with Lew Lowry and Kellogg and their friends. Almost every night there was a dinner party, or a dance, or cocktails at a friend's house, or a benefit for one of the island's many worthy organizations: the library, the hospital, the conservation group, the science museum. Since the night before Oliver's wedding, Worth had not come to Helen's bed and she hadn't gone to his. But she slept well. She realized that thirty years ago, even twenty, she would have flown at him in a jealous rage the moment she heard him talking love talk to another woman, she would have dragged her nails down his face, she would have thrown vases and broken windows, and she would have gone out and slept with every man she knew. She didn't know why she hadn't done any of that now. It was not simply a matter of having less energy. It was not that she didn't care; when she thought about her husband with another woman, it hurt so terribly it took her breath away. So she did her best not to think about it, but she felt her anger building inside her like a storm.

She had arrived at the long gravel drive leading from the main road to the waterfront and Nona's house. As she turned, she slowed, and waved at Suzette, who was at the farm stand, chatting with a customer as she filled a brown paper bag with lettuces and tomatoes. Suzette was hugely pregnant now, so full-bellied that Helen wondered if perhaps the young woman had gotten her dates wrong. Suzette looked as if she could go into labor any day.

They were pretty much prepared, Helen thought. There was plenty of baby furniture in the house—a cradle, a change table, a high chair, and so on, but Mellie had laid claim to them in no uncertain terms. "These are Wheelwright baby things, and at least we know my baby is a Wheelwright!" Mellie had hissed when Helen brought up the subject of the furniture. Mellie was going to have her baby in a hospital in Boston and wouldn't be using the furniture for weeks, if she came back to the island at all, but Helen didn't argue. She, Suzette, Teddy, and Charlotte went into Marine Home Furniture and indulged in an orgy of shopping: a crib, blankets, baby towels, paper diapers, and many unnecessary stuffed animals. Teddy had carried everything up to the third floor, for even though Helen had protested that Suzette wouldn't feel like climbing so many stairs after having a baby and should move to the second floor, Teddy and Suzette herself had insisted they preferred it up there. That way, Suzette said, her crying baby wouldn't wake everyone else in the house—only Charlotte, who said she slept like a log.

Helen carefully steered the convertible into its spot at the end of the gravel drive—on the far side, where no other vehicle might scratch it—gathered up her purse and book bag full of committee papers, and walked beneath the arch in the hedge into the garden.

Gathered on the shady patio was a small party—it only took a few members of the Wheelwright family to look like a party—Worth, Kellogg and Grace, Mandy and Claus, and Nona, snuggled in her wicker rocker and looking at her family with affection and happiness. Christian knelt on the slates by the far wall of hedge, running a model dump truck into the mulch and making growling noises. Baby Zoe lay nestled in her bouncy chair, watching everyone with bright eyes.

"You're all here already!" Helen said. Automatically she went to Worth and pecked a kiss on his cheek. She always did this when Worth arrived; she'd done it for the thirty-one years of their marriage, and it was expected. She kissed Nona's cheek, too.

Worth was still in his work clothes, although he'd discarded his suit jacket and rolled up his shirtsleeves, as had Kellogg and Claus. "The city is steaming. The air conditioners can't keep up. It was too muggy to think."

"Come on, Worth," Kellogg said to his brother-in-law. "You just wanted to arrive in time for a sail."

Worth grinned. "True. It's supposed to turn stormy this weekend, and I want to get in a sail while I can. Anyone want to join me?"

"I do," Kellogg said.

"Me, too," said Claus.

"I've got to get the kiddies fed and bathed," Mandy said.

Helen said, "I'm going to see if Glorious needs help pulling dinner together. Shall we say around nine?"

The men went off to change into swim trunks, then walked down to the shore, waded out into the water, hoisted themselves onto the boat, and set sail. Helen went to her porch, changed out of her committee clothes into a T-shirt, sarong, and flip-flops, and went down to the kitchen to confer with Glorious.

"I've got all the potatoes and salad I need," Glorious told her, "but I only have enough chicken for four or five people. I could thaw a frozen one—"

"I'll just zip back into town and get some fresh fish," Helen told her. "We haven't had any for a while."

"Oh, Helen," Glorious said, "you don't want to be making that long drive again."

Helen grinned. "I'm driving the convertible, remember? Teddy's got the old Jeep. Want to come with me?"

Glorious started to shake her head and then smiled. "You know, I think I will. It would be nice to get out in a breeze."

*Helen loved being* with Glorious. The young Jamaican woman seemed to think that everything about the Wheelwrights was humorous, and she was tender and patient with Nona. Glorious was engaged to a Jamaican man who worked as a carpenter on the island. They were in no hurry to get married, but then Glorious didn't seem to be in a hurry about anything.

As they drove the beautiful old convertible in to town, Helen turned on the radio, which still, amazingly, worked, and they listened to Ella Fitzgerald singing jazz, which was perfect for this summer evening. They went to Sayle's and conferred about whether to buy cod, halibut, or sole, chose the cod, and carried their purchase, wrapped tidily in white paper, out into the evening. The road back was narrow and winding. In summer the traffic moved like molasses, and sometimes this irritated Helen, but tonight with the soft music and the soft air and Glorious's easy companionship, she relaxed and enjoyed the drive.

They were almost home when they noticed the car in front of them swerving back and forth over the road, and with an electrifying shock of fear Helen realized that it was Nona's old Jeep. Of course, the island was crowded with old hunter-green Jeeps, but this vehicle had a row of Trustees of Reservations stickers on the back bumper. Helen was sure Teddy was driving.

"Oh, no," Helen breathed. "That's Teddy. And I think he's drunk."

As she spoke, an SUV rolled around a curve from the opposite direction, and even though the Jeep was quickly corrected and aimed for the right side of the road, the driver of the SUV laid on his horn, filling the gentle night with its piercing blare, then leaned out his window and yelled, "What the hell is wrong with you?"

"Dear God, dear God," Helen prayed aloud.

"We're almost home," Glorious said reassuringly. Reaching out, she patted Helen's hand, clenched white on the steering wheel.

They rounded the final curve, and Nona's white gravel drive came into view. As they watched, Teddy made the turn, but he was going too fast, and he steered too sharply to the left. With a shriek from the tires as he slammed on the brakes, the Jeep hurtled across the road, rammed the old farm-stand table up onto its bumper, and plowed into the trunk of an ancient pine tree. The bang of impact was loud.

Helen steered the convertible onto the drive, switched off the ignition, and jumped out. The Jeep had come to a stop with its nose smashed against the tree trunk. The hood was buckled and steam hissed from the radiator, spiraling up into the air.

Helen ran around to the driver's side. "Teddy?"

The driver's door opened and Teddy stumbled out with a big grin on his face. He held up his arms like an athlete who'd just performed an astonishing feat, as if expecting applause. "Ta-da!"

Helen reached out to steady him. "Teddy, are you all right?"

"I'm fine, Mom, be cool." He didn't have so much as a cut or a bump on his head.

"Be *cool?*" Seeing her youngest child completely intact sent shock waves of relief through her, and then all at once she wanted to shake him. "Teddy, you're *drunk!* You just wrecked the Jeep!"

Even in her frantic state, she realized exactly where the accident had taken place. "Teddy, look where you are!"

Teddy staggered, held out his arms, and gave a bewildered smile. "I'm here, I'm not injured, and no one was hurt. Don't be so dramatic."

"Oh, Teddy," Helen said, and began to cry. "Look, for God's sake! You've smashed up Charlotte's farm stand. Thank God they've already closed up for the day. Fifteen minutes earlier, and you might have hit your own wife!"

Her words seemed to sober Teddy slightly. Then a familiar stubbornness possessed his features. "But the farm stand is closed!" he argued.

Helen felt an arm around her. "It's okay, Helen," Glorious said.

Helen breathed out, trying to expel her fear and anger. "Teddy, we're going to drive to the house. You can walk. It might sober you up a little. And while you're walking, you can think of what you're going to say to your father."

When they got to the house, Glorious went on into the kitchen with the package of fresh fish. Nona was in the den, dozing in front of the television set. Helen looked out the window and saw the catboat just returning to the dock. Charlotte and Suzette were in the living room, talking with Grace about their day in the garden. When she went upstairs, she heard Mandy singing a lullaby to Christian, and for a moment Helen just leaned against the wall, remembering the days when she could tuck her children lovingly into bed, knowing they were safe.

She went into the sleeping porch, shut the door, and sank onto the daybed, holding her head in her hands. Her headache was back. It had been a long time since she had suffered from one, but this was intense. She didn't need a psychiatrist to tell her that she was anxious, not just about Teddy and his drinking but about her husband's reaction. She had read books and attended meetings and talked to other parents about tough love, but she still didn't know what to do. How did anyone ever know what the right thing was to do? Did Teddy drink because his father was so judgmental? Or was his father so judgmental because Teddy drank? Or was something slightly awry with his body chemistry? Everyone else in the family could handle alcohol. But there were no easy answers, and right now her concern was for Teddy's wife and her unborn child.

When would be the best time to tell Worth about Teddy's newest escapade, before dinner? After dinner? Should she let Worth fix himself a nice relaxing alcoholic drink first? She had been in this situation more times than she could remember over the past few years, and she knew she would leave Teddy to face his father by himself, if she weren't so afraid of how it would affect Teddy's wife.

She went into the bathroom, splashed water on her face, smoothed her tousled hair, and went downstairs and into the kitchen where Teddy sat at the table, drinking a cup of coffee while Glorious stood at the counter, slicing vegetables.

"Let's go into the den," she said to Teddy.

Teddy squirmed. "Nona's in there." The coffee seemed to have sobered him up.

"Well, your grandmother needs to know you've wrecked her Jeep," Helen told him. "Would you rather go into the living room with your Aunt Grace and Uncle Kellogg?" Without waiting for an answer, Helen said, "Glorious, if Suzette comes down, will you please tell her to come into the den? And give us about thirty minutes before you start dinner."

"You got it," Glorious replied easily.

Just then Worth and Kellogg came into the kitchen from the mudroom. Worth's hair was windblown, and the tan on his nose and cheeks had been burnished with fresh sun, giving him a healthy glow. He looked relaxed and happy.

"Worth, could you come into the den for a minute?" Helen asked. "We need to talk." She kept her voice as pleasant as possible, but even she could hear the tension tightening her tone.

Worth frowned, puzzled. "Sure."

In the dark den, the television set droned out the evening news. Nona was asleep. Helen walked to the other end of the room, where a complicated jigsaw puzzle had been laid out on the long refectory table a few days ago when it was raining.

"Teddy has something to tell you," Helen said.

Worth looked wary. "Why do I think I'm not going to like this?"

Teddy lifted his chin defiantly and pasted a cocky look on his face, but Helen could see how his fists were clenched by his side. "Dad, I wrecked the Jeep."

"Because you were drunk?"

"Yes, I was drunk. A little bit. But let me tell you why I was celebrating! I sold a nineteenth-century oil painting for ten thousand dollars! George had been trying to get rid of the old albatross for years, and I convinced the buyers that it was a masterpiece. By the time I was through sweet-talking them, they were so thrilled to possess it that they insisted on buying a few bottles of champagne and bringing them back to the shop. We drank them in the store in some Waterford crystal that I gave them as a little gift. What was I supposed to do, say, Sorry, I can't drink with you? George was there too, and after the buyers left he did everything except dance with me, he was so pleased. So it's not like I was staggering around in some dirty alley drinking a pint bottle of rotgut."

"Bottom line, Teddy, you were drunk." Worth ran his hands through his hair. He looked somber. He looked sad.

"You have to tell him the rest," Helen said to her son.

"The rest?" Worth's face darkened.

Teddy stuck his hands in the back pockets of his chinos and looked down at the floor. He looked like a little boy kicking rocks as he muttered, "I wrecked the Jeep when I ran into a tree. It just crumpled the hood, it's not totaled, and I'll pay to get it fixed."

"Did you hurt yourself?"

"No." Teddy's voice trembled slightly. "But Mom's freaked out because the tree is at the end of our driveway right where the farm stand usually is. I kind of smashed up Charlotte's old table."

"Yes, well, that freaks me out, too," Worth said, and now he was angry. He paced a few steps, turned, and paced back. "Teddy, we have been through all this before, too many times. When you got drunk at your brother's wedding, I wanted to toss you out of the house then. It's not that I don't love you. You know I love you; that's not the issue. The issue is that you're an alcoholic, and as long as your mother and I allow you to remain under our roof, we're abetting you in your drinking. We've given you second chances, we've given you third, fourth, and fifth chances, you can't say we haven't, and every time you disappoint us. And now you've upped the ante. Jesus Christ, what if you'd hit Charlotte—"

"But Dad, I *didn't!*" Teddy cried out.

"You were driving drunk." Worth's voice was icy with rage. "Teddy, you were driving drunk. You could have killed someone. That is not acceptable. That is not forgivable. We've put up with you *being* drunk, but I will not put up with you *driving* drunk. You are never driving a vehicle belonging to this house again. I want you out. I want you and that—and *Suzette* out. I want you gone. I want you both off the island."

"Worth." Helen put out her hand to intercede.

Worth's head whipped around as he looked at her. "You talked me out of this last time, Helen, and look what happened. Teddy hasn't gotten better. He's gotten worse."

"Worth, Suzette is going to have a baby. She's pregnant, she's vulnerable, she's in no state to travel. And Teddy has a job. It's been six weeks since he had a drink. You've *got* to give him another chance. You can't throw him out, not now."

Worth glared at Helen, grinding his teeth, breathing like a bull faced with a red flag. "Helen. Are you going to protect this boy forever? You need to face the facts. Teddy is a drunk, and he hasn't changed, he is not changing, he's not capable of changing. The woman he brought with him may or not be his legal wife, and that baby you're so excited about is probably not even Teddy's child. You and I have spent years forgiving Teddy and giving him more chances, and every single time he disappoints us. We have talked to counselors. We have gone to meetings. You know their advice. Teddy has to take responsibility." He leaned on the end of the long table: imperious, a corporate director giving orders. Seeing Helen's tears, he softened. "Look. I'll give Teddy some money. He can go somewhere and start over. But he is leaving this house tonight and taking that woman with him." He crossed his arms over his chest, adamant. "I am not changing my mind this time."

Helen hadn't planned her next words. She was even surprised at herself when she spoke. She was surprised at how calm she sounded, too. "Well, Worth, I think you should consider this decision carefully. I think you should try to be a bit more compassionate. Your son has a weakness for alcohol, that's true. But many people are weak, and many people make mistakes. Some people, for example, have a weakness for *sweet cakes*. Some people indulge in too many *sweet cakes—and find they've lost everything.*"

Worth blinked; then he went very still, as if his anger were now an icy emanation that froze him. Teddy gawked at Helen as if she had gone mad.

"Teddy is improving," Helen continued, her voice softening. "Suzette is a good influence on him. He's holding down a job, he's worked reliably for weeks now, but I agree something has to be done about this latest incident. Drunk driving is a serious matter. But he and Suzette shouldn't be forced to leave Nona's house. And it is Nona's house, Worth. It's not yours."

Worth took a deep breath. "Helen—"

"Worth." She cut in before he could say another word. "Really, Worth, think about it. If you, for example, got really fat, and ill, maybe with diabetes, which is a result of enjoying too many *sweet cakes,* wouldn't you expect me to forgive you? Wouldn't you expect your children—Oliver and Charlotte and Teddy—to forgive you?"

For a few moments, the only sounds in the room came from the television set. Teddy's eyes went back and forth between his parents; he looked bewildered.

Worth looked confused and caged, as if anything he said would cause a trapdoor to open beneath him, and drop him into a void.

Kellogg wandered into the room, freshly showered, carrying an icy gin and tonic. "What are you all doing in here?"

"Family conference," Helen said.

"It's over," Worth decreed. "I'm going up to shower." He strode from the room without another word.

Teddy asked, "What was *that* all about, Mom?"

It wasn't so very often that Helen got the upper hand in an argument with her husband, and she was stunned and also kind of high on the experience. Her headache was completely gone and her vision seemed crystal clear.

Calmly, she said to her son, "It was about giving you another chance, Teddy. Now listen. I'm going to drive you in to work and pick you up every evening, just as if you were a child. It's humiliating and it will be a drag for me, but I am just as horrified as your father is that you drove drunk. I'm going upstairs now, and I want you to drink more coffee, and call a tow service, and arrange to have the Jeep repaired, and I want you to pay for it out of your own earnings. Do you understand?"

Teddy nodded. He looked properly chastened, but Teddy was always a good actor.

Kellogg said, "Teddy wrecked the Jeep?"

"Ask Teddy," Helen said to her brother-in-law, and swept from the room.

Worth wasn't in his bedroom, but she heard the shower water running, so she waited, pacing the floor, feeling like a small boiling human volcano on the verge of erupting. When Worth came back into the room, he was naked except for a towel wrapped around his waist. His hair was wet, his chest hair was damp and curling, and he looked intensely physical and male. She felt the charge of sexual attraction she often felt for her husband, and this infuriated and oddly embarrassed her.

"We need to talk," she said, keeping her voice low.

"Let me put some clothes on first." Worth dropped the towel and moved around the room, uninhibited by his nakedness.

333

Helen sank onto the bed and thought of how many times over the years this very scene had played out—her waiting on the bed while Worth ranged around the room naked. Often they'd be changing for a party, but sometimes she would be waiting for him to make love to her. She would be naked herself, although she tried not to walk naked in front of him. She was too self-conscious, aware of cellulite and sags.

Worth pulled on a clean, ironed pair of boxer shorts, a fresh rugby shirt, and his chinos. He zipped them up, and again the act seemed sexual.

"All right," he said. He didn't come over to the bed but lifted his briefcase out of the chair, set it on the floor, and sat down by the window. "What's going on?"

"How long have you been having an affair?" Helen asked.

Her husband stared at her. She did not look away. She was still riding the energy of her anger.

"It's nothing," he said at last. And his face changed, sinking in on itself slightly, so that in only a second or two he suddenly looked older.

"It's something to me," Helen assured him.

"I don't know what to say." He looked crushed, as if Helen had betrayed *him*.

"Tell me her name," Helen said.

"Oh, Helen, come on. Look, it's just a—a fling. A stupid mistake on my part. An old man's folly."

"Tell me her name," Helen repeated, with iron in her voice.

"You don't know her," Worth insisted. "You've never met her. She works at the bank. She's a teller. She's—she's just nice, and fun, and pretty."

Each word out of Worth's mouth had suddenly become an arrow, an ax, chopping against the wall of icy anger surrounding Helen, and the word *pretty* sliced right through everything, so that her protective layer shattered and she was vulnerable and wounded. She did not want to cry in front of Worth, but tears pressed insistently.

She felt Worth's gaze on her face, her old, lined, sagging face, and she wanted to fling her hands up to cover it, she wanted to run from the room, lumbering along in her overweight unpretty body. Why had she started this? Why had she forced this scene upon them? Why hadn't she kept quiet, let Worth's affair run its course, and allowed the united front of their marriage to exist—or at least *appear* to exist?

Worth sighed. He pressed his fingers on either side of his nose, a sign of his emotional state. He said, "Cindy. Her name is Cindy."

Such a sweet name, Helen thought. A terrible thought possessed her, and her terror froze her tears. "Do you want to marry her?"

"God, no!" Worth looked appalled. "Helen—"

A sharp rap came at the door, and Grace stuck

her head in. "Hey, you guys, dinner's ready. We're all starving. Come on."

"We'll be right there," Worth told his sister.

Grace looked at him, then at Helen, and quirked an inquisitive eyebrow.

"For God's sake, Grace, give us some privacy," Worth told his sister. "We'll be right down."

With a sniff, Grace pulled the door shut.

"Look," Worth said, keeping his voice low, "I'll end it. It's nothing, Helen, and I'll stop seeing her. Okay?" When she didn't answer right away, he said urgently, "You know we can't settle everything right here and now. We can't really talk with everything going on in this house. Let's just go down to dinner, okay? We've got enough to deal with right now with Teddy and the Jeep."

Helen stood up. She felt as if she'd aged a hundred years, she felt as if she had just been struck with the plague. *Cindy.*

"How old is she?" she asked.

"Oh, Helen, stop this!" Worth rose, too, and paced the room angrily. With his back turned to Helen, he admitted, "She's thirty-nine." When Helen didn't respond, he turned to look at her, and then he came toward her, as if he wanted to take her in his arms. "Helen, I love you. You know that."

She cringed and backed away, averting her head, making it clear she didn't want him to touch her.

Worth held out his hands beseechingly. "Helen. Please. Let's talk about this later, okay?"

Helen said, "Okay. You go on down, Worth. I don't feel hungry. You can tell them I'm not feeling well." She looked at her husband. "That's the simple truth, after all."

## *Twenty*

*Helen is changing,* Nona thought.

Nona had sensed a deep, active silence in Helen this summer, a kind of waiting. Helen was an attractive woman, and she had an artistic spirit that was not one of the gifts of the Wheelwright genetic legacy. Worth was handsome enough, and he could be charming, but, as in most marriages, with the passing of years Worth directed the energy of his charm to the outer world and expected his wife to make do with whatever was left over. And Worth was becoming dictatorial. Both Grace and Worth had always been bossy; perhaps that was their mother's example, Nona thought, for she was never much of a follower.

Kellogg had the temperament of a cow—not a bull, a cow, a contented animal plodding in a field full of fresh green grass, and the lashes of his wife's commands touched but never stung his thick hide. Nona was very fond of Kellogg. And she guessed that, whatever transpired between her daughter and her husband in front of others, a real tenderness and even a kind of passion existed between them in private. With Helen and Worth, she was not so sure.

Here was Kellogg now, bending down, taking her hand. "Nona? Dinner's ready. May I help you into the dining room?"

More and more it seemed to cost Nona physical effort simply to get from where she existed, cradled among her thoughts, out to the interaction considered normal by others. She took a deep breath. "Kellogg. Thank you. But I wonder if Glorious could bring me something on a tray."

She wanted to tell him the truth, that she was simply too tired to make the journey from this chair into the dining room, too weary to sit at the table smiling at her family and hoping she wasn't dropping food on her bodice. But if she admitted that, Kellogg would tell Grace, who would rush in, alarmed, and try to energize Nona, for her own good. So Nona explained.

"There's a television show I want to watch."

Kellogg turned to look at the TV set, and to Nona's immense relief an old *Murder She Wrote* was just beginning. "Of course, Nona."

Kellogg went off.

Pretty soon Glorious arrived with a tray, to set up a folding table next to Nona. "We're having fish tonight," she informed Nona.

Nona said, "How nice."

"And I brought you this, also." Next to the plate

piled with healthy fish and vegetables was a small glass of Scotch.

Nona smiled. "Thank you, Glorious."

Glorious left the room. Nona roused herself enough to sip some of the Scotch, which flowed into her system like liquid sun, warming her old bones, relaxing her. She lay back against her chair. From the rest of the house came the laughter and calls of her children and grandchildren. On the TV set in front of her, Angela Lansbury entered a beauty salon to chat with Ruth Roman. Ruth Roman. No one knew who she was these days. Was the actress even alive? The past rolled around Nona like a beautiful sea.

## 1945–1946

*November 1945*

*Dear Anne,*

> *Here I am, seated behind a desk in an office at our temporary military headquarters in Bremerhaven, Germany. You have no idea what a luxury it is to be able to type this letter without wondering whether the ceiling's going to come crashing down on my head. I even have the use of electric lights.*
>
> *So things are better. Still, everyone wants to go home as soon as possible, and who can blame*

them? The vast majority of our troops have already been redeployed to the Pacific or sent home for discharge.

But we need a good solid U.S. presence here in Europe, and the Army of Occupation has been charged with many significant tasks. We have to protect potential sabotage targets and be prepared for any possible rogue-German military resistance. We have to guard all the stores in military government custody, which include artwork, literally tons of records, and tank cars loaded with mercury. Our men have to lay out billeting areas, establish lines of communication, and set up checkpoints at bridges, ports, railroads, and other facilities.

In addition, there's the gargantuan task of redeploying troops. I'm sure you know about the Adjusted Service Rating: eighty-five points and you can go home! As you can imagine, all this takes a heck of a lot of paperwork and causes no end of grumbling. I have seventy-five points, but right now I'm glad to be here, doing what I can.

Morale is low for those who remain behind, waiting and waiting for months on end. The army has done its bumbling best to deal with morale problems by establishing training, education, and recreation programs throughout the theater. Of course, that means even more paperwork and more guard stations to check passes!

I want to go home just as much as the next

man does, and I know I could talk to some people and pull some strings, but I have been lucky and feel a responsibility to continue on just a little longer to do whatever I can to help.

While we're waiting to get out of here, we've got DPs—displaced persons—and prisoners of war being shipped in from Russia and Poland. If you could see the hundreds of thousands of displaced persons and prisoners of war, with all they have left in the world on the back of a cart pulled by a starving horse, wearing rags, sleeping on the ground, grateful for the slightest bit of bread, you would understand how useful our Army of Occupation is. From my point of view, this work is more important than fighting battles. Not everyone feels that way, however, and I can understand the men who are struggling to return home to their loved ones and their lives.

I am comfortably billeted here in Bremerhaven, living with a German family in their nice house. My life is probably not so different from yours. I rise every day, put on my uniform, and go to the office, where I try to organize the arrival and dispersal of the multitude of foodstuffs and other necessities to be sent out throughout Europe. Bremerhaven, by the way, is in the northwest of Germany where the Weser River meets in the North Sea. You can find it on the map.

*I miss you, and I assure you that I am safe and eating well, and I'll be home soon.*

*Love, Herb*

Anne had spent Christmas with her in-laws, but no amount of holiday goodwill could make her forget her mother-in-law's bizarre and intentional cruelty back in August in allowing all those plants to die, or her smug satisfaction at Anne's distress. She felt trapped by her in-laws, and she missed Herb terribly. She needed to be with *him,* not with his parents, and so on January 2, 1946, Anne marched into Gwendolyn Forsythe's office at the Stangerone Freight Company.

Anne leaned on Gwen's desk and announced without preamble, "I want to go to Germany *now.*"

"I know that." Gwen didn't even look up from the pile of papers she was sorting. "And you know we've been trying to find you decent quarters for passage."

"I don't care about decent quarters. I want to go as soon as possible."

Now Gwen looked at Anne. She stuck her pencil over her ear and sighed. "I understand your frustration, Anne, but I don't think you have any idea just what kind of a mess it is over there."

"You can't talk me out of this, Gwen, I've made up my mind. I'm a married woman who has spent far too little time with her husband and far too much time with his parents. Besides, Herbert is doing important work—"

"You're doing important work here," Gwen reminded her.

"I know, and I can continue to do it and be just as much help, maybe even more, over in Bremerhaven."

Gwen swung her desk chair around and looked out her window, down at the wharves, where a multitude of dockworkers scrambled to load overseas provisions. She took the pencil from her ear and used it to scratch a spot on her scalp. "You are so young." She smiled at Anne. "You have the energy for something like this, and it's true we can use you over there. You've learned our system and we can trust you. All right. We've got a freighter making the trip to Bremerhaven in two days, carrying supplies. If you wish, you've got passage on it. You won't have a stateroom; you'll be lucky to have a bunk."

"I want it!" Anne said.

The crossing was rough, with wintry gales howling on the open decks and slamming what felt like tons of rock-hard waves into the lower decks of the freighter. Anne spent two days lying in her bunk, miserably seasick, but the last three days were calmer. At last she saw land lying like a long dark shadow in the distance, but it took another day of traveling through the North Sea before they drew close to the wide mouth of the Weser River. As they neared land, she saw sinister gray submarines and ominous militant destroyers riding the ocean swells like watchdogs at the entrance to the long harbor, straining at the leash, foaming at the mouth in their eagerness to attack. She knew the war was over, but she still felt a surge of fear. With a visceral bite, she gained a more realistic understanding of what Herb had been through.

The freighter rumbled as it slowed to make passage up the Weser River toward Bremerhaven, and then they arrived at the port. In many ways, the landscape seemed familiar, with piers extending out into the water and every sort of vessel docked there: tankers, tenders, aircraft carriers, destroyers, cruisers, herring trawlers, and motorboats of every size and kind. Customhouses and warehouses lined the waterfront, the same red brick as those in Boston harbor, but unlike Boston's buildings, most of these were bombed-out shells. Brick walls rose alone from piles of rubble; stone warehouses gaped roofless to the sky. It looked as if a gigantic angry child had hurled his building blocks down on the city. Then she saw the word STANGARONE in large gold letters above the entrance to one of the larger and mostly intact buildings.

The freighter shuddered to a stop, and dinghies and tenders motored out toward it, looking like a series of paddling ducks compared to the mammoth ship, to take the passengers aboard before the freighter went into the difficult task of docking and making ready to unload.

In a way, Anne couldn't believe she was really here. Everything had happened so quickly. She had debated whether or not to write Herb to tell him she was coming, but a letter wouldn't have reached him in time. She knew from experience that nothing ever went as planned when it came to shipping overseas, and she didn't want to get his hopes up by sending a telegram and then being told she wouldn't arrive for another week or another month. Then, as she thought about it, and let her imagination soar free, she realized how wonderful it would be, how amazing, if she arrived secretly, walked into his office one afternoon, and surprised him. He would be dumbfounded. It would be a story to tell their children.

She joined the single file waiting to climb down the ladder to the boat below. First stop, Stangarone's warehouse. She'd introduce herself, ask how to get to Herb's place on Goethestrasse, and tell them she could be at work tomorrow. She took a small suitcase with her. She'd arrange for someone at Stangarone's to transport her trunk.

During the long entrance up the harbor, she had noticed a lessening of the noise of the throbbing turbines that drove the ship, but now as she was helped to step up onto the dock, new sounds accosted her ears. Different languages shot past her like signal flares, vivid, loud, confusing. Men in uniform strode past, shouting orders, men in rags wheeled dollies laden with boxes along the wooden dock to the brick street, fishermen in wool caps and rain slickers hefted giant wicker baskets filled to the brim with slippery fish onto the pier. At the next pier a vessel was undergoing repair work, and the banging of metal on metal rang through the air.

She'd thought she was pretty cosmopolitan, pretty savvy, for Boston and its docks were not exactly a pastoral scene, but as she squeezed her way through the crowds, it was the different languages, not the people or the buildings, that made her understand that she was far from home. Someone shouted at her, at least she thought they were shouting at her, but when she turned she saw only backs and shoulders and head scarves and uniforms. She pressed on until she'd reached a brick building to lean against as she caught her breath and decided what to do next. She tightened her grip on her purse.

It wasn't going to be as easy as hailing a cab. Vehicles rumbled down the side streets, but they were bikes or trucks or wagons pulled by horses. An old woman in a man's overcoat and a head scarf labored past Anne, pushing a baby carriage full of bags of potatoes. A motor scooter backfired like a gunshot. An emaciated child shuffled past, bent double over a wheelbarrow laden with fish and shellfish. The January wind whipped off the water, filling the air with a frigid mist that almost froze on her face. Clouds were gathering overhead, and she could tell the sun, hidden by the city's broken walls, was setting on the darkening harbor waters. She had set her watch ahead one hour each day on the trip over, but her body wasn't quite ready for evening; the thought of being here in the dark frightened her and impelled her away from her wall. She spotted the heavy gilt Stangarone sign again and fought her way through the shoving crowd toward it.

Gwen had been right, she was naïve and impetuous to come here like this, but she had done it and there was no turning back. And she was so close, so close to seeing Herb again! To holding him in her arms! The thought of the look on his face when he saw her gave her the energy and courage to surge onward, and at last she was at the solid brick edifice of the shipping company.

She knew better than to try to enter by the harbor side. She could hear men yelling and the creak of ropes as cranes swung the massive containers onto the shore. Skirting a pile of bricks, she made her way up a narrow brick street and around to the front of the building. Here the devastation was worse. What had once been a square bordered by offices and warehouses was a landscape of ruined walls and glassless windows, naked and open to the air. One side of Stangarone's had been ripped open to the elements. Heaps of bricks rose like dunes against the one side that was left. Boards had been nailed over most of the exposed façade, and the door was nearly hidden by the rubble.

Anne opened it and went inside. The space was frigid and gloomy, but she could make out the staircase to the second floor. She hurried up, came to an intact office, knocked on the door, and waited. She heard voices and stepped inside, to find a wooden desk, wooden filing cabinets, stacks of colored bills of lading, a black telephone, a woman who looked American, and—oh, heaven!—an American soldier standing guard by an inner door.

"Hello!" she cried brightly. "I'm so glad someone's here. I'm Anne Wheelwright. I work at Stangarone's in Boston. I just got off a freighter, and I've come over to work here."

"Well, Anne Wheelwright, I'm glad to meet you!" The woman stood up, reached over the desk, and shook Anne's hand. "I'm Georgia. And I'm dead beat! Why don't you come with me. I'm going home. We'll find someplace for you to camp out for a while."

"Oh," Anne said, flustered. "Thanks, Georgia. But first of all, I really would like to see my husband. He's in the army, and he lives at this address." She took a piece of paper from her purse and, knowing she would mangle the German pronunciation, handed it to Georgia to read.

"Oh, Goethestrasse, I know where that is. It's a ways out. It'll be a long walk." She glanced at Anne's face. "Tell you what. We'll grab a couple of bikes, but you've got to be sure to bring yours back early tomorrow morning." Grabbing a mangy fur coat off the coat rack, Georgia pulled it on and haphazardly stuck a crimson wool hat shaped like an overturned bucket on her head. She cuffed the soldier on the shoulder. "See you tomorrow, Pete."

Anne followed her guide as she clattered down the wooden stairs. Georgia yanked open a wooden door, exposing a coatroom crammed with clothing, boxes, and several bikes. She wheeled one over to Anne.

"You follow me. It's hard going out there and the cobblestones will bump your teeth right out of your head, but it's faster than walking by a long shot. Don't talk to anyone else, and if someone tries to take your bike, don't hesitate to scream." Seeing Anne's expression, she added, "You'll be fine. It's a madhouse out there, but in a few days you'll be just another daffy inmate. I reckon you'll stay with your husband tonight and all, so he can help you get back here tomorrow. Eight o'clock, okay?" Without waiting for an answer, Georgia slammed the closet door and wheeled her bike outside.

Outside, it was cold, windy, and fully dark. Anne locked her eyes on Georgia's hat as she pedaled her way through the throng. People no longer appeared as individuals but simply as hulking shapes converging and separating on the narrow brick lane. Bombed-out buildings loomed like turrets from nightmares, and the air was loud with the sound of cursing and occasional sobs. The air smelled of brick dust and kerosene. It was bizarre past her wildest imaginings. Here she was in her nice rose wedding suit, in her nicest high heels, seated on a rickety old bicycle, her nylons ripping as she strained to force her way along a maze of narrow, gloomy streets. Now she understood why Gwen Forsythe had looked at her oddly, why she had said, "You're young." You needed the energy of youth to stay sane in this dark world.

Georgia weaved along, making a sharp right here and forking left there, past houses where windows flickered with candlelight and shops with beautiful signs and no windows, past entire blocks of rubble piled in fantastic mountains, around cold heaps of stone. The façade of a church rose, strong and eternal, its spire ascending to the heavens, but as Anne passed it she saw that behind the façade was only wreckage. The farther they biked from the harbor, the more German Anne heard being spoken, until finally all she heard was the guttural, harsh German speech.

"Okay." Georgia slammed on her brakes and pointed down a long lane paved in bricks. "This is Goethestrasse. I think the house you're looking for is about three blocks down. Have a nice reunion, kid, and I'll see you tomorrow."

"Thank you, Georgia," Anne said, but Georgia was already pedaling in the opposite direction.

No streetlights shone, but some of the houses she passed flickered with light, sufficient for her to see her way. She walked her bike, because the street was full of potholes, and she wanted to read whatever numbers still remained on the buildings.

And then she was there: 91 Goethestrasse. A handsome brick house, all its walls intact. A few of the windows were boarded up, but compared to what she'd seen, this was a citadel. Her coat and suit were rumpled from sitting on the bike and she took a moment to smooth them down. Her heart was beating crazily, partly from the exertion of her bike ride, but mostly from the excitement of knowing she was about to see her beloved Herb again.

She knocked on the door. She heard voices. She waited.

The door opened. An angel stood there. Or, for a moment, she looked like an angel to Anne. Certainly she had never seen such a beautiful woman before, except perhaps at the cinema. The woman was tall and slender, with luminous blue eyes and silver-blond hair. She was obviously German and she was very pregnant.

"Yes?"

"Hello!" Anne said, smiling eagerly. "Do you speak English?"

"I do."

"Oh, thank heaven! My name is Anne Wheelwright. I'm Herbert Wheelwright's wife. I've just arrived from the United States. I have this address. Is he here?"

The dim light from the back of the house illuminated the other woman's face. And that was all it took, a moment in the shadowy light, the recoil of the other woman's body, the way her hands flew to cover her mouth. Anne knew.

## Twenty-one

When they heard the raised voices coming from the den, Charlotte and Suzette exchanged a worried glance. Then Charlotte helped Suzette up off the living room sofa, and together they made their way into the kitchen. The den was off the kitchen, and they could overhear the argument without being caught gawking. Suzette sank onto a chair while she listened, and Charlotte paced the floor. Glorious had diplomatically removed herself to her own quarters, as she often did when tempers flared in the family. Charlotte saw Suzette's face fall as they overheard the cause of the argument. Teddy, drunk again. The second time in less than a month.

Uncle Kellogg ambled in, drink in hand, nodded at Charlotte, and continued into the den. Soon she heard her mother shouting—about *sweet cakes?* Her mother wasn't making any sense at all. Then Charlotte's father stormed from the room, passing through the kitchen without seeming to notice Charlotte or Suzette, and then her mother flashed through, her face violently flushed. Charlotte had never seen her mother look so angry. Uncle Kellogg left the den next, casting an embarrassed smile at Charlotte, and went into the hall and up the stairs, no doubt to inform his wife of Teddy's latest infraction.

Finally, slowly, Teddy emerged from the den into the kitchen. When he saw Charlotte and Suzette, he grinned sheepishly, stuck his hands in his jeans pockets, leaned against the refrigerator, and said, boyishly, "Oops."

"For, God's sake, Teddy, it's not funny and you're not cute!" Charlotte snapped.

To her surprise, Suzette spoke up. "It's this family."

Charlotte gawked at Suzette. "What?"

"It's this family. Teddy stayed sober when he was with me in Arizona. We come here, and he gets drunk."

Charlotte started to retort, then bit her tongue. She was aware that Aunt Grace and Mee and Uncle Kellogg had come down the stairs and were hovering in the hall, listening, and she would be damned if she was going to add one more argument to the ongoing fray.

"I'm going out to see what shape the table's in," Charlotte said.

"I can tell you what shape it's in," Teddy announced gaily. "It's trashed."

She didn't dare look at him. "Then I'd better move it. I don't want my customers to find *trash* where the farm stand was."

She stormed through the mudroom, out the door, and up the driveway. It was a long walk, but she needed it to help her calm down. Things had been going so well, she'd been loving this summer, she'd felt pleased with herself, even a bit virtuous, to be involving Suzette in the garden, to give her work that made her feel useful and part of the family and provided money, as well, to buy whatever little things she wanted. And it had been fun, having Teddy back. He was so lively and entertaining. During dinners, while Aunt Grace and Uncle Kellogg and the Ms had all the sparkle of a congregation of pilgrims, Teddy had brightened the room with anecdotes about his day at the antiques shop. He did fabulous impersonations, and when he got going he could be hysterical. Even the Ms laughed. And Charlotte's mother had been so happy, having Teddy back and with a grandchild on the way. Why did Teddy have to ruin things? Was Suzette right? Was it being around his family that caused him to fall off the wagon?

She arrived at the end of the drive. There, right where she always had her farm stand, was the old Jeep, its hood up, its grille crushing the wooden table against a tree trunk. She could see that the table was broken in half, and splinters and cracks razed the surface. Fury ignited inside her. Somehow it seemed so *personal.* Certainly it was an ugly, destructive sight, and she chewed on her knuckles as she circled the Jeep, checking out its condition. Its tires had ripped two muddy streaks in the cool green grass.

She climbed into the Jeep. Teddy had left the key in the ignition. She turned it, and the battery kicked, but nothing else happened. She sat there for a moment, feeling utterly defeated. Suzette's words echoed in her mind. "It's this family." Perhaps Suzette was right. Maybe there was something slightly off about her family—but no, that wasn't true. Oliver was pure and simply wonderful. Of course, Oliver never stayed at Nona's house in the "bosom of the family" for more than a couple of days at a time. So—had Oliver escaped, and in this way also avoided any sins that being with this family caused? Charlotte remembered her great transgression; her entire body flushed with heat as she thought about it. She had been so bad, so wrong, and it would not have happened if she had not worked at the bank, which was another way of being right in the heart of the family. But she also had to admit, at least to herself, that she did have a rebel streak, and so did Teddy. She loved her family, truly she did, but all her life she'd felt an urge to mutiny, if only she could do it without hurting anyone else.

Her cell phone rang, and she jumped. She'd forgotten she had it in her pocket. She answered and heard Coop's voice.

"Hey, you. Where are you?" His lazy voice was full of laughter.

"Oh, Coop. Gosh, what time is it? I'm out at the end of our driveway." In the background, she heard a woman's voice. "Where are *you?*"

"In your living room. Having a drink with Mee. I walked over on the beach. We decided it would be fun to drive to the theater in your family's old Chrysler convertible." When she didn't respond immediately, he prompted. "Remember?"

"Oh, Coop!" Charlotte hit herself in the forehead. "I didn't really forget, it's just that Teddy had an accident—"

"I've been hearing all about it."

"Well, he smashed up my farm-stand table, and I need to get it cleared out and find a new table to use. I'm sure we have one somewhere in the house, probably in the attic—"

"Look, forget about that for now. We should be leaving any moment. I hate being late for the theater. It's just rude."

"Oh, Coop." Charlotte paced around the wrecked Jeep as she talked. "Coop, I can't go. I've got to get this mess cleaned up before tomorrow morning."

"But hey, come on, I bought tickets! And there's the benefit party afterward. You don't want to miss that. It only happens once a year."

"I know, I know, it will be great, but Coop—"

"Look, Teddy made the mess, let Teddy clean it up."

Charlotte snorted. "Right, because Teddy is so responsible."

"Come on, Char," Coop urged, his voice silky, "take an evening off. Everything will get done sooner or later, and who is it really going to hurt if a few people have to wait until nine instead of eight to get their lettuce?" He laughed. "You need to put things in perspective."

Charlotte hesitated. She wanted to remind him that her customers were flighty, fickle. If what they expected wasn't there when they had made the effort to drive out into the country, they would be miffed and simply go somewhere else. She needed to build a reputation of reliability. She didn't want any of them to see this jumble of wrecked wood and steel where her charming farm stand, portraying serenity and health, should be.

"Coop—"

In the background, she heard a woman speaking. Perhaps her mother, offering to help find a new table?

"Listen," Coop said, his voice still easy and

light, "Mee just said she'd go to the theater with me. This way I won't waste the tickets and you can stay here and do whatever you need to do."

Charlotte found herself looking at her cell phone, as if it had suddenly zapped her into an alternate universe.

Suddenly Mee's voice was on the phone. "You won't mind, will you, Charlotte? Coop can take me to the party, and maybe I'll meet some nice eligible bachelors!"

Charlotte understood the tacit message: *I'm not trying to steal your man.* "No, Mee, I don't mind. Have fun."

Coop's voice came on again. "Good luck with your stand." He clicked off.

"I phoned the tow truck!" Teddy came sauntering down the drive, waving at her. "They're on their way."

Charlotte gawked at him. She was exhausted and hungry and thirsty and confused and angry, she felt rumpled and grimy and overheated and rejected, and there Teddy was, ambling along with his good looks and his easy innocent smile. For that moment, she pure and simply hated him.

"Teddy," she said, and she was on the verge of tears, "Teddy, you *drove drunk.*"

"Maybe I wasn't so very drunk." Teddy continued to smile as he leaned on the Jeep. "Maybe it was a Freudian thing, like most of the things in our family. Sort of semi-on-purpose. Maybe I resent the fact that you've stolen Suzette from me and made her part of your world."

"*Stolen* Suzette?" Charlotte threw her hands out in exasperation. "No, Teddy, I'm not buying that *at all.* You've seen way too many psychiatrists, and you've learned how to warp their theories to suit your transgressions. You were drunk. Just drunk. Admit it."

Teddy shrugged, and his smile faded. "I'll admit it. But I have to say there is something about this family that would drive a saint to drink."

Just then they heard the familiar rattling of the old Chrysler convertible as it came along the drive. The top was down, Coop was at the wheel, Mee in the passenger seat, a scarf around her hair and a gigantic smile on her face.

She leaned out over the door. "Aren't we just the most glamorous people in the universe?" She blew Charlotte a kiss.

Charlotte laughed and blew a kiss back. It was wonderful seeing her cousin so ebullient and animated.

"I thought *you* were dating Coop," Teddy said.

"I am." Charlotte glared at her brother. "*I* was going to the theater with him tonight, but instead *I* have to clean up your mess."

"Then why isn't Coop out here helping you?"

"Why should he be? He has tickets. There's a gala afterward. I'm glad Mee's going with him."

"Yeah, right." Teddy snorted.

Before Charlotte could retort, the tow truck came roaring down the road. Two burly men jumped out, surveyed the wreck, pronounced it not so bad, hooked the Jeep's bumper to a chain, and rumbled off with the Jeep bouncing along behind. Teddy helped Charlotte lift the broken bits of table away from the tree. They hauled them back to the barn, stashing them next to the half cord of winter wood. They searched Nona's house and found an old card table that could be used until something better was found. Charlotte preferred a long rectangular shape to a square one, but this would suffice. Teddy helped her lug it out to the road, where they leaned it against a tree in preparation for morning.

As they worked, Teddy sobered up, and his silly, lighthearted mood changed. Charlotte could sense the dark mood sinking into him like a stain.

"Hey, Teddy," she said, as they walked back to the house. Light was leaving the sky. Birds were calling good night. Even the breeze had settled down. "It's no tragedy, losing that table, you know. And for what it's worth, I'm sure you wouldn't have steered into it if someone had been there, Suzette or me."

Teddy nodded. "Thanks, sis. I don't know if that makes me feel better or worse. I mean, I *have* been jealous of how close you are to Suzette."

"Then you should have talked to me about it. I could have reassured you. I mean, I like her, and we talk about the garden and girly stuff and baby stuff, but Teddy, Teddy—*you're her guy.* She adores you. The rest of us are just trying to make her feel at home."

"I don't want her to feel at home, not here. I hate the way we are, we're like a herd of lemmings crawling all over each other." He sighed deeply. "Well, I love Nona, I do. And I love you, Char."

"I know that."

"Oh, well, I guess I love everyone, but I just feel claustrophobic in this family. Everyone's pressuring me to be something I'm not. I'm so busy trying to escape I can't figure out where I want to go."

"But you've found Suzette," Charlotte reminded him. "*You've* found *your* person. Don't be so down on yourself. Most people don't know what kind of work they want to do. Most people don't even get to choose."

"I know, I know, I'm fortunate, I'm rich, I'm educated—" His voice caught the edge of a whine.

"Stop it, Teddy. You're a husband and you're about to be a father. You've got a place to stay while your wife has her baby, and before long you can all move back to Tucson, or wherever you want. Gosh, you could leave now if you wanted to. No one's stopping you."

They reached the end of the drive. Suzette was there, leaning against the big concrete vase with the spilling fuchsia. "Existential crisis?" she asked.

Charlotte gaped. Suzette was continually surprising her. She didn't look like someone who had ever read Sartre. Before she could answer, Suzette reached out and pulled Teddy to her.

"Let's get some food into you. Then bed. You've got to get up early for work tomorrow."

Charlotte followed them into the house. Collapsing on the bench in the mudroom, she unlaced her boots, then just leaned against the wall. She was tired. Plus, she had melancholy. She envied Teddy his particular sin. She envied him because everyone knew about it, and their anger or indignation was, if nothing else, a clean, true reaction. Her own offense was still a secret. She couldn't imagine telling anyone in her family, and there was no reason to; it would only cause hurt and distrust by cracking open a family chasm. Besides, it was over now. It was done. She couldn't change it. She could only go forward. And what she had done, really, had not been so terribly bad. She was not the devil. She wished she had someone to say, as she had said to Teddy, "Don't be so down on yourself."

*Later, she raided* the freezer, indulging in a pint of ice cream for dinner, then taking a long soaking shower. She fell asleep the moment she tumbled into bed. But she woke several times during the night, wondering if she heard the old convertible crunching along the drive and hearing only the silken sound of the island breeze.

*The next morning,* she was weeding in her garden when she looked up to see a familiar lean figure loping toward her. Not Coop, Whit. Whit in white ducks, a blue cotton shirt with the sleeves rolled up, and a baseball cap shielding his face from the sun.

He held up a plastic bag. "Just bought some of your arugula."

Charlotte unfolded herself from her squat in the dirt, rose to standing, dusted off her knees and rear, and brushed several stray hairs from her face. "Hi, Whit. Thanks for the business."

Whit looked around. "This is really something. I can't believe you're doing it all with just one helper."

"I've got two now. Suzette's manning the farm stand." Charlotte put her hands on her back and leaned into them, stretching her spine. "If business keeps growing, I'll have to hire another worker."

"Do you want it to keep growing?" Whit stopped a few feet from her, his cap shading his eyes.

"Of course I do." She furrowed her brow at him.

"It's just that you never called about meeting the woman from *Eat Local.*"

"What woman?"

"Laura Riding. I gave Mee the information on the phone yesterday. Laura wanted to have lunch with you today, to get to know you, probably initiate an interview and an article for her magazine."

Charlotte's jaw dropped. "This is the first I've heard about it."

"I guess Mee forgot to tell you."

"I guess she did! What an idiot! Whit, I'd love to meet her—is it too late?"

Whit looked at his watch. "I'm meeting her for lunch in thirty minutes."

"I'll come with you. Can you give me a few minutes to change?" She looked down at her grimy shorts and shirt. "I think this is just a little too authentic!"

"My car's parked by your farm stand. I'll get it and drive you up to the house."

Charlotte raced to the attic, stripped off her work clothes, pulled on a filmy skirt and clean T-shirt, let her hair loose, slipped on a pair of turquoise earrings, and hurried back downstairs. She caught glimpses of some of her family as she went, but she didn't see Mee.

*Laura Riding was young,* passionate, and energetic, and she possessed an encyclopedic knowledge of plants, farming, and food. They sat in the shade of the back patio at Even Keel, talking about local crops and Nantucket's unique gastronomic heritage, and every word Charlotte said—*mesclun, blueberries*—sent Laura off on a quixotic soliloquy about a culinary utopia where everyone ate local, all diseases vanished, and small town economies flourished. She spoke with charming intensity, caused perhaps by her topic but also, Charlotte quickly realized, by what seemed to be a gigantic crush on Whit. She touched his arm, his hand, she actually batted her eyelashes at him, and when he spoke she was completely captivated.

Charlotte was so engrossed, watching Laura flirt with Whit, that she almost missed Whit's words: "—why we're opening a branch of the bank on Nantucket."

"Wait a minute!" Charlotte forgot all etiquette and waved her hands to interrupt him. "I didn't know this!"

Whit aimed his steady deep blue gaze at her. "No? I'm surprised. Your father and your uncle and your cousin's husbands have been doing most of the groundwork."

"But—but does that mean someone will have to live on the island year round? To oversee things?"

"Yes." Whit smiled. "That would be me."

Charlotte's jaw dropped. "I didn't know you wanted to live here year-round."

Determined not to be ignored, Laura leaned forward, gushing, "Oh, it must be *wonderful* to live out here in the winter! So *atmospheric*! And think of the food! Fresh fish! Shellfish! Mussels right off the jetties' rocks. And I've seen the town at Christmas, with all the little trees lit up, so sweet. I'd love to live on the island!"

Somehow, by the end of lunch, Laura managed to return her focus to Charlotte and arranged to come out to Beach Grass Garden with her photographer on Friday.

As Whit drove Charlotte home afterward, she found herself gazing at him assessingly, as if she'd never seen him before, as if she hadn't known him all her life. He was handsome and powerful-looking, relaxed yet confident. He was sexy. Oh, dear. He was very, very sexy.

"So, that was a good meeting, right?" Whit asked. "Good publicity for your business?"

"It was great. Thank you." Charlotte looked over at him. "That young woman has quite a crush on you, Whit."

He shrugged. "She's a good kid."

His answer exasperated Charlotte. She snapped, "Oh, come on, Whit! Don't always be so—so *noble*."

He frowned. "What are you talking about?"

"Oh, I don't know." Charlotte shifted uncomfortably in her seat, puzzled by the force of her irrational irritation.

"Would you prefer I be a cad?" Whit was still smiling, and suddenly he waggled his eyebrows and said in an oily voice, "Yeah, that Laura can't keep her hands off me, wants to jump my bones."

Charlotte laughed. "I'm so grateful to you, Whit, for fixing up the introduction and coming out to get me for the lunch."

"Glad to do it." His voice was warm, affectionate.

Suddenly she blurted out, "Teddy got drunk last night."

"That's too bad. What happened?"

"He says he drank champagne in the shop with some customers. Then he drove the Jeep home and smashed into the farm stand. Totaled my table and crunched the hood of the Jeep."

"Wow. I'm sorry to hear that."

"Dad's furious. Mom insists on driving Teddy to and from work every day."

Whit was quiet.

"I know what you're thinking. She's enabling him. But Whit, what else can she do? What *should* she do?"

"I don't think anyone knows what to do, Charlotte. I think your mother's doing the right thing. It's good for Teddy to work, and it's good for Suzette to have some relatives around to help her."

"But?"

"No buts."

"Oh, come on, Whit, don't you want to say that our family is a convoluted narcissistic mess that probably drives Teddy to drink?"

"Perhaps, but Charlotte, I don't think your family is all that different from mine." He tapped his fingers on the steering wheel, thinking. "We've got this strong central core. I've always felt as if my sisters and I were kind of like planets, revolving in a ring around the sun, and sometimes that track feels comfortable and right, but a lot of the time it feels like an awful rut and I just want to get out and get away."

It was shocking to hear this, to know that Whit, perfect Whit, might actually chafe at his family ties. Charlotte turned on her seat to face him. She'd never heard Whit talk this way before. Well, she'd never gotten to know Whit, she realized, she'd never looked past that familiar façade. "What do you do when you have to get away?"

Whit grinned at her. "I go off climbing two or three times a year. A completely selfish and expensive experience, if that makes you happy. I spend a lot of money for no good but my own pleasure. Last year I went to Norway and Switzerland and New Zealand."

"Wow." Charlotte found herself looking at his long muscular thighs, so elegant in his white trousers. "I didn't know that." She lay back against her seat, conjuring up images of foreign terrain, fierce peaks thrusting into the sky, crystalline blue air. All that open empty space. "That must be great."

"It's amazing."

"I've never been mountain climbing."

"You should try it." They were almost to Nona's driveway. "What do you do for pleasure, Charlotte?"

She thought of Coop. Bed with Coop. She knew

she was blushing. "Oh—well, I've pretty much worked on Beach Grass Garden for three years now."

"Perhaps it's time you had some fun."

Suddenly she was foolish, tongue-tied. She'd never been this way around Whit before, but then she'd never really gotten to know him. She felt so close to him now, and the desire to touch him was stunning.

"Whit—"

They'd arrived at the turnoff to Nona's house. Whit brought the car to a halt at the end of the driveway. Under the shade of several pine trees, Suzette sat on a lawn chair, her feet propped up on another lawn chair, her belly like a beach ball. The card table, covered in the checked cloth, was almost bare. Only two flower arrangements and a bag of lettuce remained.

Suzette waved lazily from her chair. "Charlotte, we had a rush about an hour ago."

"I've got some new potatoes and some tomatoes to pick," Charlotte called. "I'll just change clothes."

"Scallions, too," Suzette said. "Someone asked for scallions."

Whit drove on up to the house and stopped the car at the circle drive. "She's really coming into her own, isn't she?"

Whit's words delighted her. "Oh, yes, Whit. It's so nice to see her flower like this."

Whit hit the button to roll down the windows. He turned off the engine and leaned his arm along the back of the seats. The silence of the summer afternoon enclosed them. For a moment she felt very happy to be right where she was. She felt—on the verge of something. She turned toward him. "Whit, thank you so much for everything."

He turned toward her. "Are you going to Sarah Chamberlain's wedding?"

"Oh, gosh, I'd almost forgotten about it. Yes, of course." She chewed her lip, suddenly engrossed with garden thoughts. Could she leave Suzette to man the farm stand and Jorge to weed without her overseeing them all day Saturday?

"I'll see you there, then." Whit leaned over and kissed her cheek.

She stared at him. The attraction between them was like a gravity, a heat. "Whit—"

"Hi, guys!" Mee strolled up to the car, wearing only a little bikini. "What are you two up to?" She leaned on Whit's window, looking in, her posture pushing her breasts up into appealing pillows.

The private moment vanished. Annoyance flashed through Charlotte. "Whit just took me to the lunch with the magazine editor who wants to do an article on me," she said, forcing herself to sound calm. "The lunch you forgot to mention to me."

Mee shrugged, making one of her straps slip fetchingly down her shoulder. "Sorry." She directed her gaze at Whit. "I'm just going down for a swim. Want to come cool off?"

"No, thanks." Whit turned on the ignition. "I've got some work to do."

"Places to go and people to see." Mee stepped away from the car as Charlotte got out and shut the door. "Want to got for a quick dip, Char?"

"Maybe later," Charlotte said. "I've got some garden stuff to do." She looked at Whit. "I'll see you tomorrow at Sarah's wedding."

"Me, too!" Mee called to Whit. "*I'll* see you there, too, Whit!"

Whit waved at both women and drove away.

# Birth

# Twenty-two

*S*arah Chamberlain's wedding was held on the long swoop of lawn at her parents' house in Sconset. The sky was cerulean blue, the air sweet and calm. A rose arbor had been erected to frame the ceremony, and white folding chairs ranged on either side of a pink carpet scattered with rose petals. For this outdoor occasion, women needed to shade their faces from the sun's rays, and pastel flower-trimmed hats bobbed in the congregation like dozens of giant cupcakes.

Helen often cried at weddings. Today, when Sarah and her groom, Marcus, came down the aisle, Sarah was holding their six-month-old daughter in her arms. Baby Guinevere wore a christening gown whose long skirts trailed over Sarah's arms more beautifully than any bridal bouquet, and Helen was moved to tears. Sarah and Marcus were young, strong, optimistic, and madly in love. And Ruby Chamberlain, Sarah's mother, had a granddaughter. *O greedy, envious heart,* Helen thought, chiding herself as she wept. *Stop longing just for a moment, and wish them well.*

After the ceremony, everyone went to the yacht club for the reception. Earlier that morning, Grace had driven Charlotte and Helen out to the airport, where they each rented a car. Helen got a Saab, Charlotte a Jeep. Helen drove Teddy and Suzette to the yacht club. Charlotte drove Worth. Grace and her family went in their own SUV and Volvo. At the club, one of the larger tables had their name cards on it, and Helen swiftly rearranged them so that Teddy was seated between Suzette and Charlotte.

Since their argument about Sweet Cakes, Helen and Worth hadn't spoken, except for the necessary words exchanged in front of Worth's sister and her family about the events of the day. Worth's protestation of love for Helen had been given angrily and under duress, and although he'd said he would break off with Sweet Cakes—with *Cindy*—Helen felt as if Cindy were still there with him—with them—poisoning their marriage. And of course she was. Even if he never saw her again, Worth would be able to remember the other woman's body, the smell of her, the sounds she made during passion, the hue and silk of her skin. *Thirty-nine.* Would it have been less painful if Cindy were fifty-nine? Yes, Helen admitted to herself, she thought it would.

She'd assumed that once she confronted Worth she would feel less burdened, less pressure-driven by the secret, and there *was* a lessening of anxiety. But it was replaced by a constant searing pain beneath her breast. Worth had confirmed her suspicions. He had given a name and an age to the other woman. She did not know where they would go from here. She did not know where she wanted to go.

For now, she was glad to be out in a crowd. It was natural for her not to be chatting with her own husband, and it was a relief to be away from Grace's curious gaze. Helen settled at the table next to Suzette. Teddy went off to fetch drinks—sparkling water for him and Suzette, champagne for Helen. Leaning back in her chair, she surveyed the crowd. Joe Abernathy was chatting with Lew Lowry. Joe was a handsome man in a completely different way from Worth. Short, compact, bulky, he looked like a retired wrestler but sounded like an Episcopal minister. He caught Helen staring at him and winked. Helen smiled back.

Joe started shouldering his way through the crowd, coming toward Helen, and her heart skipped a beat. It had been a long time since she'd felt this, this unsettling jolt of sexual attraction. In fact, she'd assumed she was past feeling such things.

Years ago, when Teddy, her youngest child, had finally turned five, old enough to attend kindergarten, when the hot intense chaos of nursing, rocking, soothing, and entertaining babies and toddlers had passed and she finally had space and time to catch her breath and pay attention to the adult world around her, Helen had enjoyed all sorts of playful flirtations. At dinner parties, after doubles tennis, on the ferry coming to the island, during any social engagement with other mommies and daddies, Helen had sensed a man's interest and felt that knock of engagement, that swift force of desire, and sometimes she'd let herself go with it, as if stepping into a flooding channel of water and allowing herself to be swept off her feet, carried downstream, buffeted and lifted and turned by sensation. But it was always only play. The attraction to another man might be powerful enough that she conjured up fantasies of making love with him, even of running away with him, when she and Worth were making love. But she'd never so much as kissed another man. She'd had opportunities, of course, but she'd always gotten out in time—she'd thought of it as getting out, as *escaping*—and she'd felt the hot wash of relief that she'd not betrayed Worth, that their marriage was intact, that she truly loved him, and for months after her flirtation she would be fiercely passionate with her husband. In a way, their marriage was stronger for her occasional imaginary wanderings.

Now Worth had changed everything. He was unfaithful in reality, having sex with another woman—with Cindy. Surely Helen was free to do the same. She even *deserved* an affair, something to make her feel young again, attractive, radiant with sexuality, and she wouldn't just feel it, she would *be* that way, for she knew how love could light up a woman's life and make her glow.

Joe bent and whispered in her ear, because the band was so loud. He asked her to dance. Helen smiled and rose shakily, suddenly nervous. The band was playing a set of fifties love ballads: "In the Still of the Night," "My Prayer," "Unchained Melody." All around them couples danced, holding each other tightly, surrendering to the dreamy mood. Joe pulled her close. She rested her head on his shoulder and allowed herself to relish the man's body, so different in length and breadth from Worth's, against hers. His strong thighs touching her thighs. His broad chest against her bosom. She saw Sarah Chamberlain in her sweeping white bridal gown snuggled up against her new husband, both of them deep in private rapture. She could not quite remember such bliss. Joe's hand, warm against her back, caressed her as he pulled her closer, and he moved his hand down until he was touching the cleft of her lower back. Joe was divorced. His ex-wife lived on the West Coast; she never came to Nantucket these days.

*I could do this,* Helen thought. *I can do this.*

The music ended. She stepped back and met Joe's eyes. The look he gave her caused a rush of heat low in her belly, a flood of desire.

Helen said softly, "Oh, dear."

Joe said, "When can I see you?"

She answered, "Monday. Worth goes back to Boston on Monday."

Now the music started again, this time fast music that had people twisting and shouting. Joe kept his hand on her arm as he ushered her back to her table.

"My house," he said. "What time?"

"In the afternoon. I'll say I'm shopping." Even as she spoke, she regretted it. She was sure she wouldn't show up.

*"Mom."* Charlotte clutched Helen's wrist.

Helen's heart lurched guiltily. Was she being so obvious?

"Mom," Charlotte said again, "listen. Suzette's having contractions."

Helen looked across the table. Suzette was crouched on her chair, hands on her abdomen, frowning and panting. Teddy knelt next to her, his hand on her back, his face blazing with alarm.

"It's too early." Helen spoke her thoughts aloud, trying to make sense of what she saw. "Maybe they're Braxton-Hicks. False labor," she explained to her daughter.

Forgetting about Joe, Helen hurried around the table. She knelt next to Teddy, her scarlet skirt pooling around her. "Suzette? Have you been timing your contractions?"

"They're five minutes apart," Teddy told her.

Suzette's face glistened with sweat, but as a contraction lessened, she took a deep breath and whispered desperately, "I don't want to lose the baby. Helen, I'm scared."

Helen put her hands on Suzette's shoulders. "Don't be afraid. You'll be fine. Your baby will be fine. Teddy is here, and I'm here, and we're going to get you to the hospital right now. Can you stand up?"

Suzette's eyes were wide, the whites showing like a frightened animal's. "I think so."

"Teddy, take her left arm."

Helen took Suzette's right arm. She and her son levered the young woman up and slowly walked away from the ballroom. Helen was vaguely aware of the glances from people sitting at other tables. She could feel the buzz of conversation resonate at this end of the room. They managed to get Suzette out into the lobby before another contraction gripped her, and she moaned and bent double.

"Hold her, Teddy," Helen instructed her son. "Take as much of her weight as you can."

"Helen," Suzette gasped. "It *hurts*."

Helen kept her arm around the young woman's back. "Yes, I know, but that's natural, that's all right."

"Oh, no." Suzette shuddered, her body swayed, and her knees buckled. Helen heard the splash of liquid, and saw moisture spreading beneath Suzette's feet.

"Your water broke, Suzette. You remember your childbirth classes, right?" Helen looked over Suzette's head at Teddy. His face had gone white. *"Teddy."* When her son glanced at her, she said, "It's going to be just fine. This is all normal."

Grace swept up to them, her neck stretched, jaw pointing outward, nostrils flared. "What in the world are you all doing? So rude, leaving the reception—oh, my God!" Grace stared at the puddle of blood-tinged water at Suzette's feet. "Of course you would have to do that *here*."

For one brutal moment, Helen wanted to slap her sister-in-law. Instead, she ignored her. "Teddy, we're going to drive Suzette to the hospital. It will take less time than calling an ambulance and waiting for it to arrive. We're going to walk Suzette out to the porch. I'll get the car. You keep supporting her."

And then, all at once, Worth was there, resplendent in his tux, strong and tall. He said to Helen, "She's in labor?"

"Yes. Her water just broke."

"Ooooh." Suzette tried to stifle a moan as her body was cramped by another contraction. She sagged between Helen and Teddy.

"Let me hold her," Worth told Helen. "I can support more of her weight. You get the car."

"Oh, for Pete's sake!" Grace exclaimed, to no one in particular.

Helen eased herself from Suzette's heavy grip as Worth slid next to her, wrapping his arm around her just beneath her shoulders. Helen turned and ran out of the club, through the large parking lot, until she found the rented Saab. She yanked open the door and dropped down into the driver's seat, clumsily knocking her knee against the door as she did. Her hand was shaking so hard she could barely stab the key into the ignition, but finally she managed it; she hit the gas and the car roared to life. She steered it to the porch, where Suzette, Teddy, and Worth were waiting. As they helped the pregnant woman into the car, Helen saw Charlotte come running through the lobby. Whit Lowry was behind her.

"Oh, wow!" Charlotte looked in the window. "Suzette, I'm coming to the hospital. I'll be right behind you." She glanced around frantically.

"I'll drive you," Whit told Charlotte, and they ran to the parking lot.

Teddy was in the backseat, Suzette half seated, half leaning on him. Helen drove away, her hands trembling on the steering wheel.

From the passenger seat, Worth reached over and put his warm hand on Helen's. "Take a deep breath. Focus, Helen. The hospital is only a few minutes away. Suzette is young and healthy. She's doing fine. We're all doing fine."

His voice was low and calm, and the words he spoke were very much like the words he had said to her when she was in labor with their three children, especially the first time. But each time she had been frightened anyway; it was the unsureness of it all. She had never remembered how ferocious the pain was. The pain always seemed so violent, Helen had thought it indicated a problem, something wrong with the baby or the labor, and her fear had intensified her agony.

"Teddy," Worth said, turning to his son, "take a deep breath. Breathe evenly, and help Suzette get her breathing in control. She's going to be fine."

Teddy nodded, but just then Suzette cried out in agony and her body arched upward on the seat.

"Dad, Dad!" Teddy yelled. "What can I do? What can I do?"

"I'm going to die!" Suzette screamed. "Help me, please help me!"

"Listen, Suzette." Worth's voice was calm but forceful. "You're not going to die. This pain is normal. This pain is natural. You are not going to die. You might be in transition." He glanced over at Helen, whose hands were clamped for dear life onto the steering wheel. "Doesn't this sound like transition?" He turned back to Suzette. "If this is transition, you'll have your baby any moment now. Look, here we are, almost to the hospital. Teddy, take deep breaths. Suzette, hold Teddy's hands. Squeeze them when the pain is the worst."

Helen sped into the hospital parking lot, braking to a halt next to the emergency room door so hard the car nearly skidded. In the backseat, Suzette screamed and screamed, while Teddy yelled, "You'll be all right. We're at the hospital. You'll be all right."

Before she'd turned the engine off, Worth jumped out of the car, ran into the hospital, and came back with a wheelchair. Suzette was in the throes of a contraction, so they could only wait patiently until it had ended. Then Worth helped Teddy ease Suzette from the car and into the wheelchair.

"I'll park the car," Worth told Helen. "You go with them."

She was so grateful to him for understanding her need she almost wept. "Thanks."

They entered the hospital through the automatic doors. An orderly was there to help Teddy steer Suzette down the long hall to the elevator. Helen stopped at the desk to fill out the necessary forms, then raced off to the maternity ward, holding her long skirt high as she pounded up the stairs, too anxious to wait for the slow elevator. The second floor of the small hospital was quiet and dark—it was after ten o'clock—and Helen was led to Suzette's room by the sound of her shrieks. She stepped into the room but stayed by the door.

Two nurses were with Suzette, who had been somehow maneuvered onto the high hospital bed. They were helping her undress and don a hospital gown. Once she was resting against a pillow, a nurse did a pelvic check. "Six centimeters."

"No!" Suzette cried. "That can't be right! I'm in transition! They said I was in transition."

"You're not in transition," the nurse insisted. "You shouldn't push yet. You've got a while to go."

"But I can't!" Suzette wailed. "I can't do this anymore!"

"Sure you can," the nurse assured her pleasantly. "You're young. You'll be fine."

Helen spoke up. "Her due date isn't for another month."

"Oh, an eager baby," the nurse cooed. "I love eager babies." She smoothed Suzette's hair. "We're going to put the fetal heart monitor on you now. It won't hurt you, and it won't hurt your baby. Standard procedure."

"Oh, no!" Suzette screamed. "Here it comes again! Fuck this!" She arched her back in anguish.

"Father," the nurse said to Teddy, "could you go to the other side of the bed, please? And perhaps you might help her focus on her breathing. Talk to her. Show her how to breathe."

Worth entered the room, breathless from running. "How is she?"

Helen told him. "Six centimeters."

Charlotte rushed into the room, followed by Whit. "How is she?"

The nurse looked up from the monitor. "Too many people in the room."

"Right," Helen said. "Let's go out in the hall."

Charlotte reared back with alarm when she heard Suzette shriek. "Is she all right?"

"She's in labor," Helen told her daughter. "She's in pain, but the answer to your question is yes, she's all right."

They remained in a cluster by the door, all of them straining to hear, longing to help, feeling helpless. A doctor they didn't know swept past them and into Suzette's room.

"He looks annoyed," Worth said.

"Probably had to leave a party," Charlotte told her father. "It *is* Saturday night."

"Babies can be *so* inconvenient that way," Helen said jokingly.

Suzette's scream peaked, then softened. After a few more minutes, Teddy came out into the hall. He'd undone his tie, and it hung limply against his shirt. His blond hair stuck out in odd places, as if he'd been pulling it. "They're going to give her an epidural. They said it could still be hours yet before the baby comes."

"You're kidding!" Charlotte cried.

Helen put a steadying hand on Teddy's arm. "Is there anything we can do? I know. We'll go home and get you a change of clothing."

Teddy wore a lightweight navy blazer that had once belonged to his grandfather Herb. He grinned. "Oh, I don't know, Mom, I kind of like the idea of dressing up for my child's birth."

"Will you phone us the minute the baby's born?" Helen asked.

"Absolutely." Teddy answered his mother but looked at his father when he said, "Thanks for helping us tonight."

Worth nodded brusquely, and then, surprising Helen and Teddy, too, he leaned forward and hugged his son. "Good luck in there."

"Thanks, Dad." Suzette screamed again and Teddy turned. "I'll call." He disappeared into the labor room.

The others lingered for a moment, and then Whit said, "Well, I guess I'll be going. Charlotte, let me know if you've got a niece or nephew, okay?"

"Of course." Charlotte went up on tiptoes to kiss Whit's cheek. "Thanks for driving me."

Whit strode off down the hall. Helen, Worth, and Charlotte discussed who would drive which car; Charlotte's rented Jeep was still parked at the yacht club. They decided that Helen would drive Charlotte back to the club, and Worth, who had ridden in with his daughter, would go home now with Helen. When they arrived back at the yacht club, Worth got out to hold the door open for Charlotte.

"The party's still going on," he told Charlotte. "Go enjoy yourself."

Charlotte smoothed down her pink silk gown. "Really? That seems so heartless. I feel like I should be—oh, I don't know, pacing the hospital floor and wringing my hands."

"That wouldn't help Suzette," Helen told her.

Charlotte looked uncertain. "Well, okay. I've got my cell phone in my bag. Call me the minute you know anything." She waved at her parents and went into the club.

Helen and Worth were alone in the rented Saab. For a moment Helen was intensely uncomfortable, as the silence and the dark evening settled over them like a kind of tent, enclosing them from the rest of the world. She did not want to be in this close, intimate space with her husband. Sharp pin-pricks of anxiety, excitement, and a strange and private exhilaration—Joe Abernathy!—stabbed her mind. Part of her still lingered at the hospital, in that room with Suzette, in labor with Suzette, for the young woman's cries had summoned up a surprising sense of envy and desire. She wanted to lean back against the seat and close her senses against the present and remember her three deliveries. Suzette's screams had made Helen viscerally recall her own labor pain. The intensity. The passion.

"I can't help but think of the night Oliver was born."

Worth's voice made Helen jump. Giving herself a little shake, she steered the car out of the parking lot and onto the road.

"I remember how hard you clutched my hand," Worth said in a low musing tone. "I had bruises—"

But Helen did not want to play that sweet game. "Does *Cindy* have children? Did she describe her birth experiences to you?"

Worth went quiet. They rode through the dark streets, past the various shops and restaurants, and then they were at the rotary, leaving the commercial buildings behind.

"Cindy doesn't have children," Worth said at last. "Helen, I'll tell you anything you want to know about her, but I don't particularly want to talk about her. I've told her it's over between us, and I don't want to think about her anymore. I want to think about you, us, our family. I'll do whatever it takes to convince you that I'm sorry. I want our marriage. I need our marriage."

Helen listened to him, and his words did give her heart ease.

"Say something," Worth urged.

She almost snorted. All their lives, she had been the one coaxing Worth to talk, she had been the one babbling out her innermost thoughts. "Worth, it helps to hear you say you need our marriage. I'm glad. But you know what? I think I'm over-whelmed. My fuses are all blown. I'm so excited and concerned about Suzette and her baby, I'm not sure I can think clearly about anything else."

His voice was terse, as if he'd been rebuffed. "You were the one who brought Cindy up."

She didn't reply. They drove the rest of the way in silence.

*At home,* Helen changed out of her satin skirt and silk top and into practical clothes, white capris and a loose lightweight navy cotton sweater, so that she would be dressed and ready to rush to the hospital the moment the call came. She lay down on the bed, telling herself she knew she wouldn't sleep but would rest, *should* rest, and the next thing she knew, the sun was spilling through the windows. She sprang up, alarmed. It was so late! Surely

Suzette had had the baby by now. Why had no one told her?

A look at the clock calmed her down. It was only five-thirty. Stepping quietly, she made her way through the upstairs and down to the kitchen. She was the only one awake. She couldn't believe she'd slept through the night. She thought of Suzette, still in labor. She thought of Worth. She thought of Joe Abernathy, his warm, thick, muscular body against hers.

"Well, you look like the cat who ate the cream." Charlotte came in from the mudroom. "Any news?"

"The phone hasn't rung. Or at least I didn't hear it. Do you suppose I should call?"

"I don't know. I suppose. Are you making coffee? I'd love some." Charlotte fixed herself a bowl of cereal, sank onto a chair, and with the lithe grace of the young and slender, pulled up her legs and crossed them Indian style. She looked like a child. "I don't suppose you'd man the farm stand for me this morning? Suzette's been doing it, and it's August, and I'm swamped."

"Of course," Helen told her daughter. "It will help me pass the time."

*The call came* at eleven-thirty. Helen was enjoying herself at the stand, exchanging friendly banter with the customers, some of whom she knew, when the Chrysler suddenly came down the

391

dirt driveway, Worth at the wheel. He was beaming. "It's a girl. Six pounds. All her toes and fingers."

Helen jumped up so fast she nearly knocked over the table. "Oh! Oh! Oh, Worth, a little girl!"

"Come on, get in," Worth said.

Charlotte drove up behind Worth in her rented Jeep. "Go on, Mom," she called. "I'm going to close the stand." She held up a hastily contrived sign:

BEACH GRASS GARDEN CLOSED TODAY AS WE WELCOME BRAND NEW BABY GIRL WHEELWRIGHT!

Helen jumped into the convertible with Worth, grateful that the top was down. Conversation was always hard with the wind rushing over her head. Never had the road seemed so winding and long, never had they had to slow so often for dawdling vehicles, never had her heart beat with such impatience. A granddaughter!

Finally they peeled into the hospital parking lot. Helen was out the door before Worth had taken his keys from the ignition. His long strides made up for her quickened steps, so they entered the hospital together and raced up the stairs.

"Wait for me!" Charlotte called, only a few feet behind.

"Hurry!" Helen called back to her daughter. She felt absolutely childish with glee and anticipation.

They burst into the maternity ward and were

directed to the same room Suzette had gone into the night before. The door was closed.

"Quiet," Helen cautioned. "They might all be sleeping." She grasped Worth's hand hard; it was like clutching the bar on a Ferris wheel or roller coaster.

They went through the door. Suzette half lay, half sat on the bed, her multicolored hair limp against her skull. She looked up at them, her blue eyes shining. Teddy sat on the side of the bed, gazing down at the bundle in Suzette's arms.

"Hey," he said to his parents. "Come meet Dawn. We named her Dawn. She was born right at dawn." He slipped off the bed so his parents and sister could get close to his wife and new daughter.

Helen eased her hand from Worth's. She moved close to the bed and peeked down, then said to Suzette. "May I hold her?"

"Sure." Suzette lifted her baby up.

Dawn was coddled in white blankets, which Helen pulled away slightly, so she could see more of the infant, the little arms, the wrinkled neck. "Oh, she's beautiful."

Charlotte squeezed up. "Let me see her."

Worth stood behind them, pressing to see. After a moment, he said, "She has black hair." Looking into his son's blue eyes, he added, "She has black eyes."

"Like blackberries," Helen cooed. "Worth,

remember, babies' eyes are generally dark blue at birth. And their hair can fall out and another color come in."

But Worth turned without another word and left the room.

## *Twenty-three*

*I*t was Grace who broke the news to Nona. Of course, Nona thought, it would be.

Nona was in her wicker chair in the garden, toying with the lunch Glorious had brought her on a tray. A disgustingly healthy lunch, basically a salad with some chicken breast cut up in bits. And a piece of seven-grain bread, nicely buttered. Glorious took great responsibility for the state of Nona's bowels. Nona was grateful, but she would have preferred a club sandwich.

"Nona!" Grace actually tripped on the threshold as she rushed from the house out onto the patio. "Suzette had her baby!"

Nona's old heart leaped. "Tell me everything!"

"It's a little girl. Only six pounds, but all her bits and bobs intact."

Nona clapped her hands together. "How lovely!"

"Maybe not," Grace said, trying to sound solemn but unable to disguise the satisfaction in her voice. "She has *black* hair and *olive* skin. Suzette and Teddy both have blue eyes and blond hair—well,

Suzette *would,* if she ever let the natural color grow back."

Nona let the information float in the air between them. "How is Suzette?"

"Oh, I think she's fine. It was Helen who phoned, and she said Suzette's kind of bleary from the experience, but she's okay. Well, she should be, she's so young. And I'm not so sure that baby was a month early, not when she has eyelashes and fingernails and all. Nona, I don't want you to be upset, but I'm not so very sure this is your—um, great-grandchild, your blood relative. From what I've heard, she doesn't look a thing like anyone in our family."

"Oh, Grace," Nona said. She meant it as a rebuke, but Grace took it as disappointment.

"I know, I know, it's unfortunate. But apparently Teddy isn't upset. Maybe he's just being nice to Suzette. Anyway, Charlotte's taking photos with her digital camera, and she'll be here any moment to show them to us."

"Mom!" Mellie waddled out onto the patio. "You promised you'd take me shopping! There's a trunk show at the jeweler's."

"Suzette had her baby," Grace gushed. "A little girl. With *black* hair and *olive* skin!"

"Oooh," Mellie cooed. "A little girl. How's Suzette?"

"She's fine," Grace snapped impatiently, disappointed by her daughter's response.

"After we go to the jeweler's, we can buy some cute little pink things for the baby," Mellie said. "And some flowers! Come on, Mom, I don't want to be late."

Nona's daughter and granddaughter scurried away. Nona let her head fall back against her chair. Suddenly she was exhausted. If she had the energy to call Glorious, she'd ask her to help her back to bed. But she was too tired even to call out.

Perhaps she dozed. She heard Grace's car roar off, and then silence.

It seemed only a moment later that she heard the Chrysler's familiar purr. She looked around. The shadows had shifted on the patio, so she had slept, time had passed.

She heard the slam of car doors and the crunch of gravel. Then she heard Worth and Helen, and they were arguing.

She played possum, shutting her eyes again and letting her head fall sideways.

They came through the hedge. Worth sounded furious. "That baby is not my grandchild."

"Lower your voice. Nona's sleeping." Helen spoke softly, but her voice shook with rage.

"Helen, how can you disagree with me about this? Any moron could see that child is not Teddy's."

"No!" Helen's voice cut like a whip. "Any *moron* could see the love on Teddy's face when he looks at that little girl!"

"Why are you so eager to claim a child who has no blood relation to you?" Worth demanded. "Charlotte will get married someday. She'll give you grandchildren. Hell, Suzette might even have a baby with Teddy!"

"Don't be disgusting. Teddy loves Suzette. Clearly he loves the little girl. So what if she's not his genetically. He'll adopt her."

"That doesn't mean I have to call her my grand-child." Worth was almost snarling.

They didn't speak as they walked past Nona and stepped over the threshold and into the living room.

Just inside the French doors, Helen said, "Worth. You've said you want us to stay together."

*"Of course I do!"*

"If that's what you want, what you really want, I'm telling you this in no uncertain terms: You can have it, if you will stop being such a total jackass and accept this baby, this baby Teddy *loves,* into our family."

Worth's voice turned bitter. "You're black-mailing me, Helen. Even if I say whatever you want me to say, I can't change the way I *feel.*"

"Oh, yes, you can. You want me to change the way I feel about certain matters, don't you? You'd like me to live out the rest of my life as if certain thoughts and sorrows and imaginings didn't press on my heart like stones. You'd like me to love you again, right? Really love you?"

Worth grumbled, "The two—*sins*—are not equal."

"Worth," Helen said, and her voice was adamant, "I will divorce you."

Nona's heart jumped. She held her breath and strained to hear.

"For God's sake, Helen."

Helen remained calm but unyielding. "I mean it. I will divorce you."

There was silence. When Worth spoke again, his voice was conciliatory. "Let me put it this way, Helen. You want a grandchild. I want an *heir.*"

"That little girl could be your heir."

"No."

"Then we're at an impasse."

Helen, then Worth, stormed through the living room, into the hall, and up the stairs.

*I must tell them now,* Nona thought. *I only hope I'm not too late.*

### January 1946

"*Ilke? Wer ist es?*" Even with the German words, the man's voice was familiar.

Anne remained frozen on the threshold of the house. Perhaps it was the wrong house, she thought. Perhaps it was the right house and this woman lived with her husband and Herb had been given a room here. Perhaps—

The German woman stepped back into the

shadows just as Herb strode down the hall to the open door. He wore his khaki uniform, with his tie tucked inside his shirt between the third and fourth button. His hair was shorter than she'd ever seen it, parted on the left, combed into blond furrows. When he saw Anne, he slammed to a halt, lurching backward, as if he'd run into a pane of glass. His jaw dropped.

"Anne?" His expression showed surprise and then, quickly, not joy, not delight, but consternation. "Anne, is that really you?"

She took one step forward, reaching out her hand to touch him. "It's really me, Herb. I came on a Stangarone freighter."

"My God." Herb lifted his arms to receive her as she pressed herself against him, but he did not bend to kiss her lips. "My God, Anne."

When he did not kiss her, her fears were confirmed. Still, she tried to sound normal—what was *normal* now?—as she moved back from her husband and, with a bright smile, asked, "And who is your beautiful friend?"

"Anne." Herb stumbled over his words for a moment, and then gathered himself. "Anne, this is Ilke Hartman. The army requisitioned a spot in her home for me. She—she has been very good to me over this past year."

*Well,* Anne thought, *that was ambiguous.* She forced herself to smile at Ilke. "It's nice to meet you, Ilke." Rats, she thought, I sound like Herb's mother, all prissy and polite. But how did you talk to a German, anyway?

Ilke did not return Anne's smile. Instead, she spoke to Herb in German, her words rushing together in a stream of guttural explosions. Herb replied in German. Ilke turned, then, and slowly climbed the stairs to the second floor.

Herb reached forward to shut the front door of the house. Then he put his hand on Anne's arm. "Come into the kitchen, Anne. Are you hungry? Thirsty? How did you get here; I mean, how did you find the house? You must be very tired."

She told him about Georgia and her bike ride as he towed her along down the dark hallway.

"You left the bike on the street?" Herb demanded, sounding almost angry. He left her, ran down the hall, and out the front door. The bike leaned against the brick wall. Herb picked it up and carried it inside. "Nothing is safe here. You have to remember, people will scavenge anything, they need everything. A working bike with all its parts is like gold."

She said, "I didn't know."

"No, of course not, I'm not scolding, I'm just telling you."

He led her into a warm room smelling of baked bread and bacon. A kettle steamed softly on the stove and a cat lay curled in one of the kitchen chairs around a long wooden table. Herb shut the door to the hallway and gestured to a chair.

She laughed. "Herb! Herb, I don't want to sit down! I didn't just come three thousand miles in order to sit down and have some *bacon!* I want to hold you, Herb, my goodness, I want to cover you with kisses. I've missed you so much, I couldn't live one more minute without you!"

His face did not lighten. He frowned. He moved away. He ran his hands through his hair. "Well," he said, and a weight of guilt was in his tone. "Well. It's not—" He looked at Anne. "How do I tell you this?"

"Just say it."

"That woman you met. Ilke. She's carrying my child."

Now Anne did sit down, because her legs would no longer support her. The information flew into her like a flaming arrow, piercing her with flame.

"I'm sorry, Anne. I never meant—you have to understand. The war, the winter—it was hard. So much death and devastation, the world was black to me. And then to be here in a kind of civilization, and Ilke was so kind—and you have to understand, Anne, I was so weary. So stunned. Even then I didn't know for sure that I would live another day."

Anne nodded. She was gripping her hands together, but she struggled to keep her voice pleasant, not accusing, not injured. "So was it comfort with this Ilke? Comfort, not love?" *If he says yes,* Anne thought, even as her belly burned with jealousy, *I can survive this.*

"Yes. Yes, Anne, it was comfort, not love." His skin went blotchy with emotion. "I'm not proud of that fact."

"And she got pregnant."

"Yes."

"Did she know you are married?"

"Yes. She knows all about you. I showed her your picture."

The thought of Herb and the other woman bent together over her picture, the two of them in a kind of conspiracy, increased the pain in her heart. For a moment she was too overwhelmed to speak. Finally, she asked softly, "And what are your plans?"

Herb surprised Anne by laughing, a bitter laugh she'd never heard from him before. "My *plans?* My plans are simply to live through this day and the next."

"The war is over," Anne protested.

"But not the danger. We are occupying German territory. Unexploded bombs are everywhere. Some Germans hate us, and who could blame them? Three days ago a sixty-year-old cobbler killed the American who was billeted with him, in revenge for the death in the war of his own son." Seeing the alarm on Anne's face, he hurriedly continued. "No, I fear no harm from Ilke."

"Because you are lovers."

He didn't reply.

"When is her baby due?" The words were glass shards in her heart.

"In six weeks."

"It is your baby."

"Yes." He looked at Anne with old and weary eyes. "Her parents were killed during a bombing of Bremerhaven. Her fiancé was killed at Normandy. Her brother was killed in the Bulge." He made a gruff noise. "For all I know, my men could have been the ones to kill him."

"What will you do once the baby is born?" Anne asked.

"I haven't thought that far."

"Do you plan to divorce me? To marry the mother of your child?" *Please,* Anne prayed, *please God, help me.*

"No," Herb said, quietly. "No, of course I don't want to divorce you. I love you, Anne. But the baby—I don't know."

Anne buried her face in her hands. Tears poured from her eyes. She thought the pain would destroy her. Desperately she wondered what to do next: flee this house where her husband had been living with a beautiful German woman? Try to live in this town with Georgia and work at Stangarone's? After all, her own situation was hardly significant in the scope of the damage wrought by this war. She didn't even know where she would sleep tonight. How many bedrooms were in this little house, how many beds? Was Herb sleeping with Ilke? Would he lie down next to the beautiful blond woman while Anne lay awake, writhing with jealousy, in the next room?

"Herb," she choked out, because she had to say it, "Herb, that woman is *German*. How could you sleep with a German? How could you?"

Herb said sadly, "The war is over. Ilke is not just a German. She is, first of all, a human being."

"Oh, *damn* you and your piety!" Anne grabbed the first thing she saw—a small cut-class bowl of sugar on the tabletop with a matching small pitcher of cream—and threw it across the room. It smashed against the wall. With a yowl, the cat leaped up and darted out. "How convenient for you, to see her as a *human being*. You are not King Arthur, Herb, you are not a damned knight in shining armor, an open-minded, generous, kind-hearted saint! You're just another man who's played around on his wife and got caught!" Her rage was fully unfolding within her. She rose and paced the small room, flailing her arms in the air. "Don't you think I longed for *comfort,* too? Don't you think I had opportunities to sleep around? Not every attractive man was overseas, you know. There were plenty—but I wanted only you!" Her final words cut through her anger with a broad swath of grief, and she collapsed, knees buckling, sobbing. "I wanted *only you.*"

Herb came to her. He wrapped his arms around

her and helped her stand, and he held her close to him, patting her back, murmuring softly, "Anne, oh, Anne."

"Why couldn't you want only me?" she cried.

"It was the war, Anne. It was the war."

His embrace soothed her. Hearing his voice with her ear pressed against his chest reassured her. It was so familiar. And it was loving, she could feel his love like a balm, soothing her burning pain. After a while, her tears stopped. Herb asked her to sit down. He put food on plates for them both—an odd little meal of bread and bacon and potatoes fried in bacon fat. Anne couldn't eat hers, but she finally drank the tea, and when Herb saw that she really had no appetite, he put her food on his plate, and ate it all.

"You learn never to waste food here," he explained.

He asked about his parents, and her parents, and Gail, and the island, and he seemed to come into focus as they spoke. Anne sat back in her chair and studied him. He was very thin, almost gaunt. Blue half-circles of tiredness lay across his cheeks. She felt a twinge of guilt for her own selfish tirade. What did she really know about the war, about the conditions of his life these past months?

When he'd finished eating, he pushed his plate away and leaned back in his chair. For the first time, he relaxed. "I can't believe you're really here." He looked at his watch. "You must be tired."

She shook her head. "I suppose. I've got so many emotions raging inside me, I don't know how I feel."

"You should sleep. I should sleep. I have so much work to do tomorrow." Seeing the alarm on her face, he said, "There are two bedrooms upstairs. Ilke is in her parents' room. You can have the back bedroom. No one has been sleeping there."

*Meaning,* Anne understood, *Herb hadn't been making love to Ilke on that bed.*

"I'll sleep on the couch in the front parlor," Herb continued. Again he picked up on her reaction. "I don't suppose you want me sleeping with you tonight. And no, I haven't been sleeping in Ilke's bed for some time now. She's too restless with her pregnancy. I've been on the sofa. I actually like the sofa. I like having the security of the back against my back. It makes me feel safe."

Once again Anne felt a stab of guilt that opened her up to a kind of understanding of what Herb's life had been like during the war. She wanted the security of him in her bed. He wanted only the security of a safe place to sleep. So things were reduced to the elementary here, to primitive needs. The desire to console him fought with her jealousy and anger.

"Yes, all right," Anne said. "I understand."

They both rose. She was surprised when he carried their dishes to the sink and began to wash them. She found the dish towel and dried the dishes.

After a moment, Herb said, "I don't know how we're going to work this out, Anne. I feel responsible, I *am* responsible, for the baby Ilke is carrying. She has lost so much; her best friend died in the bombing of Bremerhaven. I want to be here to help her until she has the baby."

"And afterward?" Anne asked.

"I don't know. She has other friends, a married couple who live on the edge of the city. And she is a librarian; she worked at the library until a month ago." He ran his damp hand through his hair. "I hadn't thought, Anne. It's been a matter of living day to day. I suppose I mean to support her financially, support the child financially. It's the least I can do. More than that. . . ." He sagged against the sink.

Anne touched his arm. "You're tired. Show me where I should sleep."

She followed him up the stairs and down a carpeted hall into a surprisingly large room filled with handsome furniture. The bed was covered with a fat down quilt, unlike any she'd ever seen before, and she felt a visceral knock at this reminder that she was in a foreign country. Herb showed her the one bathroom in the house—an unimaginable luxury, he said—and took a fresh towel from a wardrobe in the hall.

As they moved around, Anne's senses were alert. Would Ilke come out to talk to them? What would she say? What would Herb say? If Herb spoke to the other woman in German, Anne thought she would die of jealousy, she would throw something at him, and not a sugar bowl. But the door was closed tightly on the room at the front, and all seemed quiet within.

"I'll see you in the morning, Anne," Herb said. He looked at her for a moment; then he briefly, quickly, kissed her forehead. "We'll work this out, somehow."

He went down the stairs. Anne had carried her toothbrush and her comb and brush in her purse. Her luggage had been transferred, she hoped, to Stangarone's. Tonight she would sleep in her underwear and slip. She remained dressed as she used the bathroom, for the house was cold.

She stepped out of the bathroom. Across the hall, the door to the big bedroom was open. Ilke stood there, clad in a rose-colored flannel nightgown. She looked like a very large fat child.

Anne hesitated. What could she say to this woman, her husband's lover? *I hate you. I wish you didn't exist. You have ruined my life.*

Before she could say anything, Ilke spoke. Her voice was low but compelling. "He always choose you," Ilke said. "I know he always choose you." Then she shut the door.

Anne waited, feeling unfinished, wanting to say or do something—but what? If she were Gail, she'd snap back, "You've got that right, toots." But she wasn't Gail. She stumbled to the bedroom, dropped her dress, peeled off her ruined nylons, and slipped under the down quilt. She was asleep at once.

In her dreams, a woman was crying. Anne woke slowly. For a moment the dream stayed with her and she wasn't sure just where she was. In her Boston bed? On Nantucket? On a rocking bunk? No, in a German bed.

And a woman was crying. From the other room came a deep and primal lowing, almost a mooing. Anne sat up and swung her legs over the bed. Some instinct inside her, something she'd never known existed, urged her to listen. To *react*.

Through the window, the sky was bright blue. She glanced at her watch. It was after nine! She pulled on her clothes and hurried into the bathroom, then down the stairs and back to the kitchen. A pot of tea had been made, but it was cool now. Herb had already gone to work.

Upstairs, the urgent sounds, deep and primitive, continued.

*Buck up, Anne,* she told herself. She climbed the stairs and knocked on Ilke's door.

"Come!"

Cautiously, Anne peered into the other woman's room. Ilke was lying on her side, her arms wrapped around a pillow. She had part of the pillow stuffed into her mouth.

Anne asked, "Are you all right?"

Ilke's body suddenly arched and stiffened. Her

fingers went white as she clutched the pillow like a life preserver that would keep her from drowning in her pain. The bed linens were tousled, the quilt fallen in a heap on the floor at the foot of the bed. Ilke's flannel nightgown had ridden up in a bunch around her hips, exposing long thin legs and a thatch of pale brown pubic hair. Anne looked away, embarrassed. Then the long low moaning began, partly stifled by the pillow. Anne clasped her hands. What should she do? What *could* she do?

After a moment, Ilke relaxed. Panting, she said, "My labor has started."

"But isn't it early?"

"Yes. But it happens."

"We need to call the doctor."

To her amazement, Ilke laughed. "I don't need a doctor. I am only having a baby." She began to moan again.

Anne found herself wringing her hands in response. "What can I do?"

When she could catch her breath, Ilke said, "This could go on all day."

"Good God."

"You could bring me water."

Anne took the glass from the bedside table and hurried across the hall into the bathroom. She had heard stories about the agonies of labor, but this was the first time she witnessed someone enduring it. It frightened her; it made her wonder whether she would ever want to bear children herself, if it meant undergoing such extreme pain.

Back in the bedroom, she knelt by the bed, slipped her hand beneath Ilke's head, and supported her as she drank thirstily from the glass. Ilke's hair was as soft as silk.

"Thank you," Ilke said. "It is a help to me that you are here."

"Is there someone I could call?"

Ilke grimaced. "We have no telephone."

So this was up to Anne. She couldn't go off and leave the woman alone. She pulled a chair up to the side of the bed. For the next two hours, Ilke writhed and panted and growled, no longer bothering to stuff the pillow into her mouth, but groaning, her throat arching upward, her head falling backward, her hands clutching the sheets. Her hair grew damp with sweat, and from time to time Anne would lean over to dab a moist cool cloth against Ilke's forehead. It seemed a foolish, silly thing to do, in the face of the woman's pain, but Ilke, when she could talk, thanked her.

When the contractions eased, Ilke rested. Anne surveyed her surroundings. The floor was covered with a thick wool Persian carpet, so Anne assumed Ilke's family had had money before the war. The drapes were heavy and glossy, patterned with cabbage roses and swirling vines. Framed portraits of relatives hung on the wall, and on the dresser stood a photograph of what must have once been

411

Ilke's family, parents and brother, all of them standing on some seashore, smiling in the sun. Ilke had lost them all.

Anne bent her head. What would she do if she lost her parents? She seldom saw them, wrote to them only occasionally, but they were the center of the spinning earth to her, they were gravity. Herb was—at least Herb had been—her sun, her moon, her stars, her wind and weather. But her parents were the profound security of her sense of life; they provided the reliable ground she walked upon. To lose them? Unbearable.

Her thoughts were interrupted by a new noise from Ilke, a shout.

Ilke rose up in bed, now obviously frantic. She yelled at Anne in German, loud, guttural, gut-wrenching noises.

"What can I do?" she asked.

"Help me!" Ilke screamed. "*Gott in Himmel!*"

To Anne's surprise, Ilke propelled herself off the bed. She leaned her arms on it, bracing herself as she planted her feet wide on the floor. She was *bellowing* now, and she did not rest; her yelling was long, continuous, agonized. Anne saw that the bed linens were soggy with blood and mucus and water, and Ilke's legs shone with moisture. Ilke pulled her gown up to her chest, exposing her taut swollen belly and her thin flanks. Anne was embarrassed and helpless and terrified.

She knelt next to Ilke. She had to yell to make herself heard. "How can I help you?"

"Get blankets. Get scissors. This baby is coming. You must catch the baby."

*Catch the baby?* Anne stared, confused.

"Scissors on the dresser. Now! *Scheiste*!"

Anne was surprised people weren't pounding on the door, running up the stairs, demanding to know what was happening here. Ilke's screams were earsplitting. She gathered herself, stood up, found the scissors, and brought them back. In the moment that she had stepped away from Ilke's side, the other woman's face had turned scarlet, almost purple, as she expelled her breath in a long continuous grunt.

A flood of bright red blood splattered onto the floor between Ilke's legs.

"Help me!" Ilke pleaded. "Hold me. Support me."

Anne knelt behind the other woman. She braced her hands on Ilke's hips and felt the earthquake shuddering of her body. Ilke was screaming, and Anne had the mad desire to scream, too, to scream in terror and sympathy, and then Ilke's legs moved, as if she had suddenly become bowlegged, and her body seemed to crack, and Ilke yelled, "Baby coming!" and Anne moved her hands beneath Ilke's swollen crotch and felt the wet silk of a baby's head.

All she had to do was keep her hands there. The

baby, slippery as a seal, slid out into Anne's hands. It was red and slimy with mucus and blood, and its umbilical cord was like a red, pulsing vine. It opened its mouth and cried, the sound high and weak compared to its mother's shouts. Somehow Anne maneuvered the baby around so that Ilke could see it. As she did, the afterbirth spilled out onto the floor, staining the rug with red.

Ilke was panting now, and her entire body trembled. She crawled up onto the bed and held out her arms.

Anne gave her the tiny, squirming, wailing baby. She said, "You have a son."

## Twenty-four

*Nona needed* to do this with great care, and she could not take time for planning, for shaping her words. She had to do this now.

Rising on her shaky old legs, she slowly made her way from the terrace and into the house. "Glorious?" She hated the quaver in her voice.

Glorious appeared. "Did you call me?"

"I'd like to go upstairs, dear. Could you help me?"

Glorious was at her side at once. With the other woman to lean on, Nona made it across the living room and the hall and began climbing the stairs. It helped, having Glorious there. Glorious loaned her strength, and that kept fear of falling from slowing her down.

When they reached the second floor, they could hear, from behind Worth's bedroom door, the sound of argument.

Glorious didn't mention it; she was good about that. But when she finally had Nona settled in her chaise by the window, she asked, "Would you like a little Scotch?"

"I'd love it," Nona answered.

She lay back against the chaise, resting. She felt ancient and very tired, and she was dreading what she was about to do. But the time had come.

"Here you are." Glorious came into her bedroom, set the highball glass on the table near Nona, and nodded. "Anything else?"

"Yes, Glorious. I'd like you to open the bottom drawer of my dresser. Yes, that one. See the old quilted photo album? Put it on the table next to me, please."

Glorious did as she was requested.

Nona took a fortifying sip of Scotch. "Now. Will you please ask Worth and Helen to come see me?"

"Surely."

Glorious left the room, returning with Worth and Helen behind her. Their faces were still flushed from their battle.

But Nona smiled. "Good. Worth. And Helen. I want to talk to you both. I have something I need to tell you."

"All right, Nona." Worth pulled up a chair for Helen and one for himself, almost touching Nona's knees, so she would not be troubled to project her voice, which was shaky this morning. "We're all ears."

Nona cleared her throat. "Now that the time has come, I find it harder than I expected." Emotion hit her hard. She lifted her hands and covered her face. "Oh, dear, oh, dear."

Worth reached out to put a reassuring hand on Nona's knee. "Mother. It can't be that bad, whatever it is."

"Perhaps not. We'll see." Nona dropped her hands and struggled to straighten in her chair. "Very well. Worth, on the table there, the burgundy quilted photo album. Could you open it, please?"

Worth obeyed. The album was old, the pages made of black construction paper, with black-and-white photos attached by glue and yellowing tape.

"Hey. Is this Dad's World War Two album?" He studied the first photo, of several soldiers standing on a cobblestone street. "Why didn't he ever show this to us?" He found his father, slim and young and handsome. He put his finger on his father and looked up at Nona. "Here's Dad."

"Turn the page," Nona said.

Worth turned the page. This was a black-and-white interior shot. Herb Wheelwright was seated at desk piled with papers, a chrome ashtray, and two black telephones. Herb wore a khaki shirt and tie and a dress blouse with the battalion insignia and stripes on his arm and on his lapel the bar of a first lieutenant.

Behind him stood two other army officers, one leaning casually on a wooden file cabinet, the other looking jaunty, hands in pockets, grinning. Behind Herb stood a thin, bald, older man in a suit, his face taut and serious. Between the standing men were two young women. One wore a flowered dress and her dark hair was arranged in marcelled waves. The other, a blond woman, wore a simple white shirt and a dark skirt. Her shoulder-length hair was almost white, her eyes luminous, her figure voluptuous.

"Wow, the blonde is a beauty!" Worth exclaimed.

"Yes," Nona agreed. "She is. Look at her carefully, Worth. That woman is your mother."

Worth wrinkled his forehead and shot Nona a look of gentle, benevolent concern.

"Mother." He closed the album. "Perhaps we shouldn't talk about the past. Perhaps it's upsetting you—"

"Worth, I haven't had a stroke and I haven't developed a full-force case of senility overnight. I'm telling you the truth. You need to *hear* me. Your father and I discussed this when it happened, and many times since, and now is the time for you to know."

Worth looked apprehensive. "What would you like for me to know?"

Adrenaline flooded Nona's body. She was not as anxious as she was invigorated. Perhaps everyone felt this way when they remembered a dramatic, life-changing event.

"You know your father was an officer in World War Two. You know he remained in Germany, in the Army of Occupation, for two years. You know that I joined him. You were born in Bremerhaven in 1945. But not in August. In January."

Nona watched Worth shoot a quick look of disbelief at Helen. She was glad that Helen was here to share this—this *bombshell.* The pertinence of the word made her bark out a kind of choked laugh, which made Worth look even more worried.

She continued. "These are the facts, Worth. Perhaps we should have told you before now. Or perhaps I should never have told you. You must understand how much thought I've given this."

Worth said, gently, "Mother. You and Father were married in 1943."

"We were. And we were separated for almost two years by the war. Your father saw terrible things—men fighting, men dying—and for months he was on the battlefield, living in the harshest conditions, eating dreadful food, sleeping on the cold ground, not knowing whether he would live or die. I'm not trying to excuse what he did. I'm trying to explain. When the war was over, he was sent to Bremerhaven to head up the organization and dispersal of supplies arriving in that port city and sent throughout a devastated country. He was billeted in Ilke Hartman's home. That woman, with the white-blond hair, that is Ilke Hartman. That is your mother."

Irritation rasped in Worth's voice. "You really should stop saying that."

"You really should listen to me." Nona's voice was sharper than she meant it to be, but it silenced Worth. "I sailed to Bremerhaven in January, to work at the European end of the Stangarone shipping offices. When I arrived, I found your father living with Ilke, and she was pregnant, she was pregnant by your father. He told me they had been lovers. He told me her child was his. She gave birth in January. I was there. Worth, I was there at your birth. I saw you born."

"But Nona." Helen's tone was urgent. "If this Ilke Hartman was Worth's mother, why was Worth raised here in the United States?"

The accumulated buffer of years dissipated from around Nona like a sea mist, allowing so many emotions to return vividly to her, so many sights and sounds and wounds and terrors. "Because Ilke was killed by a UXB." Seeing their confusion, she added, "An unexploded bomb. They were everywhere in Europe."

Now the memories were beginning to coalesce, to weigh upon her shoulders and her lungs. "Ilke knew a butcher in another part of town, a man who had been a friend of her parents. Her parents, her entire family, had died in the war. Ilke's milk was not abundant, and she decided to go see the butcher, to see if she could convince him to sell her a piece of meat. It was a Monday morning. The baby—you, Worth—was only two weeks old. He was sleeping, and she did not want to carry him with her, because the streets were difficult to walk on, with the rubble in the way, and people were often unruly, shoving in their haste to get to something, anything. The streets were always dangerous. And she knew the butcher well. It seemed a reasonable thing to do." Something thick clogged her trachea. She tried to cough it away.

Helen leaned forward. "Would you like some water, Nona?"

Nona touched her throat, her crepey, turkey-wattle throat. "I've got something here, dear." Nona sipped her Scotch.

"Go on," Worth urged, his voice quiet now.

Nona gazed at the sixty-year-old man, handsome, silver-haired, healthy, sitting before her. "I was taking care of you, Worth. We had not yet decided what we would do, your father and I. He loved me, he had not stopped loving me, but the war . . . the loneliness, the hardships . . . I could understand. I could forgive. It was the war, you see; it was another world. And you were a beautiful baby, vulnerable, innocent, precious. Herb told me he would remain my husband. We would return to the United States eventually. But he intended to claim you as his son and to support Ilke and you. I commended his decision. I knew it was the right thing to do. For two weeks, we three adults managed to live together in—well, you could call it a kind of peace. We understood without saying it that you were the focus of all our lives."

Worth waited in silence.

Nona clasped her hands together, directing her gaze at him. "When you hear an infant cry, Worth, you want to comfort it, feed it, ease its distress. Inside that house, it was such a strange, hot, intense world—did I tell you that the baby was premature? You. You were premature, Worth, you were seven and a half months old when you were born. You were bald and had no eyelashes or eyebrows, no fingernails. We could not weigh you, but I'm sure you weighed no more than five pounds. You were *tiny,* Worth. Absolutely beautiful, but so defenseless. Ilke did not have enough milk for you. Herb managed, through his army contacts, to procure formula, and bottles, and the three of us took turns feeding you, because you were always hungry." Nona leaned forward, her voice suddenly strong, powerful with the force of her emotions. "Try to envision it, Worth. Outside the little brick house spread devastation and ruin and chaos. Buildings were still collapsing, beams and roof slates and window glass giving way as houses and shops and churches and hospitals settled.

Unexploded bombs were everywhere. You could not trust the ground to lie still beneath your feet. Trees lay across sidewalks, their roots dry and crooked, reaching out like the arms of the dead. And the dead were everywhere. You never knew when you might see a hand extending from a pile of debris. You never knew when you might see rats gnawing at something in a mound of broken timbers. Women roamed the street weeping, tearing their hair, their skin. Men staggered through the streets. Some of them howled."

"Nona," Worth cautioned, "you're upsetting yourself."

"No. I'm upsetting *you,* and I mean to. I want you to try to see, really see, what it was like, for me and for your father and for your mother. We lived in a world utterly changed by war. We lived in a world of ruin and shambles. And here you were, a new life, helpless but alive and kicking, giving us all something to hope for. You were like a flower, sprouting from a field of wreckage."

For a moment, the three of them sat quietly, reverently. Nona's old heart was racketing around in her chest like a squirrel trapped in a cage. She forced herself to take deep breaths. She took another sip of Scotch.

Gathering her strength, she continued. "It was a friend of your father's who told us about the bomb. The bomb that killed your mother. Your father wept. I wept, too. I had not come to know Ilke well. I was there only two weeks, after all. But from the beginning she had understood how I felt about the baby, about you. She was so generous with you. She let me help take care of you, she let me rock you and carry you, and after the first week, when it became evident that you needed more nourishment than she could supply, she allowed me to give you the bottle." Tears she could not prevent fell down Nona's face. "We should have hated each other. I suppose, any other time, we would have. At least *resented.* She was so beautiful, Worth. Look at the picture. She was much more beautiful than I. And her laugh—it was like silk. Her speaking voice I didn't find so attractive, all those gutturals and coughing sounds. But her laugh . . . and when she sang lullabies to you, her voice was as sweet as honey. She was very young. She was twenty-one when she died."

Helen reached over and lifted the album from Worth's hands. She studied the photo of Ilke Hartman. "She was beautiful, it's true. But not more beautiful than you, Nona."

"You're being kind. But believe me, I know the truth. Look at her eyes. Look at the shape of her eyes, and the light eyebrows, and how they wing upward at the outside. Like Worth's. Look at the picture, and then look at your face in a mirror, Worth."

Worth shook his head. "I don't know if I can take this all in."

"Give yourself time," Nona advised.

Helen asked, "So you adopted the baby?"

Nona said, "I *claimed* the baby. I stayed in Bremerhaven, with your father and Worth, for two years. In August we wrote home that I had had a premature baby. And Worth *was* a frail, sickly infant. In fact, he was small and under average height for the first five years of his life. He was slow to crawl, slow to walk, he didn't even speak until he was three." She shook her head, remembering. "Imagine our surprise when you suddenly shot up, a strong, healthy, active boy."

"Did the Wheelwrights never suspect?" Helen asked.

Nona laughed. "Not once. They were only too eager to believe that I had given birth to a weakling. And then, as Worth became a person, they fell in love with him, just as everyone did."

Nona sank back into her chaise. Her heart had eased, the pounding receding to its calm and regular beat. She had done it. She had finally told Worth the story of his birth. She studied his face, searching for a sign of his reaction.

Worth had taken back the album and put on his glasses and scrutinized the photo. He raised his head, slipped off his glasses, and folded them. His face was calm when he said, "I know what you're doing, Mother."

"Oh?" She raised an inquisitive eyebrow. "And what is that?"

"You're trying to persuade me to accept Suzette's baby as my own blood."

"Well, yes, I suppose I am. I suppose that's exactly why I chose to tell you this now."

Worth shook his head. "I admire your inventiveness. This is quite a fabulous story you've concocted, and it makes me appreciate even more your own opinions on the matter of this new baby, but it doesn't make me change my mind."

"Oh, Worth." Nona closed her eyes against his disbelief, his stubborn righteousness. What could she do? She had a thought. "Worth, I will take a DNA test. That will prove you are not my son, won't it?"

At this, Worth sagged in defeat. He ran his hand over his face.

Helen asked, "Did Ilke name her son?"

Nona nodded. "She did, of course. She named her baby Hans."

"Hans!" This spurred Worth into a kind of helpless action. He rose from his chair and strode around the bedroom, shaking his head like a bull trying to shake off spears. He clenched his fists, needing to hit something, having no available target. Turning suddenly, he shouted at Nona, "How could you love a child named Hans? How could you love a *German?*"

Nona's reply was simple. "How could I not love *you?*"

Worth wrenched his gaze to Helen. "You know

what this means, don't you? If Nona is telling the truth, it means our children are *German*."

Helen offered a gentle smile. "Oh, Worth, I don't think so. I've never noticed a proclivity for sauerkraut or beer. They can't yodel. They don't—"

"How can you be flippant at a time like this!" Worth thundered. Facing Nona, he demanded, "Why didn't you tell me this before?"

Nona stretched out a beseeching hand, but Worth would not take it. "Your father and I discussed it often. But then again, not as often as you might think. Our lives were busy. You favor your father in your looks: the strong square jaw, the set of your head on your neck, the angle of your ears, your straight patrician nose. Only your eyes are like your biological mother's, but of course I have blue eyes, too, as did Herb. We could not think what good would come of telling you. At first you were too young, and then you were too much *yourself.* Had there ever been a medical exigency, we might have told you, but Worth, think about your life, remember it. When could we have told you? When should we have told you? And why? You are my son. I love you as much as I love Grace. I always have. In fact, I know that Grace believes I favor you. Isn't that right?"

Worth didn't reply. Exhaustion was weighing down on Nona's chest and shoulders. It was as if this secret had filled her life and her body like a second set of lungs, and now it had been excised and she was empty. She was hollow. She wanted to say, *Worth, do you know I am too feeble to carry even baby Zoe across a room? In that same way, I can no longer carry your pride, your anger, your pain, in my heart.* But she only said, "Do you know, my dear ones? I am suddenly very tired."

Helen asked, "Would you like us to help you back to bed?"

"Thank you, no. I think I would prefer to rest on my chaise. But my shoes—" She looked at her son. "Worth, would you help me, please?"

His jaw was set in a lock Nona knew so well. For a moment he hesitated. Then he asked, coldly, politely, "Would you like me to remove your shoes?"

"Please."

He bent on one knee to unlace and slip off her shoes, and Nona saw the top of his head, saw the bald spot beginning in the midst of all his silver hair, and she saw as if through layers of time, how his hair had been thick, white blond, slightly wavy, and once, so long ago, how his scalp had been bald, delicate, defenseless, an infant's bare scalp with its vulnerable fontanel. He had been a sickly baby, relentlessly crying in a thin, high wail, needing constant attention, sleeping only when someone held him.

They had taken turns, Herb and Anne, rocking and walking the infant, for those first few days when Ilke rested, recovering from the sudden birth. Nona could remember the speckled pattern of linoleum on the kitchen floor, the rag rug in the hall, the handsome ivory and green oriental carpet in the parlor. The framed photographs of Ilke Hartman's parents and sister on the mantel. The curtains, heavy striped silk. The comfortable chair, upholstered in velvet and stuffed with horsehair, where she had often sat, for the few moments the infant would allow her to rest. Outside the house had been chaos and destruction. Inside the house was warmth and order and new life.

Anne had not slept with Herb those two weeks. He remained on the sofa and left for work every morning and returned every evening, bringing whatever food supplies he had scrounged from army supplies or bought on the black market. Anne never went to work at Stangarone's. She was too busy keeping house, making stews; women today had no idea how much time the preparation of meals used to take. And how everything had to be saved. She could make one chicken last the three of them for four days. First, the luxury of roasted chicken. Then, a casserole made with back meat and noodles. Then, a stew from the bones and flour dumplings. Finally, a soup, with whatever vegetables could be found to add.

The lion's share of the food went to Ilke, who was nursing the baby, or trying to, not very successfully. Anne lost a great deal of weight while she was in Germany, but so did everyone, and the good news was that Ilke's parents had a wine cellar, so every night she and Herb allowed themselves a glass or two, and that luxury settled their nerves. She did not touch Herb. He did not touch her. When they spoke, it was only about the baby, or the outside world; the news from America, the docking of more ships, the arrival of more displaced persons.

The second week, when Ilke rose from bed and declared herself fit and put on a maternity dress that hung off her, displaying her newly slender figure, that week Anne had not been jealous, but she had been, perhaps, on guard. Ilke washed her hair, and what had been matted with sweat and tangled from her writhing in labor now lay in shining pale gold silk, framing her beautiful pale face. Ilke did not seek out Herb. She seldom spoke to him, and when she did, it was in English, her broken, faltering English, and Anne appreciated this, because she knew that Herb understood some German, and Herb and Ilke could have conversed in a language Anne did not comprehend. But Ilke's love and energies were all directed toward the infant. She walked him, she nursed him, or tried to, and she wept with frustration when her milk was not ample.

Nona suddenly recalled another kindness of Ilke's. Whenever she handed the baby over to Herb, she said the same thing she said when she handed the baby to Anne: *Here, little one, go to your friend.* Or, *Now your friend rocks you, my love.* She never called Herb "Papa." Perhaps it was not really a kindness so much as a matter of self-defense. Perhaps she did not believe that Herb would claim and support the child throughout his entire life, or perhaps she didn't, in her secret heart, even hope for that. Perhaps she hoped Herb would return to America, forget the child, and she would marry a German who could claim the baby as his own.

For Anne, it had been a through-the-looking-glass experience. Nothing seemed quite real. Each day was isolated from every other, each moment devoted to the necessities of the present, with no time to plan for the future.

Nona remembered piercingly how pleased she had been when she lifted the baby from Herb's or Ilke's arms, and the baby had grown calm as she gently jiggled him, walking her path through the house. The baby had responded to Anne as if he understood that she was keeping him safe. Herb was not always so successful, although he tried. Perhaps his uniform was too stiff against the infant's cheek, perhaps his male voice was too brusque or deep or loud, perhaps, like many men, he did not feel comfortable and capable with an infant, and the baby sensed this. But in a way, Anne felt chosen by the infant. She loved him. She purely loved him.

She did not feel sexually attracted to Herb. She

was always busy, and she was always very hungry, and she felt occupied and capable and *alive*. When Ilke's nipples became cracked from the baby's demanding and unsatisfied suckling, it was Anne Ilke came to, not Herb. In those days men did not share such experiences. Anne remembered a friend who had used A & D ointment, and Ilke had some in the house and used it sparingly and found relief. How proud Anne had been of herself! She had been so pleased that, when Herb came home, she told him about Ilke's cracked nipples and her own advice—and Herb had blushed scarlet and left the room, grumbling under his breath. She had remembered then that Ilke's breasts, Ilke's nipples, had once been objects not of milky sustenance but of sexual pleasure. Had Herb lain next to Ilke, suckling her, fondling her? Of course he had. Jealousy had twisted through her then. She had gone to her bedroom and wept, stuffing the pillow in her mouth to hide her sobs. Oh, she had not been without jealousy and bitterness. But then she slept. And then the baby cried, and Ilke asked her to walk him so she could sleep, and Herb was already asleep in his room, exhausted from his day's work. And Anne had taken the baby in her arms, and looked down into his face, and everything but a profound and amazed love had disappeared.

Now her son, her sixty-year-old son Worth, finished removing her shoes. He rose. His face was stiff and closed. It would take time for him to heal.

"One question," Worth said. "Are you going to share this news with anyone else? I'm sure Grace will be thrilled. But what about Oliver, and Charlotte, and Teddy? Will you tell them?"

"I won't tell anyone else," Nona assured him. "It is my duty, I believe, to give you this information, and Helen, as your wife and the mother of your children, should know as well. It's up to you, the two of you, to decide whether or not to tell your children."

Worth snorted angrily. "Teddy's going to laugh his ass off."

"Worth," Helen remonstrated softly.

"Teddy loves you," Nona assured her son. "He idolizes you. He believes he can never live up to your standards."

Worth shook his head. "Well, Nona, it seems that *I* don't even live up to my standards."

"Then perhaps," Nona suggested, "the standards need to change."

Worth scrubbed his face with his hands. He looked angry and anguished, and Helen rose and went to him. "Worth. We can—"

Abruptly, he threw her hand off him. "I can't deal with this. I'm going back to Boston."

Helen started to object and then nodded. "Yes. Perhaps you should."

# Twenty-five

*During the intense heat* of the late Sunday afternoon, Charlotte strode along a furrow, furiously hoeing the weeds out of the beds of kale and eggplant and chard.

"No, too hot, too hot!" Jorge had called, rushing up to her. "I hoe. I hoe!"

"Not today," Charlotte told him. "I need to hoe today. You can go work on the beans."

Catching her look—she was clearly not in the mood for argument—Jorge had hurried off to another part of the garden.

During the ride from the hospital after seeing the newborn baby, her parents hadn't spoken, but anger oozed from their pores until Charlotte thought she could actually see the air turning a bilious green. Clearly they did not want to talk in front of Charlotte. But she knew what the argument was about. Her father did not want to accept Suzette's baby as his grandchild. Deep in her heart, Charlotte was glad her mother was standing up to him.

But when she had been lacing up her work boots in the mudroom, her parents did talk, and Charlotte had overheard them. Her mother had actually threatened divorce—and the words had been like a hard kick in Charlotte's stomach. They took her breath away. Would her mother actually leave her father? It couldn't happen. A frantic energy filled her, but she didn't know how to use it. Her mother had stormed up the stairs, and her father had followed, and she knew this was a battle they had to fight out by themselves.

Well, the garden always, *always* needed weeding, and today she was grateful for the work. Charlotte took down the CLOSED sign at the farm stand, put out some lettuces and vegetables so they wouldn't go to waste, then stomped into the garden with a hoe.

A taxi came slowly up the lane toward Nona's house. Charlotte stared. It had no passengers, so no one was arriving. Anyone who would be leaving would be driven by Grace or Helen, so this was a little odd.

She continued to work but stopped again when, a few minutes later, the taxi came back down the lane toward the main road.

Her father was sitting in the back, alone.

"Dad!" she called, waving her hands.

He didn't seem to hear. The cab bore him away.

She set back to work, hoeing with maniacal energy.

Sometimes Charlotte allowed herself to wonder about her family, about its genetic makeup. Why were she and her brothers such fuckups? Perhaps that was too strong a word. Or imprecise. Oliver, for example, was a great success, both in his loving long-term relationship and in his work, but he had clearly abandoned his family and any part he might have in it, choosing to live as far as possible from the East Coast. Had he been drawn there simply by career opportunities or did he just not want to deal with the whole Wheelwright business? Someday, Charlotte would ask him.

Perhaps *rebel* was a better word than *fuckup*. She'd grown up watching Mellie, Mandy, and Mee following their parents like mindless but very cute fluffy little ducklings, paddling politely through the pond of life without making a ripple, and there her family was, Charlotte, Teddy, and Oliver, splashing and dunking one another and trying to fly, clowning around, dashing in different directions, and disappearing for months at a time. Charlotte wondered whether there was a genetic kink passed on by their mother—for clearly their mother was the outsider—that caused the three of them to rebel. She knew she would not have done the terrible thing she did if she hadn't been trying so hard to live within the cold hard lines of her father's rules and feeling so imprisoned, so caged.

"You look like a lady who could use a cool drink."

Startled, Charlotte looked up to see Coop standing there, in shorts, T-shirt, baseball cap, and deck shoes.

"Hey, Coop." She realized she was dripping with sweat. *Attractive.* "What time is it?"

"Time for me to kidnap you and carry you away."

"Oh. Well, I still have—"

"It's after six. Jorge's gone home. There's nothing left to sell on the farm stand. You need a break."

"Coop—"

"Okay, you're forcing me to do this." With one swift lurch, Coop bent, grabbed Charlotte's legs, and threw her over his shoulder.

"Coop!" Writhing, she dropped her hoe. "I need to put my tools away."

"They're fine out here. No one's going to take them."

It was hard to breathe with his shoulder wedged into her abdomen. "Coop, put me down!"

"Will you go with me nicely?" Staggering under her weight, he stomped down the long garden row, trying to keep in the furrow but occasionally stumbling sideways, his foot smashing down on a plant.

"Yes! Yes! Put me down!" She beat on his back with her fists, and when he'd trodden down a luscious Brandywine tomato plant, she went quiet, submitting. "Please, Coop. Put me down."

He did, awkwardly unloading her onto more tomato plants. She felt the juice squirt and the stalks snap beneath the weight of her body. Coop grabbed her hands and pulled her to her feet.

"You need to relax," he said, pulling her close. "And I know just how to relax you."

"Coop," she protested, "I need a shower. I'm all—"

He wrapped his arms around her. "Hey, I like my women hot and bothered."

"Would you stop this caveman stuff!" She stomped her foot but it hit only the soft ground and made no noise. "Honestly, Coop, this is *not* turning me on!"

At once he dropped his arms and stepped back. "Sorry. Sor-*ry*. I was just playing." He shrugged. "I was just—listen, if you're not interested, all you have to do is say so."

She took a deep breath. "Oh, Coop, I'm sorry, too. And I am—um, interested. I've just got so much to do." She felt like hitting him. She felt like crying. She almost said, *My parents are fighting, Mom's talking about divorce, and Suzette's baby has black hair.* Instead, she surrendered. "I guess I do need a drink."

Coop took her by the hand and led her out of the garden. It almost killed her to leave her damaged plants lying broken in the dirt. She only wanted to run back, tuck them back into the safe ground, do what she could to save them, but she allowed herself to be tugged along. She shut and latched the gate. They walked down the lane until they came to the road and the farm stand. Everything she'd put out had been bought. Charlotte emptied the basket of money. Coop helped her fold up the tablecloth and the card table and tuck them up next to the tree. He put a comradely arm around her shoulders as they walked over to his drive and down to his house.

"Why not take a quick shower?" he suggested. "When you get out, I'll have a nice cool drink waiting."

"That sounds wonderful. Thanks."

She went into his bedroom, stripped off her clothing, and, stepping around various piles of discarded clothing and towels, made her way into the bathroom and the shower. She lathered her hair and body, then let the water pound down on her, and it was such a relief, such therapy. Afterward, she wrapped herself in a huge towel, tied it above her breasts, and padded barefoot out to the deck where Coop sat, a drink in his hand. His dogs curled at his feet. An iced glass was on the table for her, and a board of cheese and crackers.

"This is nice, Coop. The shower was lovely."

"And look at the view. Peaceful, huh?" Coop lounged in his chair, lanky and calm.

Charlotte looked at the view. Blue water swept over to the far shore, green with beach grass and wild roses, and off to the western horizon, past the sandbars, to the town, which appeared, from this distance, in miniature, a toy village.

She did not want to talk about her family. "What did you do today?"

Coop stretched. "Played tennis. Sailed." Glancing over at her, he grinned. "I know, it's a hard life, but someone's got to do it." Seeing her smile, he asked, "Have you ever seen Harrison Clark play tennis? He talks through the entire game. And he's killer competitive." Coop assumed Harrison Clark's clipped accent. "I should have gotten that. Why didn't I get that? My backhand's gone all to hell. I need more practice. Was that out? I think it was out. All right, I'll let you have that point since you swear it was in, but I still think it was out. I think you need glasses. I think I need glasses. Damn, I stubbed my foot. My ankle hurts. Why does my ankle hurt? I'm too young to have my ankle hurt."

His imitation of Harrison was so perfect, Charlotte lay back in her chair and laughed. Coop told her about Peggy Windruff's new fifty-one-foot sloop, describing its teak decks and sleek lines, its electric stowaway mast and state-of-the-art electronics, the handsome staterooms. He told her about his trip in February, down to the Bahamas with his friend Jimmy Jackson—what a paradise it had been, sailing for a month in clear water, catching fish to grill for dinner, kicking back toward nightfall to watch the stars freckle the sky and the moon rise so full and close it seemed that, if they set sail, they'd reach it by morning.

His voice and the images he called up lulled Charlotte, reminded her of the beauties of the world and the luxury of sailing. After a while, Coop asked her if she wanted another drink, and she said yes, and he fixed her one, but when he returned to the deck, he didn't hand it to her but held it just out of reach, teasingly, and so he coaxed her out of her chair and into the house and into the bedroom. Her towel fell away from her naked body as she lay back on the bed, and he put her drink on the side table, and they both forgot about it completely.

*Charlotte woke at sunrise.* Next to her, Coop sprawled naked and snoring. She'd slept through the night, and she felt easy in her body and eager to start the day. She rose and quietly slipped into her clothes. Once again she left Coop sleeping as she padded out of his house. At home, she took another quick shower, dressed in clean clothes, and hurried out to her garden. The morning was warm, the air misty. Birds sang and flitted from bush to tree, and everything seemed succulent and lush. She sang lighthearted songs from *South Pacific* and *The Sound of Music* as she roamed through her garden, gathering up lettuces, eggplants, beans, and onions for the farm stand.

Then she came to the row where she'd been working the night before, where Coop had swooped down to steal her away. Four or five hearty tomato plants, snapped off at the stalk, sprawled in the dirt, where ants and flies were feeding on some of the crushed tomatoes. The sight appalled her. She scolded herself for her overreaction; they were only tomatoes, she reminded herself. Still, as she bent in the furrow to lift off any tomatoes that were still intact, a sense of remorse settled on her.

*Consequences.* Hadn't she already learned that every act has consequences, and, while repentance exists, it can't erase the damage set in motion?

She worked hard, rerooting the plants that could be saved, pulling up those that were past saving. She carried her baskets full of glossy vegetables to her shed to rinse and package. Jorge arrived, checked the schedule she usually kept up to date, and set off to work. She went into the house for breakfast.

Glorious was at the stove, putting a pot on to boil. "Good morning, Charlotte. I'm doing potato salad today. Got any extra scallions?"

"Absolutely. I'll bring them in right after breakfast." Charlotte washed her hands, took down a box of granola and filled a bowl, and then rummaged in the refrigerator until she found a box of blueberries and added them. "How is everyone?"

Glorious shook her head. "I don't know about *everyone,* but I'm worried about Nona. She's fretting."

"Really? That's too bad."

"She won't eat breakfast, says she's not hungry, and I can tell she didn't sleep a wink."

"Oh, Glorious," Charlotte sighed. "You must think our family is a mess."

"Honey, I think all families are a mess. But look

at it this way. If the Good Lord hadn't made us all so cantankerous and feeble, we wouldn't have anything to do and He wouldn't have anything to laugh at."

Charlotte laughed appreciatively. Over the years, Glorious had somehow decided to keep her opinions light, and Charlotte was grateful.

Christian clattered into the room then, trying to walk with one foot stuck in a plastic dump truck. Mandy followed with baby Zoe in her arms.

"Are your hands clean? Great." She plunked the baby in Charlotte's arms. "Do something with her, would you? She's grousing."

Charlotte stared down at the pretty baby girl. For a moment, the baby stared back, then wrinkled up its face and wailed. "I don't think she likes me," Charlotte said.

"Nonsense. She's just crabby. She's teething. I've got drool all over my clothes. Christian, stop butting that truck into the wall. Do you want some blueberries? I need something s-w-e-e-t. Glorious, do we have anything s-w-e-e-t?"

"We've got some nice oatmeal raisin cookies," Glorious replied.

*"Cookies!"* Christian yelled.

"Where is everyone?" Charlotte asked.

"Mellie's lying on her bed, wallowing like a pig. Mee's down at the beach. Mom's changing the sheets and gathering laundry. I don't know where your mother is."

442

"Mm." Charlotte tried to appear nonchalant.

Mandy looked amused. "I hear the baby has black hair."

Charlotte almost said, *You know what, Mandy? When I was a girl, I adored you. I wanted to be just like you when I grew up. Well, I sure don't want to be like you anymore!* She bit her tongue. This house already had enough aggravated vibrations zinging through the air.

She satisfied herself by replying virtuously, "The little girl is a beauty and the important thing is, she has all her fingers and toes." Focusing on baby Zoe, she cooed, "Just like you!" Carefully, she lifted a dimpled fist and kissed the baby's fingers.

*Charlotte worked hard* all day in her garden, realizing not for the first time how the space allowed her to be part of her family and yet separate. They all spent too much time together, she decided, that was the problem. Most of the time they rubbed along quite happily, but it was natural that they'd argue and compete and bicker. They were only human. Sometime soon she'd invite Coop over for dinner, not a social occasion with everyone on her best behavior, but a casual family meal with Christian sticking a French fry up his nose and Zoe filling her diaper and her parents sniping at each other and Aunt Grace preening herself self-righteously and Uncle Kellogg not saying a word. Coop was an only child. How would he like being around such a horde and, after all, what did Charlotte care?

She cared, she realized, because even though she and Coop were so brand new with each other, she was having sex with him and enjoying it, and she had never slept with any guy unless she thought she might be serious about him, might establish a long-term commitment with him, might—just say it, Charlotte!—might marry him. Right now she didn't even know if she loved Coop, and she was pretty sure that if she said the word *love* to him he'd back up so fast he'd fall over.

Still . . .

Still, she reminded herself with a mental kick in the derriere, she should stop mooning about the future and remember that she'd agreed to go out with Coop tonight. He was arriving at seven. She put her tools away, closed up the farm stand, and raced to the house to get showered and dressed.

*Her feet felt light* in her clever little sandals after being encased in heavy work boots, and her dress swirled around her in a girly-girl way that pleased her as she skipped down the stairs and into the living room.

Coop was there, sitting on the sofa, and Mee was there, too, sitting next to him, her entire body turned toward him, her low-cut dress positioned for maximum exposure. They were both laughing. When Mee saw Charlotte enter the room, she jumped, pretending to be startled, as if she'd been caught doing something wrong.

Coop rose. "You look great, Charlotte."

She twirled. "Better than the overalls?" She took Coop's arm possessively and fluttered her fingers at her cousin. " 'Bye, Mee. See you all later."

"Have fun." Mee waved back, but she looked terribly alone sitting there, and Charlotte flushed with guilt.

*Outside the movie theater* was a small bistro where Coop had booked a table. Tonight the place was packed, as always in the summer, and Charlotte allowed herself a moment's regret at the lack of intimacy and then a moment's pleasure at being seen with such a handsome man. They ate fresh fish and—from Charlotte's point of view—day-old veggies, and as she sipped her wine, she felt a glow of well-being. It was still summer, and right now she felt golden.

Coop regaled her in his humorous, slightly sardonic manner with an account of his day sailing with an old college friend. Charlotte laughed, delighted to be entertained, and she was smiling at him with great warmth, reminding him without words but with her gaze that they had slept together the night before and would sleep together tonight, when out of the corner of her eye she noticed a familiar figure enter the bistro: Whit Lowry. Fiona O'Conner was with him, and her curly red hair tumbled down her back, which was bare almost to the waist. She slid into the banquette across from Whit, and Charlotte saw Fiona was smiling at Whit just the way she was smiling at Coop.

*Well,* she thought. *Well!*

*Well, what do I care?* she reminded herself, and aimed her gaze back at Coop.

The theater had air-conditioning, but it was a small room packed with people, and now and then during the movie, the August heat, her hard day of work, and the two glasses of wine told on Charlotte and she found herself dozing off. Each time she glanced guiltily at Coop, but he was engrossed in the movie and didn't notice. Afterward, they went down to the Club Car for a drink, and even though Charlotte would rather have gone to home to bed, she didn't say so. It wasn't, after all, that she was mad with lust for him. She was just tired. But the bar scene didn't have the charm it had held when she was younger. It was steamy and noisy, people were crushed together, stepping on one another's toes, and the music was so loud it hurt her ears. A quartet of men whom Charlotte knew vaguely from sailing joined them at the bar, boisterously recounting their adventure sailing a sloop up to Maine. They were funny, Charlotte allowed, but not as funny as they were drunk. *For heaven's sake,* she scolded herself, *you're still young. Stop being such an old lady!*

At midnight, she pulled Coop close to her so he could hear her when she yelled in his ear: "Coop! I have to go home! I get up at four-thirty tomorrow!"

His breath was perfumed with gin when he yelled back. "Hey, give yourself a break. Sleep in. The garden won't go anywhere." He turned back to the sailors.

"Fine!" Charlotte slipped off her bar stool and slung her little purse over her shoulder. "I'll take a cab."

Coop caught her arm as she tried to pass by. "Hey! Hang on! Don't get all hot and bothered!" With one lanky smooth move, he dismounted his stool. "Gotta go, guys. The little lady has work tomorrow."

The four men roared at the same time, all of them condemning work and anyone who spoiled the summer doing it, but Charlotte kept moving and Coop followed. They walked in silence to the car. Charlotte sank back on the infinitely soft seat of Coop's Lexus and let the silence of the night soothe her jangled nerves. For a while, they drove in silence.

"Have you fallen asleep over there?" Coop asked. His voice was tight.

"No. No, I'm just enjoying the peace."

"Charlotte, can I ask you something?"

"That sounds ominous." She stirred herself, turning toward him, smiling. "Sure."

"Has it ever occurred to you that you're going a little overboard with this garden thing?"

She counted to ten before she answered. "No, I don't think I am. I'm serious about the garden, Coop. I want to—"

"Do you mean you want to keep it going for the rest of your life?" He sounded amazed.

"Well, the rest of my life is a pretty long time. I'm thinking more of, say, ten years. And then we'll see. But I like the idea of providing organic veggies and doing my bit to keep the earth green. It sounds idealistic, perhaps, but if we don't all try to do something—"

Coop interrupted. "Ten years! Are you kidding me? Charlotte, you're thirty years old! What about marriage, what about a family? You won't be able to take care of babies if you're out digging in the dirt, plus you are always working, so how will you ever have time to have a private life?"

Surprised by his vehemence, Charlotte replied softly, "You sound just like my parents."

"Well, I think your parents are right. I really just don't *get* this garden business. You're an educated, wealthy, intelligent woman. You could do anything. And come on, Charlotte, get real. What's going to happen when your grandmother dies?"

"Nona's fine!"

"Now she is, and I'm glad. But she's *ninety.*

What's going to happen when she's gone and the property is divided among all of you? You're not going to be able to keep your garden; *you're* not going to inherit all that land. What if your family wants to sell the place?"

Charlotte was stunned. Everything he said was so—so *informed.* It wasn't like Coop to care about such matters, at least what she knew of him, and it was becoming quite clear to her how little that was.

And then, with a bright flash in her brain, she got it. "Mee. You've been listening to Mee."

He didn't deny it. "Mee's concerned about you. Your family's concerned about you. If you were a naïve adolescent, it would make sense, but—"

"Okay, Coop, stop right there." She was trembling. "When you say *your family,* please remember that my cousins and I have always been different. We love each other, but we're different. And none of us knows who's going to inherit what, not that that is any of your business anyway! And no one is going to sell the place!"

He kept his eyes on the road. "With all that acreage, you could make a stupendous amount of money."

"So could you, with your property," she shot back.

"Believe me, I'm trying to talk my parents into selling. I wouldn't have to worry about money for a long time."

"But you're not worried about money now!" Charlotte argued. "Coop, you're young, and you have your software business, you can support yourself; isn't the house, that beautiful view, your way of life, your land and beach, isn't that worth more than money to you?"

They reached the spot where Coop's drive met the road. Several yards on, the Wheelwright drive joined the road. Coop steered the Lexus into his drive, put the vehicle in park, released his seat belt, and turned to Charlotte. Gently, he touched her cheek.

"Are we having our first argument?"

Her emotions were all over the place, but she couldn't dismiss the suggestion implied by his words, that they were in the midst of a relationship, that they would have other arguments, other discussions. "Coop. Look. I'm sorry if I'm overwrought."

"I wouldn't say overwrought." Coop knew how to turn on the charm. "Maybe just *wrought*."

She smiled. "You know, I've had the garden for three years now."

"I guess I knew that. I'm not sure I really paid attention." He caressed her cheek. "And three years is a long time. It's a commitment. I understand that. And I apologize for getting into such heavy stuff so soon. I don't mean to be intrusive." His hand dropped to her neck; he stroked it with his fingertips. "Actually, I would like to be intrusive. . . ."

His tone was easy, his touch alluring. *But I'm so tired,* she reminded herself.

At the same time, he said, "You're tired. Let me take you home with me, rub your back, and make you feel all better."

She did.

# Confessions

# Twenty-six

*Tuesday morning,* Helen drove in the newly repaired Jeep to retrieve her son and his family from the hospital. She couldn't keep from smiling as she carried duffel bags and two vases of flowers behind the little procession making its way out of the maternity wing and down to the first floor and outside. Teddy and Suzette carefully tucked Dawn into the required car seat. They filled the back with the new paraphernalia that had seemed to blossom into Teddy and Suzette's life overnight—plastic bags of gifts from the hospital, duffel bags of clothing and flowers from family and friends, and a diaper bag full of necessities for Dawn.

Suzette and Teddy talked nonstop during the drive home, regaling Helen with information: Dawn was a champion nurser, a greedy little girl who had learned how to latch on to the nipple immediately. And she'd slept four hours straight! And the hospital had given them many new baby gifts, but Suzette didn't intend to use formula ever, so should they take it to the church food pantry?

Helen smiled and smiled, loving it all, and found herself wishing that Worth were with them, sharing the day with her.

But of course, this moment would not bring Worth joy.

When she turned into the drive, she saw Charlotte kneeling among the annuals, cutting flowers, and stopped the Jeep in the lane. "Come see!"

Charlotte ran down between rows of tomatoes, unlatched the gate, and hurried over. She peeked in the window at the sleeping infant, tucked in a pink blanket and strapped safely into a car seat.

"Oh, *sweet*," she gushed.

"I hate that she has to be in a car seat," Suzette said. "It's state law, but look, she's so tiny, her little head bobbles over."

"We'll have her back in your arms in less than a minute," Helen said, and drove off to the house.

It took almost an hour for Teddy to get Suzette and the baby settled in the living room. Then, while they napped, Helen drove Teddy into town, to return to work at the antiques store. She drove back to Nona's house—some days were like this; Helen had often joked that she should buy a chauffeur's cap—and all the driving provided her plenty of time for thinking. Too much thinking, too much imagining. Finally, she turned on the radio and let music relieve her overactive mind.

Back home, she stopped in the lane and called out to Charlotte. "You look hot. Did you have lunch?"

Charlotte stretched and rubbed one aching shoulder. "I forgot," she admitted.

"Jump in," Helen told her. "You can rest awhile and I'll make you a sandwich."

They returned to the house. Helen followed her daughter in through the mudroom. "Suzette's in the living room with Dawn. Go sit down. I'll bring lunch in."

The kitchen was empty, and in the humid heat of the early afternoon Helen knew several of the family were taking their after-lunch naps—baby Zoe and little Christian, Mandy and Mellie, and Nona, too. Glorious was in her room, probably watching one of her soap operas. Helen moved quietly as she prepared the sandwiches.

Charlotte padded in barefoot, poured drinks, set them on a tray, and headed off to the living room. Helen followed with the sandwiches. Suzette was stretched on her side on a sofa, little Dawn nestled in her arms.

"She's awake," she told Charlotte. "Would you like to hold her?"

"Oh, yes, please." Carefully Charlotte lifted the baby and snuggled her close. She sat down on a chair close to Suzette. "Can I look at her toes?"

"Sure."

Charlotte gently lifted the light blanket away from the infant's body. She touched the end of each perfect toe and stroked the curled fingers. "I don't think she's as yellow as she was."

"She was jaundiced. Lots of newborns are." Suzette spoke with a newfound authority. "But it's fading."

Helen said, "Charlotte, chicken salad sandwich

457

for you. And lemonade. And Suzette, the same for you. I didn't know if you were hungry—"

Suzette laughed. "I'm always hungry."

Helen arranged the food within easy reach, added another pillow behind Suzette's back, and settled into a chair.

"Look, Mom." Charlotte held the baby toward her mother. "She's gotten as pink as a new Dawn rose. Isn't her name perfect?"

Eagerly Helen reached out. "Let me hold her while you eat."

As she looked down into the infant's eyes, she was overcome with a sense of quiet joy and profound gratitude. A new child was the world's greatest mystery and, Helen thought, the world's greatest hope.

*Worth did not* phone her that night.

Or the next night.

Or the next.

Helen was determined not to phone him. Because she couldn't spend every waking moment gazing at Dawn, she forced herself out of the house. She played tennis and sailed, went out for dinner and drinks with friends, saw a couple of plays, and early in the morning she went for long walks on the beach.

Glorious told them all that Nona had a slight cold, not anything to be worried about but something to be watched. Nona needed to rest. Helen was glad that Nona had the cold, or was pretending to have it, because it would not be fair for Helen and Nona to discuss things without Worth present. It would seem as if they were ganging up on him. Helen appreciated Nona's diplomacy and tried to adapt her own behavior accordingly. She checked in with Nona once a day, kept her conversation light, and focused on general matters: her tennis game, her plans for the day, her committees.

But every moment, truly, Helen was waiting for Worth's call. She knew him well enough to predict that he wouldn't phone her right away. He needed time alone to think, to retreat like a wounded animal into his lair to lick his wounds. He had a lot to deal with, Helen had to admit that. Not only Nona's enormous news but the complicated existence of Teddy's child. And, of course, Helen's ultimatum.

She hoped he took her seriously. It had not been a ruse on her part, not a game. When she assured Worth she would leave him if he did not accept Suzette's baby, she had been absolutely serious.

She had already envisioned how it might play out. She had considered who she would choose for a divorce lawyer, where she would set up her own new single home—in Boston, on Commonwealth Avenue, near the Public Gardens—and how she would keep herself from grieving—by taking a job at one of the many art galleries in the Back Bay and by seeing her granddaughter as often as possible. She went as far as to decide that she would buy a house in a leafy suburb for Teddy, Suzette, and the baby. Teddy would find work in an antiques store, and Helen could babysit; the city would be better for Teddy in the winter than the island, which could be a trial, with its fog, cold, isolation, and lack of cultural activities.

And she would travel! Instead of being tied for three months to the island, the family rituals, and tennis and sailing, which were all lovely, but still . . . she would be free to spend a few summer weeks in France, England, or Italy.

And Joe Abernathy. Well. Perhaps nothing would come of his attentions, but all she wanted really was a light flirtation, someone to play with. Even a few dates with him would serve to prevent her from being labeled "Poor Helen," deserted by her husband for a younger woman—for she did not fool herself. If she and Worth divorced, Worth would not be alone for a minute.

The thought made her heart ache. At night she wept into her pillow like an adolescent girl losing her first true love.

*On his sixth evening* away from Nantucket, Worth phoned.

"Can you talk?" he asked.

"I can. Just a moment. Let me shut the door." She was on the sleeping porch, getting ready for bed. It was after eleven.

"I called earlier. You didn't pick up."

She started to tell him that she'd been at a play. But she didn't want to give him even that much. "I'm here now."

A deep sigh. Then, "Helen. God, what a summer this is."

"Yes."

"I'm having trouble dealing with it all. Teddy claiming a baby that isn't his—"

Helen interrupted. "Or perhaps is his."

"And Nona—this incredible story Nona told me. That she's not my mother! My God, Helen, it's as if I don't belong to anyone."

She started to speak, then kept her silence. Perhaps he belonged to Cindy. He needed to figure it out himself.

"Helen, I miss you. I miss the family, the island. I miss Nona." His voice broke on his mother's name.

She couldn't help it; her heart twisted with pity. "She is still your mother, Worth."

He cleared his throat. "Not really."

Helen thought carefully about her next words. "What if Charlotte's infertile, Worth?"

"What? What kind of question is that? Why would you even think such a thing?"

"I'm thinking all sorts of things these days. My mind is ranging pretty free. I want to be open to all possibilities. And one possibility is that Charlotte might not be able to have children."

"That's ridiculous."

"Worth, infertility is a serious problem these days. I'm not saying Charlotte is going to be infertile, I'm saying only that it's a possibility. Or perhaps she'll never marry. I mean, she's thirty and not serious about a man, no potential fiancé in sight—"

"She's dating Bill Cooper."

Helen laughed dryly. "Get real. You know Coop's reputation. He doesn't get serious with anyone. And while we're on the subject, I'm seeing Whit with Fiona O'Conner everywhere. So that little dream of ours about Whit and Charlotte is going to have to fade away, I'm afraid. To return to my point: what if, for any possible number of reasons, Charlotte doesn't have a child? Oliver isn't going to, we know that much. Will you wait until Teddy and Suzette have another baby, a pale little blond one, and call that child your heir and still ignore Dawn?" She allowed urgency to color her voice. "Worth, you are living in the past. It's the future we need to think of. Can't you separate yourself from this gigantic looming shadow called Family and think of yourself alone? I have, just recently, and I've got to tell you, it feels pretty wonderful."

"Thanks a lot," Worth muttered.

"Listen to me. Really *listen*. Stop thinking about the all-important *Wheelwright legacy*. Think about yourself. You are sixty years old. How much longer are you going to live? How much longer are you going to be able to have fun, to try new things, to travel, to pay attention to something new? The world is changing, Worth. Has changed. The bank is not just a neighborhood bank anymore, and your position there is not essential."

"Oh, come *on!*"

"It's *not.* You know it's not. And whatever your father and grandfather did when they ran the bank, it's not something you're able to do now. I'm not even sure it's something you want to do. Are you? Are you sure? Stop a minute, Worth. Think about what I'm saying. Do you want to spend the rest of your life putting on your suit and going in to work and dealing with numbers and getting home late?"

"I'm not ready to retire and fill my days playing golf."

"No, I know that. But that's not the only option."

"You're getting off the subject."

"The subject is a pretty all-encompassing one." She was quiet a moment. "You matter all by yourself, Worth. Your life is your own. Your happiness is your own to choose. The bank, the family. . . . They don't have to be all that matters."

"They *aren't* all that matters!" Worth protested. "But the bank—if I weren't at the bank—" He sputtered, unable to finish his thought.

"—the bank would continue without you," Helen finished for him. "Kellogg is doing a good job. And Claus and Dougie."

After a long silence, Worth said, "I would feel as if Grace had won."

Helen was surprised that he would admit that much. "Yes, of course you would. But *you* would have won your freedom, Worth. You would have won your own life."

"Why haven't you ever talked like this before?"

"Perhaps because I've never thought like this before." Helen was trembling slightly; she was a little bit frightened and a little bit exhilarated. To calm herself, she thought of the face of the new baby girl, fragile and beautiful and entirely vulnerable.

"Somehow we've gotten off the subject," Worth said. "Listen, I'm tired. The bank, and all this; I can't talk anymore. I'll call tomorrow."

Helen's voice was cool. "Fine."

"Helen, I don't want you to think I'm with Cindy. I've broken up with her. You need to remember that."

She thought of Cindy's reaction when Worth told her it was over, how she must have pressed herself against Worth, weeping, passionately kissing his mouth. She put the phone down so that the sudden tears in her voice would not betray her.

*As he'd promised,* Worth phoned the next night. "I want to talk about Teddy."

Helen was in her robe, curled up on the sleeping porch. A sweet breeze rippled through the screens, playing over her skin like running water. "Okay."

Worth said, "I worry about Teddy."

"I think we'll always worry about Teddy. He has a drinking problem. From everything we've read and heard, that means he'll always have a drinking problem. You and I can't change that. We can't fix that. Suzette seems to have a steadying influence on him."

Worth's voice tightened. "I think Suzette saw him as a meal ticket and latched on to him."

Helen opened her mouth to disagree, then gave herself time to consider his words. "Maybe Teddy *needs* someone to latch on to him. Maybe Suzette and this baby will ground him."

Fiercely, Worth said, "Teddy got drunk twice this summer."

"And how many times did you sleep with Cindy this summer?" Helen shot back.

"Damn it, Helen, the two events aren't comparable!"

"That's true," Helen replied softly. "Teddy didn't break anyone's heart when he got drunk."

After a moment, Worth said quietly, "It breaks *my* heart to see my son drunk."

"Because it hurts your sense of family pride? Because it embarrasses you in front of Grace and Kellogg? Because he's showing weakness?"

"Maybe. Maybe all those. But also because it makes me think that somewhere deep inside, Teddy's hurt. And I don't want my son to be so terribly hurt."

Tears stung Helen's eyes. She pulled her robe around her, tucking it beneath her bare feet. "But, Worth," she said, as a thought occurred to her, "the second time Teddy got drunk this summer was when he'd made a huge sale at the antiques shop and the buyers brought in some champagne to celebrate their acquisition. Perhaps Teddy is hurt inside, but hey, we're all hurt somehow inside, right? Isn't that just part of the human condition? Teddy's alcoholism is also a result of his physical chemistry. He just can't drink. Do you see what I'm saying? It's a *problem,* but it's not a *tragedy.*"

Worth was quiet for a few moments. Then he asked, keeping his voice level, "Why are you so intent on claiming Suzette's baby as your grandchild?"

"Because Teddy's claiming the baby as his child. Because Teddy is happier and steadier—not always sober every minute, but steadier—when he's with Suzette. Because I've watched Teddy and Suzette; they are good together. Because I saw Teddy's face when he held the baby. Because the future matters more than the past. Because I want to choose happiness. Because I want to open up my world."

"You're taking a big risk. You could get disappointed in any number of ways."

"Really? Gosh, I never knew the people you love could disappoint you."

"Helen, Teddy has always disappointed me. You know that."

"And Teddy knows that."

"I think Teddy was born hating me."

"Oh, Worth, no."

"Teddy and I have always had a difficult relationship, you know that. If I say left, Teddy turns right. If I say up, Teddy says down."

"We've talked about this, Worth. Teddy had to make his own identity as the third child with perfect older siblings."

"Yes, yes, I know. He's the rebel in our family. But you have to admit, he takes his rebelliousness out on me more than on you or Charlotte or Oliver." When Helen didn't answer immediately, Worth asked, "Are you still there?"

"I'm thinking." After a moment, Helen said, "It's true. Teddy has always struggled against you. But you have always made it clear that he hasn't measured up."

"But he hasn't! Helen, you know he's as intelligent as the others, but he wouldn't apply himself in school. His grades were terrible. He kept doing stupid damn things that got him kicked off sports teams and suspended from school. And he thought it was all *funny*."

"That's true," Helen admitted. "But let's think about the present. Let's think about Teddy and Suzette and their baby. This is serious, Worth. Even Teddy wouldn't claim a baby just to irritate you."

"I'm not so sure," Worth muttered.

"Teddy loves Suzette. He loves the baby. He's worked steadily and done well at the antiques shop. Oh, Worth, think about this. Think about how hard you've tried all your life to measure up to your father. You've tried so hard to be your father you haven't ever figured out how to be yourself. You need to accept yourself, warts and all, and then you need to accept Teddy and the people he loves as your own. I think that's what Teddy wants from you."

Worth's next words surprised her. "Will you accept me, warts and all?"

After a pause, Helen said softly, "I don't know, Worth. I'll have to think about it."

*Helen kept herself busy* during the day, helping Charlotte with the garden stand, rocking baby Dawn so Suzette could grab a nap, doing errands, shopping for household necessities like soap and toilet paper, and stocking the pantry and cupboards.

In her mind she carried on a conversation with her mother-in-law, one just between her and Nona. *How did you go on loving Herb after learning about his affair with Ilke?* Helen wanted to ask. Helen could understand loving the baby. Babies were helpless, innocent, lovable. The question was, how did Nona—Anne—manage to go on after learning that her husband had slept with another woman? Did she ever trust Herb again?

It had been wartime. Of course that made an enormous difference. And, Helen thought with a rueful smile, it probably was some help that Herb's lover was dead. Helen didn't wish death on Cindy, but it would be nice if the woman would move to another country.

*When Worth phoned* that night, he said, "I feel like my entire world has fallen apart. I don't know who I am. I don't know where I've come from. And I don't know who the baby—"

"Her name is Dawn," Helen reminded him.

"—Dawn is. I keep wondering how I can accept the baby—Dawn—as my own grandchild."

"Perhaps it will help to remember how Nona accepted you."

Worth coughed, or choked, or, perhaps, sobbed. "How could she do that? How could she have loved me?"

"She just did. She always loved you. Worth, think about it. Did you ever feel that she didn't love you? You know you never once felt that way. If anything, you always thought she loved you more than she loved Grace."

"I know. I know." He sounded hurt and lost and miserable. After a long silence, he said, "I want to accept this baby. But I can't do it without you."

*This* was what she wanted to hear. She wanted to

believe him. She wanted to trust him. "How do I know you won't have another affair?"

Worth's voice was urgent. "Because I won't. I promise."

Helen felt as if she were picking her way carefully through a dark maze of thorns and roses as she spoke her thoughts aloud, coming fresh to her realization. "So we both have to choose. We have to choose faith over doubt and trust over suspicion."

"Yes," Worth said. "Yes, I suppose you're right."

"We have to choose love over fear," Helen said.

"Yes." Worth's voice grew stronger. "I can do that. Can you?"

"I *want* to do it." She was surprised at how hope broke open inside her like a radiance, softening her sorrow and anger. Perhaps all along she had been hiding from herself just how much she wanted to remain with her husband. "Yes, I *can* do it."

"Thank God," Worth said. He cleared his throat. "Look, Helen, I've got to take care of some matters at the bank tomorrow. But I'll come to the island Tuesday, probably afternoon, as soon as I can get away. All right?"

"All right," Helen replied.

"Helen," Worth said, and then she heard him draw in a deep breath, and when he spoke again, his voice was clear and strong. "I'm coming back to see you, and my mother, and my granddaughter."

"Oh, Worth," Helen replied, and for a while she couldn't speak because of the tears that fell. But she held on to the phone, and in the silence she knew that Worth was there, too, connected to her still, connected to her again, through the mysterious elements of air and electricity and the even more mysterious magic of love.

## Twenty-seven

*Charlotte felt* like a volcano just below boiling point, or a hurricane picking up speed, and she tried to use the energy her emotions generated to fuel her work. She *was* working hard in her garden, but for once the good hard physical labor would not calm her buzzing thoughts. Every night she tossed and turned, waking exhausted and cranky. She told Coop she was too busy and tired to see him and stayed until dark in her garden, even though people were beginning to leave the island as the summer slowly drew to an end.

Perhaps it was anxiety about Nona, Charlotte thought, that was keeping her on edge. Nona didn't leave her room all week, and when Charlotte slipped in to say hello, she found her grandmother looking especially old and withered and tired.

Perhaps it was just the heat, as Nona claimed. The late August weather was thick, humid, scorching.

But no, Charlotte thought, as she automatically

filled a basket with plum tomatoes for the garden stand, it was more than the weather. She didn't feel good about Coop. Things were just too *blurry* with him. He was irresistible, he was sexy and funny and lovable. But she didn't trust him, and she didn't like herself when she was with him. She needed to pay attention to those feelings.

And she was worried about her parents. It was Monday. Her father had been gone over a week. Her mother said he was in Boston, dealing with yet another crisis at the bank, but always before, every summer, he had spent weekends on the island. He loved his carefree weekends; he always said he *needed* them. She loved her father so much, but she loved her mother, too, and she loved Teddy, even though she wanted to shake some sense into him—but she'd always felt that way.

She lugged her baskets of fresh veggies over to the farm stand and set them out. All the lettuce was already gone; she would have to pick more. But first, she had to grab something to eat. And perhaps take a quick swim to cool off.

When she entered the kitchen, she found her mother there, tossing an enormous salad.

"Oh, good," Helen said. "You can join us for lunch! Look." She pointed with her wooden spoon. "I've made my own version of a Cobb salad, with lobster instead of chicken."

"Wonderful." Charlotte grabbed a drink and followed her mother into the living room, where

Suzette reclined on the sofa with her baby in her arms.

"Lunch," Helen announced. "I'll hold Dawn while you eat."

"Thanks." Suzette lifted the infant high. Helen bent to hold her and settled in the corner of the sofa, gazing down.

Charlotte set Suzette's plate in her lap. For a while the three women talked lazily about the heat of the day, Dawn's sleeping patterns, Charlotte's garden.

Charlotte ran an appraising eye over Suzette. "You're looking good, Suzette. How are you feeling?"

"I'm tired," Suzette told her, "but also sort of euphoric. High and dizzy and mellow all at the same time."

Charlotte's food lost its taste. She glanced at Helen to see if her mother thought what she thought—that Suzette's description sounded a bit druggy.

Suzette caught the change in Charlotte. She put her food down and wriggled on the sofa, facing Helen and Charlotte. "Okay. I think it's time I told you some things."

Charlotte's mother shook her head. "Don't feel you have to. You don't—"

Charlotte interrupted her mother. "Tell us."

Suzette took a deep breath. "Yes, I used to do drugs. Pot and hash and some cocaine. Oh, and alcohol, of course. But I haven't done drugs for years."

"For *years?* But you're so young! How old were you went you started?" Helen looked dismayed.

Suzette lifted her chin defiantly. Speaking carefully, she said, "I was twelve when I started drinking and fourteen when I first smoked pot. But I had a lot of clean months and years. Most of the time I've been clean."

"Oh, *honey.*" Tears welled in Helen's eyes.

Suzette leaned toward Helen. "I haven't had a drink for years. I haven't done drugs for years. *Look* at Dawn. She's fine." She ran her hands through her hair, then began again.

"My father left home when I was a child, and I have no idea where he is. My mother—drank. She had a hard time raising me, and I was alone in the apartment a lot, and I never had the advantages Teddy had. I could have gone to college—I mean, my grades were good enough—but the year I graduated from high school my mother died, so I had to go to work. I had one really bad year, the year my mom died, and I drank and did drugs, and I was not a pretty sight. But I joined AA, and I got cleaned up, and I stayed clean for three years, and then I met Teddy."

"I'm so glad," Helen said softly, gazing down at the infant in her arms.

Charlotte asked, "Are you and Teddy married?"

Suzette cast her eyes down. Quietly, she said, "No."

"No?" Helen looked stunned.

"Look. Let me explain." Suzette clasped her hands together in her lap and sat up straight, as if she were applying for a job. "I got to know Teddy through AA meetings, so I've heard Teddy talk about his family over and over again. Teddy's problems start right here, with his family."

"Oh, please," Charlotte protested. "We're not monsters!"

"I didn't say you were. I'm just saying that Teddy doesn't think he can measure up to the rest of you. He thinks you're all so perfect. Oliver is brilliant, and Charlotte has made such a home in the middle of the family here on Nona's land, and Teddy's father and uncle work in the bank, and so do Mandy and Mellie's husbands, and all those men do everything right." She glanced at Helen. "Teddy thinks you love Oliver best, and Charlotte, he thinks his father loves you best."

Helen shook her head. "That's not true!"

"Well, Teddy thinks it's true, he *feels* it's true. And I fell in love with *Teddy,* but I wasn't sure I could deal with everything else. With all you Wheelwrights. He is so—what's the term psychologists use—wrapped up?"

Charlotte supplied the word. "Enmeshed."

"Right. Teddy's so enmeshed with his family."

Helen interrupted, "But that's what families are all about! Being enmeshed! Being a messy, snarled, confusing cluster of people, people you love the most and hate the most sometimes, too."

Suzette said, "Okay. I agree. But it took me a long time to escape from my own snarled cluster. I wasn't sure I wanted to take on another train wreck."

"You see us as *a train wreck?*" Charlotte demanded.

"No. I didn't say that. I'm not explaining this very well. I just know that the circumstances of my family made me into a drunk, and I wasn't sure I was strong enough to deal with a family as, as—*complicated* as Teddy made you sound."

Charlotte could see how Suzette was struggling, and she wanted to help her somehow, so she said, lightly, "Well, we certainly are a *complicated* family. And there certainly are a lot of us here in the summer."

Suzette flashed Charlotte a grateful smile. "That's true. *So.* Before we came here, I told Teddy I didn't want to marry him, I wouldn't marry him, until we'd spent some time here at the summer house. I mean, the summer house and all the cousins and the perfect family and everyone knowing everyone else's secrets—it scared the shit out of me. If you were as—difficult—as Teddy made you sound, well, I wasn't sure I wanted you all around my child. But because of the baby, Teddy wanted everyone to think we were married."

Helen almost whispered, "Is the baby Teddy's?"

"Yes. Absolutely."

But Charlotte was annoyed. "Let me get this clear. The baby is Teddy's, but you would have kept her from us if you didn't like us."

Suzette stared steadily back. "That's my right."

"This is terrible." Helen had gone pale. "To think that Teddy feels so wounded by his own family . . ."

"And what did you decide?" Charlotte asked, crossing her arms defensively over her chest. "*Are we good enough for you?*"

"Charlotte, please." Suzette reached out a beseeching hand. "*I* didn't say *good enough*. It's about *my* own capabilities, my own fears. And my concerns for Teddy. And Dawn is Teddy's child," Suzette confessed, her voice softer now. "She couldn't possibly be anyone else's. I don't know why her hair is so dark. My parents both had dark hair . . . But look, Teddy was right. Mr. Wheelwright is furious because he thinks Dawn isn't Teddy's child."

Charlottle turned to her mother. "She's right. Dad left the island after he saw Dawn, and he hasn't come back."

Helen kept her voice low as she held the baby against her. "It's true Worth was upset when he saw the baby's dark hair. And he has been concerned about all of this—the baby's paternity and whether or not Suzette and Teddy are married. I don't think that's so very terrible. These are profoundly serious matters, after all. But Worth has other issues to deal with. I don't mean the bank. I mean personal matters."

Charlotte's gaze whipped to her mother's face. "What personal matters?"

Helen shook her head. "It's up to Worth to tell you that. All lives have passages of time when—"

Charlotte interrupted. "Are you and Dad getting divorced?"

A faint smile crossed Helen's face. "No. We are not. In fact, your father is coming back tomorrow afternoon. And he's decided—no, that's the wrong word. It sounds too cold, too cerebral, and this is a choice Worth is making with love—he has *accepted* Dawn as his grandchild."

"That will mean a lot to Teddy," Suzette said.

"And it will mean a lot to Worth," Helen countered, "when you and Teddy tell him about Dawn."

"So, wait," Charlotte said. "Suzette, you didn't answer my question. *Are* you accepting us?"

"Well, yes, it's obvious, isn't it? That I—like—Teddy's family." Suddenly shy, Suzette's voice fell to a whisper and she flushed pink with emotion. "Nona is wonderful, and you two have been so good to me. And Teddy is happier here than he has been for a long time. I mean, I know he got drunk, but he's an alcoholic. We both are. We both will be working on this all our lives."

"Are you going to marry Teddy?" Helen asked.

Suzette nodded. "Yes. I told Teddy I will marry him, as soon as he wants."

"Here!" Charlotte cried. "Have your wedding here!"

"At the summer house," Suzette said. "Yes, we could do that. I think Teddy would like to do that. Although we don't want to live here, I mean, in the summer house. We'll find a place on the island, and then we'll take it one day at a time."

"You're going to stay on the island?" Helen's face was bright with hope.

"I think so." Suzette couldn't help but smile at Helen's expression. "Teddy really loves his job. He's good at it. And he has friends here."

"And *you* like *us!*" Charlotte teased. "Admit it!"

Bashfully, Suzette said, "I do."

Dawn began to whimper. Suzette stretched out her arms and Helen gently handed over the baby. "You look tired," she said to Suzette. "We'll let you rest."

Charlotte rose. "I've got to get back to work."

Helen stood, too. "Can we get you anything, Suzette?"

"No. I think I'll just snuggle down here," Suzette told her.

Charlotte carried the tray into the kitchen. Her mother followed her. Together they stacked the dishwasher and cleaned up. Charlotte assumed her mother's thoughts were still bound up in the good news of Dawn's paternity. But to her surprise, her mother asked, "Would you like me to man the farm stand for a while?"

Charlotte grinned. "I would *love* that, Mom."

*That evening,* her friend Katy phoned to remind Charlotte that they had hardly seen each other all summer and to beg for a girls' night out.

"That's *exactly* what I need!" Charlotte cried.

She showered and slipped on her most frou-frou summer dress and piles of tinkling bracelets and drove into town to meet Katy. They had drinks and dinner at the Ropewalk, and then strolled around the docks, looking at all the splendid yachts, and allowed themselves to linger in town, listening to the street musicians and gazing at the beautiful people. They talked about their summer dramas— Katy called it "parallel play" like toddlers had. They didn't solve any problems, but Charlotte went home feeling greatly cheered about life.

*Tuesday morning,* Charlotte knew part of that cheer had been inspired by too many strawberry daiquiris. Her head ached steadily, like some kind of engine, and her mouth was dry. She sat at the kitchen table, drinking orange juice and wondering whether she should go back to bed.

Aunt Grace peered into the room, saw Charlotte, and jumped, looking guilty.

"Good morning, Aunt Grace," Charlotte said.

"Oh! Oh, hello!" Aunt Grace skittered away

down the hall, leaving Charlotte curious. *Now* what was going on?

Rising, she rinsed her coffee cup and set it in the dishwasher and was turning to leave when Christian thundered into the room, waving a robot and yelling, "Me want Cheerios right now!"

Mandy followed with baby Zoe in a sling. "Lower your voice, Christian, people are still sleeping," she instructed, then saw Charlotte, and jumped. "Oh! Oh, good morning, Charlotte!"

Charlotte reached up to take the cereal from the cupboard and found Christian's Winnie-the-Pooh bowl from another shelf. "What's wrong with everyone?" she grumbled, as she helped Christian into his chair. "You all act like I've turned green."

"Auntie Charlotte turned green!" Christian chanted, knocking himself out with laughter.

"Is there coffee?" Mandy sank into a chair and put her feet up on another chair. "Thanks for helping, Char, I'm beat."

Charlotte set the bowl in front of her nephew, found his special spoon for him, and fixed Mandy a cup of coffee the way she liked it, with a lot of cream and sugar.

"Really." Charlotte sat down across from her cousin and stared at her. "What's going on?"

Mandy jiggled Zoe, who whimpered and fell back asleep. She made a face, squeezing her eyes together and wrinkling her forehead. "Um. Mee's with Coop."

"What?"

"Well, Mee was bored last night. When you went out with Katy. So she walked over to Coop's. And she hasn't come home."

Charlotte frowned. "Well, I'm not sure . . . I mean, you don't know—"

"I do know, actually. Mee phoned me on her cell last night. At about eleven o'clock. She was in Coop's bathroom, and she was whispering. She said if anyone was worried that she wasn't home, it was because she was spending the night at Coop's."

Charlotte just sat there, mouth open.

"Well," Mandy quickly reminded her, "it's not as if you were engaged or anything."

Still trying to absorb this information, Charlotte replied mildly, "No. No, we're not."

Mandy tilted her head, appraising Charlotte. "I thought you'd be upset."

"You *hoped* I'd be upset," Charlotte shot back.

Mandy bridled. "Well, *that's* a terrible thing to say!"

Charlotte started to argue, then shrugged. She rose. "I've got to get out to the garden."

"Charlotte, wait." Mandy scooped a pile of errant cereal from the table and dumped it into Christian's bowl. "Eat that before you get more," she said to her son. Looking back at Charlotte, she said, "Mee didn't want to hurt you. I mean, she's not—doing this—to hurt you."

Charlotte sighed. "I know that, Mandy. The only motivation any woman needs to—do what Mee is doing—is just to look at Coop."

"But you never did seem serious about him."

"I've only dated him this summer. I haven't had a chance to get serious about him." She didn't want to have gooey girl talk with her cousin right now, even though Mandy was practically panting for it. "I've got to get to work."

"Charlotte—so you're okay?"

"I'm fine."

In the mudroom, she laced up her work boots, applied more sunblock, and stuck her sun hat on her head. She strode out of the house and down the drive to her garden shed. So this is why she'd been so unsettled, so edgy, so nervous. This thing, this *event,* was unrolling toward her, and now it had happened. She wondered whether this was enough. Had she paid off her debt? Had she earned her freedom? Or did she have to *tell* someone about what she had done, to make it more real, more complete? If so, who would she tell? Not Mandy. None of the Ms could ever keep a secret. Not her mother, who would too easily forgive Charlotte, and certainly not her father, who would think Charlotte was even more of an idiot than he already believed. She needed someone involved with the family, someone who would comprehend the magnitude of her transgression and could provide a sensible reaction, and then perhaps she would be able to set herself free.

*Whit,* she thought all of a sudden. *Whit.* She dug her cell phone from her pocket.

*Whit met her* at Altar Rock. No one ever came to the moors in August, it was just too hot. But Whit knew a secret place, a shady grove beside a hidden pond. They left their cars at Altar Rock and walked down a dirt road bordered with crooked scrub oak smothered beneath wild grapevines. She was surprised when he suddenly ducked beneath a branch and motioned for her to join him. She followed him through a green tunnel of leaves, along a narrow path worn down by deer, and found herself on the edge of a small blue body of water adorned with water lilies. An island covered with a multitude of wildflowers rose from the center of the pond. It was cool in the shade, and still, except for the occasional rustle of leaves.

"Whit, this is beautiful!"

"I know. And private. Whatever you've got to say won't be overheard out here." As he spoke, he flapped an old blanket out onto the ground.

Charlotte helped him smooth it out. She settled, cross-legged, on the blanket, and took her thermos out of her bag. "Iced tea?" She poured them each a plastic cup. Now that the moment had come, she regretted her impulse. Yet she also knew she couldn't continue her life one more minute without removing the secret that was strangling her life.

"All right. Here goes." She shifted, angling away from Whit. It would be easier to tell him if she didn't see his reaction. "About four years ago I did something pretty bad. I haven't told anyone else. I thought I could—oh, somehow work out my own schedule of atonement, and somehow I'd feel better, but it hasn't turned out that way." She cleared her throat. "All right," she said again. Then, in a rush, she told him. "Whit, I had an affair with Phillip. When Mee was still married to him."

Whit didn't respond. She glanced at him, but he was staring out into the distance.

"It's not why Mee got divorced," she added quickly. "Mee never knew. It didn't have anything to do with Mee. It hardly had anything to do with Phillip. I was just so unhappy and confused at the bank. I kept making mistakes. I was working in his department then—commercial loans—and I kept making stupid mistakes, and Phillip was so nice about it. He didn't make me feel like an idiot. He *helped* me." More quietly, Charlotte added, "He didn't tell my father how I kept messing up."

Whit picked up a twig and snapped it into equal lengths, considering. After a moment he said, "You know, don't you, that Phillip had affairs with a lot of women at the bank?"

Charlotte pulled her knees to her chest and hugged them, dropping her face down into her arms. Her voice was muffled as she said, "I heard that about him. And I'm not saying that I was such a fabulous experience for him that I caused him to leave Mee. I mean, it was four years ago, and it didn't last very long, and I broke it off. But I did have sex with a man who was married to my cousin, and that is just *shabby*."

"Yes," Whit agreed quietly, "it is."

Charlotte sniffed. "I've been trying to—oh, this sounds corny, but it's the only way I know how to say it—I've been trying to live *virtuously* ever since. I didn't have sex for years, and I worked in my garden and spent my free time with Nona—not that I don't adore Nona, I do, but I haven't had much of a social life. I thought—I *knew*—the time would come when I would wake up one morning and realize I'd paid my debt. I would be free to move on. And this morning—well, this morning, Mandy told me that Mee spent the night with Coop. She's still with him."

"Really?" Next to her, Whit broke into a big smile. He turned to look at Charlotte. "How do you feel about that?"

"I'm glad." Charlotte lifted her head and wiped the back of her hands across her wet cheeks. "I won't deny I've always had a kind of crush on Coop. But over the summer I've gotten to know him, and we're so different it would never have worked out between us. And I know how bad Mee has felt since her divorce, she's been feeling unattractive and unloved and all of that, and now she can feel superior and smug and ravishingly irresistible because she's 'stolen' Coop from me." Charlotte looked up at Whit. "What I want to know, what I *need* to know, is whether or not I should tell Mee that I slept with her husband. I mean, I don't want her to feel guilty about Coop."

Whit studied her face. "You've got quite a complicated system of checks and balances going on inside your head."

She nodded, agreeing.

"It seems to me," Whit said slowly, "that Mee 'stealing' Coop from you shouldn't make Mee feel as guilty as you feel about sleeping with her husband. Plus, Mee is just a bit—this is only an observation, not a criticism—Mee's less complicated than you. I don't think she'll feel guilty about Coop. So I don't see that it would do any good to tell her about you and Phillip."

"Oh, thank heavens." Charlotte sighed. "I think you're right. Oh, you have no idea how good I feel now—how *free!*"

"I'm flattered that you've come to me with this, Charlotte."

"You *are* sort of like family," she told him.

With a smile in his voice, he said, "I'm not sure if that's a good thing or bad."

Carefully, Charlotte chose her words. "I *love* my family. I've realized that I can't be like Oliver and just move away to another part of the world and live my life separately. For better or worse, my life is going to be influenced by my family. For a while I fought against that, and I know some people would say I'm too—what is the pop word these days?—*enmeshed.* But I love my family. I love my mother and father, and I adore Nona, and I want to help Teddy, and I'm getting terribly fond of Suzette, and I'm irrationally wild about their baby, and I'm not sure I love Uncle Kellogg and Aunt Grace, but I do love my cousins and I'm glad they're so temperamental about Suzette's baby and my using Nona's land, because it just makes them human and weak and fallible, and that makes me feel better about myself." Charlotte was crying again. "Oh, Whit. I'm an *idiot.*"

"True, but a very attractive one," Whit told her. Reaching out, he put his arm around her and pulled her next to him in a brotherly hug.

Charlotte leaned against him, grateful for his strength, his maleness, his calm, and cried for a while, in the shelter of his arms.

*After a while,* Charlotte said reluctantly, "I have to get back to the garden."

"All right," Whit said, but he didn't take his arms away.

"Whit?"

"Mm?"

"Could we have dinner tonight?"

"Damn. I can't. I've got plans. And may I hasten to add, *family* plans."

"Oh. Oh, well. . . ." Charlotte pulled herself away from him and stood. She began to gather up the thermos and cups.

Whit rose, too. "How about tomorrow night?"

She looked at him, aware that her face was streaked with tears and her hair was probably all over the place. In spite of that, she sensed his desire for her. It was as certain as the sunlight.

"Dinner? Tomorrow night? Sounds wonderful."

They walked beneath the low green ceiling of leaves and branches up out of the secluded glade and back along the dirt road to Altar Rock and their cars. All around them, beach plums and rose hips glistened among the heath and low bushes, and a hawk wheeled high overhead in the flawless blue sky. Charlotte felt as if she were suddenly possessed of a rare, clear, pure happiness—it was a delicate gift, almost liquid, contained within her heart like elixir in a sacred vessel. She wanted to be motionless; she wanted to simply exist, feeling this way. Cleansed. And new.

## Twenty-eight

*Helen steered* the old Chrysler into a parking spot in the airport lot and took a moment to check her reflection in the mirror. When Worth phoned this morning to tell her he would be arriving at five-thirty, he sent her into a kind of young love fit of jitters. She tried on several outfits, finding them all wrong—the shirt with the low bodice was too suggestive, the khaki trousers were too prim, and her favorite sundress seemed too dressy. She settled on the sundress finally, carefully put on makeup, and then hurriedly washed it all off.

She was lucky she'd made it to the airport in time.

As she walked toward the terminal, her heart began to leap and bound. And when she saw Worth coming from the baggage section, his duffel bag in his hand, she almost giggled with nervousness. Had she forgotten how handsome he was, how striking?

He scanned the crowd, and when he saw Helen he smiled.

She waited as he made his way toward her.

"Hi," he said simply, and bent down to kiss her lips.

It was only a quick, neat, familial kiss—Worth did not like public displays of affection—but Helen nearly swooned like a schoolgirl. *My goodness,* she thought, *how the body goes along just doing what it wants to do!*

He took her hand as they left the terminal and headed toward the Jeep.

"Good flight?" she asked.

"Easy," he told her. "Ah, the island air is so much nicer than the city's. It's good to be here."

"It's good to have you here," she said, then bit her lip at the formality of her words.

When they reached the Jeep, Worth hesitated. "I have an idea."

"Yes?"

"Let's stay at an inn. Let's stay at an inn, and eat dinner out, and not go back to Nona's until tomorrow."

Helen said the first thing that came into her mind, "But in August! During high season! It will be so expensive."

"It will be so *private,*" Worth countered. "I want to spend some time alone with you."

Helen flushed. "We'll have to phone them or they'll worry. What will we tell them?"

"I'll call them. I'll tell them we're spending the night in town and will be home tomorrow. That's all they need to know."

"I don't have a toothbrush," Helen said weakly.

"We'll buy one." He held the car door. "Come on. Let's go."

The drive from the airport to the center of town was only a matter of a few miles. Worth choose an inn halfway between the Jetties Beach and town. It was larger than the cozy B&Bs and it had parking. There was a vacancy, and they were given a room, and before Helen had really accustomed herself to the idea, they were walking down the long carpeted hallway. Air-conditioning blew, tempering the air, and the silence was sheltering. Worth keyed the door open, ushered Helen inside, and shut the door behind them. The room was comfortable, clean, and anonymous. They were closed away from the world.

A jealous thought popped into Helen's mind: *Was this the sort of place Worth had taken Cindy?*

*Stop it!* she mentally ordered herself. *Love over fear, remember?*

"Let's go to bed." Worth held out his hand.

Helen hesitated. Suddenly, she felt shy. She put her hand in his.

Worth led her to the king-size bed. Together they turned back the covers. He crossed the room to pull the draperies shut, but a streak of daylight still striped the room, and Helen felt even more timid. She did not want to be judged and found ugly in comparison to a younger woman. And yet this was such a new moment between them, she didn't want to spoil it with her jealousy.

Worth quickly stripped off his clothes and slid naked into bed. She undressed too and got into bed, pulling the covers up.

Worth turned on his side to look at her. "Come here often?" he asked.

She laughed, grateful for his attempt at humor. Reaching out, she put her hand on his chest. He was so warm.

Worth pulled her to him. At first she was awkward, insecure, and too occupied with her thoughts, but her husband wooed her with his hands and mouth until she surrendered to the moment, and then they were together, warm and tender, familiar, but excitingly just a little strange, a little new. In the heat of the moment, she wept, and her husband kissed her tears.

Afterward, they slept.

When they woke, it was evening.

"Hungry?" Worth asked.

"Starving." Helen stretched her limbs in the bed, which, after her nights on the sleeping-porch daybed, felt luxurious. "Should we walk into town?"

"Do you suppose they have room service?" Worth asked.

Helen grinned. "I bet the Red Sox have a night game."

"You're right," Worth admitted.

He rose from the bed and stalked naked across the room to the desk where the leather portfolio lay. "Ah. They do. Have room service." He looked at Helen.

"It sounds lovely," she said.

Worth phoned in their order, and then, at Helen's request, dialed Nona's number.

"Ah, Glorious, it's you. *Wonderful.* Look, Helen and I are spending the night in town. We just wanted to let everyone know so you don't wonder where we are." Worth grinned as he listened to the voice clamoring around Glorious. "No, thank you, Glorious, we don't need to talk to Grace. We're fine, and we'll be home tomorrow, around noon. Would you please tell Nona this yourself? Thanks."

"Poor Grace," Helen said, not without a bit of pleasure. "She must be crazy curious."

"It will be good for her," Worth said.

"Well, we're only an old married couple having room service and watching television," Helen said.

Worth smiled at her from across the room. "Two people, together," he said.

*Wednesday morning,* Helen and Worth walked into town, ate a long satisfying breakfast at Fog Island, then sauntered up and down the cobblestone streets like a pair of tourists. Worth bought *The New York Times* and Helen bought a toothbrush. It was fun to be in town in the morning along with all the other people—families, dog walkers, and lovers, young and old—strolling along, enjoying the bright day.

But when the hour came to check out of their hotel room, reality descended. It was time to return to the summer house.

Worth drove the old Chrysler, and Helen sat in the passenger seat. As they drove along the winding road, Helen studied her husband's face. "How do you feel about Nona's news?"

"I'm still processing it. And it's still hard. I don't think I'm ready to tell the children yet."

"Do they ever need to know?" Helen asked.

"Yes. Yes, I think they do. Sometime. And Grace should know, too. But Nona took her own sweet time telling me. I don't want to rush things. We've all had enough drama this summer."

"Yes," Helen murmured. "That's certainly true."

Worth reached across and took Helen's hand. "I want to talk to Teddy and Suzette. I want to tell them I'm sorry I acted like an asshole. I want them to know I'm ready to love their baby—"

"She's very easy to love," Helen said.

"—and maybe we can just have a normal family life for a while."

Helen laughed. "If there *is* any such thing as normal family life!"

*Drooping heavily* with leaves, the roadside trees and abundant bushes made a green tunnel of the road. In the verge, asters and wild daisies and Queen Anne's lace dotted the green with yellow and pink and white. They arrived at Nona's driveway, turned onto the dirt lane, and suddenly slowed.

"What's that hellish noise?" Worth asked.

Helen listened, frowning, to an unnerving shrill whine, vibrating, shaking the air. "I don't know, Worth. I can't imagine."

Worth stepped on the gas, sending the Chrysler speeding over the dirt road. As they grew closer to the house, the noise grew louder and more intense.

They came to a halt in the middle of the drive.

Two enormous dump trucks blocked the way.

One had a chipper attached behind it. A man wearing heavy black earphones was feeding branches into the machine, which screamed shrilly as it ground away, spitting chips into the truck bed. Behind him, two men wielded chain saws as they sliced branches off the privet hedge. Already one side of the hedged garden had been removed. Bare stumps protruded from the ground. The sun flooded in on the slates, warming ground that had been shaded for generations.

Worth and Helen jumped out of the car and ran down the drive, around the trucks, and into the house.

Nona was in the living room, seated on her chaise, watching through the closed French doors as the men worked. She looked wonderful. Her cheeks were pink and her eyes bright with excitement. She wore a pair of white fur earmuffs. Seeing Worth and Helen, she yelled, "It's the only way I can tolerate the noise. It's all too fascinating *not* to watch!"

"Nona!" Worth cried. "What's going on?"

"Exactly what you see, dear. I'm having those hedges taken down. I've wanted to do it all my life. I have no idea why I've waited so long. It's going to be awfully noisy here for a few days. Once they get all the branches down, they've got to dig out the stumps. And then, then, my dear, we'll plant a real garden, full of dahlias and cornflowers and roses."

She held up an ancient pair of mink earmuffs to Helen. "Want some?"

Helen took them and settled them on her head. The day was hot, and fur on the head was not the wisest choice, but the earmuffs did soften the noise considerably.

Nona yelled, "What do you think?"

"I think it's fabulous!" Helen yelled back. "Look at all the sunshine!"

"I'm thinking about all the flowers we can plant now," Nona said. "I want to talk to Charlotte about this. She'll know what sorts of things grow well in full sun."

Worth yelled, "Where's Grace?"

"Oh, Grace has gone off in a flap. She's afraid I've gone nuts. Perhaps you can calm her down."

Helen exchanged a look with her husband. "I'm not sure Worth is up for any more family responsibility these days."

"That's all right," Nona said. "*You* are. Oh, look." She pointed. "That tree is about to go."

The air shuddered with the noise of the chain saw as a small privet tree, freed of its lower branches, was cut down. It toppled slowly to one side, letting the sunlight illuminate another rectangular portion of Nona's land.

# Full Bloom

# Twenty-nine

*Charlotte slipped* into her shed, where the noise of the saws was slightly diminished, and started to punch Whit's number into her cell phone.

She hesitated. Was this the right thing to do? Was she just grasping at any excuse to see him again? She would see him tonight. Couldn't she wait? *Shouldn't* she wait?

She hadn't slept well that night—but it had been a happy insomnia, filled with sensations and desire and a kind of terrified hope. This morning it had felt good to rise early and stalk out to her garden, to pick and wash vegetables and set them on her farm table.

Then the tree service arrived with their chain saws and trucks and chippers, and her concentration was destroyed.

She'd raced up to the house to see what was happening. Nona was sitting just inside the French doors, watching the work and looking absolutely beatific. Grace fluttered around wringing her hands and fretting while Mandy shadowed Christian, who was fascinated by the workers and their tools. To escape from the noise, Suzette carried her baby down to the little beach where Glorious had set up some chairs, and after a while pregnant Mellie joined her, with Mandy's daughter Zoe in her arms. Grace drove Teddy to work and returned home to phone Kellogg in Boston, begging him to come home and help her—she was afraid Nona had lost her mind.

Charlotte returned to her garden, but now in the dazzling sunlight her thoughts flew around her head like brilliant butterflies. Nona was taking the hedges down! It was amazing.

Actually, it was *monumental.*

And she wanted to share it with Whit.

She punched in the final number. The phone rang. Whit said, "Hello?"

"I'm sorry to bother you," she said, "but could you help me survive one more family event?"

*Whit came* immediately. He parked on the side of the drive and met Charlotte just outside her shed.

"What's going on?" he asked.

"Come see." Taking his hand, Charlotte led him up the drive.

The air was filled with the buzz and shriek of machinery, and sawdust filled the air as branches and limbs fell to the ground.

Whit shouted something at Charlotte, but she shook her head and pointed to her ears. "Follow me!" she yelled. "My room's at the back of the house, so we'll be able to hear ourselves speak."

She took him in through the living room where Nona and Glorious sat, wearing earmuffs, watching the hedge fall. They all waved hello. Charlotte drew Whit up two flights of stairs to the attic. She pulled him into her room and shut the door. It was probably twenty degrees hotter here than on the ground floor, but a fresh breeze swept off from the ocean into the small gabled chamber.

There was only one chair in the room and it was covered with clothes. She gestured to Whit to sit on the bed while she paced the floor.

"Whit, what do you think?"

"Nona looks like she's having the time of her life," Whit said.

"Yes. Why, yes, you're right, Whit. Oh, I'm glad you're here. Nona does look happy, doesn't she? I mean, I don't need to worry about her, do I? But Whit, taking down the hedge is such a stupendous event! It's been there for at least two generations! Shouldn't Nona have discussed it with us? Or, at the very least, had some kind of family ceremony, maybe with champagne? This is all so casual! So weird!"

Whit thought about it. "Well, it seems to me that Nona's at the age where she doesn't have control of much. Her body's giving out, and her family continues to change. This is something she can control. She probably likes making one huge event happen."

"You're right. I know you're right. But I still feel restless. Unsettled."

Whit asked, "Because of the hedge?"

Charlotte turned from the window. For a moment, she pushed back all her fears and concerns and allowed herself to just *look* at him. She'd always known he was handsome, and that had irritated her, and now she had to admit that what she'd designated as irritation was really an intense physical connection that scared her half to death. But she was also oddly calmed by his presence. She liked it that now, in the midst of all the chaos in her house, he had focused on the personal, the immediate, the physical.

"I'm not sure," she admitted. "Maybe it's not the hedge. Maybe it's my life."

He didn't speak but looked at her steadily in a way that made her legs go weak.

"Maybe it's you," she said quietly.

"That would be good."

Charlotte sat down on her bed, next to Whit but not touching. Looking at her hands, she said, "I never wanted to be attracted to you, Whit, and I guess I've figured out it was because it would have been what my father wanted me to do."

"I'm not surprised."

"But now I'm thinking, Well, that's not such a bad thing. Making my father happy."

"It *would* be a bad thing if you married me only because it would make your father happy," Whit said.

Charlotte blinked and looked up at him. "How did we get to the subject of marriage?"

Whit said, "When has the subject ever been anything else?"

"Well!" Charlotte hugged herself nervously. "Well, Whit. I mean, we don't even know if we're compatible."

"Yeah, we do know," Whit assured her. "We're compatible. Think of yesterday. Talking. Just being together."

It felt like her lips were freezing. And her fingertips. "But maybe we're not compatible . . . sexually?" She could hardly get out the final word.

Whit said quietly, "We'll just have to research the question, won't we?"

"Will we?" She couldn't breathe.

He took her face in both his hands and tilted it toward his. He put his mouth on hers, gently, his lips open, and she could feel the warmth and stirring of his breath. She put her hands on his chest. Beneath his shirt, his heart was racing, and this gave her courage. It meant as much to him, then, as it did to her. He was not faking it, trying to please his father by joining the two families. Right now he wanted her, and everything about him assured her that his desire was real and urgent.

Together they lay down on the bed, pressing their bodies together. She put her hands on his shoulders, on his back, and slid her hands down inside his shorts. He drew a sharp breath.

"Perhaps we should wait," Whit said.

"Perhaps we shouldn't," Charlotte answered,

attempting to sound light but really sounding almost desperate as she unzipped her shorts and wrestled her body out of them.

Whit hooked his thumbs in his shorts and yanked them and his boxer shorts off. He moved above Charlotte, bearing his weight on his elbows, his legs pressed against her legs, his long penis resting against her belly and thighs.

"I don't have any condoms," he whispered.

Charlotte smiled. "That's okay," she told him. "My mother wants lots of grandchildren."

Whit smiled back. "So does mine."

# Thirty

*Nona awoke* with a start. She'd been dreaming she was in a hot-air balloon, drifting above the island, gazing down at her family and the house and the serene blue water.

But something had changed. Looking around, she saw the terrace, littered with leaves. Light flooded down on the slates outside the house, brightening the living room as never before. It was late afternoon.

One of the landscapers, a rugged tall man with burnt cinnamon skin, came to the French door, opened it, and leaned in. His entire body was plastered with small privet leaves.

"Mrs. Wheelwright?" he said. "We couldn't get it all done today. We'll be back tomorrow morning about seven. Should be able to finish it then."

"That's wonderful, Carl." Nona raised her hand in a kind of wave. "Thank you." She lifted the earmuffs off her head, flinching as they got caught in her hair.

Helen came into the room. "Nona, you're awake."

"Hello, dear. Where is everyone?"

"Let's see. Grace and her crew have gone off to the yacht club for dinner."

"I didn't know they were planning that." Nona shoved and wrestled her body around, trying to organize herself into a standing position. "Would you mind helping me to the bathroom?"

Helen came to her side and let Nona lean on her as they slowly shuffled along. "I don't think they planned to go out, but Grace felt she needed a change of scenery."

"Grace will be okay once the hedges are all down and we can put in new plantings," Nona said. "Where's Charlotte?"

"Charlotte and Whit are down on the beach. Charlotte and Whit have set up a casual picnic dinner there."

Nona stopped still. She peered at Helen. "Charlotte and Whit, did you say?"

Helen smiled. "Charlotte and Whit."

"Let's not get our hopes up," Nona advised.

"Wait until you see them together," Helen answered smugly.

Nona shuffled into the bathroom, used the toilet, and washed her hands. Looking in the mirror, she saw that her hair had come out of the chignon and flew about her head in wisps. She tried to pat it back in place, then made a face at herself—funny old self, she could not believe she was so old!—and went back out into the hall where Helen was waiting.

"Has Glorious left?" she asked Helen.

"She has. Big date night for her."

"And the others?"

"Suzette's at the beach and Dawn is sleeping in a little wicker basket, like a baby from a fairy tale."

"And Worth?"

"He's down there, too. He carried Dawn down, in fact."

Nona looked at Helen. "He did?"

Helen smiled. "He did."

"Where's Teddy?"

"He's catching a ride home with a friend. He'll be here any time. He knows we're down at the beach."

"Well, then, let's go."

Nona surrendered some of her pride and allowed herself to lean heavily on her daughter-in-law as they progressed through the house, out the doors, and onto the lawn.

The heat of the day had diminished, and the air was clear and sweet. The groomed lawn was soft beneath Nona's feet, and birds called and flew among the trees that bordered the land.

"I'd almost forgotten how lovely it is out here," Nona said.

Helen kept a firm arm around Nona's waist and held Nona's hand with her own. They arrived at the strip of sand shaped by the wind into low dunes. Tall narrow blades of beach grass grew in the dunes, and wild roses twined everywhere in lush profusion. The perfume was heavenly.

"Stop a moment," Nona told Helen. "Let me just breathe."

Helen waited, staring out at the water, until Nona said, "All right, dear. I'd better sit down."

It was only a few more feet, and then they were on the beach.

Charlotte and Whit were at the water's edge, squatting in the sand, whispering and laughing softly as they compared shells. Suzette was ensconced in one of the new clever canvas chairs that had arms with a cup holder and a little platform where she could rest her legs.

Worth sat in a beach chair, holding Dawn, wrapped in several light blankets, in his arms.

"My, it looks like a party," Nona said, as she sank gratefully into a beach chair.

"It *is* a party," Suzette agreed. "Look at all the food Glorious made."

Nona accepted a glass of wine and a plate of cheese and crackers and sliced vegetables from

Helen, who poured herself a glass of wine and sat cross-legged next to Worth's chair. Nona sipped the wine and felt remarkably content with life.

"Look at the water," Helen said. "It's as still as glass."

They all gazed out at the harbor. A few sailboats drifted idly in the distance, and a kayak sliced a white trail.

"The silence is lovely," Helen said.

"Yeah," Suzette agreed. "What a lot of noise those saws made. But Dawn just slept through it all."

"Babies can do that." Leaning over, Helen looked at her granddaughter. "She's so beautiful."

Nona said, "Her head comes to a point."

"Nona!" Helen was shocked. "How can you say that?"

Nona said, "Her head comes to a point and she's beautiful."

"Hello, everyone!"

Nona turned to look. Teddy was striding down the lawn, undoing his tie as he walked.

"Oh, good, drinks on the beach. Heaven." Teddy squatted down in front of Nona and put a hand on each arm of her chair. "Nona, I think taking the hedge down is a brilliant idea. It's going to look great."

"I'm so glad you think so." Reaching out, she caressed Teddy's cheek. How she loved this man, her second grandson.

Teddy stood up and walked to the drinks table. Nona forced herself not to look, but she couldn't help it; she peeked, and from the periphery of her vision she saw Teddy pour himself a glass of sparkling water.

Teddy said, "Hey, Dad, let's go for a walk. I've got some things to tell you."

Worth raised an eyebrow, then said, "Okay." Carefully he handed the baby to Suzette. He bent and removed his loafers.

Teddy kicked off his shoes. He and his father walked away, along the sloping beach. Helen brought her knees to her chest and hugged them.

"Summer's almost over," Suzette said, gazing out at the water.

"And fall is about to begin," Nona said.

"Some days it's as if life is just starting, brand new," Helen observed.

"Well, it is," Nona agreed. "Every day."

# ABOUT THE AUTHOR

NANCY THAYER is the *New York Times* bestselling author of *Moon Shell Beach, The Hot Flash Club, The Hot Flash Club Strikes Again, Hot Flash Holidays, The Hot Flash Club Chills Out*, and *Between Husbands and Friends*. She lives on Nantucket.

**Center Point Publishing**
600 Brooks Road ● PO Box 1
Thorndike ME 04986-0001 USA

**(207) 568-3717**

**US & Canada:**
**1 800 929-9108**
www.centerpointlargeprint.com